PERMISSIBLE
LIMITS

Also by Graham Hurley

FICTION
Rules of Engagement
Reaper
The Devil's Breath
Thunder in the Blood
Sabbathman
The Perfect Soldier
Heaven's Light
Nocturne

NON-FICTION
Airshow

PERMISSIBLE LIMITS

Graham Hurley

ORION

DORSET COUNTY

1999

LIBRARY AS

This edition first published
in Great Britain in 1999 by Orion
An imprint of Orion Books Ltd
Orion House, 5 Upper St Martin's Lane
London WC2H 9EA

A CIP catalogue record for this book is
available from the British Library

Typeset in Great Britain
at The Spartan Press Ltd,
Lymington, Hants
Printed and bound by
Clays Ltd, St Ives plc

For Darina and Erik
with love

Acknowledgements

My thanks to those individuals whose generosity and knowledge helped make this book possible.

Carolyn Grace, with whom I made a number of films, planted the seed for the idea. Her gutsiness, and her airmanship, have been a constant inspiration and she won't mind me saying that absolutely none of what follows has any connection with any events in her own life.

Paul Bowen, Director of the Royal International Air Tattoo, opened countless doors in the aviation world. Rod Dean, Mustang pilot extraordinaire, gave me an enormous amount of time and help, as did Bernie Forward, recently of the Air Accidents Investigation Branch. Tony Houghton and Eddie Seagrave of Goodwood Aerodrome offered invaluable advice, while John Tilling, Simon Howells and Andrew Edie explained the mysteries of aviation insurance. Paul Coggan, of Warbirds Worldwide, took a lively interest in the project, as did Brendan Walsh and Norman Chapman of Intrepid Aviation, who introduced me to the glories of the Harvard, the YAK, and a stripped-down Merlin. My thanks, as well, to Susie Cameron and Roger Edwards for sharing their memories of life in the Falklands.

My agent, Antony Harwood, and my editor, Simon Spanton, have been unflagging in their support, as has Christina Waugh, a good friend and a shrewd critic. To Bill Flynn, Ellie Bruce and I owe a special debt. He believed in both of us and for his faith this book is all the richer.

Lastly, a huge thank you to my wife, Lin. Wingman is too small a word . . .

Find the enemy and shoot him down.
All else is nonsense.

Baron Manfred von Richthofen

Prelude

People who came to say goodbye to Adam always talk about the swans.

We held the memorial service in a lovely little church within sight of the sea. It was a cold March day with fitful sunshine and a bitter wind. After the service, we gathered in groups on the gravel path that led down to the lane. Drifts of early daffodils brightened the shadowed gravestones and I remember how empty the service had seemed without a coffin or a body. The fly-past had been scheduled for half past three. Already, we could hear the Mustang coming.

The aircraft appeared a minute or so later. Harald was at the controls and I could see his face looking down at us as he dipped a wing in salute. Some of us bowed our heads. One or two of the men were weeping. For that single moment, even the wind seemed to stop.

After the Mustang had peeled off to the south, it was quieter again. Conversation seemed somehow pointless. There was nothing to say, nothing to add. We began to walk towards the gate, little black clusters of us, grim-faced, awkward, and it was then that I heard the swans.

They were on exactly the same heading as the aircraft. I saw their shadows first, dancing across the pale stones of the church, then I looked up, catching my breath at their beauty and their grace. There were nine of them in all and they disappeared towards the undercliff and the sea in perfect V formation, untroubled, leaving us to the cold and the single tolling bell.

The memory of those swans has never left me. I can hear the beat and sweep of their wings as I write. Adam, I think, would have loved them.

Chapter one

I got the news about Adam by phone. It was a Thursday afternoon. The builders had been in since Christmas and our latest extension for yet more guest suites was nearly complete. For once, we looked like being ready for the new season.

The nearest phone extension was in the kitchen. A man's voice I didn't recognise asked whether I was Mrs Ellie Bruce. Bad news is like a smell. You scent it.

'My name's Clark, Mrs Bruce. I'm a police officer. We've had a call from the Distress and Diversion Cell up at West Drayton.' He paused. 'Do you know what these people do?'

'Of course'

I bent to the phone, trying to fight the waves of panic. The Distress and Diversion Cell co-ordinate the rescue services when an aircraft gets into trouble.

'Sandown have reported your husband overdue,' the policeman was saying. 'Jersey booked him out at 10.45. It seems his flightplan gives an ETA of 11.40.'

I did the computations in my head. Sandown is our local airfield, a single grass strip tucked beneath the shoulder of St Boniface Down. Transit time from Jersey to the Isle of Wight in the Cessna Adam had borrowed would be around fifty-five minutes. Eleven forty sounded exactly right.

'He hasn't turned up?'

'I'm afraid not.'

I glanced at the big clock on the wall over the sink. Five to four. Adam had phoned only this morning. Weather permitting, he'd promised he'd be back in time for a late lunch, though that – I knew – could have meant anything.

There was an ominous silence at the other end of the line. I could sense there was worse news to come.

'Is your husband an experienced pilot? Do you mind me asking, Mrs Bruce?'

I blinked. Six years in the Fleet Air Arm. Supply work out to the

North Sea rigs. Contract after contract in southern Africa. Helicopters. Fixed-wing. Single-engined. Twins. Even, for a couple of months, an ancient DC-3.

'He's got thousands of hours,' I said, 'God knows how many.'

'And he's used to flying over water?'

'Of course. He does it all the time.'

I was sitting down now. One of the builders gave me an inane grin through the window. Four o'clock was time to put the kettle on.

'West Drayton are in the process of reviewing the radar tapes, Mrs Bruce,' the policeman muffled a cough, 'and I'm afraid it's not looking brilliant.'

'What isn't?'

It was a stupid question. I'd once paid a visit to the Distress and Diversion Cell, a small, darkened, busy room at the main air-traffic control centre near Heathrow. There's a big display screen on one wall and smaller consoles facing it. The guys behind the consoles can pinpoint an aircraft to within a couple of hundred metres, anywhere in UK airspace. Impressive, unless you happen to be on the end of a conversation like this.

'What's happened? What did they see?'

'Apparently your husband's aircraft was carrying a transponder.'

'Of course.'

'Would you happen to know what it was squawking? They're saying seven thousand.'

I had my eyes shut, trying to visualise the big wall display. A transponder is a little radio transmitter carried on board an aircraft. It sends out a coded four-digit signal which registers as a trace on the radar screen; 7000 is the code you enter in transit when your aircraft is no longer receiving an air-traffic service. The people in the Distress Cell were right. Once he'd left Jersey's air-traffic control zone, Adam's transponder should definitely have been squawking 7000.

'So what happened?' I asked again.

'Seven thousand's off the plot.'

'When? When did it happen?'

'Exactly?'

'Yes, please.'

'Hang on. I wrote it down.'

The builder had given up with the tea. He was back beside the big window in the extension, his shirt tail flapping in the wind. I watched him slopping primer on the frame, my mind a complete blank. Adam couldn't have just disappeared. Not the way this man was saying. He was far too clever, far too wily. My old fox. My young cub.

'Eleven twelve.'

I felt my stomach lurch. Eleven twelve was more than four hours ago.

'Maybe there was some problem with the transponder,' I said quickly. 'Maybe he turned back. Have you tried the French?'

I had a sudden picture, extraordinarily vivid, of Adam in a little café on the edge of some French airfield tucking into steak and frites, but even before the answer came, I knew I was fantasising. Had Adam really turned back, he'd have been on the radio in seconds, and even if the radio had gone U/S as well, he'd have made contact again after landing. He was far too good a pilot to have left the situation unresolved.

I clung to the telephone. According to the policeman, checks on airfields on the other side of the Channel were still awaiting the arrival of someone who spoke French. Now, he was talking about a search-and-rescue operation.

'Lee-on-the-Solent have put up a helicopter. They're in touch with a freighter fifteen miles to the east of the impact point, and the Bembridge lifeboat's on standby.'

Impact point? My grip tightened on the phone. I couldn't get the bloody wall display out of my head.

'But the trace,' I insisted, 'the squawk, seven thousand. Tell me exactly what happened.'

'Ah . . .' He paused for a second or two, apologetic, regretful. 'I'm afraid I can't, Mrs Bruce. I'm simply relaying the facts. They say he's gone, disappeared. I'm afraid we may have to assume the worst.'

'But there wasn't a radio message?'

'Not as far as I know.'

'*Nothing?*'

'No.'

'So where was he? Whereabouts did it happen?'

Another silence. Then the policeman was back again.

'He was just crossing the fifty-degree north line. Does that make any sense?'

I nodded. The fifty-degree north line was almost exactly mid-Channel. If this nightmare conversation was real, if Adam had indeed ditched, then he'd be out there now, a tiny dot in the ocean. At the height of summer, with no injuries, he could have paddled round for hours but in early February, even with his luck, I knew the prospects were bleak.

The policeman was asking me to stay by the phone. He might have more news within the hour. Before he rang off he was nice enough to ask me if there was anyone close who could stay with me. Lying, I assured him there was.

I remember very clearly the morning when I first met Adam. I was still living down in the Falklands on the sheep settlement where I'd grown up, a rather solitary, introspective nineteen-year-old, much given to moody, day-long excursions on one or other of the farm's horses.

My favourite was a sturdy chestnut called Smoko. Like me, she had a passion for striking out across the trackless peat and the endless acres of tussock, riding for miles and miles until we were satisfactorily lost. Somehow, we always managed to return in one piece but the magic of the Falklands was the chance to be so overwhelmingly alone, and it was into that solitude that Adam, quite literally, dropped.

It was July 1982. Smoko and I had been reined in by the Argie occupation, and by the war that followed, and this was the first time since April that my father had judged it safe for us to venture out. Even so, we had to stick to areas declared mine-free by the army people and I was deep in one of the maps we'd been issued when I first heard the helicopter.

It was flying very low, following the contour of the hills from the direction of San Carlos Water. I remember shielding my eyes against the low winter sun, watching the little black insect grow quickly bigger. Despite the events of the past few months, Smoko had never quite got used to the clatter of the helicopters and I had to gentle her as the chopper circled us a couple of times before settling on to a nearby stretch of track. It was one of the big Royal Navy helicopters, squat, heavy, the dark-grey bulk of the cabin streaked with salt and oil. They called them Sea Kings and they were forever flying low over the settlement, frightening the sheep.

Even when the rotor had stopped turning and it was quiet again, Smoko was still nervous. We watched the pilot studying us from the cockpit. At length he unstrapped himself and appeared at the rear door. He stepped down on to the track and stamped some of the stiffness out of his legs. He was tall, well over six feet, and when he lifted an arm to wave I felt Smoko twitch beneath me. He walked over towards us. He'd taken off his helmet by now and his hair was flattened against his skull the way you look when you come out of the shower. He had a nice grin – spontaneous, unforced – and when he got close and took off his aviator sunglasses, I remember the colour of his eyes. They were the lightest blue, a shade my mother always referred to as 'mischievous'.

He introduced himself, keeping his distance from the horse. Like most of the service people we'd seen, he looked exhausted, his pale face darkened with stubble.

He wanted to know which settlement I came from. When I told him, he grinned again.

'Gander Creek?'

'That's right.'

'The Tranters?'

I have two sisters, one older, one younger. We've all been fortunate in our physical inheritance, absorbing a mixture of my mother's long-legged Scandinavian good looks and my father's wind-buffed York-shire sturdiness. I don't think any of us thought of ourselves as beautiful – I'd much rather have had blue eyes than brown, and my smile is decidedly lop-sided – but we were all still single in '82 and it was plain that navy intelligence had spread the word.

Adam was gesturing back towards the Sea King. In a couple of days' time, it was his winchman's birthday. He said he owed the old bugger a decent night out and he wondered whether he and his crew and one or two others might drop over for a party. He'd seen the settlement from the air and he knew we had a community hall. He and his boys could muster plenty of Scotch, oodles of vodka, and the winchman had a sackful of disco tapes. They'd been fighting the war for longer than he cared to think about, and now the Argies had jacked it in, there was the bloody weather to contend with.

His mention of the weather made me laugh. Living in the islands all my life, I'd got used to the incessant wind and sudden curtains of squally rain. The thought that a Falklands winter might offer some kind of ordeal was wonderfully novel.

'We've got a date, then?'

Rather cautiously, I told him it might be possible, but when he said he'd prefer Sunday to Saturday I realised that for him, at least, the party was as good as fixed. He gave me another grin, then extended a gloved hand close enough for me to reach down and shake it.

'Nice horse,' I remember him saying, 'I'll try not to frighten it next time.'

It was dark before the police phoned back. I'd been forcing myself around the house, coupling one job to another, fighting the temp-tation to think too hard about Adam's wretched Cessna. There had to be some way the West Drayton people had got it wrong. Either that, or Adam had already been picked up. Some fishing boat or other. Some passing mermaid. Anyone, as long as he was still intact.

'Nothing, I'm afraid.'

'Nothing at all?'

For the first time, I was close to tears. Tears are what happens when you can no longer find the words to keep the lid on all the stuff bubbling up inside. When the policeman came back with another of his sensible questions, I sank into the nearest chair, choked with emotion.

'Was he carrying marker dyes?' he asked for the second time. Dyes stain seawater red. Or green. Or yellow. Damn all use if it happens to be dark. 'Mrs Bruce?'

'I'm sorry.' I reached for a tea towel, the kitchen a blur. 'Give me a moment.'

He faltered, then told me that the coastguard would be in touch if there was anything to report. The search was resuming at first light but realistically, unless something exceptional had happened, they were looking at an MPD. Official jargon always gives me the shivers, how cold it can be, how brutally efficient. MPD means Missing Presumed Dead.

I was trying hard to focus on the Aga. Adam used to stand there, I thought. It was his favourite spot, the place he chose to warm his bottom, and unzip his flying suit, and talk me through his latest sortie in the Mustang, or the Harvard, or even my little Moth. Our whole life had been built around these moments, sharing our respective days, comparing notes, swopping stories, sharing a glass or two of scrumpy from the farm down the lane before I busied around with the oven gloves and dished up supper. All that laughter. All that warmth. Gone.

'There'll be a reference to the AAIB,' the policeman was saying, 'So you should expect a call from them, as well.'

The AAIB is the Air Accidents Investigation Branch. Until now, thank God, it had been nothing more than another of those eternal aviation acronyms.

'Of course,' I said dully. 'I expect I'll be here.'

After the policeman had rung off, I went upstairs to the bedroom. Since we converted Mapledurcombe, Adam and I had been living in one wing of the house, a little self-contained suite of rooms off-limits to guests. Having no children, nor much in the way of visiting friends, this corner of the house had been ours to keep exactly as we pleased. The fact that it was so scruffy, so lived-in, was – I suspect – a delight to both of us. The business we'd chosen to run imposed the highest standards. Here, we could be ourselves.

I lay on the duvet in the darkness, my hands stretched out above my head, my fingers tracing the shapes carved in the bedhead. We'd had the bed longer than we'd had the house. It was French, a big, solid, handsome thing that weighed a ton. Adam had found it in an auction room on Jersey, and shipped it back to the mainland. Like the Aga, and my old bike, and a couple of dozen other items, it had become part of the geography of thirteen years of marriage: comforting, ours, always there. Alone, without Adam, I realised that none of it meant anything.

I must have drifted off to sleep. I awoke to hear the phone ringing downstairs. It was Harald. It was half past midnight. He was in Cowes. He wanted to come over.

By the time he arrived, I had the water boiled for coffee. I heard a car crunching up the drive and I opened the front door to find Harald getting out of the taxi. He bent to the driver's window.

'Give me fifteen minutes,' I heard him say.

In the hall, Harald held me at arm's length for a moment or two, then enveloped me. His leather jacket smelled of oil, Avgas and the little black cheroots he occasionally smoked. To my surprise, he was trembling.

'Shit,' he said twice.

I almost asked him what was wrong but the question, of course, would have been idiotic. Over the last year or so, Adam and Harald had become very close. Adam called him a buddy, which for him was rare. Like me, he took few risks with real friendship.

On the panelled wall beside us I'd recently hung a painting that I'd commissioned for Adam's last birthday. It showed the Mustang skimming the top of a bank of cotton-wool clouds. The nearside wing was slightly low and the artist had done a wonderful job on our sleek silver bird, but I'd been especially pleased with his figurework. The pilot was sitting well back in the cockpit, and the grin on his face could only have belonged to Adam.

Harald couldn't take his eyes off the picture. He'd been to Mapledurcombe a number of times but the last couple of months he'd been back in the States and I don't think he'd seen it.

'Spooky.' He was still looking at Adam. 'You know something?'

'No.'

'I think he knew.'

'Knew what?'

Harald glanced round at me. For a man in his late fifties, he didn't carry an ounce of spare flesh.

'I think he knew the way he'd go, the way it would happen. He'd never make old bones. Those sort of guys never do.'

I stared at him. I had the feeling it was meant as some kind of compliment, a reassurance even, but it had exactly the opposite effect. What Harald was telling me was unambiguous, a big, fat full stop at the end of the worst day of my life.

9

'You think he's dead?'

'I think he's happy.'

'*Happy?* What a horrible thing to say.'

'Not at all. He was the best. Believe me, the best.'

We had coffee at the kitchen table. Harald never drank alcohol but I helped myself to a tumbler of Adam's precious malt whisky. I'd never tried it before and I've never touched it since. Even now, just the smell of malt is enough to make me want to throw up.

Harald had flown over from Jersey and taken the hydrofoil to Cowes. He'd been in St Helier on business and had seen Adam for dinner only last night.

'How was he?'

'Fine, just fine. We had sushi at that new Japanese place. You know Adam. Try anything once.'

I nodded. I wanted a message, some kind of indication that I'd been on Adam's mind, but I knew Harald wasn't the kind of man to ask. Too guarded. Too buttoned-down. Unlike the husband I'd so obviously lost.

'So what . . .' I shrugged hopelessly, '. . . happened?'

'I don't know. No one knows. He borrowed Steve's Cessna. That's where the story begins and ends.'

'You've talked to Steve?'

'You bet. I was over there this afternoon. The guy's shattered. You can imagine.'

I swallowed another mouthful of malt. Steve Liddell was as plane-crazy as the rest of us. He ran a small engineering business on the edge of Jersey airport. He did maintenance and stuff for private flyers, and Adam had used him for one or two routine jobs on the Harvard and my Moth. Adam had talked about him a lot recently, and had gone as far as suggesting that we take a stake in his business. Given our other commitments, I hadn't been wild about the idea.

'The Cessna was OK? As far as Steve knew?'

'Absolutely. He says he signed off the last fifty-hour check only a couple of days ago. The aircraft was a hundred per cent, engine, electrics, instrumentation, the lot. No problems. Clean sheet.'

'So what happened?' I repeated.

'Christ knows.' Harald shook his head. 'We're not talking some rookie pilot here. The guy's a veteran, born to it. Lucky, too. It just doesn't happen this way. Not even a radio call? Excuse me –' He broke off, tipping his head back, swallowing hard, and I realised that grief embarrassed him. Join the club, I thought grimly.

Harald had regained control, suddenly businesslike. He said he'd chartered a boat from some contacts in St Helier. They were at sea now, pushing down towards the crash site. Harald had ordered them to scour the area until further notice. Money, as ever, seemed to be no problem.

'But what about the search-and-rescue people?'

'They'll be scaling down. By midday tomorrow, they'll probably call a halt. We're talking serious assets here. Helicopter time ain't cheap.'

'But you'll stay there?'

'For as long as it takes.'

I looked at him for a long moment, my eyes swimming, then his hand found mine on the table. It was surprisingly warm.

'He's dead, Ellie.' He gave my hand a little squeeze. 'The question I'm asking is why.'

After Harald had gone, I poured myself another malt, moving from room to room, a ghost on the long, shadowed first-floor gallery that overhung the hall. I was grateful for Harald's visit. The days ahead were going to be a trial and I needed that kind of candour, that kind of support, the knowledge that there was someone out there who – in his own way – had known Adam nearly as well as I did.

Harald Meyler had changed our lives at a point when I knew we were facing financial disaster. Adam would never have used that kind of language – it simply wasn't the way he'd chosen to lead his life – but I was closer to the figures than he was and I didn't need an accounting degree to realise that we'd gone way, way over the limits we'd set for ourselves.

Thanks to Adam, and five years of flying mercenaries around southern Africa, we'd been able to buy Mapledurcombe House, a sprawling Elizabethan manor with sensational views across the Isle of Wight. The place had needed a lot of attention, but even so there'd been just enough cash left for Adam to bid for a couple of World War II aeroplanes at an auction in southern Ireland.

One of the planes was an old two-seat trainer called a Harvard. The other, in even worse condition, was the shell of a classic American fighter, the P-51 Mustang. It had always been Adam's dream to rebuild vintage aircraft but the sheer cost of the project had shaken us both. A hundred and twenty thousand pounds is a lot of money for two crated wrecks and a truckload of bits and pieces, but the purchase price quickly seemed a bargain once we'd hired an engineer and started putting the aeroplanes back together again. Spares cost a fortune, as did the premises we leased, and the various certifications we needed. There were certain weeks, I told Adam, when you could stand very still, and cup your hand behind your ear, and listen to the trickle of money draining from our precious company account.

I paused for a moment in the little timber-beamed bedroom we called the Mitchell Suite. This was the first of the rooms we'd converted for the American guests we were sure would flock to Mapledurcombe. The idea, brilliant in its simplicity, had been Adam's. Rebuild the Harvard first, give Mapledurcombe a lick of paint, offer gourmet cooking, car hire, free membership of the local golf club, and – best of all – the chance to make one last sortie in the rear seat of the sturdy wartime trainer.

This package would be targeted at ageing USAAF veterans, men who'd flown against the Germans in the war. Retired now, they'd have the time and the money to treat themselves and their loved ones to a very special vacation. With his air transport pilot's licence and our rebuilt Harvard, Adam would put the Americans back in the air over Europe. With a pile of cookery books, and a bit of local help, I would offer them the softest of landings.

We called the company Old Glory. In our first summer season, we took enough money to make a hefty dent in the costs of the Harvard rebuild. The letters that arrived from the States guaranteed an even better second year. On the promise of these advance bookings, Adam – ever impulsive – gave Dave Jeffries, our engineer, the go-ahead to start on the Mustang. The Mustang ate money like the thoroughbred she proved to be. By the time the fighter was airborne, we owed the bank £177,000.

Adam, of course, said it didn't matter. The rebuild had gone way over budget but that was because we'd decided, rather late, to go for the full dual conversion. Most Mustangs, including ours, were single-seat. Enlarging the cockpit and adding a second seat had confronted Dave Jeffries with the kind of engineering problems that could only be solved, alas, by massive injections of cash. To Adam, who was nerveless when it came to money, this was simply an investment. With two spare seats – one in the Harvard, one in the Mustang – we could double our takings. That, in turn, would mean yet more bills to pay for extra bedrooms at Mapledurcombe, but in Adam's eyes this was the clinching evidence that we were finally on a roll. Spend money to make money, he'd murmur, hunched over his flying maps on the kitchen table, plotting the best route back to Schweinfurt or Berlin.

After a fashion, it worked. But as successful as Old Glory became, we still hadn't paid off even half the overdraft. Adam had incorporated our little enterprise in Jersey to protect us from the Inland Revenue but I don't think it had occurred to him that bank managers in this offshore low-tax paradise were just as canny and unforgiving as their brothers in the UK. When it came to the crunch, the message from our accountant in St Helier was brutal. Adding three extra rooms to Mapledurcombe had returned the overdraft to six figures. Insurance rates on the aircraft were going through the roof. We needed someone to invest a lot of cash. Quickly.

That someone was Harald Meyler. He'd been in touch with Adam before, the result of an article in one of the aviation magazines about our Mustang rebuild. Harald had appeared within weeks, curious to know a little more about the aircraft's history. The log books we'd acquired from the auctioneers were incomplete but the aircraft had flown with 336 Squadron, part of the US Eighth Air Force, and this fact had duly been noted in the article. Harald, who knew a great deal about classic aircraft, had stayed long enough to spend a couple of evenings with Adam and it was these conversations, I'm sure, that laid the foundations for what followed.

Harald fascinated Adam. He was an American, with homes in Florida and Switzerland. He was older than we were, fifty-five according to the passport I once saw, and he'd built the kind of life that invited lots of questions. How come he was so wealthy? What, exactly, did he do for a living? And why had he put together, in his phrase, 'one of the neatest collections of fighter planes in the free world'?

The planes evidently included a Thunderbolt, two Hellcats, a Lightning, three Mustangs, a Trojan, a Tigercat, two Warhawks plus a handful of early jet fighters. The aircraft were quartered on a remote airfield in Florida and Harald flew them all. The latter impressed Adam no end – envy as well as admiration – but what struck me was the sheer outlay involved. Nursing just two of these casualties back to health had forced us dangerously close to bankruptcy. Maintaining a small airforce – as Harald obviously did – compelled serious respect.

The problems over the bank loan came to a head in 1994 and it was Harald who rescued us. Impressed by the quality of the rebuild, he'd already made Adam an offer for the Mustang. At the time, determined to keep his nerve, Adam had turned him down. But when the company's survival was finally on the line, the two of them met up again and a lengthy negotiation gave us the breathing space we needed. At first, Harald had wanted to buy the Mustang outright. In the end, he settled for a forty-five per cent share, reviewable after three years, at a price of $405,000, payable in three instalments. The first $135,000 saved us from going under. I, for one, was profoundly grateful.

I was back in the kitchen now, still thinking about Harald. Unlike the other Americans we'd got to know – eager, open, friendly – he'd never once invited us back to the States, or opened even the smallest door to his heart or his past. Put this way, Harald sounds charmless, even cold, but like Adam I found him compelling and oddly likeable. There was something in his face that spoke of a great deal of pain. He looked weathered, emotionally, and in a small way I became fascinated by the kind of life he must have led. After the negotiations over the Mustang were done, Adam started calling him our Guardian Angel, and though it's a daft phrase I knew exactly what he meant. He had strength. He was one of our kind. And he'd saved Old Glory from spearing in.

It was three in the morning before I finally went to bed. I slept badly, waking twice to swallow water from the tumbler at my bedside. I dreamed of some nameless, godforsaken piece of ocean. It was always rough, always grey, always cold. From time to time the outline of a ship drifted by, and there came the sound of a child's voice calling for help. I awoke in tears, the pillow wet beneath my cheek. Downstairs, the phone was ringing.

It was the police again, a woman this time, relaying a message from the coastguard. They'd had a helicopter up since dawn. An hour and a half ago, more or less where they'd expected, the crew had seen one or two bits of wreckage in the water. The chopper had marked the position and passed the data to the rescue co-ordination centre. A naval frigate, on exercise off Dorset, had been asked to investigate.

I clung on to the phone. My head hurt.

'This wreckage . . .' I began, '. . . was it an aircraft?'

The silence told me everything. After the policewoman had said how sorry she was, I thanked her and put the phone down. Harald had been right. Even without a body, I knew that Adam was dead.

Chapter two

The television people arrived at lunchtime. They'd phoned earlier, asking for an interview, and I think I'd been too dazed to say no. They parked their Volvo estate by the front door and carted in all kinds of equipment, setting up light stands in the little snug that Adam and I used during the winter.

I'd met the interviewer before. She was a slim, pretty redhead who'd recently done a feature on the Mustang, and I knew she'd taken Adam's eye. The interview wasn't very long – five minutes at the most – and I was handicapped by knowing so little about what might have happened. It turned out they'd already talked to the coastguard and they had pictures, too, of the search-and-rescue helicopter returning to Lee-on-the-Solent. Given all this footage, the most I could contribute was a kind of numbed incomprehension, but it occurred to me as they left that this was exactly what they'd come to record. They'd rearranged the furniture a bit, and hung the painting of the Mustang on the wall behind my chair, and after they'd gone I was left alone in the snug, staring at a pile of old photos I'd let them film, realising just how hard it is to voice something as raw and powerful as grief.

There were more calls from the media during the afternoon, newspapers mainly, and by five o'clock, weary of explaining that Adam hadn't gone down in the Mustang, I decided to flee for a couple of hours. One of the calls I had to make on my own account was to Adam's parents. They'd emigrated to Vancouver only last year and I knew I had to break the news as soon as possible. If I was back in Mapledurcombe by eight, my call would probably find them preparing for lunch. In the mean time, I could gather what strength I had for what I knew would be a difficult conversation.

Ralph Pierson lived by himself on the island's south coast. He had an immaculate chalet-bungalow on a wooded lane that wound down to the lighthouse at St Catherine's Point. His garden unrolled from the back of the house and from the patio he'd built he could look out across the broad expanse of lawn to the undercliff and the sea.

Adam and I had known Ralph for nearly three years. He was in his mid-seventies, still fit, still alert, a fund of wonderful stories. As a young pilot, he'd flown Spitfires and Typhoons during the war and had contacted us after news of the Mustang rebuild had made a paragraph or two in the local paper. We'd liked each other on sight and after the sudden death of his wife, he and I had become close friends. I'd lost my own father at about the same time and I can't pretend that Ralph wasn't something of a substitute.

He was waiting beside his open front door when I got out of the car. He was a tall man, nearly as tall as Adam, and he was wearing the blazer and slacks he favoured for semi-formal occasions. He put his arms round me, and kissed me on top of the head, and then led me inside. There was a tray of tea on the low table beside the sofa and he'd even found the time to rustle up some crumpets.

I stood beside the big picture window, staring out. The sea looked grey and forbidding and I couldn't get rid of the memory of the voice in my dreams. All day I'd heard it. Calling and calling.

Ralph must have seen me shudder. He insisted I had the armchair that looked inwards, towards the fireplace. He stooped to the glowing logs and gave them a poke.

'Unfair,' he said simply. 'Damned unfair.'

I nodded in mute agreement, already glad I'd summoned the strength to phone and then drive over. Ralph had the rare gift of making me feel completely at home. No fuss. No drama. Just the readiest kind of intimacy, wholly natural, wholly sincere.

'I'm going to hang on to the Mustang,' I said suddenly, 'if it's the last thing I do.'

'Because?' Ralph was still on his knees by the fire, coaxing a crumpet on to a toasting fork.

'Because it was Adam's. Because it meant so much to him.'

'And you think that's possible? Or even wise?'

'I've no idea. But that's what I'm going to do, I promise you.' I broke off, surprised at my own vehemence. Keeping the Mustang felt like a decision I'd been waiting to make all day, something positive, something to remember him by, something to preoccupy me and keep me busy, just the way my marriage had done. Adam and the Mustang were two of a kind. As Ralph knew only too well.

'It's early days, Ellie,' he said quietly. 'Things may change. You should take a deep breath, give yourself a bit of time. Here –'

He juggled the crumpet from hand to hand while I found a plate. I watched the butter melting on top, remembering the day he'd phoned to tell me about his wife, Sally. She'd died of a heart attack in her sleep. He'd awoken to find her lying dead beside him.

16

'It's horrible,' I said slowly. 'Really horrible. I'd no idea.'
'Death?'
'Losing someone.'
Ralph nodded, sombre.
'You're right,' he said. 'But you have to go on.'
'I know, but . . .'
I looked round the room, desperate for something else to talk about, only too aware how every conversation returned again and again to Adam. Alive, I hadn't minded at all. He was that kind of man, vital, ebullient, turning heads, compelling attention. Dead, though, I couldn't bear it.

Ralph kept his desk in the corner of the long lounge, tucked in beside one of the smaller windows. Amongst the pile of books, I spotted *The War Diary of the Mighty Eighth*. The Mighty Eighth was airman's slang for the US Eighth Air Force. Since last year, Ralph had been helping us by putting together a detailed history of our Mustang.

'How's it going?' I enquired lightly. 'The research?'
Ralph was spreading jam on another crumpet. He looked, if anything, relieved at the sudden change of subject.
'Is that a serious question?'
'Of course.'
'Then it's going well. In fact it's going beautifully. I meant to phone you yesterday. One or two developments, I'm happy to say.'

I smiled, glad of the warmth this lovely man spread so effortlessly around him. It was something to do with a largeness of spirit, a whole-heartedness that I'd never quite met in such measure before. Adam had always seized life by the throat but Ralph – older – had a softer, subtler grip. He was never downcast, never cynical, never pessimistic. He had immense dignity and a kind of quiet strength. The way he'd managed to cope with the loss of his wife had always, to me, been remarkable.

I licked the butter from my fingers and retrieved the *War Diary* from the desk. It weighed a ton and when I got back to the chair and opened it, half a dozen photos fell out. I picked them up and went through them one by one. They showed a Mustang. By the shape of the cockpit and the bulge of the big underbelly radiator, it looked like a P-51D.

'Is this ours?'
'Yes.'

I returned to the photos, fascinated. They were in grainy black and white, the corners curling where they'd been stored in direct sunlight. In the first couple of shots, our fighter looked scruffy and battleworn.

They were air-to-air shots, but the aircraft was up-sun and the pilot was visible only as a silhouette in the bubble cockpit. In the third photo, the aircraft was back on the ground, parked in front of a big pair of hangar doors. A gaggle of pilots stood beside the cockpit, laughing. The stocky one in the middle was explaining some combat manoeuvre, his gloved hands out in front of him, the left hand closing on the right. He was still wearing a leather helmet and a parachute harness. His flying jacket was half-unzipped and I wondered just how much time he'd had to knot the scarf around his neck.

Ralph was watching me.

'His name's Karel Brokenka.' He pointed to the pilot in the middle of the group.

'He flew the plane?'

'Yes.'

'Our plane?'

'Yes. And he scored in it, too.' Ralph joined me, perching himself on the arm of the chair. 'According to Brokenka, it was '45, New Year's Day. Fourth Fighter Group were flying daylight escort with the B-17s. They came across some Me109s on the way out and bounced them. There was a helluva dogfight and 336 accounted for at least four.' Three-three-six was the USAAF squadron to which our Mustang was attached. I was still looking at the pilot in the photograph. He had a chubby face and a slightly lop-sided grin.

'And you're sure he was flying the Mustang?'

'So he says.'

'And these came from him?'

'Yes. Along with some other bits and pieces.'

It was Ralph's turn to go to the desk. While he rummaged in one of the drawers he told me how his letters to the air force archive in Washington had finally produced a list of names and addresses. Karel Brokenka was living in a nursing home in a suburb of Chicago. On the phone, he'd confirmed that P-Popsie had indeed been his aircraft. WD-P was the squadron designation of our Mustang. He'd called it *Little Ceska* or 'Little Czech'.

Ralph returned with a file. Inside was a collection of photocopied A4 sheets, neatly stapled together. On the front sheet was one of those stick-on address tags. The nursing home was called Shoreview.

'I explained to him that the log book was incomplete. I told him about the missing page. He thought that was very funny.'

'Why?'

'He said he'd torn it out. Thought they'd never catch up with him.'

'And did they?'

'No, but I did.'

Ralph was smiling now. Brokenka had evidently kept the missing page as a souvenir of his one and only kill. I began to go through the photocopied sheets. Each one carried a big blue stamp. 'USAF Archive', the stamp read, 'Certified for Release'. Ralph's hand hovered over mine. I was looking at a grid of dates, aircrew names and aircraft types.

'These are extracts from the squadron's Operations Record Book. Look –' Ralph's finger moved down the column of dates until we got to 1 January 1945. Beneath the details of sortie or flight, neatly typed, was the entry: *Penetration Target Withdrawal Support, Derben-Stendal-Genthin. 4 Me109s destroyed.* I looked back along the line. On 1 January, P-Popsie had indeed been flown by 2Lt. Karel Brokenka. I mouthed the name to myself. It had a nice feel.

'What's he like?'

'Pleasant enough chap. My sort of age, seventy-six, seventy-seven.'

'Married?'

'Divorced, but I gather his ex-wife still pops in to see him at the home. He had some kind of stroke. Nothing too serious but he says he's pretty much confined to a wheelchair these days.'

I turned the photograph over. Someone had scribbled the pilots' names. There were five in all. Left to right, Brokenka was the third. I looked at the photo again, checking the sequence. Karel Brokenka was very definitely the chubby one in the middle, the pilot who'd drawn blood in our Mustang, and I stared at him for a moment or two, trying to imagine him at the controls, the same seat, the same stick, the finger on that gloved hand closing on the firing trigger as the Me109 fattened in the gun sight. We'd been hoping against hope that Ralph might unearth something like this. It would give the Mustang so much character, so much extra pedigree. Not simply an aeroplane. But an aeroplane with a history. I must tell Adam, I thought at once, picturing his face when I gave him the news.

Seconds later, I felt Ralph's hand on mine. From somewhere or other he'd produced a handkerchief. I took it, shameless, grateful, blowing my nose.

'Crying helps,' Ralph said quietly. 'I'll pour you some more tea.'

Later, after I'd pulled myself together, we talked again about the stuff that Karel Brokenka had sent over. Adam had planned for a full-scale book on the Mustang, listing every flight, every pilot, every unit with which the aeroplane had ever had contact. Lavishly illustrated, handsomely bound, we'd offer the book as a souvenir for visiting guests, and if it was any good, there might even be sales on the open market. Either way, Adam visualised the history as yet another brick in the wall we were building around Old Glory, and Ralph – with time on his hands – had been only too pleased to volunteer his services.

I was on my third cup of tea. Karel Brokenka's family had evidently fled their native Czechoslovakia after the Germans moved in. They'd rented a single room in a Chicago tenement and as soon as he could, young Karel had volunteered for the air force. By Christmas 1943 he was back in Europe, flying with 336 Squadron from Debden, an airfield in Essex.

Ralph was showing me the combat report Brokenka had filed after his outing on New Year's Day. The squadron had made its rendezvous with the bombers at 11.25. An hour later, a flight of Mustangs had peeled off, bouncing the Me109s in the Ulzen area. Brokenka, in *Little Ceska*, had singled out a target, and chased it in a near-vertical dive. He'd closed to less than two hundred metres, loosing off three-second bursts of fire. At 3,000 feet, bits of the Me109 began to disintegrate. Seconds later, it was ablaze. Brokenka had seen the pilot bale out but was too busy pulling out of the dive to register a parachute.

I looked up.

'What about the German?' I queried. 'Does Brokenka have a name?'

'No. But we've got the date now, and the mission details, so the rest shouldn't be too difficult.'

'What will you do?'

'Write to the Bundesarchiv. That's the German lot. Their records are over in Berlin. I gather they're pretty helpful and I promised Karel I'd get back to him the moment they come up with something solid.' He tapped the file containing the squadron records. 'It's all elimination, of course. Their pilots filed reports, just like ours. I imagine the chap we're after's probably dead, but if he survived . . .' He frowned. 'Are you sure you want to keep the Mustang?'

'Positive.'

'Only now's the time . . .' Ralph's eyes were back on the mountain of books on the desk.

I shook my head and told him again that the aircraft was staying in the family. The phrase made him smile and he patted my arm before returning to his chair by the fire. The archival detective work, he said, had been a real pleasure, but a revelation, too. So many letters. So much cross-checking. So much light to be shed on those faraway days he remembered so well. For an hour or so, happily, I listened to him musing about his own little corner of the war, the aircraft he'd flown, the friendships he'd made, the moments when he'd battled for a kill, the conclusions he'd come to about exactly what it was that put the best fighter pilots way out ahead of the rest.

'And what was it?'

'Ruthlessness. Single-mindedness. Tunnel vision, if you like. The chaps who made it, really made it, were mostly bastards. They didn't care about anyone else, just themselves. Funny that. They'd do well whatever line of country they went into. Peace or war, it wouldn't matter.' He nodded. 'You had to get in close, as close as you could, and you had to have a certain kind of courage. Not normal courage, not what you or I would call courage, but something else.'

'What, exactly?'

'I don't know, Ellie. It's something I've thought about and thought about. A lot of these people were almost psychopathic. They had a sort of immunity.'

'To what?'

'Fear. They were pitiless, cold. You could feel the chill in them. It was as if something inside didn't work properly. They had a kind of madness. Do you know what I mean?'

I told him I didn't. He looked thoughtful, gazing at the glowing coals, and I was suddenly struck by a very different Ralph, altogether less sure of himself than perhaps I'd imagined.

'What about you?' I asked gently. 'Were you up there with them? These aces you talk about?'

'No.' He shook his head, regretful.

'Did you try?'

'Yes.'

'And it didn't work?'

'No.'

'Why not?'

He thought about the question, still looking at the fire, then he sighed, favouring me with a rueful smile.

'I never got close enough,' he said, 'if you want the truth.'

I told him it didn't matter. Not to me. Then I was struck by something else.

'What about Adam?' I asked him. 'Would he have made it?'

He gave the question some thought. Then he shook his head.

'No,' he said slowly. 'He wouldn't.'

'Why not?'

'You really want to know?'

'Yes please.'

'Because he was too human, too eager, too much in a hurry. And because he let his attention wander. You couldn't afford to do that. Not if you wanted serious kills.'

I nodded, thinking of Adam, my puppy, my playmate, the glorious man who'd filled my heart, and shared my bed, and turned my life upside down.

'You're right,' I conceded. 'But that's why I loved him.'

Ralph smiled.

'And needed him,' he said quietly.

Adam had been away in Africa a month before I realised what it was that I hated about Britain. We were still living in a draughty terraced house in Aberdeen, our first proper home after we'd married and Adam had got a job flying supply helicopters out to the North Sea oil rigs. The job only lasted nine months or so – Adam got bored – but it was through American contacts he met on the rigs that he landed the contract with the South African people. This new assignment took him out of the country for spells of three months or longer, and while he was away I did my best to make friends locally. We'd been out with several couples when Adam was still at home but I quickly discovered that operating as a single woman does absolutely nothing for your social life. The result, predictably, was loneliness.

This, to be honest, came as a surprise. At home, in the Falklands, I'd never given the need for company a thought. By choice, I was often out with Smoko on my own, but I'd never once felt lonely. Back at the settlement, I had two sisters, a mum, a dad, and good buddies amongst the young shepherds and roustabouts who lived in the cookhouse. A day's ride away, there were more settlements, more friends, more conversation. But in Britain, where you couldn't move for people, there didn't seem to be the same sense of kinship. People were cautious, wary, suspicious even. The way you dressed, which supermarket you went to, how much your husband earned, all these things appeared to matter. Packed into a big city, each of us seemed infinitely more isolated and cut off than I'd ever noticed in the emptiness of the Falklands.

With loneliness came a longing to be home again, and on the gloomier days I began to drive out into the mountains, desperate for an hour or so when I could tramp around, and feel the wind on my face, and kid myself that I was back at Gander Creek. It never worked, of course, because there was always the drive back to Aberdeen, and the traffic jams on the ring road, and news of yet another stabbing on the TV once I'd got myself locked and bolted behind my nice big front door. As the weeks went by, I began to hate this half-life, and in my letters to Adam I must have said so because the moment he came home on leave he came up with the answer.

'I'll teach you to fly,' he said. 'We'll start next week.'

And we did. He'd made friends with one of the managers out at Dyce airport. The guy was also ex-navy and he had shares in an old Tiger Moth. A Moth is a biplane, one big wing on top of the other, and it's got a little metal skid at the back which makes it, in Adam's phrase, a tail-dragger. There are simpler ways of learning to fly than starting in a biplane but Adam, who was seldom less than sure of himself, wouldn't entertain the thought of anything modern. An open cockpit, he assured me, was the very best introduction to what he promised would be a life-changing experience.

It was early April when we started, a raw, bright day with a chilly wind blowing in off the sea. We were flying from a private farm strip up the coast, about a forty-minute drive from Aberdeen, and when we got there I was delighted to find how rudimentary the set-up was. A scruffy old Portakabin. Fuel hand-pumped from forty-gallon drums. And a youth on a tractor to clear the cattle from the strip whenever someone wanted to take off or land. This was a world to which I needed no introduction. Gander Creek. Definitely.

I got changed in the Portakabin. It smelled of the fertiliser the farmer had stacked in bags at one end. Adam had found me a flying suit from somewhere or other but it was at least a size too big. Wearing an extra pullover filled up most of the space inside, and after I'd rolled up the trouser bottoms and the sleeves I felt like a badly wrapped parcel. Adam had produced a leather helmet, too, and a pair of goggles, but it wasn't until we were walking out across the grass that I realised he was serious about me wearing them. Like the plane itself, with its struts and its wires, and the worn leather trim around the cockpit, the helmet and the goggles seemed like props from some period movie.

Adam helped me put them on, tightening the helmet strap beneath my chin and then adjusting the goggles so they sat snugly on my face. For this first flight, he'd let me sit in the front cockpit. Later, once the real training started, we'd swap seats. When I asked why, he said something complicated about the aircraft's centre of gravity. In a month or so, fingers crossed, I'd be going solo. Flying solo, you always sat in the rear cockpit.

'So why don't I sit in the rear cockpit now?'

'Because you'll get a better view from the front.'

'What about you? Don't you need the better view?'

'No problem. Just promise me you won't throw up.' He gestured at the open cockpit. 'First time I flew, I covered the guy behind in breakfast.'

The story made me laugh and I clambered into the front cockpit, making myself comfortable while Adam ran through the controls. I did my best to memorise the basics – stick, rudder, throttle – but sitting there listening to Adam explaining the way the seat harness buckled and unbuckled, I remember thinking how odd the whole exercise was. Another reason for being so fed up with living in Britain was because of the restrictions, the feeling of being so hemmed in. Yet here was my beloved husband, binding me hand and foot on the promise that flying would give me back my freedom.

He finished the briefing with a word about the parachute. If we got into trouble, he'd let me know on the intercom. If the intercom didn't work, he said playfully, he'd reach forward from the rear cockpit and tap me on the shoulder. Three taps meant bale out. Two taps meant stand by.

'And one tap?'

I remember him squeezing my gloved hand.

'Means I love you.'

The bellow of the engine terrified me. I hadn't expected it to be so loud, so obviously powerful. The propeller was a blur in seconds and the wind gusting back around the cockpit suddenly tasted of burnt petrol. We bumped out across the grass. It had been raining for most of the winter and over the cackle of the engine I could hear the wheels squelching through the puddles of standing water. Because of the way the aircraft's nose was tilted up, neither of us could see a thing and Adam had to weave the plane from side to side, checking left and right to gauge the turn for the marked strip down the middle of the field that constituted the runway. The Moth seemed clumsy, ungainly, poorly balanced, lurching from side to side every time we hit a divot or a rabbit hole, and I remember thinking how unnatural the whole thing felt. Smoko and I had been friends in seconds. Flying, on first acquaintance, seemed a pretty grim substitute.

Hard against the hedge at the end of the strip, I listened to Adam murmuring to himself as he ran through some kind of checklist. He seemed completely at home, completely happy, and after he'd told me to adjust the little rearview mirror attached to the top wing, he gave me a grin and a thumbs-up before revving the engine and turning the aircraft into wind. The Moth began to gather speed and I became aware of the control stick moving between my legs as Adam pushed it forward to lift the tail. I gazed out, feeling the slipstream tightening the skin around my goggles, watching the grass blur beneath the wing. We were racing along now, the bumping beginning to ease, then suddenly we were airborne, the little biplane crabbing sideways for a moment or two until Adam kicked it straight.

I felt myself grinning, and I looked back, straining against the harness straps, watching the Portakabin, and the tractor, and our battered old Sierra grow smaller and smaller until they disappeared altogether. I'd flown a lot in the Falklands, sometimes in planes little bigger than this one, but flying in the Moth, with its open cockpit and churning engine, was something so different, so new, that I began to understand why Adam had recommended it with such vigour.

The needle on the altimeter was passing 1,200 feet. Away to the west I could see the shadowed wall of the Cairngorms. Beneath us, a perfect line of breaking surf stretched north towards Peterhead and Fraserburgh. Adam was singing now. He had the worst voice in the world, and absolutely no memory for lyrics, so he made them up the way he improvised so much of the rest of his life, and he was still murdering one of the early Beatles numbers when he dropped the little biplane's nose, revealing a fishing boat and a cloud of seagulls several thousand feet beneath us. I watched the boats get bigger quickly. The note the wind was making in the wires that cross-braced the wings got shriller and shriller. Then the stick came back towards me, and my stomach fell away, and Adam pulled the nose of the Moth up and up until I could see nothing but sky. For a moment we were upside-down, the beat of the engine much slower, then the Moth came off the top of the loop and I watched the coast revolve around us, a whole 360 degrees, until we'd levelled out, the engine churning away again as if nothing had ever happened. The noise Adam could hear in his earphones was quite unprompted, a spontaneous round of applause, my own glad admission that – yet again – my lovely husband had been right.

'What's going on?' he yelled.

'Nothing.' I tried to stop giggling. 'You just changed my life.'

Later, we flew inland, up the valley of the Dee towards Balmoral and Braemar. I sat hunched in my cockpit, glad of the leather helmet and the extra sweater, fascinated by how responsive and alive the aircraft felt beneath my fingers. Adam had given me control after half an hour or so. I was to fly straight and level, ignoring the instruments in front of me, selecting a landmark way ahead and keeping it lined up with a point on the aircraft's nose. The landmark I chose turned out to be the shoulder of Lochnagar, a distinctive mountain easy to spot amongst the surrounding peaks, and I watched it drift slowly closer, nudging the biplane back on course from time to time with tiny little movements on the stick or rudder.

The feeling of being in charge, of being able to float up or down in three dimensions, was quite overpowering and after a while I became bolder, experimenting with the rudder pedals, marvelling at how I could crab the Moth sideways with a little pressure from my right or left foot. It was fun, this new game, but it was scary, too. Climbing over Lochnagar, we disappeared briefly into windblown rags of cloud. They tore past the open cockpit, plunging us into a very different world – cold and grey – and I was glad to be out in the sunshine again, the Cairngorms still beneath us, the bare shoulders of rock and heather mottled with those same clouds.

We landed back on the coast forty minutes or so later and Adam, I think, was pleased. That night, in bed, he said what a good pair of hands I had, and when we talked about how delicate flying was, how it needed a lover's touch, I understood at once what he meant. In my head, the Moth was already stabled with Smoko, my beloved horse. Airborne, it had become a friend.

Blessed with clear weather, we flew for the rest of April. Delighted with my progress, Adam deferred his departure for the next contract, and after twelve hours of instruction, I went solo. Three months later, with Adam in Africa, I sat the various tests for my Private Pilot's Licence. Oddly enough, the first leg of the Navigation Flight Test took me back towards the mountains. The examiner was flying in the front cockpit. I had control from the back. The first leg was pretty undemanding – fifty miles on the same heading – and I had time to look down, still fascinated by how slowly the landscape seemed to unfold beneath us, still amazed at that strange, God-like feeling that flying imparts.

Adam had been right. The Moth had uncaged me. I was free again. I was happy. I had lots to think about, lots to confront. Learning to fly had never been less than a challenge but instinctively I felt at home in the aircraft. I loved the feeling of freedom she gave me, the feeling that we could outrun the wind and the weather, scroll glorious pictures in the sky, cheat gravity itself. We trusted each other. We respected each other. We'd see each other through to wherever this extraordinary journey might take us. Poetic? Of course. But real, too. More real than I have the talent to describe.

An hour or so later, when I side-slipped into Dyce for a perfect three-point landing, I knew the Nav Test was in the bag. I was right. More tests followed. I passed those, too. And when the examiner finally confirmed that the PPL was mine, I couldn't wait to tell Adam.

Trying to get a line through to Angola, where he was based, was a nightmare, and when the international operator told me she'd given up, I sat down and wrote him a long letter. In it, I tried to express what flying had come to mean for me. It was a way of saying thank you, of course, but it also obliged me to take an honest look at the first twelve months or so that we'd spent together. Our marriage was fabulous but I'd made a pretty rocky start in the UK and I knew it. I'd been weak. I'd been feeble. I'd let myself buckle under all the pressures that most people seemed to take for granted. Now, though, things would be different. Whatever Adam wanted to do with our lives, I was with him. Whatever he planned, I promised to make it work. And I did.

Chapter three

By the time I got back from Ralph's, it was nearly nine o'clock. I fed the cats, brewed myself a pot of tea and then sat beside the ansaphone, wondering whether I had the strength to cope with the fourteen recorded messages. Some, doubtless, would be friends and relatives, all of them well-meaning, few knowing quite what to say. One or two, judging by this afternoon, would probably have come from the media, yet more bids to tear a little flesh off the bone and expose it to the public view. For that, I had no taste whatsoever, and I finally solved the problem by phoning Adam's parents in Vancouver.

The last time I'd seen them was back in September, the morning we'd driven them to Heathrow. Adam's father, himself ex-navy, had run a yacht brokerage in Torquay. Far too honest for his own good, he'd finally tired of Thatcher's England, sold the business, and swapped a view of the River Dart for an acre and a half on Vancouver Island. He was a hard-working, intensely practical man and in her letters home Adam's mother had written glowing reports of what he'd been doing to transform the garden. With a little boat and a mooring in the nearby anchorage, their new life would be complete. They'd been incredibly lucky. In five brief months, they'd found their feet. Canada already felt like home.

When I got through, it was Adam's father who answered the phone. He sensed at once that something was wrong. When I told him what had happened, he didn't say a word. For a moment I thought he'd rung off, or put the phone down, then I heard him clearing his throat. When he spoke again, it was an old man's voice, tired, almost resigned, as if I'd given him news he'd been expecting for years. He wanted to know, absurdly, whether I'd be OK for money. I gulped. Money was the last thing on my mind.

'Fine,' I said, 'I'll be fine.'

'You must promise to let us know,' he said, 'if things get sticky.'

'Of course.'

We talked about a funeral. I said that there wasn't a body. He said we'd have to have a memorial service. I said I supposed we would.

Then he went quiet again and the next voice on the phone was Adam's mother. She sounded shocked, and when I explained again she said she didn't believe it. At that point I was back in familiar territory and after we'd both finished crying, she said she was sorry, so sorry, but she'd have to ring off. We'd talk again soon. There'd be so much to sort out. Would I be sure to keep eating? Would I be getting in touch with Leslie, Adam's sister? I said yes to everything, keen to end the conversation, and after we'd said our goodbyes I began to wonder about Adam's father again, how well he'd cope. He'd always come across as immensely strong but I was beginning to realise that even a lifetime of military service and self-discipline can't shield you from the shock of losing a child.

Across the hall from the snug is the room that Adam and I had converted to an office. I'd gone in to check Adam's sister's number but the moment I got to the desk I saw the fax waiting in the machine. At first I thought it was a booking confirmation from the States but then I realised it had come from Dennis Wetherall, our accountant in Jersey. He'd been trying to get through since mid-afternoon but there'd been no response to his pleas for me to ring.

I turned on the Anglepoise over the desk and sank into the chair. The second paragraph was even brisker than the first. He'd heard about Adam. He was very, very sorry. But there was a problem with the company's liquidity and certain steps had to be taken at once. Urgent, he added, wasn't a term he ever used lightly.

After the longest weekend of my life, fending off more media phone calls, I flew to the Channel Isles. The early-morning Monday flight out of Southampton was booked solid and it was nearly midday before I got to Jersey. Dennis Wetherall was waiting for me inside the terminal building.

Dennis has never looked like an accountant. He's short and slightly squat in build. He goes in for designer jeans, cowboy boots, collarless shirts, and he wears his hair in a long ponytail, secured with a length of scarlet ribbon. Amongst his clientele he numbers a couple of rock stars and a millionaire novelist or two, and he seems to view the rest of his profession with a kind of bemused resignation. Adam, predictably enough, loved him, and socially he was never less than amusing. The occasions he came to stay at Mapledurcombe, we were rarely in bed before three.

Dennis drove me into St Helier in his new Porsche. Blunt as ever, he spared me the laboured consolations I was beginning to dread.

'Can't think what got into him,' he said. 'Not his style at all.'

'Spearing in?'

'Dying.'

'Exactly.' I nodded. 'So what happened?'

Dennis shot me a look. Even in winter, he affected top-of-the-range Ray-Bans.

'I don't know,' he said at length. 'But I'm glad you got the fax.'

He took me to lunch at a restaurant overlooking the Inner Harbour. It was called Le Corniche and he'd booked a table in the long, sumptuous conservatory that seemed to suck in the light. Just sitting there with him, I began to feel a bit better, a little passing bubble he wasted no time in puncturing. From his briefcase, he produced a file. I saw our names on the top right-hand corner.

'Here.'

He passed me a photocopy from the file. I found myself looking at some kind of form.

'What's this?'

'A loan guarantee.' His finger stabbed at a line near the bottom. 'And that's your signature.'

I stared at the scrawl. Ellie Bruce. It certainly looked like my signature but on closer inspection the 'B' and the 'r' of the surname weren't quite right. I sign with less of a flourish.

'Not me,' I said.

'Are you kidding?'

'No.'

Dennis tried to reclaim the form. I hung on to it. Adam's signature was down there too, though this time it looked genuine. I began to study the rest of the form. According to the neatly typed figures on the third line, we'd guaranteed a bank loan of £300,000.

'Where did you get this?'

'From a bank.'

'Here in Jersey?'

'Yes.'

I was still staring at the figure. It was enormous.

'Who's all this money for?'

'Steve Liddell. Like it says.'

Dennis drew my attention to the top line. He was right. For reasons I didn't begin to understand, we'd staked our all on Liddell Engineering, Steve's company.

I looked up. Dennis and I talked regularly on the phone. When it came to business, we'd established a certain candour.

'How long have you had this?'

'Twenty-four hours.'

'It's dated last October.'

'I know. I can read too.'

'So why didn't you know before?'

'Good question.'

Dennis was staring at me, openly belligerent, and I realised that this was some kind of test. As our accountant, he had a right – indeed, an obligation – to know everything about our financial affairs. So why were we risking the business by helping out Steve Liddell? When we'd only recently been in such lousy shape ourselves?

'I know nothing about this,' I said carefully. 'That's definitely not my signature.'

'You're telling me someone faked it?'

'Yes.'

'Like who?' He was still staring at me. I refused to answer. At length, he took the form and laid it on the tablecloth between us. Butter from his finger left a greasemark beneath Adam's name.

'Is that signature genuine?'

'Yes, as far as I can see.'

'You're sure?'

'Yes.'

He nodded, tearing at the remains of a bread roll.

'That's what the bank manager says, too.'

'How would he know?'

'He watched Adam sign it.'

I looked again at the form. I'd never heard of Gulf Banking Services Corporation.

'Who are these people?'

'It's a small offshore outfit, incorporated in the Caymans. They do a lot of business here, most of it high-risk.' He paused. 'You're serious? You've never dealt with them?'

'Never.'

'And Adam didn't mention the name ever?'

'No, I'm sure he didn't.'

Dennis pushed his chair back from the table and brushed crumbs from his lap. The hostility had gone. I'd evidently passed the test.

'It gets worse,' he said. 'Did you hear about Steve Liddell?'

I shook my head. Steve Liddell was the young engineer who'd lent Adam the Cessna. I knew he'd recently moved into brand-new premises on the edge of Jersey airport, but this was the first time I'd realised that we were underwriting his business expansion plans. Adam, it's true, had once suggested that we take some kind of stake in his company, convinced that servicing classic warbirds would be immensely profitable, but when I'd said no, I'd assumed that would be the end of it.

31

'So what happened?' I asked. 'To Steve?'

'He had a fire. A week or so back.'

'Serious?'

'Serious enough. He was working on Harvey Glennister's Spitfire. Apparently there's not very much of it left.'

It was my turn to stare. Harvey Glennister was a Lloyd's broker who dabbled in warbirds, one of a growing number of the new rich for whom a classic fighter like the Spitfire had become the ultimate fashion accessory.

Dennis had started on another bread roll. He said he was amazed I hadn't known about the fire.

'Didn't Adam tell you?'

'No.' I frowned. 'Maybe he didn't know.'

'Come on, Ellie.' Dennis barked with laughter. 'He was over here for most of last week. He was in and out of that hangar, I know he was. There are scorch marks up to the ceiling. Part of the roof practically melted. Hell, I was up there myself a couple of days ago. Even then you could still smell it.' He picked up the bank form, then let it flutter to the table. 'Not know? With a third of a million quid at stake? Are you kidding?'

I could feel a deep chill inside me. This was news I didn't want to hear, not from Dennis, not from anybody. Adam forging my signature was bad enough. This was even worse.

I leaned forward, sparing Dennis the obvious question, knowing I had to confront it.

'So why didn't he tell me?'

'About the Spitfire?'

'About everything.'

'Pass.'

The waiter arrived with the food. After Dennis had finished telling me about Steve, I couldn't face the scallops.

'So he wasn't insured? Is that what you're saying?'

'Yep, more or less. There were certain things he saved on. That was one of them. He's got insurance, of course he has, but nothing like enough.'

'So where does that leave him?'

'He'll be down for the Spitfire. Or most of it.'

'And how much is that?'

'Half a million, probably more. It's early days but I went through some stuff he faxed me this morning. Bottom line, he's stuffed. Here. I'll show you –'

His hand was back in the briefcase. I told him not to bother.

'Your chips are cold,' I said briskly. 'Let's go and talk to Steve.'

Back in the car, Dennis tallied the worst-case options. If the damage to the Spitfire was as bad as he suspected, and if the insurance situation was indeed the way Steve had described it, then Liddell Engineering – on the most optimistic assessment – was effectively bust. No business working on a £300,000 secured bank loan could afford to absorb a bill the size that Harvey Glennister would be sending in.

'Secured?' The word sounded like a death knell.

'Yeah, on you.'

'You mean Old Glory.'

'No, you. Your assets.'

'What assets?' I laughed. Dennis and I had been through almost exactly this conversation only a year or so ago. On that occasion it had been the Mustang rebuild that had plunged us into debt and it was only with Harald's help that we'd emerged intact. Since then, a great deal of hard work plus a growing reputation in the States had won us a modest credit balance at the bank, but this – all too obviously – was now history. Thanks to Steve Liddell, Old Glory was back in deep, deep trouble.

I glanced across at Dennis. Over the last couple of years, at his insistence, I'd learned to find my way around a balance sheet. Figures no longer terrified me. Only their consequences.

'So exactly how is the loan secured?' I asked him.

'On the house.'

I nodded. The house carried a £110,000 mortgage. On a rising market, if we were very lucky, we might get £250,000.

'And the rest? What's that secured on?'

'The Mustang.'

'Does Harvey Glennister have an urge to fly Mustangs?' Dennis laughed again, then returned my look.

'Are you serious? You want to trade?'

'No.'

'Are you sure? Only . . .' He shrugged, disappointed, and for a moment I glimpsed the wheeler-dealer of Dennis Wetherall's dreams, the fast-talking entrepreneur he might have become had accountancy not given him such rich pickings.

'The Mustang's not on offer,' I said quietly. 'I'll live in a tent before I part with it.'

Dennis swerved to avoid a bicycle.

'At this rate,' he said grimly, 'you might have to.'

Steve Liddell's new premises were on the south side of Jersey airport, a brightly painted industrial unit that Dennis told me he'd taken on a three-year lease. There were big roll-up doors at the front, and the hardstanding outside gave direct access on to the airfield perimeter track.

Dennis parked the Porsche on the empty tarmac and I stood beside the car for a moment or two, watching the pilot of a passing 737 lift the nosewheel and haul the aircraft into a steep climb. Adam, bless him, had been right about flying. Once the virus is in your blood-stream, it never leaves you.

Dennis was already making for a little glassed-in porch on the side of the unit. I called for him to wait, catching him up as he pushed in through the door. Beyond the porch was a tiny reception area. Two desks formed an L shape. There was a computer on one desk and a pile of unopened mail on the other. The rubber plant in the corner needed a lot of attention.

I joined Dennis beside the computer. The screen-saver featured little cartoon biplanes flapping from one corner to another. Each aircraft towed a banner advertising Liddell Engineering and I was still wondering how much the software must have cost when Dennis nudged the mouse, returning the screen to a draft letter. The letter was evidently fending off an anxious customer. It seemed he'd heard about the accident with the Spitfire and wanted an assurance that his own aircraft, booked for routine maintenance, would be in safe hands.

Neither of us heard Steve come in. When I turned round, he was standing in an open doorway on the far side of the reception area. He was wearing grubby olive overalls. He had his hands on his hips and his face was in deep shadow under the peak of his Timberland cap. He was staring at the computer screen.

Dennis, typically, wasn't the least bit embarrassed.

'Tried to call you.' He gestured at the unmanned mini-switch-board. 'No reply.'

Steve wiped his face with the back of his hand. I'd only met him a couple of times before, when Adam and I were over on business, but I was shocked by how much he seemed to have aged. He was a tall lad, broad-shouldered, well-built, with an open, cheerful manner and a readiness to help that had always impressed me. Now, though, his body seemed to sag inside the overalls. His face was grey with exhaustion and when he extended a reluctant hand in my direction, the smile was utterly lifeless.

He gestured at the still-open door.

'Come through.'

The hangar was empty except for an old Piper Cherokee jacked up in one corner. There was a big scorchmark on the concrete and Dennis had been right about the damage to the roof. The smell was still there too, acrid and bitter. Rubber tyres, I thought, and probably the plastic coating on the wiring looms.

At the back of the hangar was another door. Beyond it lay the office that Steve used. It was sparsely furnished, a desk, a chair, an airways map taped to the wall, a *FlyPast* calendar still showing January, and two filing cabinets shrouded in polythene. On the floor beside the filing cabinets was a line of cardboard boxes stuffed with documents. A month or so after his move to these new premises, Steve had yet to unpack.

He offered us both a cigarette. Neither of us smoked. We talked about Adam for a couple of minutes and Steve repeated what Harald had already told me, that the Cessna he'd been flying had only just been through its fifty-hour checks. It was an oldish aircraft, first registered in 1968, and Steve had been looking after it on behalf of the owner, who was currently on an extended business trip to Thailand. They apparently had an arrangement whereby Steve could loan or hire the aircraft to anyone he trusted, but when I pressed him for details – more about Adam than the Cessna – he refused to meet my eyes. The thing was a mystery, he kept saying. He didn't have a clue what might have happened and as far as he was concerned the whole episode was now in the hands of the AAIB.

The police had mentioned the AAIB when they'd first broken the news about Adam. The Air Accidents Investigation Branch is a kind of government detective agency, and right now I knew that their inspectors would be wanting to find out exactly what had happened to the Cessna.

'Have they been in touch?' I asked Steve.

'They've interviewed me.'

'Already?'

'Yeah. They came this morning. Two of them.' He looked at me, uncertain, not wanting to go on.

'And?' I said.

Steve shrugged, then gestured limply at one of the drawers.

'They went through the technical logs, all the paperwork. I told them everything was fine. There wasn't a problem.' He put his head back and looked up at the ceiling. 'They wanted to know about Adam, too.'

'And what did you tell them?'

'I said he'd been fine, you know, fit, well, nothing wrong with him . . .' His voice trailed away.

'Go on,' I said. 'What else did they ask?'

'They wanted his log book. They wanted to know how much experience he'd had. I couldn't help them with the log book but I told them he wasn't . . . you know . . . exactly a novice.'

I didn't oblige Steve with the smile he wanted. Adam's log book was back at Mapledurcombe. I could picture it in the top drawer in his office desk. Mine lay beside it.

'Will they be wanting to talk to me?' I wondered aloud. 'Only I'd have thought –'

'Yeah,' Steve cut in. 'They said.'

'Said what?'

'Said they'd get in touch. I gave them your number. I didn't think you'd mind.'

'Not at all.' I frowned. 'So did you get the feeling they'd come to any conclusions?'

'About what?'

I stared at Steve, trying not to lose my temper. There were questions I was desperate to have answered but he looked so battered, so physically drained, that I almost felt sorry for him. I took a deep breath.

'About Adam's accident,' I said patiently. 'What I want to know is whether or not they've come up with anything.'

Steve shook his head.

'They've impounded the ATC tapes,' he said, 'and they told me they'd talked to the weather people at Bracknell, but I think that's about it. Adam just fell off the radar. They haven't a clue why.'

I gazed at him a moment longer, then looked away at Dennis. I'd had enough of asking questions for one morning.

Dennis returned to the incident with Harvey Glennister's Spitfire. What kind of state was it in? Where had it gone?

Steve hunted for an envelope in a drawer. He emptied the contents on to the desk, a gesture – it seemed to me – of resignation. Dennis glanced through the photos then passed them to me. They showed the burned-out fuselage and the buckled panels on the wings. The paintwork was bubbled and blistered and the canopy over the cockpit had been shattered by the heat. The cowling was off the nose and damage to the big Merlin engine was plainly visible. In photo after photo, it looked like someone had taken a giant blow torch to the aircraft, peeling back its skin, exposing the bones beneath.

'It's gone back to the mainland,' Steve was saying. 'They took it away a couple of days ago.'

'Who took it?'

'Glennister's people.'

I'd got to the bottom of the pile of photographs. Dismembered by a couple of sturdy engineers, the aircraft had been packed into containers and trucked away.

Dennis wanted to know more.

'What about the AAIB?'

'They weren't interested.'

'They knew about it? You told them?'

Steve's hesitation gave him away.

'They'd found out from someone else,' he said at last. 'One of the airport people, I expect.' He nodded vaguely in the direction of the terminal buildings in a gesture that could have meant anybody.

Dennis was getting tetchy.

'You're telling me they won't investigate?'

'There's no need. No one was hurt.'

'Half a million quid's worth of aeroplane?'

'That's not their problem.'

'No, but it might be ours.'

Steve ignored the remark, slumped in his chair behind the desk. He tapped ash into the waste bin at his feet and began to fiddle with an old altimeter he must have rescued from the skip. It was lying there on the desk beside the telephone and for the first time I noticed the small framed photo partially hidden behind it. It was angled away from me but I could see enough to register the face of a child. She looked young, pre-school certainly.

Dennis was starting to ask the harder questions. He was, if anything, even more aggressive.

'Ellie's down for three hundred grand,' he reminded Steve. 'We need to know about the status of the loan.'

Steve gestured hopelessly at the photos.

'I'm trying to sort it out.'

'How?'

'By talking to the insurers.'

Dennis muttered something terse about Glennister. The man had a box at Lloyd's. He knew the insurance industry backwards. If anyone got screwed here, it certainly wouldn't be him.

'No.' Steve nodded. 'I expect you're right.'

'So who pays?'

'I dunno.'

'Take a wild guess.'

Dennis glanced in my direction. Steve was looking even more dejected.

'Tell me about the business,' I said quickly. 'How was the rest of it going?'

'Fine, until . . .' Steve indicated the photos of the wrecked Spitfire.

'But you had customers? Stuff was moving through?'

'Yeah, absolutely. That's why I expanded. I had more work than I knew what to do with. This place was perfect, just what I needed.'

'And it took all the money? The whole three hundred thousand?'

'Not all of it, no.'

'How much, then?'

Steve ducked his head, refusing to look me in the eye, and I rephrased the question. For the time being we were talking about money. All too quickly, as Dennis kept warning me, we could be talking about bricks and mortar.

'This matters to me, Steve. I want to know exactly how I stand.'

Steve said nothing. Dennis stirred. He had a big topaz ring on his little finger, and when he was angry he had a habit of twisting it round and round.

'It's been a bad week, Steve,' he said softly. 'On Thursday, Ellie lost her husband. Next, it could be her home. You hearing me?'

Steve looked up.

'It won't come to that,' he said quickly.

'How do you know?'

'I just do.'

'But how can you?'

Once again, Steve had no answer. Conversationally, he seemed like a man with one hand tied behind his back. There were moves he couldn't make, things he wouldn't say. So far he'd told us practically nothing.

I heard myself asking about the fire. How did it start? When did it happen?

'Couple of weeks ago.'

'But when? Exactly?'

'The middle of the night. Around one in the morning.'

Dennis took up the running.

'And the thing just burst into flames? Just like that? Spontaneous combustion?'

'No one knows.'

'Might someone have got in? Was the place locked up?'

'Of course.'

'You *know* that?'

'Yes. I locked up myself. This place is really secure. It's one of the reasons I took on the lease.'

Dennis brooded for a moment. He still had the ring in the fingers of his other hand, twisting and twisting.

'And you were the one who discovered the fire?' he said at last, 'Is that the way I hear it?'

'Yes.'

'How come?'

Steve glanced up at him, then looked down again.

'I've got a van,' he said softly. 'Old VW combi. It's parked round the back.'

'You *sleep* here?'

'Yes.'

'Why?'

Steve shook his head.

'Doesn't matter,' he said. 'But it's lucky I did. The place is alarmed, smoke detectors, proper rig. By the time I got inside the Spit was well alight but at least I managed to contain it. There were other aircraft in there, a couple of them jacked up. I couldn't have got them out. No way.'

'Contain it?' Dennis barked with laughter. 'How the fuck did you do that?'

'I had fire extinguishers, four of them. The airport fire crew were here pretty quickly, too. They were the ones who really dealt with it.'

'And what did they say? Afterwards?'

'Same as me. They didn't know.' He shrugged. 'Electrical fault? Fuel leak? You tell me.'

Dennis nodded very slowly. Plainly, he didn't believe a word.

'Thanks,' he said. 'Let's go through this three hundred grand again.'

On the way back to St Helier, I asked Dennis about the framed photo on the desk. Whose child was it? What was her name? Dennis said he didn't know, and by his tone of voice it was obvious that he didn't much care. What interested him far more was Steve Liddell's next move.

Pressed by Dennis, Steve had told me again that my £300,000 was safe. To Dennis, who lived in the accountant's world of black and white, this was simply evidence that the boy was either in denial, in shock or clinically insane. The figures, he said, spoke for themselves. The first year's lease had cost Steve £35,000. Tooling for three mechanics, another £33,000. Round it up for rates, office equipment, services, wages and all the other demands on the cash flow, and you were probably looking at about £100,000 in start-up costs. Add to that the interest payments on the loan, plus Steve's probable liability for the Spitfire, and there'd be precious little change from the third of a million that Adam had so gaily underwritten.

'But Steve's still trading,' I pointed out. 'He's still got the premises and the tooling and all the rest. Doesn't that count for anything?'

39

Dennis, wedged behind a tractor, enquired whether I, too, was mad.

'What's the foundation for any business?' he rasped, sounding his horn for the third time. 'Christ, Ellie, you should know.'

I frowned, trying to concentrate. For some reason I couldn't stop thinking about the photo on Steve's desk.

'Good will,' I said vaguely. 'And reputation.'

'Yeah, and something else,' he said. 'Confidence. That's number one. You've got to believe in yourself, believe you're the very best. Did you see the guy just now? Did you take a good look? And does he strike you like a man way out in front?' He shook his head, contemptuous, dismissive. 'Defeat's a smell, Ellie. And that guy stank of it.'

He finally made it around the tractor and I closed my eyes for a moment or two, glad of the silence between us, fixing the image of the young child in my mind. As we'd left the office, I'd taken the opportunity to have a good look. She had dimples, and lovely eyes, and a bright, trusting smile. She didn't look the least like Steve Liddell.

'I'm thinking of threatening the bank with an action,' Dennis said suddenly.

'What for?'

'Dereliction of duty. They were happy enough to advance the money, take the interest, accept the security on the loan.'

'So what else should they have done?'

'Notify me.'

'Have you asked them why they didn't?'

'Yes.'

'And what did they say?'

We were on the outskirts of St Helier now. Dennis slowed for the short cut down to the harbour.

'They said that Adam had told them he dealt with his own affairs. They said he had no time for fancy accountants.' He glanced sideways at me. 'Nice to be wanted, eh?'

I spent another hour or so at Dennis's office before finding somewhere to stay. Dennis was keen for me to meet the bank manager who'd fixed up the loan, and while we waited for his secretary to confirm an appointment, I dug some figures out of my own briefcase and ran through the advance bookings situation for the coming season.

So far, we'd always opened Mapledurcombe for business during the first week in June. This gave us four clear months through to the end of September, generating enough revenue to keep our heads above water while giving us the chance to maintain the standards we'd set for ourselves. Currently, we were charging £150 per night per person for accommodation and all meals. For that sort of money, quite rightly, our guests expected the very best, and so far I'd resisted the temptation to extend the season in the belief that we'd probably buckle under the strain. This summer, though, I was assured of help from a couple of wonderful women in the village and as a result we'd decided to open a month early, on 2 May. Filling five months instead of four had been no problem. Already, in mid-February, we were oversubscribed.

Dennis put the figures through his calculator. Like me, he projected the season's gross takings at £168,000.

'And that's just board and lodging,' I reminded him. 'The flying comes separately.'

'How much are you charging for the Harvard?'

'Six hundred and fifty an hour. We've just put it up.'

'And the Mustang?'

'Two thousand nine hundred and fifty.'

Dennis made small, neat notes on the pad beside his calculator. Like most accountants, sums like these made no visible impression on him. Everything on earth had a market price. If people were prepared to pay £17,000 for a day trip to Berlin and back, so be it.

'What's the bottom line on the Harvard? Costwise?'

'Per hour?'

'Yes.'

I knew the figures backwards. I'd been through them a thousand times with Adam, tallying up all the various expenses involved just keeping the aircraft in flying condition. Fuel and maintenance cost a small fortune but insurance was the real killer. For the Harvard, we were currently paying £10,000 a year. The Mustang came in at nearly double that figure.

Dennis was still waiting for the hourly cost.

'Four hundred and twenty-five an hour for the Harvard,' I said, 'And around two thousand for the Mustang.'

'And you're serious about keeping the aircraft?'

'Yes.'

'What about pilots?'

'I've got a list as long as your arm. Most of them would do it for nothing.'

Dennis, still bent over his pad, grinned. He knew as well as I did that laying hands on a classic warbird like the Mustang was every pilot's dream. We were always getting letters from would-be hopefuls, but over the years Adam had built a list of maybe half a dozen pilots he really trusted, and I knew there'd be no problem keeping both planes crewed.

I watched Dennis working through one last column of figures. He knew the average usage rate we'd established for each aircraft, the minimum number of flying hours we could be reasonably sure of selling each month.

At length, he looked up. This was a sum I hadn't done.

'For both aircraft, ball park, we're talking ninety-five grand.'

'That's over the season?'

'Yep.'

'Total revenue?'

'Total net.'

Net means profit after deducting all expenses. I tried to look pleased. In truth, it was more than I'd expected, though it didn't, of course, take into account the cost of a new pilot. What kind of price should I put on Adam? Was there enough money in the world to buy me one last hour of his time?

Dennis began to reach for his calculator again, a question on his lips, but something in my face must have persuaded him to rein in. Abruptly, he changed the subject, and he was still telling me about the powerboat he was thinking of buying when the call from the bank came through. He listened for a couple of minutes. Then his face darkened.

'How come so soon?' he growled. 'What's the problem?'

This time the answer was brisk. He glanced at his diary and then agreed to meet at ten next morning. By the time he put the phone down, I was resigned to bad news.

'They're calling in the loan,' he said angrily. 'Bastards.'

On our various trips to Jersey, Adam and I had always stayed at a little place called Au Bon Accueil, a small, narrow-fronted hotel trellised with Virginia creeper. It wasn't cheap but the service was wonderful and the food even better.

Au Bon Accueil was twenty minutes' walk from Dennis's office but by the time I got there I knew it was the wrong place to stay. We'd always booked the same bedroom – number 7 – and I knew that any sleep I managed to snatch would be haunted by memories from those glorious days. I was too exhausted for more grief and too raw for nostalgia. What I needed just now was a cheap B&B, a good night's rest and the strength – somehow – to concentrate my few resources on rescuing Old Glory from the ashes of Harvey Glennister's wretched Spitfire.

I found a B&B in a side street off Val Plaisant. There was a pay phone in the hall beside the fish tank and I phoned Dennis to tell him where I was. He'd been kind enough to offer me the spare room in his harbourside apartment out at St Aubin and I thanked him once again for the thought. We'd meet tomorrow. After our appointment at the bank, I'd probably take the afternoon flight back to Southampton.

Almost as an afterthought, I asked him for an honest assessment of our chances with Gulf Banking Services Corporation. Might they defer calling in the loan? Were banks usually this hasty? There was a silence on the line, unusual for Dennis, then he came back. Since I'd left, he'd had another call, followed by a couple of faxes. The first contained the schedule of interest payments. Three months into the loan, Steve Liddell already owed them £9,000 in back payments. That, said Dennis, was bad enough. What made it infinitely worse were the contents of the second fax, which detailed the small print of the agreement Adam had guaranteed. Most unusually, said Dennis, it contained a clause permitting the bank to foreclose on the loan in the event of a default, or under circumstances deemed otherwise non-compliant with the spirit of the agreement.

'What does that mean?' I said quickly.

'You tell me.'

'But who makes the judgement about the circumstances? Who does the deeming?'

'They do.'

'No appeal?'

'None that I can see. Unless you fancy going to law.'

'So what do we do now?'

I watched the fish circling the tank, waiting for Dennis to answer. Trapped, I thought. Round and round and round for the rest of my life.

'We'll thrash it out with them tomorrow,' Dennis said at last. 'I'll call by and pick you up.'

That night, I ate alone in a bistro round the corner from Royal Square. I ordered an omelette and a salad and a small carafe of red wine. The fog had come down outside and I was glad of the way it swallowed me up when I left, huddled in the long cashmere coat Adam had bought me as a Christmas present. My resistance softened by the wine, I gave in to my worst instincts and retraced the route we always took after supper on nights when we found ourselves staying over on the island. I knew this was hopelessly self-indulgent, exactly what I shouldn't do, but I didn't care.

Up the hill beyond Royal Square is the shell of the old Fort Regent.

43

There's a leisure centre in the middle of it now, but from the terrace on the front you can look out over the inner harbour towards St Elizabeth Castle and the gentle sweep of St Aubin's Bay. Tonight, for once, I could see nothing through the swirling curtains of sea fog, and I walked slowly along the terrace, counting the benches until I got to the end. Here was where we usually stopped. Here was where we could look down on the neat rows of moored yachts in the marina, fantasising about the moment when Old Glory would have bought us a big, sturdy ocean-going forty-footer, and we could take a year or so off and circle the globe, threading landfalls together like beads on a necklace. In my heart, I'd always known it would never happen – Adam was far too impatient to depend on anything as fickle as wind and tide – but it had become an important promise we'd made to each other and I liked the feeling it gave me, just thinking about it.

Far away, out at sea, I could hear the bellow of a foghorn. Then came another, and another, much closer. The balustrade was cold and damp beneath my hands and I shivered, imagining yet again the half-submerged shape of my poor drowned Adam, somewhere out there, wave-tossed and abandoned.

Growing up in the Falklands, you get used to death. Out on the horse, it would be a rare day when I didn't come across the carcass of a sheep, the bones picked clean by the circling buzzards, or a sick elephant seal, beached and helpless, waiting for the rising tide to claim him. Back in the settlement, when someone died, we'd dig the grave ourselves, spading down through the soggy black peat and then gathering in the late afternoon to lower the rough, newly nailed coffin and listen to my father intoning a verse or two from the Book of Common Prayer before the light failed and we went back to the cookhouse for a glum round of scones and whisky.

That had been the small print of our daily lives, something we were used to. For me, dead bodies held no mystery, no fear. But what had happened to Adam was altogether different. There was no body. There were no goodbyes. Just a heap of memories, confused, entangled, shot through with his laughter and his sheer appetite for life. On occasions, when he chose to, Adam could be as gentle as any man I've known. The day when I got the news from the fertility clinic confirming that I'd never be able to give him a child, he was kindness itself. But the Adam I treasured, the man I wanted, and won, and loved, was the Adam who'd stepped out of the helicopter all those years ago and shot me the hack old line about giving his winchman a decent party. That, of course, had been a pretext but I hadn't minded in the slightest because it spoke of boldness, and mischief, and a determination to seize the initiative that I had, in my own young life,

44

never quite managed to master. Living with Adam, getting to know him, a little of that magic had rubbed off, and I knew now – with an absolute certainty – that his death would make me stronger yet.

Quite why he'd guaranteed Steve Liddell's loan was beyond me, and it certainly hurt that he'd kept the arrangement so secret. But already, in my mind's eye, I could see him volunteering to share the load in this new adventure, scribbling a couple of signatures for the bank manager, ignoring the small print. The thought that Steve might fail – that he might come to grief – would never have occurred to him. Once Adam believed in someone, his faith and his commitment were total and there simply wasn't room for anything as boring and mundane as failure. That's why he'd been such a delight to live with. And that's why, even now – facing an interview that might rob me of everything – I could forgive him.

For some reason, I'd always been the one who woke up first in the mornings, and the thought of Adam's face on the pillow made me smile. If I listened very hard, I told myself, I could hear him now, rubbing the sleep from his eyes, telling me to get back to the B&B, and treat myself to a large brandy, and join him in bed. Nothing sounded sweeter, and I blew him a kiss, turning away from what had once been our view, glad I'd succumbed to the wine.

I was back at the B&B by nine o'clock. The woman had given me a key to the front door and I let myself in, trying to remember what she'd said about leaving the door on the latch. I was still wrestling with the lock when I heard someone calling my name. For a second or two I thought I was dreaming. Then I turned round, knowing it had to be true. Sitting on the chair by the fish tank was Harald Meyler.

Chapter four

At Harald's insistence, we went out again. As tired as I was, he said he had news for me. He'd been hanging around for the best part of an hour for my return and there were pressing phone calls waiting for him back at the hotel where he was staying. When I asked him how on earth he'd found me, he smiled and said he'd talked to Dennis. His phone calls to Mapledurcombe hadn't been returned. He'd guessed I'd probably come over to Jersey.

He had a hire car outside. We drove slowly out of St Helier, the fog still thick, while he briefed me on the latest reports he'd received from the skipper of the boat he'd chartered. The vessel, he said, had been out in mid-Channel now for the best part of twenty-four hours, trawling up and down around the position the radar people had calculated as Adam's point of impact. The word made me flinch and I half-listened to Harald's quiet speculations about tidal drift, knowing in my heart that both of us had given up any hope of finding him alive. When I said as much, Harald simply nodded. Adam, in his view, would have been dead within minutes, if not from his injuries, then from hypothermia. So far, there'd been no sign of the wreckage that the search-and-rescue people had reported, and as far as he knew the naval frigate on the scene had also drawn a blank.

'Isn't that unusual?' I wondered aloud.

Harald nodded. We were still driving through the suburbs of St Helier. An entrance to some kind of drive loomed through the fog and I glimpsed a hotel sign as Harald drove in under a big stone arch.

'It's very unusual,' he said at last. 'Which is why we have to keep looking.'

'But what does it suggest? To you?'

I could see lights ahead. Harald had slowed the car to walking pace, tapping his fingers on the steering wheel.

'He could have bellied in, stayed intact. That happens sometimes.'

'But didn't the chopper crew report wreckage?'

'They did. But they might have got it wrong. The Channel's full of trash, all kinds of garbage. Fly low enough, choose the right day, it looks like the logging season.'

'But wouldn't the aircraft float? If it was still in one piece?'

'For a while, yes. Then . . .' he shrugged, '. . . the cabin fills with water, the fuselage too. There's a bit of buoyancy in the wings, of course, but he had full tanks on departure. I checked.'

'With who?'

'Steve.' He glanced across at me. 'You were up there today.'

'That's right. How did you know?'

'Dennis told me. He said Steve looked wrecked.' He frowned. 'What did you make of him?'

I thought hard about the question. Beyond a line of parked cars, the headlights picked out the front of what must have been Harald's hotel.

'I agree,' I said bleakly. 'I thought he looked terrible. In fact I thought he looked ill.'

Harald brought the car to a halt and switched off the engine.

'You're right,' he said. 'That's why we have to talk.'

The hotel turned out to be an old manor house, beautifully furnished. It had a look and a smell that reminded me, on a much grander scale, of Mapledurcombe: wood-panelled walls, swagged curtains, oriental rugs and some lovely antique furniture. Harald led me through the reception hall. From a bar at the end, I could hear laughter.

Heads turned as we went in. For a second or two they were strangers, these men, then I began to put names to the faces. Duggie Peterson. Alan Jessop. Miles Brenton. Display pilots from the airshow circuit. Men I'd bumped into the weekends when Adam had been part of the same circus, hauling the Mustang around the sky in front of ten thousand people. He'd loved the opportunity to show off the plane, to stretch the flight envelope to its limits and pop in a trick or two that took even these veterans by surprise. On those summer days, the sky was Adam's stage, and I remembered his face afterwards, the moment when he taxied back towards the line of parked aircraft, sliding back the canopy and waving to the crowd. At first, to my surprise, the gesture had made me slightly jealous. Now, it was a memory I treasured. My pilot. My prince.

Harald did the introductions at the bar, before returning to reception to check for messages. Everyone did their best to tell me how sorry they were about Adam, and I swallowed hard, amazed at how public the knowledge had already become, and touched by how tongue-tied these men could be.

Harald returned and led me to a table in the corner. Without checking, he bought me a large Scotch. When he sat down, he had his back to the pilots at the bar.

'The guys flew in this morning,' he explained. 'We get together around now to sort out the schedule for the summer. That's why I stayed over. That, and Adam.'

He began telling me about a Fighter Meet planned for September and I half-listened, still watching the men at the bar, their body language, how easy they were with each other, recognising the breed to which Adam had belonged. They were like no other group of men I'd ever met. They had that self-confidence, that inner calm, that I'd only seen – oddly enough – in the Falklands. Shepherds have it, and drovers too. It comes with the knowledge that you're doing something challenging and difficult that makes you entirely happy. Not once, I thought, are these men ever bored. To the frustrations and tedium of real life, like gravity itself, they seem immune.

I looked again at Harald. He was one of them too, very definitely, and I bent towards him, trying to concentrate. The Fighter Meet, he said, was to end with a tribute to the Little Friends.

'You know the phrase?'

I nodded. Ralph Pierson had used it only a couple of weeks ago. It was the nickname the American bomber crews used for the escorting Mustangs which shepherded them to Berlin and back. On the big daylight raids, Ralph said, the Little Friends took care of the men in the B-17s.

'You're putting up lots of Mustangs?'

'Double figures. Fourteen at least.'

'Sounds a brilliant idea. Adam would have loved it.'

'You're right.' he nodded. 'That's why we're dedicating the Meet to him. Good weather, we should pull a huge crowd.'

I felt my eyes filling with tears and I turned my head away. It was a lovely gesture but Adam's death was too close, too recent, for me to say anything as trite as thank you.

Harald touched me lightly on the arm.

'Steve Liddell,' he murmured.

I blew my nose, wondering where Steve could possibly fit in Harald's plans for this pageant.

'Steve?'

'Yes.' Harald took a sip of his grapefruit juice. 'You've seen the state he's in. What did he tell you about Harvey's Spit?'

I recounted what little Dennis and I had picked up. Harald never took his eyes off me for a second. When I'd finished, he sighed.

'There's more,' he said, 'and if he hasn't told you then I guess I should.'

'You know what happened?'

'Yes.'

'How?'

Harald studied me for a moment. I put the shadows under his eyes down to exhaustion. And concern.

'Steve's been under a lot of pressure,' he said. 'Personal. Business. You name it.'

This was the first time I'd realised that the two men might be close. When I asked, Harald nodded.

'I like the guy,' he said softly. 'He's young, he's gutsy, he's not afraid of hard work. And when it comes to aircraft, I'd trust him with my life.'

He explained about the work he'd put Steve's way. Lately he'd been importing ex-Soviet military trainers, an aircraft called a Yak-52, and he'd been only too happy to ask Steve to check them out. The aircraft had been ferried in from an airbase in Romania, and Steve had spent days going through each one before Harald sold it on.

I'd never heard of a Yak. I asked Harald what they were like.

'Wonderful little planes, very tough, very forgiving. Fully aerobatic, too. The guys on the Yaks went straight on to jet fighters. That's how good a plane it is.'

He said he'd sold every aircraft he could get his hands on. Except one.

'And what happened to that?'

'I've kept it.'

'It's with Steve?'

'You got it.'

'In his hangar?'

'Sure. And why? Because, like I say, I trusted the guy.'

He knotted his hands on the tabletop, squeezing hard. The Yak had been in Steve's hangar the night of the fire. Harald had turned up next day to find the airport fire chief sifting through the remains of Harvey Glennister's Spitfire. The Yak, hard up against the far wall, had mercifully escaped serious damage.

'What does that mean?'

'A little blistering on the paintwork. Nothing structural. Nothing expensive.'

'But you talked to the fire chief?'

'You bet.'

'And?'

Harald took his time answering. When he spoke again, his voice had a harsher quality, an anger I'd never associated with him before.

49

'Steve phoned for the fire guys the moment he was inside the hangar. When they got there, they found the aircraft hot.'

'You mean on fire?'

'No. She'd gone up, sure, but they meant she was plugged in, powered up. Everything on the goddamned Spit was live. Filaments. Contacts. Instruments. Electrics. The lot.'

I was getting out of my depth. I tried to visualise our own mechanic, Dave Jeffries, over in the hangar at Sandown. I'd seen a lot of him during the rebuilds on the Harvard and the Mustang and I knew Harald was right. Without electricity to bring the plane to life, an engineer was dealing with a corpse.

'You're saying Steve was *working* on the plane? In the middle of the night?'

'I'm saying it looks that way.' He nodded, sombre now. 'Number one, you've got the aircraft powered. Number two, they found a bowl under the starboard fuel pipe. When they looked hard at the fuel pipe, they found a fracture. Number three, someone had run a lead light out to that same place.'

A lead light is a little inspection lamp with a wire guard over the bulb. That, at least, I knew.

'And the lead light was on, too?'

'It runs off a twelve-volt transformer. The transformer was live, yes.'

I looked at him a moment, wondering why Steve hadn't been franker. The answer, of course, was all too obvious. Harald spread his fingers wide, tallying the probable chain of events. More numbers, I thought grimly. More grief for Steve Liddell.

'What do you need for an aircraft fire? One, fuel. Two, some kind of wick. And three, a spark, or a heat source, or some damn thing to get it going.'

'Wick?' I was lost again.

'Yeah, an oily rag will do. Just anything to kindle the fire.'

'And they found a rag?'

'No, but they wouldn't. Avgas burns at a thousand degrees C. You saw the roof?'

I stared glumly at my untouched drink, remembering the melted panels in the hangar roof. There were implications here, not just for Steve but for me too.

'So what do you think happened?' I said slowly.

'You want my theory?'

'Yes please.'

'I think Steve was working on that plane. I think he was in the middle of a repair job on the fuel pipe. And I think he went outside to get his head down for an hour or so.' He frowned. 'Did he mention that van he's got?'

'Yes.'

'Then I guess that's where he was. The last month or so he's been sleeping rough, poor guy.'

'And the plane caught fire?'

'Sure.' He made a brisk gesture with one hand. 'Work it out for yourself. A fuel leak. A lead light. The aircraft already hot. That's not a situation you walk away from. Not if you're sensible.'

'But Steve is sensible. You said it yourself.'

'I said he's a regular guy. These are irregular circumstances.'

'What do you mean?'

I'd remembered the photo on the desk in Steve's office, the face of the child. Was this what lay behind it all? Had something in Steve's private life driven him to the edge?

Harald was looking at my glass.

'You don't want that Scotch?'

I shook my head, struck by something else.

'What about the insurance people? They'll be talking to the fire chief, bound to.'

'Of course.'

'So what will that mean? For Steve?'

'On paper, not much. If I'm right about the fire then it's negligence, sure, but that's why you take out insurance in the first place.'

'They wouldn't blame him? They'd still pay out?'

'Yeah. Problem is, he went for the cheapest deal.'

Harald bent towards me again, more bad news. Steve, like any engineer running his own business, had taken out cover. The policy, called 'hangar/keeper insurance', protected the premises, the quality of his own work, plus any damage that might occur to aircraft in his keeping. To keep his premium down, Steve had agreed to a limit of £500,000 on any single aircraft.

'And the Spitfire?' I asked.

'It was a Mark IX, really neat rebuild. Glennister had the hull insured for seven hundred and fifty grand.'

'That means Steve's . . .' I frowned, doing the sums, '. . . two hundred and fifty thousand short.'

'You got it.'

'So where does that leave Glennister?'

'If he's smart, and he is, he'll claim on his own insurance. They'll pay out in full. Then they'll instruct a lawyer to reclaim costs from Steve's insurers.'

'But Steve's underinsured.'

'Exactly.'

'So what happens?'

'I guess they'll claim against him. They're a quarter of a million in the hole. It's figures, Ellie. Money. They have no choice.'

'So where does that leave Steve?'

Harald drew a finger across his throat, then leant back in the chair, emptying his glass. I began to regret ever leaving the B&B. I should have stayed, I thought. I should have tumbled into bed, pulled up the covers and won myself a decent night's sleep.

Harald was watching me again. I had the feeling he'd got something off his chest. His manner had softened.

'You had some exposure to Steve,' he said.

It was a statement, not a question.

'You mean business dealings?'

'Yeah.'

I nodded, wondering how he knew. Advice wasn't something Adam had ever been keen on, but I knew he admired Harald's judgement and it was conceivable the two men might have talked.

'Did Adam ever mention it?'

'Sure.'

'And what did he say?'

'He told me he wanted to take a stake in Liddell's outfit.'

'And what did you say?'

'I told him to be damn careful.'

'Why?'

'Because it was going to be an arm's-length arrangement, at least the way he described it. And because, I guess, Steve's still a kid.'

'But you trusted him enough to look after the Yaks.'

'Sure, but that's different. As an engineer, I've never had a problem with the guy. As a businessman, he was getting in very deep, very fast. If Adam wanted to be a part of that, OK. But you need to be here, you need to be hands-on, every day of the week, otherwise it just runs away from you.'

I thought of Adam's recent visits to Jersey. Some weeks it seemed to me he practically lived there. I shared the thought with Harald. He shook his head.

'He wasn't with Steve,' he said. 'He wasn't where he needed to be. He wasn't with the action.'

'But he guaranteed Steve's loan. I know he did.'

'Sure, and right now that's not looking such a great decision.'

I nodded, miserable, lost for words. There was nothing to say, nothing to add, nothing to soften the brutal logic of what Adam had done.

'I didn't know anything about this,' I said softly. 'I knew Adam had been interested but I'd no idea he'd got involved.'

For a split second, Harald looked astonished.

'He didn't tell you?'

'No.'

'You only just found out?'

'Yes.'

'Jesus . . .' he shook his head, '. . . then I'm sorry.'

One of the pilots at the bar came across and laid a hand on Harald's shoulder. He flew commercial jets for a living but his real love was for warbirds and he could't get enough of them. Adam had nicknamed him Martini. Any plane, any time, any where.

He smiled at me and murmured an apology. Then he asked Harald about progress on the 109. Harald told him the rebuild was on schedule. Fingers crossed, his engineers were looking to May for certification. Some time in July, once the auxiliary tanks were installed, he'd ship it across from Florida to the UK. I listened to the two men discussing how they'd showcase the Messerschmitt at the Fighter Meet, glad of the interruption.

The conversation over, Harald turned back to me.

'Are you really rebuilding a 109?' I asked him.

'Sure.' He nodded. 'I've got three beaten-up hulls back home. If this one turns out nice, we'll do the other two.' He paused. 'I'd no idea about Adam not telling you. Jeez, I feel almost guilty.'

'Don't be.' I shook my head. 'It's not your fault.'

'I guess I just . . .' He shrugged. 'It was no business of mine. He wanted my advice and I gave it but in the end, hell, you do what you do.'

'Of course.'

Harald gazed at me, then shrugged again and got to his feet and glanced at his watch. We'd already established in the car that I'd eaten. Now, he apologised for fetching me out to the hotel. He'd have reception ring for a cab. I'd be back in St Helier in no time at all.

We left the bar and went through to the lobby. While we waited for the cab to arrive he promised to keep me briefed on progress with the search. He'd instructed the charter skipper to stay out at least another couple of days. The guy had worked the Channel currents most of his life. If there was really wreckage out there, he'd be the one to find it.

The cab arrived. Harald walked me down the steps. Already, I'd told him I planned to return home next day. Quite when, I'd left vague.

He opened the rear door for me, then paused, struck by a sudden thought.

'I'm going back myself tomorrow,' he said.

'Which flight?'

'Private, not commercial. I'm taking the Yak.' He reached forward, picking a ball of fluff from my coat. 'Drop you off at Sandown? Save you the ferry from Southampton?'

He helped me into the cab and smiled, not waiting for an answer.

Dennis Wetherall collected me, next morning, at 9.45. I'd slept badly, Adam's fault again, though this time his body was floating down some African river. One or two of the images echoed earlier nightmares I'd suffered when he was flying mercenaries out in Angola, and when I parried Dennis's gruff 'Good morning' with a grunt of my own, I recognised the effect events were beginning to have on me. I was getting fed up. Maybe that was a good sign.

Gulf Services Banking Corporation occupied the fourth floor of a modern glass and steel block half a mile inland from the harbour. A secretary met us as we emerged from the lift. The manager's name, she said, was Ozilio Sant'Ana.

I was still trying to commit the name to memory when she led us into a big, carpeted office at the end of the corridor. Mr Sant'Ana rose from his desk, buttoning his jacket and extending a hand. He was tall and courtly with dark curly hair and nice eyes. His skin was olive, beautifully smooth, and his smile revealed a perfect set of teeth. Used to doing business with dowdy, hard-pressed company ciphers, I was heartened by what I saw. This man oozed authority. If we made our case, I sensed he had the power to order a stay of execution.

At the other end of the office was an L-shaped sofa, arranged around a low table. Sant'Ana invited us to sit down. His voice was soft and he spoke with a light American accent. On the table, beside the waiting tray of coffee, were copies of the *Economist* and the *Wall Street Journal*.

Dennis got down to business at once, snapping open his briefcase and consulting a thickish file. He wanted to establish a chronology, an exact list of dates. When, exactly, had Steve approached the bank for a loan? How long had it taken him to draw up a business plan? What kind of revisions had the bank demanded to the plan? And at what stage had Adam's name surfaced as guarantor? Sant'Ana answered the torrent of questions with immense patience and I was still trying to put a name to his aftershave when Dennis caught my eye.

'We have a problem with one of the signatures,' he announced. 'Mrs Bruce denies ever seeing the form.'

A frown ghosted over Sant'Ana's face. He must have been in his late forties. Fit, relaxed, good-humoured, he'd have fitted perfectly into the crowd of pilots at the hotel bar where Harald had taken me last night.

He was looking at me now. He'd already told me how sorry he was about Adam.

'Your husband didn't give the form to you?'

'No.'

'It's not your signature?'

'No.'

He looked, if anything, amused, spurring Dennis to yet greater efforts. The assets against which the loan was secured were held in joint names. If my signature was indeed a forgery, then the guarantee was invalid.

'But how do we know?' Sant'Ana gestured at the photostat Dennis had laid between us. 'I accepted the signature in good faith. How can I be sure it's fake?'

'Are you calling my client a liar?'

'Of course not, Mr Wetherall, but there are protocols here. We have a formal agreement. There are procedures. They govern what we do.'

Dennis repeated that I hadn't been party to the deal. I hadn't discussed it, nor had I given it my authority. My husband had been acting on his own, without my knowledge. I listened to Dennis with a sinking heart. As far as money was concerned, despite my efforts to keep costs under some kind of control, it seemed a pretty fair description of our relationship.

Sant'Ana reached for the coffee pot. The spout hovered above my empty cup. When I nodded, he smiled.

'He sounds very Brazilian, your husband.' He began to pour the coffee. 'What would women know about business?'

'Nothing. Until they have to sort it all out.'

I regretted the comment at once. It sounded thin-lipped, embittered, not at all the way I felt. Sant'Ana was still smiling.

'Your husband treated me as a friend,' he said. 'I like to think you'll do the same.'

An hour or so later, Dennis and I were back in the Porsche. We had, in Dennis's phrase, got the beginnings of a result. The bank was aware of the depth of the hole Steve Liddell had dug for himself, but Mr Sant'Ana had given his word that nothing would happen to the collateral on the loan until the insurance picture was a good deal clearer. Perhaps Steve's insurers would pay out on the claim. Perhaps Steve, given a reasonable period of grace, could trade his way back to solvency. I listened to Dennis putting his gloss on the conversation we'd just shared. Under the circumstances, he concluded, it had turned out a lot better than he'd expected. What still bewildered him was the speed with which the bank had advanced the loan in the first place. Given Steve's lack of a track record, his relative inexperience, £300,000 was a helluva lot of money.

'Thank Christ you came along, though.' He glanced sideways at me. 'He'll be asking you out to lunch next.'

'Who?'

'Sant'Ana.' He scowled. 'Just don't bloody sign anything.'

We'd come to a halt in the multistorey car park where Dennis garaged the Porsche. I said I was grateful for his support but there were things about Steve Liddell's business he really ought to know. I told him about last night, about Harald's interpretation of the accident and – worst of all – about the shortfall in the insurance.

'Two hundred and fifty grand?' Dennis couldn't believe it. 'That's even worse than I thought, Liddell's definitely stuffed.'

He gazed out of the car, shaking his head. Someone had stuck a pebble of pink chewing gum on the grey concrete pillar beside the window. Finally, Dennis sighed, and reached for his briefcase.

'Insurance companies like to move fast,' he grunted. 'It cuts down the legal bills.'

'Meaning?'

'We've got less time than we thought.' He frowned, sifting through a pile of documents. 'And while we're talking insurance, you might as well have the rest of it.'

He extracted a bound copy of our last year's accounts. With it came a photocopy I didn't recognise.

'This is Adam's insurance policy. I've been hanging on to it as a fallback.' He gave me a thin smile. 'Just in case Sant'Ana starts acting like a bank manager again.'

He handed me the policy. The print was tiny. Nothing made any sense.

'Adam took out something called Aircrew Life and Loss of Licence cover. He'd had it a couple of years. It meant that losing his licence would trigger a hefty payout. Ditto dying.' I looked away, hiding my smile. Sometimes Dennis could be so tactless, so blunt, it was almost comical.

'You're telling me there's money due?'

'Potentially, yes, but it isn't as simple as it sounds. We're dealing with the life element here. There's a problem with proof of loss.'

'Whose loss?'

'Yours.'

'You want proof?' I looked at him at last, the smile gone. 'You think this is some kind of picnic? Some kind of game? Who wants this proof? What proof are you talking about?'

Dennis eyed me for a moment. Like so many single men, he lived in a world of his own – armour-clad, secure, cosy – and I think he was genuinely shocked that he'd angered me.

'We're talking small print,' he said defensively. 'The problem is the body.'

'There is no body.'

'Exactly.'

'But there's no Adam, either. And that's because he's dead.'

'Sure, but we have to prove it. That's what they want, proof.'

'You *do* mean a body.'

'Yes, otherwise it's hard for them to deem him dead.'

'Hard for *them*. Are you serious?'

I stared at him, furious. I'd had enough of all this talk of collateral, and periods of grace, and insurance shortfalls, and remote accountants in city offices who had difficulty deeming my husband dead. I had difficulties, too. I had difficulties conceiving another week without him, another month, a whole bloody lifetime. Something had happened, something had taken him away from me, and all I could do was thrash around in a swamp of impossible six-figure debts I could never hope to pay. My life was Adam. Adam was dead. The money stuff could wait. End of story.

I reached across and slipped the life policy back into Dennis's briefcase. He was still holding the bound accounts and I could tell from the expression on his face that there was yet more bad news to come.

My fingers closed around the door handle.

'I'm going home,' I said. 'I'll be in touch.'

I phoned the airport from a pay box on the street. The next flight to Southampton was full. If I wanted to return today, I'd have to wait until the first of the evening departures. I hung up, still fuming. Then I remembered Harald's offer. I had the number of his mobile in my bag. When he answered I could hear the growl of a piston engine in the background.

'Lucky you called,' he said. 'I was about to roll.'

I took a cab to the airport. Harald was waiting for me in the Jersey

Aero Club. He was wearing a leather jacket and a pair of blue Levi jeans and he was looking pleased with himself. He kissed me as we met and said his bag was already stowed. He showed me the Yak through the big picture windows on the airside of the club house. It had a high dual cockpit, one seat behind the other, and a big radial engine at the front. Even at a distance, I could see where the red and white paintwork was darkened and blistered from the fire in Steve Liddell's hanger.

We walked out across the grass and Harald helped me into the front cockpit. Unlike my Moth, the Yak wasn't a tail-dragger and I had a good view forward over the nose. The cockpit felt roomier than I'd expected and when Harald had buckled himself into the seat behind me, and plugged in his headset, he talked me through the controls.

Somehow it hadn't occurred to me that I might be flying this machine but he dismissed my protests and started again, telling me to follow him round the cockpit, left to right. I did what I was told, my left hand gliding over the throttle, flap lever and undercarriage safety gate. The controls and instrumentation were nearly as rudimentary as the Moth, and I tightened the harness a little, settling in the bucket seat as Harald primed the engine. It burst into life, deep-throated, making the rivets dance around me, and I listened to Harald's murmur on the intercom as he went through his checks while the needles on the temperature and pressure gauges slowly rose. The gauges were calibrated in percentages, something I'd never seen before, and Harald had begun to tell me about the little plane's aerobatic capability when he broke off to request a clearance from the tower.

'Jersey tower. Golf Alpha Bravo Tango Bravo. Radio check.'

'Golf Alpha Bravo Tango Bravo. Jersey tower. Loud and clear.'

'Roger, Jersey tower. Golf Tango Bravo. Taxi.'

'Golf Tango Bravo. Taxi runway two-seven. QNH 1003.'

Automatically, I reached for the altimeter, entering the QNH. QNH is the measurement of the current air pressure. Without adjustment, the altimeter gives a false reading.

'The airframe's stressed to plus seven.' Harald was back in the world of aerobatics, 'Isn't that something?'

Plus seven is a measurement of something called g. I've never fully understood the physics but getting to plus seven means doing something very radical indeed to the aeroplane, a turn as tight as a knot, a cartoon loop, a pull-out to the vertical after a high-speed dive. Do any of these things, and your body will suddenly weigh half a ton, and the blood will rush to your head or your feet, and if you're still conscious you'll wish you weren't. At Adam's insistence, I'd pulled g in the Moth, and more recently in the Harvard, but I'd never gone further than three. Seven sounded indescribably awful and I was still gazing fondly at a taxiing passenger jet behind us when Harald completed his run-up checks, steadied the Yak on the threshold of the runway and sought permission to take off. The tower came back at once.

'Golf Tango Bravo. Clear take-off. Surface wind two-six-zero, five knots.'

The main runway at Jersey runs due west. The wind, at 260 degrees, was more or less on the nose, ideal for take-off.

'You have control,' I heard Harald say. 'Don't be shy with the throttle. Give her a hundred per cent and plenty of right rudder. You're looking for a hundred and ten k.p.h. for nose-wheel lift. She'll fly herself off. Just point and squirt.'

Point and squirt? A hundred and ten k.p.h.? Nose-wheel lift? It dawned on me that he was serious. I thought of protesting, of handing control back, but then I simply acknowledged the message. The passenger jet, a long, sleek MD-80, was waiting behind me in the queue for departure. I could see the row of curious faces pressed to the cabin windows.

My left hand closed on the throttle. My right foot pushed on the rudder pedal. I eased the throttle forward, smoothly increasing the boost until the engine was howling and I felt the lever nudge against the stop. I slipped the brakes and the Yak surged forward, the spin of the prop yawing the aircraft to the left. More right rudder, I thought. I had one eye on the airspeed indicator: 50 k.p.h. . . . 60 k.p.h. The centre line on the runway was beginning to blur . . . 80 k.p.h. . . . 90 k.p.h. I felt the aircraft yaw again and caught it beautifully. Then the needle on the airspeed dial was passing 110 k.p.h. and I eased the stick back, letting the aircraft lift itself off the runway. I held it low for a second or two, making the most of the ground effect, the cushion of air between the plane and the racing tarmac, then I pulled on the stick again and we began to climb, the end of the runway slipping away beneath the nose, the sun splintering on acres of glasshouses in the fields beyond the airport boundary.

'We're VFR,' I heard Harald say. 'Fly zero four zero. Two thousand feet will be fine.'

I banked the Yak into a shallow turn. VFR stands for Visual Flight Rules, which meant we were flying with our eyes, in clear weather, rather than on instruments, up in what Adam used to call 'the clag'. The Yak felt beautifully balanced, the controls firm yet responsive, and I looked down at the island's coastline as the starboard wing dropped. The startling blue of the sea and the lovely ochre yellow of the beach stretching away to the north never failed to excite me and I was still grinning when I heard the sudden hiss of escaping air.

'What's that?'

My eyes were racing across the instruments. Our airspeed was fine, turn-and-bank fine, rate-of-climb OK. Then I heard a clunk beneath me, and Harald's voice again. He sounded amused.

'You forgot the undercarriage,' he said. 'The gear works off compressed air. Guess I should have mentioned it.'

'Zero four zero,' I muttered apologetically. 'Two thousand feet.'

Past Cap de la Hague, for the best part of seventy miles, there's nothing but sea. We droned north for a while behind the big old radial engine, the aircraft steady beneath my fingertips. This was the kind of flying I was supposed to hate – enclosed cockpit, no contact with the slipstream and the elements – but Harald had been right. There was something about the Yak that imparted an immediate warmth. After only ten minutes, it felt like an old friend, utterly dependable. I glanced up, checking Harald's face in the rearview mirror bolted to the top of the windscreen. He was peering at the little GPS he'd Velcroed to the dashboard in the back. The GPS is a hand-held device that tells you where you are by reference to various satellites. The readout is accurate to a hundred metres or something equally incredible, and after making all the usual jokes about playthings from Toys R Us, most pilots now swear by them. Happy with the readout, Harald was looking left and right, down from the cockpit, searching for something. I did the same, seeing nothing but the sea, flecked with whitecaps, and the distant wake of a westbound tanker.

Abruptly, I felt the stick move between my fingers. Then Harald's voice in my headphones.

'I have control,' he said.

The port wing dipped and we went into a tight turn. The force of the turn began to drag at my face, the first signs of g, then the turn tightened even more and I felt the weight of my body fighting against the harness. The nose was down now and we were losing height rapidly, the windscreen a deep, deep blue as the Channel came up to meet us. Then, suddenly, Harald pulled the Yak out of the spiral dive, and we were circling a small boat. It looked like some kind of fishing smack. There were a couple of men on the tiny deck forward of the wheelhouse. We were low enough to see the glisten of spray on their yellow oilskins, and one of them waved as Harald waggled the Yak's wings in salute. The boat disappeared beneath us and we began to climb again as Harald pushed the throttle forward.

'She's called the *Frances Bevan*,' he shouted. 'The guys are first-class.'

We banked hard, still climbing, and looking out I could see the boat again, much smaller. Suddenly it dawned on me what he was talking about. This was the boat Harald had chartered to look for the remains of the Cessna. This was where Adam had gone down.

I couldn't take my eyes off the ocean. The swell was running west to east and the higher we got, the more distinct became the pattern of the waves, marching up the Channel. Thanks to the sunshine, it was an infinitely friendlier scene than I'd imagined, but it was the oddest feeling, gazing down from my seat in the gods, wondering for the umpteenth time just how Adam had speared in. He would have died in seconds, I told myself. It would have been the gentlest exit.

'Remind me about the strip at Sandown.' It was Harald again.

'Two three,' I said at once. 'With this wind.'

'Fine. You're looking for stage one flap at one seventy. Finals at one fifty. Over the fence at one forty. Just fly her on. Don't worry about the round-out.'

He was asking me to land the Yak once we got to the Isle of Wight. I was still looking down at the waves.

'No thanks,' I said numbly. 'You do it.'

We landed at Sandown at noon. I retrieved my holdall from the luggage bay behind the rear cockpit, half-expecting Harald to take off again. He was heading north, up to a small private field near Manchester. He said he had a business contact there, a BMW dealer who was interested in buying a couple of Yaks for himself and his wife. I was on the point of thanking him for the lift when he unbuckled his harness and clambered down from the cockpit.

'Wouldn't mind taking a look at *Ellie B*,' he said. 'Is my baby at home?'

Ellie B was Harald's pet name for the Mustang. He'd started calling the aircraft after me during the last year, much to my husband's amusement. Adam's preferred name, which he'd never got round to painting on the nose, was *Hot Pursuit*.

We kept the Mustang in our hangar on the south side of the airfield. Harald and I walked over together, not saying much. I couldn't make up my mind about his little detour in mid-Channel. In one sense it was pretty close to the bone. In another, given the money he was spending trying to help me, I knew I should simply be grateful.

The hangar doors were open and I could see our engineer, Dave Jeffries, standing on a pair of steps, working on the big Merlin

engine. Dave had been with us for the best part of four years. Adam
had found him at the RAF's Battle of Britain Memorial Flight, up at
Coningsby, where he'd been on the point of leaving his fitter's job,
and had tempted him south with a year's contract to work for Old
Glory. After the beautiful job he'd done rebuilding the Harvard,
Adam had retained him to work the same magic on the Mustang, and
he'd been with us ever since. Yet another reason, in my book, for not
getting over-involved with Steve Liddell.

Harald stood beside the Mustang, gazing up. He numbered three
Mustangs in his warbird collection back in Florida, but he'd always
had a soft spot for ours. The moment he'd first laid eyes on it – the
rebuild fifty per cent complete – he'd told Adam that Dave's work
had been outstanding. He'd said it matched anything he'd seen in the
States and he'd lost no time trying to buy it for himself. Adam, of
course, had said no, but when we finally agreed on Harald taking a
forty-five per cent stake, the price he paid was extremely generous.
For that, I was certain, we owed a huge vote of thanks to Dave.

'How is she?'

Harald was looking up at Dave. The two men had always got on
well. The same directness. The same disinterest in small talk.

'She's fine.' Dave gestured at the big four-bladed propeller. 'I split
the hub and replaced the spider seals the other day. Good as new
now.'

'How many hours on the old set?'

'Ninety odd.'

Dave reached for the lead light, moving it along the engine bay,
pooling light on the glistening valves either side of the exposed
camshaft, and I thought again of Steve Liddell and his empty hangar,
the concrete floor blackened where the Spitfire had gone up in flames.
Harald was talking about boost pressures now and I left the two men
to it, walking out into the sunshine and then looking back at our
precious aircraft. The Harvard was in there too, a squat, heavy
World War II trainer that I'd more or less mastered thanks to Adam,
but the jewel in our crown was undoubtedly the Mustang.

Just the shape of the aircraft, the way it sat on its big, wide
undercarriage and its neat little tail wheel, told you everything that
you ever wanted to know. The big red spinner at the front, the long
silver nose, the pert bubble canopy, the bulge of the underslung
radiator, there wasn't a line on the aircraft you'd ever dream of
changing. It was like an animal. You could almost reach out and
stroke it. You could almost feel how slippery, how fast it was.

I heard Harald laughing, something he didn't do too often, then he
was out in the sunshine again, joining me on the grass. Dave had

made a little plaque for him, a replica of the original registration on the cockpit dash, and after he showed it to me he tucked it into the top pocket of the denim shirt he was wearing beneath the leather jacket. He stood beside me, watching a young student pilot making heavy weather of a touch-and-go. Then he jerked a thumb back towards our hangar.

'You know the offer's still there,' he said. 'You only have to say the word.'

I nodded. Harald had never made any secret of his desire to buy the rest of the Mustang. He'd even named a price that would, in my present predicament, make life a great deal easier.

'Four hundred and ninety-five thousand dollars,' I murmured. 'It's written on my heart.'

'I'd go higher,' he said at once. 'We could talk about five hundred and fifty.'

'Really?' I looked at him, almost tempted, then he reached out and patted me on the shoulder, as calm and unhurried as ever.

'Think about it,' he said. 'There's no rush.'

I returned his smile. He gave me a brief hug and then said goodbye. He'd phone me if there was any news from his boys in mid-Channel. In the mean time, I was to take care. He gave me a nod and a smile and walked away. I watched him circling the Yak, bending to inspect the tyres, then I returned to the hangar. Dave was about to break for lunch and we talked for a couple of minutes while he gloved his hands in Swarfega, getting rid of the oil and the grease. For the moment, I told him, we had to go easy on the maintenance budget. Not that there was a crisis. Not that there was any kind of financial problem. But Adam's death had naturally turned things upside-down, and just now I was keen to get my bearings before taking the next step. Dave nodded and said it wouldn't be a problem. He was older than Adam and myself, barely a year off his fiftieth birthday, but he'd always liked Adam and I know the accident had shaken him badly.

Outside, I could hear the burble of the Yak's big radial as Harald ran through his engine checks. I watched him taxi to the end of the grass strip. His take-off run must have been less than three hundred yards. Then he was airborne, retracting the undercarriage and easing the Yak into a steady climbing turn, the little plane growing smaller and smaller until all I could hear was the faraway beat of the engine.

I turned away. Beside the hangar was the second-hand Portakabin Adam had bought as an office and an ops room. Over the years we'd been on the island, he'd made it his own, cluttering it with half a lifetime's collection of maps, and snaps, and odd little mementos.

Sooner or later I knew I had to go in there and start sorting things out, but I'd been putting off the moment ever since I'd first got the call from the police about the Cessna going down.

The door to the Portakabin was padlocked. I had one of Adam's several keys. I unlocked the door and let myself in. Adam's office was the smaller of the two rooms. He'd angled the prefab so one side faced south, and the sun was streaming in through the window. Like this, midday, the place felt warm and snug and cosy.

I sank onto the battered leather sofa Adam had treasured so much and looked round. Nothing, of course, had changed. The jigsaw of big airways maps that covered one wall. The framed colour shots from various airshows. Adam's Fleet Air Arm squadron badge, mounted on a wooden shield. The exquisitely painted Tiger Moth he'd assembled from an Airfix kit, dangling on a length of cotton, inch-perfect over his desk.

I got up and circled the office, tidying a pile of aviation magazines, retrieving a parachute from a hook on the coatstand, moving Adam's mountain bike so I could get at the stuff that cluttered his bookcase. Every job I started was freighted with memories and in the end I gave up, collapsing into the swivel chair behind his desk, wondering whether I really had the strength to go through his unopened mail. I decided against it, pulling open one of the drawers instead. There was a litter of bills and receipts inside, paperwork I knew I had to tackle, and I was still sorting them into separate piles when I found the photo.

It showed a girl on a beach. She had long black curly hair, and a full mouth, and she was wearing a wetsuit rolled down to her waist. The bikini top couldn't have been briefer. She had a beautiful body, deeply suntanned, and the expression on her face – fond, eager, mischievous – told me more than I wanted to know. Behind her, in the water, windsurfers stitched back and forth across a pretty bay.

I turned the photo over. The little office felt suddenly as cold as a tomb. *For you, my darling*, went the big, loopy handwriting. *From all of me.*

Chapter five

Amongst the calls waiting for me at Mapledurcombe were a couple of messages from the local police. The last time I'd had any contact with them was the afternoon they'd phoned with the news about Adam's disappearance but I didn't recognise the name on the ansaphone. A Detective Constable Perry wanted to have a word with me.

I sat at Adam's desk, trying to resist the urge to take yet another look at the photo I'd brought back from his office at the airfield. Already, the girl on the beach had come to obsess me. In ways I still find difficult to describe, coming across this tatty little snap, with its adolescent message, was an even bigger shock than the news of Adam's death. Everything I'd assumed, everything I'd loved, treasured, taken for granted, had turned – almost literally – to sand.

DC Perry drove over from Newport. He was a youngish detective with a shapeless black raincoat, bloodshot eyes and a heavy cold. We talked over tea in the kitchen. When I asked him why he'd come, he gave me a pretty vague answer about the circumstances surrounding Adam's death. When I asked him what – exactly – those circumstances might be, he became even more evasive. Finally, after he'd wolfed the second scone, I managed to pin him down.

'Is it to do with his insurance policy?'

'Why do you say that, Mrs Bruce?'

'My accountant tells me there might be a problem.'

'What kind of problem?'

I tire easily when I'm upset. This particular afternoon, I was exhausted. I stopped circling the kitchen and sank into the chair across the table from Perry, looking him in the eye.

'My husband's been dead three days,' I told him. 'It hasn't been easy trying to cope. Why don't you just tell me what you want?'

Perry had already offered his condolences, a formal, rather passionless expression of regret, but I'd put this down to the fact that he'd known neither of us. Now, it occurred to me that there might be rather more to this visit than met the eye.

'You're right about the insurance policy,' he said slowly. 'I'm afraid I've got to ask you a few questions.'

'Why?'

'Because of the nature of your husband's death.'

'You mean the way he did it?'

Perry looked briefly startled.

'Did what?' he asked quickly.

'Died.' If I sounded aggressive, it was because I meant to. Funny how betrayal breeds contempt. All men. Every single one of them. Traitors.

Perry had produced a notebook. I watched his biro racing across the page. He looked up, the easiest questions first.

'I understand he'd had the policy a couple of years.'

'Is that what the insurance people said?'

'Yes.'

'Then I'm sure it's true.'

'You're telling me you didn't know?'

'Not in any great detail, no.'

'But you knew how much was at stake? How much he was worth?'

'Worth?' I offered him a bleak smile.

Biro poised, Perry waited for me to carry on but I just looked at him, staring him out. I'd had quite enough of playing men's games. I wanted some answers of my own.

'What happens next?' I asked at last. 'My accountant tells me we need to find his body.'

'Your accountant's right. At the moment, your husband's down as a missing person. That's partly why I'm here. If he's missing, it's our job to find him.'

'He's dead,' I said flatly.

'How do you know?'

'The ATC people saw the plane go down on radar. They tape these things. There's a record. Evidence.'

'They saw him drop off the screen,' Perry said. 'That's not necessarily the same thing.'

'You've talked to them?'

'Of course.'

The expression on Perry's face might have been a smile. I glared at him. He was right about the ATC coverage. Below a certain height, the curve on the earth's surface creates a black hole, impervious to radar beams. Smugglers use it, though coverage gets better and better the closer you get to the coast.

Perry was looking at his notes.

'Your husband's plane was carrying four hours' worth of fuel.

He'd been up for . . .' he shrugged, '. . . say forty minutes. That leaves over three hours. Three hours is three hundred miles. He could be anywhere. He could have landed in some field or other . . . couldn't he?'

'Yes, he could. But why? Why would he want to do it? Cause all this fuss? All this hassle?' I flapped my hand half-heartedly, a gesture that was meant to encompass pretty much everything that had happened since Thursday afternoon.

Perry was still looking at me. At length, he asked me whether Adam had been under any kind of stress.

'None,' I said briskly. 'That I know of.'

'He hadn't been acting strangely? Nothing out of character?'

'Not at all. He had the lowest blood pressure of any man I've ever met. Nothing got to him. Ever.'

'No business problems?'

'Nothing we couldn't handle.'

'You're sure about that?'

'Positive.'

'And nothing . . .' he paused, '. . . on the emotional side?'

It was a curious way of putting it, clumsy, old-fashioned, awkward, and looking at him I couldn't get the girl's face out of my mind. The lips. The half-smile. The way the wet bikini had clung to her breasts. What was I defending here? Why was I going through this daft charade?

'We were very happy,' I said firmly. 'The relationship was fine.'

'And nothing wrong with his health? Nothing you'd noticed? Only men don't necessarily let on, you know, when things go wrong.'

'They don't?'

For the second time, my directness made him blink. He reached for his pen again and scribbled a note. What had he written? What had I let slip?

He looked up and the expression on his face made me realise that he was altogether more perceptive than I'd thought.

'These things can be hurtful,' he said quietly. 'In my line of work you get to understand that. If there's anything, anything at all . . .' he gestured at the pad, '. . . you only have to say.'

'You think there's more?'

'There's always more.'

I nodded, trying to make light of it.

'I'm sure you're right,' I said. 'But you'll forgive me, you know, if I'm a little hazy just now.'

'Of course.'

There was a long silence. Perry blew his nose, carefully folding the handkerchief afterwards, and for a moment I thought he was going to start all over again. How long the insurance policy had been active. How experienced a pilot Adam had been. Why he might have tired of married life with yours truly.

'Are you telling me my husband faked his own death?' I enquired coldly.

'I'm suggesting it's a possibility.'

'OK.' I nodded. 'Let's say he did, is that a crime?'

'Yes.'

'What kind of crime?'

'Fraud, for starters.'

'And is that why you're here? Because you think he's still alive?'

He hesitated a moment, then he had the grace to look away.

'You may not realise quite the kind of situation your husband's created,' he said. 'Because there's no body, we can only open an inquest and then adjourn it. As long as the inquest isn't over, I'm afraid he's not dead. Not officially, anyway.'

I stared at him, shocked. I'd heard some of this only this morning but I'd somehow assumed that Dennis's talk of proof of loss was strictly for the benefit of the insurers. The possibility that it might also apply to the real world hadn't occurred to me.

'So what happens next?' I said. 'Where do I go from here?'

'It's awkward, Mrs Bruce. You have to wait a year. If your husband's body turns up, all well and good. The inquest will resume, in the normal way.'

'But what if he doesn't?' I was looking at a photo on the dresser, Adam clambering out of the Mustang. 'What then?'

'After the year's up, we write to the Home Office. The Secretary of State can grant a presumption of death. Normally that takes a couple of weeks. Then we arrange an inquest – say a week or two later – and that's when the coroner can close the file. Officially, that is.'

I nodded, trying to take it in.

'But does all that matter?'

'I'm afraid it can, yes.'

'Why?'

He hesitated, then looked round. Anything in joint names, he said, would have to stay that way. Assets that I might want to get rid of – like the house – would be effectively frozen.

'You mean I couldn't . . .' I shrugged hopelessly, '. . . sell it?'

'No, not without his consent.'

'But he's dead.'

'Doesn't matter. Makes no difference.'

I felt something close to panic welling up inside. Everything we had

– the house, the business, the aircraft – was held in joint names. Did this mean I had to wait a year, a whole twelve months, before I could make any decisions? What if I had to raise money quickly? What then?

Mention of the aircraft sent Perry back to his pad. He wanted to know how much they were worth. I gave him the figure for the Mustang first.

'Six hundred grand?' There was no doubt about the smile this time.
'Yes.'
'And the other one?'
'The other two. There's a Harvard and a Tiger Moth.'

I named a price for each. He wrote them down. While he was still busy with his shorthand, I got to my feet, eager now for the interview to end.

'Maybe I did it,' I said lightly. 'Have you thought of that?'

Perry didn't look up.

'Did what, Mrs Bruce?'

'Killed him. Killed my husband.'

There was a longish silence. He was still making notes on the pad.

'You'd need a motive,' he murmured at last, 'if that's a serious question.'

He stayed another half-hour or so. He took a formal statement about Adam – basic stuff like the length of our marriage and the nature of the business we ran – and then he went into some detail about Adam's movements over the last month or so. Because I'd been thinking of nothing else since midday, I was able to help him out there, and when I'd fetched the diary from the office, I gave him a list of dates when Adam had been away.

'Where did he go?'

'Jersey, mostly.'

'Business?'

'Of course.'

'Who with?'

'Various people.'

Again, the pen faltered, and when he looked up and asked for names I had to bite my lip before I came up with Dennis Wetherall. I gave him the phone number of his office, and the address too.

'What about a Steve Liddell?'

'Him, too.'

'They were in business together?'

'Sort of. Not really. You'll have to ask Dennis.'

'But you say you ran . . .' he consulted his pad, '. . . this Old Glory together?'

'Absolutely.'

'And you didn't know about Steve Liddell?'

'Of course I knew about Steve Liddell. But he had nothing to do with Old Glory.'

I was still wondering where he'd got Steve's name. Had the Jersey police been on? Did he have a list of questions to put to me about the fire? It seemed he didn't, though before he went he confided that he had, indeed, been contacted by the CID office in St Helier. When I asked why, he simply smiled, shaking his head. The scones, he said, had been lovely, and if there was anything else I wanted to say then I just had to lift the phone. He scribbled a mobile number on the back of a card and stepped aside as I led the way out of the kitchen.

By the front door, he paused and fumbled in his trouser pocket for the handkerchief. The oil painting of the Mustang was back in the hall. Perry peered at it, then pointed at the beaming face in the cockpit.

'Was that your husband?'

'Yes.'

Perry gave his nose a final wipe, then opened the door and stepped out.

'I expect you'd like him back.' He turned round, buttoning his coat. 'Wouldn't you?'

I thought about the proposition for a moment or two. Then I nodded.

'I would,' I said. 'I'd like that very much.'

After Perry had gone, I buried myself in the paperwork I'd neglected over the past few days. Even with the two of us, running Old Glory was never less than demanding. Like any business, it needed constant attention and it was dark outside by the time I'd dealt with the latest batch of correspondence, mainly letters from Americans wanting to stay. The fact that we were already fully booked for the coming season made little difference to the workload. We'd always made a point of replying to each applicant, telling ourselves that every airmail letter represented a potential guest, if not this year then maybe next.

The work done, I left the printer to chatter away in the office and returned to the kitchen to make myself a cup of tea. Already, deep inside me, I felt a stranger in my own house. This was where I thought Adam and I had been so happy. This was what we'd built together, shared together. As it turned out, though, me and the home and the business and the Mustang hadn't been quite enough. There had, as ever, to be more – another challenge, another conquest, another ball for my greedy juggler to keep in the air.

Put this way, what he'd done didn't seem quite so gross. Indeed, the more I thought about it, the more in keeping with his character it appeared to be. Adam wouldn't have been Adam without the compulsion to tackle life at a thousand miles an hour, and if in his haste he'd stumbled over some sultry bimbo on a Jersey beach, then who was I to be surprised? Finding out hurt like hell, of course it did, and a big part of me that loved him couldn't bear the thought of sharing him with anyone else. Indeed, had he still been alive, and had I still found the photo, then I'd certainly have thrown him out and probably killed him before he'd got to the end of the drive.

The thought, oddly enough, made me smile. It was so hot-blooded, so physical, so in keeping with what we'd had. If Adam had survived my onslaughts, then I knew he'd have been back within hours, contrite, laden with flowers, a late convert to monogamy. I dwelt on the image as long as I could, imagining his laboured explanations, his pleas for forgiveness. The girl had been easy, beautiful, thick. She'd taken him to bed a couple of times but already he was bored stiff with her. The thing was over, a couple of hot weeks way back last summer, maybe a phone call or two afterwards, but nothing serious, nothing heavy. And the photo in the drawer? The heartfelt message on the back? He'd grin, and shrug, and take me in his arms. You know men, he'd say. Always hanging on to the wrong kind of trophy.

I nearly didn't answer the phone in the office. It was Dennis ringing from Jersey. He had two bits of news about Steve. One I wouldn't want to hear. The other probably explained everything.

I didn't understand a word.

'You what?' I said.

'Bad news first. Adam was in deeper than we thought.'

'What do you mean?'

'I've been going through the current accounts. He laundered some cash and put it Steve's way. We're looking at money here, Ellie. Not loan guarantees.'

'*Laundered?*'

'Yeah. Basically it was income from the Mustang, about seventy grand's worth, but he disguised it.'

'Why? How?'

'Doesn't matter. If I tell you how he did it, I'd be here all night.'

I nodded, forcing myself to concentrate. This was like life in the Blitz, I thought. Raid after raid. The masonry crashing around me.

'That's the bad news?'

'Yeah.'

'What's the other bit?'

'Steve's private life. You remember that photo of the kid you noticed? The one on his desk?'

'Yes.'

'That's his little girl. Her name's Minette.'

'Steve's married?'

'No, he had a partner. Chick called Michelle.'

'Had?'

'Yeah, she went off with some fella. Don't ask me who. Crucified Steve, though. You can see it, can't you? State of the guy?'

I was still thinking of the little face in the photo on Steve's desk. Dennis was right. No wonder Steve had looked so awful. No wonder the Spit had caught fire.

I began to thank Dennis for getting in touch again, then I stopped. The photo I'd found in Adam's office was still lying beside the phone. I tried to head off the question but there was no stopping it.

'What does she look like? This Michelle?'

'No idea,' Dennis laughed. 'Apparently she runs some kind of windsurfing school. Out on one of those nice little bays.'

She had a name, this woman. *Michelle*. I sat in the car, parked in the darkness on a tiny track overlooking the lighthouse at St Catherine's Point. This was the very bottom of the island. Beyond here, for umpteen miles, there was nothing but the trackless wastes of the Channel. Was Adam really out there? Had he really crashed? And even if he had, was there any point in caring any more?

Michelle. I wound down the window, peering into the windy darkness, thinking of Steve Liddell and the little girl he'd lost to his one-time partner. No wonder he'd been reluctant to talk about the accident with the Spitfire. No wonder he'd looked so helpless, so beaten, so physically spent.

It was cold outside and I shivered, winding up the window again, wondering whether it was late or not. Since Thursday, time had become somehow elastic, stretching and stretching, the days blurring into each other, a non-stop succession of phone calls, and half-understood conversations. With each of these exchanges it seemed to me that the news got worse and worse, tightening the corset into which Adam had strapped me. First the loan guarantee. Then the photograph on the beach. And now £70,000 he'd simply helped himself to. Where had it gone, that money? Had it gone to Steve, as Dennis seemed to believe? Or had it really been meant for Michelle? A token of my husband's affection? A down-payment on some life they were planning together, once he'd dumped one or two bits of baggage? Like me?

I shook my head, trying my best not to believe it, trying to give him the benefit of the doubt. The beam from the lighthouse swung left to right, a finger of light reaching deep into the Channel, and I found myself talking to him, murmuring questions, wanting to know the truth. Why had he done it? Wasn't I enough for him? Weren't we good together? Why blow it like that? The questions went round and round in my head, each one triggering a fresh doubt, a new uncertainty, and suddenly a phrase of Harald's came back to me.

He'd been talking about Adam's involvement in Steve Liddell's business, and one of the reasons Harald had had his own doubts about the loan guarantee was Adam's reluctance to get – in his phrase – 'hands-on'. *He wasn't with Steve,* he'd said. *He wasn't where he needed to be. He wasn't with the action.* At the time, that hadn't surprised me in the least. The small print of more or less everything in Adam's life except his precious Mustang bored him stiff. But if he hadn't been with Steve, where had he been?

The implications of this question brought tears to my eyes, but the longer I sat there blowing my nose, the more I knew that the thing – just now – was beyond resolution. Coping by myself was no longer an option. I had to talk to somebody else.

Ralph Pierson's bungalow was only five minutes away. When I rang the bell, the door was opened by a tall youth in a tracksuit and trainers. He had freckles and a mass of curly red hair. He looked about twenty.

'My name's Ellie,' I said hesitantly. 'Is Ralph busy?'

He stepped back, inviting me in. Across his tracksuit top, in white letters, it said: *Aberdeen University – Department of Forestry.*

'Grandpa's in there.' He nodded at the open door to the lounge. 'I think he's still working.'

I knocked at the lounge door. Ralph was sitting at his desk. He was wearing a baggy crew-necked Guernsey and a pair of dark-blue flannel trousers. The moment he saw it was me, he stood up.

'Lovely.' He gave me a kiss. 'What a surprise.'

We settled ourselves by the fire. He introduced Jamie, his grandson, and explained that he was staying a few days to sort out a couple of trees in the garden. Fresh from university, Jamie had found himself a tiny flat in Battersea and was trying to make a go of it as a tree surgeon. Coming from the treeless Falklands, I'd never heard the term before and I listened while Jamie explained. Trees, he said, were like people. They were living things. They needed love and attention from blokes with a bit of knowledge of the way they worked. Moving to London was a gamble, and so far the pickings had been lean, but the place was full of knackered trees and clueless owners and in the long run he was sure to make his fortune.

Like his grandfather, Jamie had a lovely manner – gentle, funny, attentive – and we talked about London for a couple of minutes longer until Jamie excused himself, leaving Ralph and me by the fire. Evidently the lad ran every night, five miles at least, and Ralph, for one, was deeply impressed.

'Lovely boy.' He nodded approvingly. 'Always has been.'

I told Ralph what had happened over the last day or so. I didn't spare him any of the details and I included finding the photo in Adam's office. Ralph listened carefully, packing the bowl of his pipe with shreds of Erinmore Flake. I think he took my candour as a measure of my desperation because after I'd finished he produced a bottle of rum, a spirit he knew I liked, and poured me a generous measure.

'To you.' He raised his glass. 'And to Old Glory.'

I didn't know quite how to take the toast. Was this the conclusion he'd drawn? That I should dig in and fight? If so, why? And with what? I arranged the questions in a sensible order and put them to him one by one, fighting to keep control of myself. Not very deep down, I felt ugly, and vindictive, and very, very hurt, but I was determined not to let it show. Ralph, of course, could see through all this but I think it suited him, too, to keep our little boat from being swamped. Just now, he said, it was important to hang on to a sense of perspective. These were early days and it would be easy to get things wrong. How could I be sure about the financial situation? How did I know that Dennis was right about the £70,000? And, most important of all, where was the proof that the girl in the photo was indeed Michelle? Lots of people went windsurfing. You didn't have to own the show to get your photograph taken.

I nodded.

'Or screw someone else's husband,' I said.

'Quite.'

This was the closest I got to expressing the way I really felt and I heard myself apologising at once. Fond though he was of me, it was no part of Ralph's responsibility to share my disgust, and I didn't blame him when he abruptly changed the subject.

After the war, Ralph had joined the BBC, moving through the ranks until he became an Outside Broadcast producer in the infant days of television. A move to one of the founding ITV companies had given him a bigger job and he'd often told me some of the more colourful stories from those pioneering days. Now he was talking about Cowes Week, the great yachting jamboree. His bosses over in Southampton had wanted him to produce the first-ever live coverage. Most of the cameras had to be afloat, mounted on launches. The technical problems were enormous and everyone he spoke to said that even half-decent coverage would be impossible.

'Impossible,' he repeated.

'So what happened?'

'We persevered. We took the problems one by one, and most of them we solved.'

'But what about the ones you couldn't?'

'We ignored them. Or we boxed around them. Or we did any damn thing, as long as they went away.'

'And did they?'

'Mostly, yes.'

I nodded, wondering quite how this early exercise in live television related to the wreckage of Old Glory and of what had once been a wonderful marriage.

'So how did it go?' I asked. 'On the day?'

Ralph laughed.

'It was bloody good. It wasn't perfect, nothing ever is, but it was lots of fun and we knew we'd given it our best shot.'

This was getting warmer. Best shot I knew about. When it came to maximum effort, to working your socks off only to see your efforts wasted, I was one of the world's experts.

'But this is different,' I insisted. 'Making your programme, trying to get it right, you knew you could rely on the people around you. I can't do that any more. I thought I could but I can't.'

'How do you know?'

'*Know?*'

I stared at him, then began to go through it all again. What Adam might have done with the money. Who Adam might have been seeing in Jersey. Where that left Old Glory. And me.

Ralph looked thoughtful, sucking on his pipe. He was a past master at pointing the conversation in new directions. Anything, I thought bitterly, to avoid discussing Adam. What a bastard he'd been. How irresponsible. How reckless.

'Remember when you took me up in the Moth?' he mused.

I nodded. We'd been flying together at the end of last summer, a belated thank you for all the work Ralph had been putting in on the book.

'That was nice,' I said defensively. 'A nice day.'

'It was better than nice. You fly well, really well. I didn't tell you at the time but maybe I should now.'

In spite of my anger, my bewilderment, I felt a little warm glow kindling inside me. Flying was something that even Adam couldn't take away. Up in the clouds, the Moth and I were beyond reach.

Ralph was talking about the Harvard.

'How many hours have you done now?'

I frowned, trying to remember. Adam had started me in the Harvard more than a year ago. After six hours I'd gone solo, and since then I'd done maybe another thirty.

'And you feel happy in it?'

'More or less. It's not like the Moth, though.'

'Bit of a carthorse?'

'Not really.' I shook my head. 'It's easy to think that, looking at her, but no, I wouldn't call her a carthorse.'

I thought hard about what I was trying to say. Adam, to his credit, had always had nothing but respect for the old trainer. Ours was one of the pre-war models and I remembered the first time he'd sat me in the big front cockpit, showing me the controls. He'd commented on the smell, a mustiness seasoned with Avgas and oil and old leather, and he'd told me it was common to every Harvard he'd ever flown. 'Sixty years of fear,' he'd grinned. 'That's what you're smelling.'

I looked across at Ralph, marvelling at his guile. He'd worked the old trick, the old magic. For a couple of minutes now, I'd thought of nothing but the challenge of keeping the Harvard airborne.

'It was the controls I couldn't get used to,' I said. 'You put in such big movements on the stick. The rudder needs a real kick. Adam used to say it was like flying a bowl of soup. It slops around everywhere and then you do something wrong, mess up the numbers, and it kills you.'

'Did he say that, too?'

'Yes.' I nodded. 'He didn't play around all the time. Not with aircraft, at least.'

The comment stalled the conversation for a moment or two. Ralph was staring at the fire.

'You really loved him, didn't you?' he said at last.

I smiled. Even now, it was a pleasure to admit it.

'I did,' I said, 'And I think I still do. That's the problem. That's what I can't sort out.'

'Then don't even try.' Ralph reached forward, shifting one of the bigger logs with the poker. 'None of us gets very much luck in this world. If you really loved him, if you trusted him, if you believed in him, then all those things matter. They're rare, believe me. Especially the love.' He looked up. 'And Adam? He loved you, too?'

'I thought so.'

'Then think so now. I didn't know him at all well. But what I saw was pretty convincing.'

'What do you mean?'

Ralph looked at me for a long time. I think he was trying to gauge how much I could take, how far he could go.

'He was transparent,' he said at last. 'What you saw was what you got. He had no side to him. He always reminded me of a young labrador. Very alert. Very boisterous. Very eager.'

I smiled again, gladdened. This was the Adam I'd fallen in love with, the Adam beside me in the wedding album. Young labrador was a brilliant description. He really belonged in a field, chasing rabbits.

'He had a darker side as well,' I said warily, 'I wouldn't pretend he didn't. He could be difficult when things didn't go his way.'

'You mean sulky?'

'No, more frustrated than sulky. He always put so much in, he expected everything to work, all the time. When it didn't, he felt . . .' I shrugged, hunting for the right word.

'Betrayed?'

'Yes, betrayed.'

I looked at Ralph for a second or two, then laughed. Full circle, I thought. Adam betrayed. Me betrayed. Maybe Ralph was right. Maybe things weren't quite as obvious as they seemed. Maybe I should look just a little bit harder.

Ralph had uncorked the rum bottle. I covered my glass with my hand, telling him I had to drive back, then it occurred to me that he, too, might have something to get off his chest. We'd never talked like this before. So intimate. So close. So candid.

'Just a splash,' I said, 'would be lovely.'

I leaned back in the chair, half-closing my eyes, listening to the silky trickle of the rum into my glass. Ralph, as ever, had dressed my wounds. Already, I felt better.

'I was married for nearly fifty years,' I heard Ralph say, 'and we pretty much went through it.'

I opened my eyes.

'Went through what?'

'Everything that you can possibly imagine. Our first baby died. We had a lot of financial problems. My wife had an affair.'

'She did?'

I was staring at him, ashamed that I hadn't asked about the baby.

'Yes.' He nodded. 'She'd been married before, of course. I don't know whether I ever mentioned it. She'd had one of those wartime marriages. He was an American airman, as a matter of fact. Navigator on a B-17.'

'What happened to him?'

'He was killed in a landing accident. To tell you the truth, I don't think Sally ever got over it.' He lifted the glass to his lips, sipping the rum. 'Years later, she took up with another American, a businessman this time. It was months before I twigged what was going on.'

'She admitted it?'

'She told me about him. The night before she left.'

'*Left?*'

'Yes.'

'With the kids?'

'Kid. We only had one at the time. Jamie's mother, Ruth. No.' He shook his head. 'Ruthie stayed.'

'And your wife came back?'

'Yes, in the end she did. But it wasn't right. Not then. Not ever, really. Not if you want the truth.'

He broke off, plucking helplessly at the crease in his trousers, and I felt suddenly swamped with sympathy, a raw, hot feeling that threatened to overwhelm both of us. I got up and perched myself on the arm of his chair. When I covered his hands with mine, I could feel them trembling.

'What are you saying, Ralph?'

He looked up at me. His eyes were a milky blue.

'I'm saying you should be thankful for what you had. It's rare, Ellie. If it felt good, it was good. That's all I'm saying.'

'But –'

He reached up, sealing my lips with his long, bony forefinger.

'I mean it. Sally and I, bless her, were never right and we knew it. Knowing it and admitting it are two different things but at my age life finds you out. In the end there's no pretending, no make-believe. You *know* what it was really like.'

'And Adam?'

'He loved you. I'm certain of it.'

I left Ralph's an hour or so later. Jamie had returned from his run, pinked with exertion, and the sound of him singing in the bathroom shower had broken the spell between us. I was more grateful than I could ever say to Ralph. I knew how much he'd risked by trying to help me and the fact that he'd succeeded was a tribute to his courage as well as his kindness.

Before I left, he showed me the latest progress on the Mustang book. A month before the end of the war, Karel Brokenka – the Czech pilot who'd downed the Me109 – had force-landed the plane in Sweden after a coolant failure. Years later, the Swedes had sold it on to the Israeli Air Force. After action in the Suez affair, Ralph said, the old warhorse had been bought by a Maltese entrepreneur and put out to grass. Quite what happened next wasn't entirely clear but Ralph was still writing letters and sooner or later he was confident of pinning down the rest of the story. To me, our little fighter's history sounded hopelessly complicated and I admitted as much as I stood on the doorstep, saying goodbye.

Ralph put a hand on my arm.

'Relax,' he said. 'You're in a spin but it's perfectly recoverable. Just take your hands off the controls and let the damn thing sort itself out.'

I was still trying to find my car keys.

'You're talking about Old Glory?'

'No.' Ralph kissed me on the forehead. 'I'm talking about you.'

Harald turned up again next day. He phoned from the airfield and I invited him over for lunch. We had pasta and a salad at the kitchen table while he told me about his trip to the north. The BMW dealer had gone up for a spin in the Yak and bought two on the spot. Harald had phoned Steve Liddell with the good news and sent various faxes to his contact in Romania. With luck, Steve should be spannering again within the week.

'You're still with him?'

'Sure. Someone has to be.'

'After everything that's happened?'

'You mean Harvey's Spit?'

I looked at him a moment, wondering whether to update him on developments, then decided against it. It was a lovely day. The pasta, to my delight, was delicious. Why let the face in the photo spoil it?

'Yes,' I said lightly. 'That's exactly what I mean.'

Harald ducked his head and reached for a napkin, wiping his mouth. He confessed a soft spot for young Steve. He said he'd decided to try and help him back on his feet. I said that sounded a pretty Christian thing to do and we were still talking about the Yak when I heard a knock on the front door.

It was Jamie, Ralph's grandson. He was wearing jeans and a lovely cotton shirt. He had a dark-green pullover draped over his shoulders, the arms knotted loosely around his neck. There was something familiar about his face, the way he smiled, but for the moment I couldn't quite place it.

'Did you run here?'

'Afraid not.'

He indicated a battered mountain bike propped against one of the garage doors. The frame was caked in mud, just like it should be.

'You rode over?'

He nodded, grinning.

'Twenty minutes, door to door.'

I invited him in but he shook his head. He had something for me. From Ralph.

He gave me a brown Jiffy bag, standing uncertainly on the doorstep.

'You want me to open it now?'

'No, of course not.'

'You're sure you don't want to come in?'

'No thanks.'

We looked at each other for a moment and it suddenly hit me who he looked like. Way back, in the Falklands, I'd had a boyfriend called Paul. Paul, at sixteen, was the image of Jamie. Same wild hair. Same white, almost milky skin. Same appetite for exercise and laughter.

We said goodbye and I watched him slip his feet into the pedal grips before giving me a cheery wave and heading off back down the drive. As I turned into the house, I glimpsed Harald at the kitchen window.

'Who was that?'

I told him about Ralph and his grandson. We resumed our seats at the kitchen table. I felt the Jiffy bag, trying to guess what might be inside.

'You mind if I open this?'

'Go ahead.'

While Harald picked at the remains of his salad, I prised out the staples in the Jiffy bag. Inside, wrapped in cotton wool, was a small diecast model of a Mustang. I held it up, showing it to Harald.

'Sweet,' I said.

I landed it beside Harald's plate, a perfect three-pointer. Harald didn't seem the least impressed. With the Mustang was a Get Well card. When I opened it, a folded cheque fell out. I left the cheque on the table, reading the card. Ralph's handwriting was impeccable, perfect copperplate. He felt the urge, he said, to cheer me up. The Mustang might do the trick and if it didn't, the cheque might help. I was to spend it on anything I liked. If I wanted to treat it as a loan, so be it. If I preferred to think of it as a present, nothing would give him greater pleasure. He'd recently cashed in some old share certificates. The proceeds had gone to myself and Jamie. Equal shares.

I picked up the cheque. It was for £5,000. I folded it again and slipped it into the pocket of my shirt, overwhelmed by the gesture.

Harald was examining the Mustang. He looked, if anything, slightly glum.

'I've been thinking,' he said, 'about your financial situation.'

'Don't.'

I began to collect the empty plates, carrying them across to the sink.

'You need money, Ellie,' Harald called, 'and I'm happy to help.'

'I'm fine,' I insisted. 'You take it black, don't you?'

I turned round to find Harald looking at me, his face twisted in a tight little smile. Convinced I'd offended him, I returned to the table.

'It's not that I'm ungrateful,' I said. 'It's just that things are hard. To tell you the truth, things are bloody awful. But just now, just exactly now, I feel pretty good and . . . well . . . that's about it.'

I picked up the Get Well card and propped it on the dresser. In the lunatic world of classic aircraft, £5,000 was small change but that wasn't the point. To Ralph, and I expect to Jamie, it was probably a fortune.

Harald's eyes followed me everywhere.

'You're sure about the Mustang? Five-fifty thousand bucks?'

'Yes, I'm sure.'

'You don't want to sell it?'

'I don't want to part with it.'

'What about some kind of leaseback?'

'What does that mean?'

'I pay you the money, then I own it. You pay me some kind of nominal fee and keep using it. That way you get to unlock the value without having to kiss the plane goodbye.'

I thought about it for a second. More small print. More contracts. More room for expensive mistakes.

'No thank you,' I said.

'OK.' Harald shrugged, reaching for the little diecast model. 'Let's say we do it another way.'

'What other way?'

'Let's say we talk about the Harvard.'

'The *Harvard*?'

I paused, en route to the kettle. Back home, in Florida, this man had a small air force packed with really sexy aeroplanes. Harvards were two a penny, especially in the States. Why should he be interested in ours?

Harald was looking thoughtful and I wondered what was coming next.

'I'll buy the Harvard,' he said. 'It'll belong to me but you can keep it here.'

'But why? Why do you want it?'

He began to drum his fingers on the wooden table top.

'Two hundred and fifty thousand,' he said softly.

'A quarter of a *million*?'

'Dollars.' He nodded. 'In one hit. Just say the word, I'll sort out the paperwork.'

I was still trying to do the sums: $250,000 was around £160,000, more than double the Harvard's market value.

'But why?' I asked again. 'I don't understand.'

'It's a nice plane, one of the first I ever flew. Put it down to sentiment, Ellie. And just say yes.'

This was beginning to sound like charity but I wasn't sure that made much difference. Just now I was in deep, deep trouble and £160,000 was a bloody good start to getting out of it.

'The Harvard stays here?' I asked guardedly.

'Sure.'

'And who pays the running costs?'

Harald hesitated for a fraction of a second, long enough for me to realise that he hadn't begun to think this thing through.

'I do.' He smiled. 'My plane. My tab.'

'So you own it?'

'Sure. And I maintain it, borrow it from time to time, prior warning of course, and you get to bank the cheque.' His fingers strayed to the little Mustang. 'Does that sound like robbery?'

'Not at all.'

'So is there a problem?'

'I'm not sure.'

I was looking at the proposal from all sides, trying to spot the angles I'd missed. One of them was the tricky issue of just who owned the plane. Technically, half of it still belonged to Adam, and if DC Perry was right about having to freeze our assets for a year, then the Harvard wasn't mine to sell. Dennis should be here, I thought. He'd find a solution in seconds.

'I need time,' I said, 'to think about it.'

'Sure.'

'You don't mind?'

'Not at all.'

Harald got up, excusing himself from coffee. The green, skintight leather gloves he used for flying were out on the hall table. I followed him, still reeling.

'You're off already?'

'I'm up to North Weald and they haven't got lights. An hour ten in the Yak. I'll just make it.' He kissed me lightly on the cheek. 'There's one thing I haven't mentioned. About the deal.'

'What's that?'

He opened the front door, then turned back to me, slipping on the leather gloves, one after the other.

'You learn to fly the Mustang,' he said softly. 'And I teach you.'

Chapter six

Two days later, my sister arrived. The first I knew was a phone call the previous afternoon from my mother down in the Falklands. The whole family, she said, had been worried sick about me. How could I possibly cope on my own? How could I grieve properly when I had a business to run? All those planes to look after? Adam's affairs to sort out? The latter phrase raised a grim smile and I was still trying to assure her that everything was under control when she told me that Andrea had already left.

'She's on the Brize Norton flight,' my mother explained, 'The Tristar took off a couple of hours ago.'

Direct flights down to the Falklands operate from the RAF airfield at Brize Norton. Brize is up in Oxfordshire and I spent the rest of the evening reorganising everything so that I could put the car on the ferry from Cowes first thing and be at the airfield in time to collect her.

Andrea, at thirty-nine, is the oldest of us three girls and had always been my father's favourite. She is undeniably the most attractive of all of us – long-legged, angular, blonde, with the kind of brooding intensity that a lot of men find irresistible. She's academically bright too, the only Tranter to stand any chance of making it to university. Maybe because of this, she's always preserved a careful distance from myself and Kate, and the news that she was flying eight thousand miles to take care of little me was, to be frank, a surprise. I was grateful, of course, and it would doubtless be lovely to see her again, but something didn't quite gel. Given the fact that we'd never been especially close, just why was she making such an extravagant gesture?

I had my answer within minutes of meeting her in the arrivals hall. The big Tristar had been half an hour early, and Andrea was one of the first passengers through. A brand-new Berghaus anorak and beautifully cut jeans couldn't disguise how much weight she'd lost. Never fat, she looked gaunt, even ill. When we kissed, her lips were cold. I pushed her trolley across the car park. It was a glorious spring morning, the sky a brilliant blue, the softest of breezes laced with the tang of aviation fuel.

'It's freezing,' Andrea complained. 'Even the bloody Falklands was warmer than this.'

I was loading her luggage into the back of the estate car. Judging by the number of suitcases she'd brought, Andrea would be with me until Christmas. I began to babble some nonsense about the weather, how marvellous it had been, how everyone was worried about drought, but when I slammed the tailgate shut and looked up, Andrea was already sitting in the car, her head wreathed in cigarette smoke.

I joined her, slipping my keys into the ignition.

'How's Hamish?' I asked brightly.

Hamish was Andrea's husband, a big, hunky Royal Marine who'd married my sister six or seven years back and traded in his service career for the post of PE teacher at Stanley's new secondary school.

Andrea was watching an elderly couple peering up at the destination board on a nearby coach.

'He's left me,' she said stonily, 'the bastard.'

We took the Oxford road out of Brize Norton. By the time I was back on the A34, heading for Southampton, Andrea had told me the whole story. Hamish, she said, had been acting strangely for more than a year. At first, she'd put his evasiveness and his unexplained absences down to the sheer size of his workload. As well as a million and one responsibilities at school, he'd taken on the setting-up of a Falklands-wide football league. The league included teams from the army base at Mount Pleasant, and there'd been endless meetings, countless crises, umpteen cancelled fixtures, pressure enough to try any man's patience.

Gradually, though, it had dawned on Andrea that there was more to Hamish's mood swings and savage outbursts of temper than disputes about pitch size and refereeing qualifications. For one thing, their sex life – evidently never brilliant – had come to a virtual halt. For another, he'd begun to drink. Not sociably, in the way that the pair of them had always drunk, but sullenly and very often alone.

'I watched him changing,' she kept saying, 'I watched him becoming someone else. Do you know what I mean?'

She looked sideways at me, her fourth cigarette as yet unlit, but I kept my eyes on the road. For the best part of an hour I'd been hunting for parallels with my own errant husband, but so far – thank God – I hadn't found a single one.

'No,' I said, 'I haven't a clue what you mean.'

'Then you're bloody lucky.'

'*Lucky?*' I stared at her.

'Yes. Men are animals. Cowards, too, when it really comes down to it. Do you know what he said when I confronted him? He said it wasn't his fault. He said I'd driven him to it. By being too strong. Too tough. *Tough?* Me? Can you believe that?'

I could. Six years away from the Falklands – not a single holiday, not a single flying visit – had softened my memories of Andrea. Now I remembered just how hard, how unforgiving she could be. For three years, as an only child, she'd been the very centre of attention, and deep down I'd always suspected she was determined to keep it that way. Hamish, I thought, might just have made a very wise decision.

I heard the scrape of a match. The other woman's name was Jacqui.

'Have you met her?' I ventured.

'*Met* her? I practically saved the woman's life when she first arrived. Hamish took her out in the Land Rover and they walked up some bloody mountain or other. Longden. Two Sisters. I can't remember. Anyway, it was raining, and the poor lamb got pneumonia.'

'You nursed her?'

'Yes, and fed her, and kept her amused. But that's what you do, don't you? When your husband brings some stray back from the airport and she's too dozy to have found anywhere half-decent to live.' She took a long pull on the cigarette, gazing moodily out at the budding hedgerows. So far, apart from a sisterly pat on the arm, she hadn't said anything at all about Adam.

'But she moved out in the end', I prompted. 'She must have done.'

'Too right she did.'

She named a new development that sprawled up towards the ridge line that looked down over Stanley Harbour. Jacqui had rented a bungalow with a couple of colleagues from the oil exploration company where they all worked. It must be cosy, I thought, now that Hamish was there too.

'Do you see him at all?'

'Of course I do. You know Stanley. It's hardly the kind of place you can hide yourself away.'

'I suppose not.' I tried to sound sympathetic, 'It must be difficult.'

Andrea reached forward, stabbing the remains of her cigarette into the ashtray.

'It's murder' she said savagely, 'Thank God I can be some use here.'

We were back at Mapledurcombe by late afternoon. The sun was setting over the distant swell of Tennyson Down and the view from the bedroom that would be Andrea's had never looked more fabulous. My sister gave it a passing glance. Fourteen hours in a Tristar seemed to have left her, if anything, with an excess of energy.

Already, in a brief tour of the house, she'd listed the items that needed attention. The little snug at the end of the downstairs hall to be tarted up. One or two bits of furniture in the dining room to be replaced. An old and much-loved rug in the room we used as a lounge to be rolled up and carted away to the dump. Life, with Andrea, had always been this way, a ceaseless assault on those little pockets of domesticity that you treasure and defend. Back home, as children, she'd always made a point of telling me exactly where to hang the Leonard Cohen posters in my room. Half a lifetime later, absolutely nothing had changed.

'You must be knackered,' I said hopefully, watching her unpack. 'We'll have an early supper, then I'll let you get your head down.'

Andrea threw me a look.

'Hamish used to say that,' she muttered, 'and now I know why.'

The next day was Friday, a week and a bit since I'd got the news about Adam's accident. In eight brief days my world had turned upside-down and it was already obvious that Andrea's arrival had given it yet another spin. We'd stayed up until one in the morning, fuelled by a bottle of duty-free brandy while she'd ranted on about Hamish. I'd done my best to make the right noises and – God knows – I was only too aware of the way she must have been feeling. Like me, Andrea had never been able to have children, and like me she seemed to have invested pretty much everything in a man who'd let her down. But at that point, I told myself, the similarities between us came to an end. Even with my own kith and kin I'd never be so open, so graphic, about my wounds. And never, come to that, would I be so vindictive about the man who'd caused them. Marriage is an on-going negotiation. Even in death, as I was beginning to discover, the process of give and take, of forbearance and forgiveness, never ends.

It was mid-morning before Andrea joined me in the kitchen. I was sitting at the table with a calendar and one of Adam's ring-binder pads, trying to draw up a schedule of things to do before the opening of the new season. When Andrea peered at the grid of ringed dates and asked me what it all meant, I told her.

'So how many people are you expecting?'

'That first week?' I consulted my list of bookings. 'Three couples and a sweet old boy from Minneapolis who's been over before.'

'*Seven?*'

Without looking, I could visualise the curl of Andrea's lip. From what little I'd told her about Old Glory, I think she must have been expecting an operation on an infinitely grander scale.

'Yes,' I said, 'seven. Our capacity's eight but we've given Mr Olafsson a whole suite to himself.'

'And charged him single rate?'

'Of course.'

'Why do that? Isn't the point of any business to make money?'

I blinked. I'd been expecting a little light flak from Andrea but nothing this concentrated, or this soon. Old Glory was mine now. I ran it. I made the decisions.

'He came over with his wife last time,' I said defensively. 'She died before Christmas.'

'Is that why he's over again?'

'Yes.'

Andrea was bending down now, peering at my list of bookings. I could feel her breath on the nape of my neck.

'And did you give them the Mitchell Suite last time?'

'Yes.'

'And that's why he wants it again?'

'Of course.' I got up, pushing back my chair a little more forcefully than was strictly necessary. 'Breakfast?'

Andrea sat on the edge of the kitchen table smoking a cigarette while I made her scrambled eggs on toast. She was much taller than me and the sight of her in one of Adam's dressing gowns was oddly disconcerting. Already, in twelve brief hours, I felt Mapledurcombe somehow slipping away from me, shadowed by her presence. Now, in what I suspected was a bid to shift the conversation back to Hamish, she asked me how it had been in my own marriage.

I heaped the scrambled eggs on to a couple of slices of toast and ground black pepper over the top.

'It was bloody wonderful,' I said quietly. 'If you really want to know.'

Andrea pulled the dressing gown a little more tightly around her. Despite the weight loss, she still had a lovely figure.

'You were always the lucky one,' she said glumly.

'You think so?'

'I know so.'

'Lucky to lose him?'

'Lucky to nab him in the first place.'

88

I carried the plate of scrambled eggs across to the table while she crushed the half-smoked cigarette in my saucer. Since that first night Adam and his Sea King crew had invited themselves over to Gander Creek for the party, Andrea had never forgiven me for what happened. She'd fancied him on sight and done her best to make a play for him. They'd had a couple of dances and shared a plate of muttonburgers, and while the boy who played lead guitar in our settlement band was mending a broken string, I'd overheard her telling Adam about her plans to try for a university place at Oxford.

At this point, of course, neither of us knew that Adam was bored witless by anything remotely bookish or academic, and when the band struck up again and Adam seized me rather pointedly by the hand and led me to the very middle of our shabby old community hall, I remember all too clearly the expression on my sister's face. There was bewilderment there, and a measure of disbelief, but as the music slowed, and Adam gathered me closer, Andrea's scowl grew darker and darker. Since we were toddlers, there'd always been a pecking order, an unquestioned acceptance of just who had first place in the queue. Whether it was the biggest spoonful of trifle at tea time, or the best ride at the annual sports weekend my father always organised, Andrea grabbed it. Adam, bless him, put paid to all that, and the insult was all the more wounding because of the way he so obviously didn't care. At the end of that glorious evening, as he tugged me towards the looming bulk of his waiting Sea King, he caught sight of Andrea standing in the lit porch that led into the community hall.

'Look after your little sister,' he yelled back to her. 'The big bird will return.'

Andrea ate scarcely half the scrambled eggs before pushing the plate away. Her cigarettes were in the pocket of the dressing gown.

'You'll miss him,' she said casually, reaching for the big box of matches I always kept on the side.

'I will.' It was a simple statement of fact. 'I miss him already. I miss him more than I thought it was possible to miss anyone. There's a hole there I can't begin to describe. He's just . . .' I shrugged miserably, '. . . gone.'

Andrea nodded, sucking in a lungful of smoke, inspecting my little confession for the point of maximum weakness.

'Divorce is like that,' she said finally. 'In fact I think it's probably worse. At least you've got your memories. That's more than I have.'

'Memories mean nothing. Not for the moment, anyway. Memories are for old people. We weren't old. We were young. We had plans. Not memories.'

89

Andrea touched the corner of her mouth with her little finger, her body bent at the table, her long legs crossed. It was a gesture and a pose I remembered from countless other conversations, the smoke from her cigarette curling upwards, her head cocked to one side, her eyes narrowed in inner contemplation.

'There must have been bad times,' she said at last. 'Must have been.'

'Very few.'

'Did you trust him?'

'I loved him.'

'That's not the same thing.' She frowned. 'Is it?'

'Yes.' I nodded. 'Funnily enough, it is. We never really rowed, not – you know – in a serious way, because there was never any point. Oh, sure, we disagreed sometimes, small things, domestic things, the business maybe, but it never developed into anything serious, anything major, because we never let it. Life was too short. And he was away a lot, remember.'

'Away?' The word was like a flash of silver after a grim morning's fishing. Andrea had baited her hook and now, at last, there was the possibility of something on the end of the line.

I made another pot of coffee and told her about Adam's adventures in southern Africa. Most of this stuff Andrea knew already – I'd talked about it in telephone calls, mentioned it in letters – but my sister had never had much patience with the small print of other people's lives and she expressed her usual grudging interest, waiting for me to bring the story up to date.

'But was he helpful?' she asked. 'Did he do his bit?'

'Where?'

'Here.' She gestured round. 'With the business.'

'Of course.'

I told her about our heroic efforts in the early days, securing the roof, putting the window frames to rights, sorting out the garden, salting my praise for Adam with the frank admission that DIY wasn't altogether his thing.

'So there *were* problems?'

'Not problems, no. Disasters, plenty of them, but never problems. We always coped. And we always laughed afterwards.'

'*Laughed?*' Andrea's head went back. 'God, we could have done with a bit of that. I don't think I can remember when Hamish and I last had a laugh, you know, a proper laugh, let our hair down.'

'It's important.' I was studying the calendar again, more in hope than expectation. 'More important than sex in some ways.'

'You think so?'

90

'Yes. Making love's, you know, wonderful but the thing I miss most is the sound of Adam laughing. He didn't even have to be here. Just on the phone would be enough. He'd laugh at the oddest things but it was so infectious. You just went along with it. Times could be hard, really hard, everything falling apart, often literally. It might be something around the house, or a crisis with the bank manager, or one of the aircraft going U/S, or a booking falling through, or any bloody thing really, but Adam would always see the funny side of it. Always. He never failed me. Not once.'

The memories caught up with me and I reached for the edge of the table, choked with emotion. I heard the scrape of Andrea's chair and I turned my face away as she got to her feet, ashamed to let her see me like this. Then I felt her arms closing around me, and I smelled the faintest hint of aftershave in the folds of Adam's dressing gown, and I buried my face in her shoulder, howling with grief. It was the first time I'd cried, really cried, since the news first came through, and afterwards Andrea sat me down, and finished making the coffee, and then fetched the remains of last night's brandy from the snug next door.

'We're in the same boat,' she said softly as she coaxed the glass into my hand, 'you and me.'

I dried my eyes. I felt weak, and cold, and empty.

'You really think so?' I queried.

We spent the rest of the day itemising all the jobs, big and small, we had to tackle before May came and the first guests arrived. I walked Andrea around the house again, a proper tour this time, room after room, and afterwards I showed her what we'd been able to do outside. In all, Mapledurcombe boasted nearly three acres of gardens, front and rear, and it had been Adam's job to turn our doodled plans into reality.

Access from the little country road that wound up from nearby Shorwell lay between a pair of big stone pillars guarded by tall wrought-iron gates. From here to the courtyard at the rear of the house, Adam had resurfaced the crumbling drive and dug wide borders on either side. Beyond the borders lay an expanse of badly neglected lawn, and it had taken Adam and a couple of young lads from the village a good month to level the ground and then returf it with fresh grass. The garden as a whole was contained by a seven-foot wall built in a wonderfully mellow red brick. The wall, centuries old, was trellised in wisteria and honeysuckle, and on certain summer evenings, after we'd all had a bit to drink, I'd swear that the wisteria looked like drifts of pale-blue woodsmoke.

At the front of the house, the land sloped away to the south-west and Adam had hired a small mechanical digger to build a succession of terraces. Some of the terraces we'd given over to rosebeds and elegant stands of lilies and flag iris. A couple, on the smallest possible scale, had provided a hole or two of pitch-and-putt. While the very bottom of the garden, carefully levelled, had given us enough room to install a modest heated swimming pool, with space on the paved surrounds for sunbeds and our one real extravagance, a rambling nineteenth-century gazebo we'd spotted at a country-house auction in Wiltshire. Dismantled, shipped south and re-erected at Mapledurcombe, the gazebo offered perfect views over the lower slopes of Brighstone Down, and the bright-yellow fields of rape that jigsawed the south-west corner of the island.

In the gazebo, on rainy days, our guests could tuck themselves in on the cane recliners, inspecting the weather as it rolled up the Channel, while Adam and I pored over the airways maps, tailoring the individual flight plans that would become – quite literally – the high spot of their vacations. These sorties back over Europe in the Mustang or the Harvard were, of course, the real reason for Old Glory's success, and as our afternoon wore on I could sense that Andrea had spotted a way we could divide our responsibilities without driving each other barmy. By now, she'd made it clear that she'd be staying for the whole summer. She couldn't bear the thought of going back to the Falklands, and in my heart I didn't blame her, but already we both knew that working together on the domestic side simply wasn't on. There was too much history between us for that. Andrea was too headstrong and impatient to bend or mend her ways, and for my part I saw absolutely no reason to abandon a winning formula just because my bossy big sister had turned up. The flying, on the other hand, was way out of Andrea's league and it made obvious sense to let me take over where Adam, all too sadly, had left off.

I'd told Andrea about Harald's offer on the Harvard, and about his insistence that I should learn to fly the Mustang. We were sitting in the gazebo, sipping tea I'd brought down from the house.

'Is it a handful then? Flying this Mustang?'

I told her it wasn't. Dozens of women had flown them during the war, delivering the planes to front-line squadrons. Some of these women had been half my age, and most of them – at least to begin with – had far fewer hours in their log books than me.

'So what's the problem?'

'There isn't one. It's a tricky aircraft. You have to work at it. And it's bloody expensive, too, if you get it wrong and bend it. But planes are planes. It's like riding a bike. Learn to fly one, you're halfway to flying the lot.'

I paused to nibble a biscuit. The confidence I'd voiced was borrowed, in truth, from other pilots. I'd heard the same theory at countless airshows, that lovely hour or so when the aerobats and the fighter jockeys gather in the beer tent or the bar and debrief each other on the afternoon's adventures. Listening to them reliving loops, or flick rolls, or stall turns in umpteen aircraft types, it was hard to believe that any of it was really difficult. But in reality, I knew different. Every aircraft I'd ever flown had its own repertoire of foibles, little lapses of good behaviour that could steal up on you, and take you by surprise, and – on a bad day – kill you. The Mustang, of course, was no exception and the flights I'd shared with Adam – a handful, three at the most – had taught me that all-important link between an aircraft's performance and your own chances of survival. The faster the aircraft, the sharper your reactions had to be. The cockpit of a Mustang was no place for second thoughts.

'What's he like, then? This Harald?'

I was still airborne, still flying the Mustang, Adam's laconic commentary piping through my headphones. Give or take the odd gentle turn, I'd never tried anything more demanding than straight and level flight but even so I'd learned enough to admire afresh my husband's flawless three-point landings.

'Harald?' I said idly. 'He's fine. He's been a good friend, especially this last week.'

'But what's he like?'

At last I gave the question some thought. Describing Harald, his build, his physical appearance, the way he dressed, was easy enough, but beyond that things got blurred. The essence of the man, who he really was, still eluded me.

'I don't know,' I said carefully. 'He's very kind. Very able. He doesn't say much. He's not very demonstrative, you know, con-versationally. He's obviously done lots with his life, he's made oodles of money, but it doesn't seemed to have changed him.'

'How do you know?'

'I don't. But he's very, I don't know, solid. I can't imagine him ever being very different somehow. He's lumbered, like we all are. Once Harald, always Harald.'

'Do you like him?'

I suppose I should have anticipated the inflection in Andrea's question. It went with a lifting of the eyebrow and the lightest of nudges in the ribs. 'Like' meant 'fancy'. Divorcees' talk. Widows' talk.

'Yes, I do,' I admitted after a second or two. 'I like him a lot. But not that way.' I looked across at Andrea. She had the grace to nod. 'I like his seriousness,' I went on, 'and I like his weight.'

'He's fat?'

'God, no. He's lean, really trim. Not thin, not fat, but just . . .' I studied my teacup, '. . . right. He keeps himself together, you can see it. He probably works out, weights and jogging and all the rest of it. That would be his style, actually. I can imagine him doing it. Same time every day. Early mornings, probably. There's something very spartan about him.'

'You're telling me he's boring?'

'Not at all. Quiet, yes. But not boring.'

'And will you . . . take him up?'

'On what?'

'On this offer of his. This Mustang thing. Learning to fly it.'

I paused again, weighing the question, recognising the subtext. Say yes, and I'd be getting myself out of Andrea's hair, giving her what she wanted, what she needed, a clear run at making Mapledurcombe tick. Say no, and I'd probably be consigning both of us to a summer of nonstop rows. That Andrea could cope with our little enterprise was beyond doubt. One of her real gifts was a talent for organisation, and she'd never been frightened of hard work. She knew her way around a lot of excellent cookery books, and when the mood took her she could be surprisingly hospitable. With her catwalk figure and her throaty laugh, our Americans would love her.

But would I really be able to master the Mustang? I looked out at the view. The morning's cold front had gone through and the weather was clearing from the west, the blue foam-flecked Channel waters pocked with the fat black shadows of the racing clouds. I thought of the last time Adam and I had been together in the air, one icy day just after Christmas, flying back from an impromptu celebratory lunch at a little country airfield near Bordeaux. Typically, Adam had insisted on taking the Mustang, telling me to forget the expense, telling me it was the least he could do to celebrate my thirty-sixth birthday. Maybe Ralph Pierson was right, I thought. Maybe Adam hadn't, after all, been in love with some sex-mad bimbo. Maybe he wasn't forever squandering our hard-earned money. Maybe he really was the man I'd always assumed I'd married. Loyal. And tender. And hopelessly, gloriously, over the top.

'Yes.' I turned round, half-convinced. 'I'll give it a shot.'

At the weekend, to my surprise, I got a call from the AAIB, the accident investigation people up at Farnborough. The caller said his name was Grover. He happened to be passing through Southampton that afternoon and he wondered whether he might pop across for a chat. Popping across, as far as Mapledurcombe's concerned, isn't as straightforward as it might seem. Add up the time you spend waiting for the ferry, making the long haul down Southampton Water, then negotiating the queues of geriatric drivers that choke the island's roads, and you're probably looking at a journey of not less than a couple of hours.

I glanced out of the window. It was a beautiful day.

'I'll fly over,' I said on impulse, 'I'll meet you by the BA ticket desk at three.'

'Ticket desk where?' Mr Grover sounded surprised.

'Southampton Airport.' I heard myself laughing, 'Will that be OK?'

Grover turned out to be a small, rotund, cherry-faced man in his mid-fifties. The shoulders of his suit were flecked with dandruff, his shirt collar was slightly too tight for his neck and he had a nervous habit of continually feeling for his watch. The fact that I'd rolled out my beloved Moth and hopped across from Sandown seemed to have put him at a disadvantage, because he insisted on taking me across to the restaurant and buying me a huge cream tea.

I was halfway through my second scone before we abandoned the inevitable small talk and turned to the real reason he'd asked to meet me.

'Your husband,' Grover sounded almost apologetic, 'I'm afraid I haven't quite got a fix on his background.'

I began to work my way through Adam's flying career, beginning with his years in the Fleet Air Arm. Across the table, Grover was making notes. When I got to the bit about the Falklands War, he looked up.

'Did you bring his log books by any chance?'

'Yes.'

'May I?'

'Of course.'

I dipped into my bag and laid them carefully on the table. Log books tally every hour of a pilot's flying career, an exhaustive A to Z listing every aircraft flown, every journey made, every landing survived. In Adam's case, the total hours flown exceeded seven thousand, and I watched Grover thumbing through the entries for 1996, taking tiny sips of tea as he did so.

Finally, he stole a look at his watch and then glanced up.

'I'm afraid I'm going to have to hang on to these. I'll give you a receipt, of course.'

I began to protest but thought better of it. Over the last ten days, Adam's log books had acquired an almost religious significance. They were sacred to me, relics I'd guard with my life. In the absence of the real thing, they were the closest I could get to that succession of adventures that had been the story of our marriage. Open these pages, and I could hear Adam's voice, see him grinning as he capped his biro, and undid his harness, and levered himself upwards out of the cockpit.

'Will I get them back?'

'Of course you will. I just need to go through them properly.' He gestured around. 'This isn't really the place. Nor the time.'

We looked out across the concourse, suddenly busy with dozens of newly arrived passengers. I watched one woman standing on tiptoe, searching for a familiar face. When she saw him, she waved, and plunged through the crowd, throwing her arms around him, and I turned away, engulfed again. Grover was talking about the trips he'd made to Jersey. So far, he'd been twice.

'How well do you know young Liddell?' he enquired.

'A little,' I said, hunting for a tissue. 'Adam knew him much better than I did.'

'And the Cessna he was flying?'

'That was Steve's. Or in Steve's care.'

'But your husband hadn't flown it before?' Grover's hand tapped the log book he'd been examining.

'No, not to my knowledge. He'd flown Cessnas before, of course, but not that one.'

Grover nodded. He had a little smear of cream at one corner of his mouth. I wanted to tell him, to point it out, but there was something about the man that slightly intimidated me. DC Perry, I thought, had talked to me this way. Endless questions. Serious eye contact.

'So what do you think happened?' I asked.

Grover was frowning at the last of the scones.

'To tell you the truth I don't know. The 172's a simple enough aeroplane. Your husband had lots of experience. There's nothing that stands out.' He took a last look at the scone then screwed his napkin into a ball and stowed it neatly on his plate. 'We got an aftercast from Bracknell as well. That didn't tell us much either.'

'A what?' I'd never heard the term before.

'An aftercast.' For the first time, Grover smiled. 'It's the opposite of a forecast. We ask for the weather at a particular time and place and the Met people at Bracknell do the honours.'

'And what did they say?'

Grover gazed at me a moment then flipped back through the pad beside his plate.

'Broken cloud,' he said. 'Ten knots of wind from the west. Sea state moderate.' He looked up. 'Nothing dramatic there, I'm afraid.'

We gazed at each other for a moment, another avenue blocked, another explanation off the list. The air/sea rescue search had been abandoned after the first forty-eight hours. To the best of my knowledge, Harald's chartered fishing boat was still out in the Channel, but so far they'd found nothing.

'Say there's no wreckage,' I began. 'Say nothing ever turns up. What then? Do you look on the seabed? Send a submarine down?'

Grover shook his head and sighed.

'I'm afraid not. A passenger aircraft? Something off the public transport list? Almost definitely. On this occasion? A Cessna? One on board? Sadly not. If resources permitted, I dare say I'd give you a different answer but the way things are just now . . .'

He trailed off and I looked out at the concourse again. The man and woman I'd seen earlier had disappeared. Grover, meanwhile, had changed tack. He wanted to know about Adam's state of health. I reached for my bag again and produced the envelope I'd found in one of the files in Adam's office. The envelope contained his licences, complete with all his ratings certificates, the results of the various exams he'd taken, plus copies of his medical reports.

'My husband had an ATPL,' I said. 'The last time the medic saw him was back in October.'

An ATPL is an Air Transport Pilot's Licence. To stay in compliance, Adam had to undergo a medical examination every six months. I watched Grover thumbing quickly through the contents of the envelope. These, too, he said he'd have to take away.

He glanced up.

'GP?'

'What about him?'

'I just wondered whether your husband was registered or not.'

'Of course.' I tried to remember our GP's name. In three years at Mapledurcombe, we must have been to the surgery – at most – a couple of times. 'His name's Jennings,' I said at last. 'Why do you ask?'

Grover took his time pinning the documentation together and returning it to the envelope. Then he frowned.

'It's just that sometimes the GP has a different story,' he said.

'To who?'

'To the CAA medic, the chap who does the ATPL test. The one may know more than the other. It's a question of disclosure, really.'

97

'You're suggesting my husband may have kept something back?' I was beginning to resent this conversation.

'Not at all. Though it does happen, Mrs Bruce.' Grover's fingers were back on his watch, twisting the metal strap. 'Stress, of course, is something we can't properly measure. But equally it's something we shouldn't ignore.'

'You're saying he was under stress?'

'Not saying, no. It's a question, not a statement.' He shook down the cuff of his shirt, hiding the watch. 'You see, there's no such thing as an inexplicable accident. In fact, strictly speaking, there's no such thing as an accident. Everything has a cause. Causes have effects. There's a logic tree, an order of events. Stress can be a component, often is.' He frowned. 'Were there any signs at all? Something you might have noticed? Looking back?'

I thought long and hard. Not about whether Adam had been under stress or not. But whether I owed this man the truth.

'He wasn't under any stress,' I said at last. 'At least, not as far as I know.'

'No financial problems?'

'None.'

'Business going OK?'

'Yes.' I returned his smile as best I could. 'Our business was fine.'

Grover nodded and reached for his pen. After scribbling a line or two he closed the notebook and returned it to his briefcase. The moment we'd met he'd said how sorry he was to hear about my husband. Now he said it again. In his line of work, he met all too many widows, women whose lives had suddenly been changed utterly. Thirteen years back, when he'd joined the Branch, he thought he'd get used to the trauma and the heartbreak. Now, older and wiser, he knew better. Sudden, unexpected death, he said, was beyond comprehension. Some women never got over it.

'Thanks,' I said.

'That's not the way I meant it.'

'No, but –' I shrugged. I'd had enough. I wanted to go home. He reached across the table and put a restraining hand on my arm.

'There are other women,' he said gently, 'who cope. Their courage never ceases to amaze me. It can happen. I promise you.'

He asked about my plans for Old Glory. Someone on Jersey must have told him a fair amount because he seemed to know exactly what we offered. I explained that the business would go on. Bookings were excellent. Our first guests would be arriving in a month or two. Between us, my sister and I would – in his phrase – cope.

'Good, I'm glad. If I may say so, this Old Glory of yours is a brilliant idea.'

I gazed at him, heartened. He sounded genuine. In fact he sounded positively supportive. He was inquiring about pilots for the forth-coming season, asking who'd be flying our guests in place of Adam. I named a couple of pilots from the airshow circuit, people he seemed to have heard of.

'Do they have commercial licences?' he asked.

'I've no idea. Should they?'

He smiled at me, lowering his voice to a conspiratorial whisper. I realised he was marking my card. It seemed we were friends.

'They most certainly should,' he said. 'Otherwise the CAA get very shirty.'

'Shirty?'

'Yes, my dear. It's a very grey area. Your husband was fully certificated. Use a pilot who isn't and they'll come down on you like a ton of bricks. Believe me. I've seen it happen.' He tapped the side of his nose and got to his feet. For a second I stared at his outstretched hand, then it dawned on me that he was off. 'Mother-in-law's coming to dinner,' he explained, extracting a card from his wallet and slipping it into my hand. 'The wife gets upset if I'm not there to carve the joint.'

We walked out of the airport terminal together. His Rover was parked in the lot opposite. He extended his hand again and gave mine a little squeeze.

'Take care flying back,' he said, 'and do ring me if anything comes up.'

By the time I got back to Mapledurcombe, it was nearly six o'clock. Andrea had the lights on in the kitchen and I stood in the gathering darkness for a moment or two, watching her scrubbing the paint-work around the big stainless-steel extractor hood we'd installed over the Aga. She'd found a pair of collapsible steps from somewhere or other and she was balanced on the top, her body bent forward, attacking the heavier stains with the kind of manic concentration I remembered so well from our days at Gander Creek. Judging by the transformation in the rest of the kitchen she must have been at it all afternoon, and I wondered how much of her anger with Hamish she'd managed to work out on our newly gleaming surfaces.

She glanced over her shoulder as I walked in.

'It's there on the table,' she said. 'I meant to give it to you yesterday but I forgot.'

She returned to her scrubbing while I opened the letter. I

recognised my mother's handwriting at once. The letter ran to half a dozen pages. There was lots about Gander Creek, including a very funny account of the traumas of this year's wool clip. Kate, my younger sister, had fallen in love with one of the shearers and was threatening to elope with him to Australia. This, in my mother's view, would be disastrous, not least because Kate still lived at home and helped my mother out with the thousand and one jobs that always needed attending. Subdividing the holding the way my mother had done after my father's death had certainly made life easier, but a glorious week in Montevideo had recently given her a taste for civilisation and reading between the lines, I could sense that she might soon be leaving the Falklands for good. Whether that would mean she'd come to the UK was anyone's guess but I suspected that sooner or later it was inevitable.

Curiously, there was very little in the letter about Andrea, except a rather brisk dismissal of Hamish. 'Your father never really trusted him,' she'd written, 'and on reflection he was absolutely right.' At the very end of the letter, as if she'd been working up the courage to broach the subject, my mother had written about Adam. What bothered her was the absence of a body. It was terribly important, she wrote, to say a proper goodbye. Only then would I be able, in her phrase, to turn the page and start a brand new chapter. I wasn't altogether happy about the implications of this particular metaphor – did she mean a new relationship? – but I knew she had my welfare at heart.

Andrea had finished with the paintwork. She clattered down the steps and tore off her rubber gloves.

'Well? What does she say?'

'She wants me to arrange a memorial service.'

'Can you do that?'

'I've no idea.'

I read the last page of the letter again. A memorial service, according to my mother, would be the right and proper way to confer God's blessing on the man who'd meant so much to me. The phrase 'God's blessing' surprised me. We'd never been especially religious at home, practising a rather cheerless form of Anglican worship when the occasion demanded, and this sudden gust of godliness was wholly out of character.

I read the last few sentences aloud. Andrea was hunting for an ashtray.

'She wants to come and stay,' she said when I'd finished, 'Best hat and frock.'

*

That evening, I took Andrea over to meet Ralph Pierson. My mother's suggestion had planted a seed in my mind and the more I thought about a memorial service, the more convinced I became that she was right. But just how should I go about making the arrangements? The last occasion that Adam and I had seen the inside of a church was years back, for the christening of a friend's baby. Ralph, on the other hand, was a regular churchgoer.

When we got to St Lawrence, and I eased the car in through Ralph's front gate, I found an ancient Escort in the drive. The car must have belonged to Jamie. When he opened the door to my knock, his face creased into a grin and he was still smiling when I stepped aside and introduced Andrea.

'My big sister,' I explained. 'She's staying for a while.'

Ralph, as ever, was warm, and cheerful, and immensely helpful. Jamie busied around with the drinks while I explained about my mother's little wheeze. Ralph pondered the suggestion over a stiffish whisky then finally told me to leave it to him. He'd be up at the local church the following morning for Sunday matins. He knew the vicar well. He was sure something could be arranged.

Throughout this conversation, I was aware of Andrea and Jamie perched together on the sofa beside the fire. Andrea had adopted her usual pose – eyes narrowed behind a gauzy blue veil of cigarette smoke – and without too much coaxing Jamie was telling her all about the frustrations of trying to make a living in London. The world of the tree surgeon, like pretty much every other world, was unbelievably cut-throat. Guys with forestry degrees and proper insurance and hundreds of pounds' worth of the right equipment were being underquoted by cowboys with nothing but a head for heights. After nearly six months, Jamie had begun to suspect that making even a half-decent living was near-on impossible. All in all, he'd had enough.

Andrea, I could tell, was intrigued. I can read my sister like a book and the way she kept tipping back her head and smiling her inscrutable smile told me everything I needed to know.

On the way home, I checked I'd got it right.

'You really suggested we might offer him a job?'

'Suggested, yes. A thought, that's all.'

'But there's nothing wrong with our trees.'

'That's hardly the point. He's young. He's strong. He's eager. And he's obviously had enough of London. Are you telling me we couldn't find work for someone like that? Wouldn't *need* someone like that?'

'Depends what you have in mind.'

I let the comment rest between us. Andrea was sitting low in the passenger seat, her feet propped on the dashboard, her hands clasped round her knees, totally relaxed. Without checking, I could picture the smile on her face.

'He just seemed so nice,' she said at last. 'So willing. So enthusiastic.'

'He's twenty-one,' I pointed out.

'So?'

It was a challenge. I ignored it. We drove on in silence. Minutes later, I slowed for the turn into Mapledurcombe. At the end of the drive, beside the steps to the front door, I pulled the car into a tight turn and killed the engine. For a moment, neither of us spoke. Then Andrea stifled a long, lazy yawn.

'You do the flying,' she murmured. 'Just leave the rest of it to me.'

Chapter seven

Next morning, on impulse, I pulled on a skirt and a half-decent jacket and drove back to Ralph's. I parked outside his bungalow, and when he answered the door I asked him whether he minded me joining him for matins. He said he'd be delighted to have company, and we walked the half-mile or so to St Lawrence Parish Church.

The church was a disappointment, a damp, forbidding Gothic pile beside the main road. Stands of wilting daffodils dotted the grave-yard and I stood by the door, shivering, while Ralph chatted to a succession of worshippers he obviously knew well. One or two of them were couples but I was struck by the number of single women, most of them elderly, who struggled slowly up the path from the gate. St Lawrence, I thought, was obviously no stranger to widowhood.

Ralph, it turned out, was a server at the church, which meant that I had to sit alone. The interior of the building was a definite improvement on what I'd seen of the outside, much warmer for one thing, and before Ralph disappeared to robe up he found me a seat in a pew near the back. While I waited for the service to start I counted the heads in front of me, trying to imagine how Adam's friends and family would fit into this cavernous semi-darkness. Ralph later told me that a congregation of seventy-odd was a good turn-out for a morning service, but even this number left the church looking bare and empty.

When Ralph finally appeared, he was second in the procession up the aisle. He was wearing a rather nice blue cassock and he gave me a smile and a wink as he carried his candle towards the altar. The first hymn we sang was 'Eternal Father, Strong to Save', the stirring plea for lost souls at sea, and it was Ralph himself who softened the irony when we met again outside.

'Vintage stuff.' He gave me a smile, 'Adam would have loved it.'

I told him he was probably right. We'd been joined by the vicar, a tall, thin figure, much younger than he'd somehow appeared during the service. He had a full black beard and his face was pitted with acne scars, but it was the eyes that held my attention. They were the kindest eyes I think I've ever seen, a deep, deep brown, full of life and something I can only describe as a kind of innocence. The way he smiled, and clasped my hand, triggered in me a feeling of profound well-being. I could trust this man. He'd listen.

We walked around the south side of the church. Beyond the trees I could see glimpses of the sea.

'Well, what do you make of us?'

The vicar had found a little pool of sunshine beside a row of mossy gravestones. Ralph had obviously had a word or two because he seemed to know about Adam and the accident. I told him I was glad I'd come. The service had been very high church, incense and lots of candles, an experience so novel it had almost felt like watching a play.

'It's theatre,' the vicar agreed, 'with one tiny exception.'

'What's that?'

'We all know the words. And that, believe me, makes a difference.'

Ralph chuckled. I could tell that the two men were friends. The vicar was still looking at me.

'But what about the setting? The feel of the place? That's important, too.'

I hesitated long enough to give myself away.

'To tell you the truth –'

'You hate it?'

I stared at him, amazed.

'Not hate it, no. That's much too strong. It's just . . . a bit . . .'

'Too dark? Too gloomy?'

'Yes.' I could feel the blood pinking my face. 'And to be honest that's not quite right. Not for what I have in mind.'

The vicar nodded and took me gently by the arm. We walked back down the path to the gate and waited for a bus to go past before crossing the road. A child on a bicycle had appeared, pedalling furiously towards us, and she braked to a halt at the kerbside. She had curly black ringlets and the vicar's eyes.

'Mum says it's nearly ready,' she panted.

'Tell her half an hour.' The vicar turned back to me. 'Can you spare a couple of minutes?'

'Of course.' I was still looking at the child. 'But shouldn't you be . . .' I gestured helplessly down the road, '. . . going home?'

'Absolutely. And so I will. Come with me.'

Ralph had beaten a tactful retreat, disappearing back inside the church. The vicar and I began to walk again. A hundred yards or so down the road a gap in the hedge led to a path. I had time to glimpse a signpost, then we were walking upwards, our bodies bent against the gradient. As the path steepened and steepened, conversation died. Privately, I'd always considered myself pretty fit but after a minute or so I was struggling for breath.

The vicar glanced down at me. He was smiling again.

'It's worth it,' he said, 'I promise you.'

At the top of the path, quite suddenly, we were standing beside an old stone wall. At the far end of the wall was a wooden gate, waist-high, immensely sturdy. Inside the gate, a flagstoned path skirted one of the loveliest churches I think I've ever seen.

Back home, down in the Falklands, our picture of England had been built piecemeal from a jumble of chocolate-box images that I'd realised only later had absolutely nothing to do with contemporary Britain. The England exported in the pages of *Country Life* is a pretty fib, a confection. It doesn't include the grimmer bits of the West Midlands, or Portsmouth, or inner London, and where it exists at all it tends to be the preserve of the rich. This, though, was something very different, a tiny little church, tucked away at the end of a path you'd hardly notice, a glorious secret, shared just now by myself and this immensely patient cleric I was keeping from his Sunday lunch.

'It's twelfth-century,' he told me. 'We call it the Old Church.'

I pulled the gate towards me. The wood felt smooth and warm to my touch.

'May I look inside?'

'Of course.'

The path led between a jumble of headstones towards a tiny porch. The names and the dates on the headstones had been weathered away and I had to stoop to peer in through the narrow windows along the side of the church. I stepped back, hearing voices. The vicar was talking to a passer-by at the gate. He saw me out of the corner of his eye, saw my uncertainty, and told me to take my time. Lunch today was cold. He'd lost his reputation for punctuality years ago. Everything would be fine.

I took him at his word, circling the graveyard, pausing to examine the church from every angle. Its very smallness lent enchantment. The steep pitch of the slate roof. The little stone belfries at either end. The jigsaw of gravestones in the hummocky grass. The way the over-hanging trees framed every view, every perspective. Just being there bred an instant peace, a blessing so tangible it made me smile.

I picked my way between the gravestones. Steps led down to an extension, a kind of terrace that reminded me a little of Mapledur-combe. There were more headstones here, tucked up against a beautifully trimmed hedge, and there were a couple of young trees, flowering cherries, in early bloom. I looked around, taking my time.

Up beyond the graveyard was a steep fold of downland, the smooth sweep of the ridgeline broken by a single tree, while behind me, beneath the clouds of milling seagulls, lay the undercliff and the blue, blue waters of the English Channel. I walked slowly on, reading the names on the newer headstones, knowing that for Adam this little church was perfect, and I paused beside the smaller of the flowering cherries, looking up again at the swell of the down. I wanted the Mustang to appear up there, cresting the down. I wanted a slow pass, a dip of the wing, and then a new course, a new heading, out to sea.

I turned round. The Channel stretched away towards the horizon. I'd come back with a map and a compass, I told myself. I'd phone Grover, the man from the AAIB, and I'd get the precise location of the accident, the spot where Adam dropped off the radar screen, and I'd have the Mustang vectored exactly there. Adam's family would be with me here in the graveyard, and his friends too, and every one of them would be bonded to him by that single moment. It would, in the vicar's phrase, be a piece of theatre. Except that, on this occasion, we wouldn't need any words.

The vicar was waiting for me by the porch. We ducked our heads and stepped down inside. The interior of the church was tiny. Nine rows of wooden pews, simple whitewashed walls, grey flagstoned floor, little vases of fresh flowers brightening the deeply recessed windows. At the far end, beyond a wooden rail, lay the altar and – inset in a deep arch – a single stained-glass window. I stood at the back of the church, wondering whether I should offer a prayer of thanks. As a place to say goodbye to Adam it was – quite literally – a godsend.

The vicar was standing beside me. He, too, was looking at the altar and his expression was almost childlike. To look at his face, you'd think he'd never been up here before.

'Isn't it marvellous?' he whispered at last.

I agreed that it was. When I asked whether it was still used for services, he nodded.

'Whenever we can,' he said. 'It's too precious to become just a photo-opportunity.'

I smiled. I liked this man a great deal. I liked his innocence and the hint of steel that lay beneath that simple phrase. Photo-opportunity summed up the bits of England I'd been thinking about earlier. So much better, I thought, to have a living, breathing church. Old stones. Young hearts. Real needs.

'You know about my husband,' I said. 'I think Ralph told you.'

'Yes. And I'm sorry.'

'Thank you.' I ducked my head. Simplicity again. Balm for my broken heart.

I explained about the lack of a body, and the difficulties I faced in the real world.

'Real world?' The smile was back on his face, inquisitive this time, the skin around his eyes creased with a hint of mischief.

I told him about my exchanges with the police and the official view that Adam wouldn't be dead, not properly dead, for at least a year. He listened with his head bowed, his long white fingers intertwined in the folds of his cassock. At length, he frowned.

'And how about you?' he asked. 'How do you feel?'

'About what?'

'About your husband, Adam.'

I took my time trying to frame an answer, something that would exactly define the way I felt.

'He's dead,' I said at last. 'He's gone.'

'And that's why you're here?'

'Yes.'

'To mark his going?'

'Yes.'

'Then that sounds real enough to me.'

I looked up at him, almost in wonderment. All my anxiety, my pain, had gone. Adam's death, in some infinitely mysterious way, had suddenly become something I could cope with, no longer jagged and discordant and horrible, but wholly natural, an episode in a much, much bigger story.

I tried to share the thought, develop it a little, look for bearings on this new bit of the map. I wasn't a practising Christian. I couldn't claim the help of dogma or faith. I didn't believe, for a single second, in miracles. Yet it had happened, all the same.

The vicar laid a hand on my arm. I half-expected the line about God moving in mysterious ways, but he simply told me he was glad. Later, when I felt the time was right, I could drive back over and have a bite of tea with himself and his wife and then we could discuss how best to arrange the service. The church itself could hold about seventy people. With a microphone and a couple of loudspeakers, there was room for maybe a hundred extra mourners outside. When I mentioned the Mustang, and the possibility of a fly-past, he said it was a lovely idea. Earlier in his ministry, in a parish in the north, he'd done something similar. A local lad had killed himself skydiving. To mark his passing, at the end of his memorial service, six of his mates had staged a memorial drop. One had even landed in the churchyard, narrowly missing the church spire.

The vicar chuckled. We were back in the porch.

'And you don't mind?' I asked.

'Mind what?'

'Mind that I don't normally go to church? Mind that . . . you know . . . when it suits me I come asking like this? You don't think that's . . .' I frowned, hunting for the right phrase, '. . . a bit feeble?'

'Not at all.'

He pulled the door shut behind us. I could hear the clang of the iron latch echoing inside the church. I paused, suddenly struck by another thought.

'One thing –' I began. 'What happens if I'm wrong about Adam? Say he isn't dead. Say he turns up, way after the service. What then?'

The vicar smiled again, shepherding me up the steps and into the churchyard. We walked back down the path in silence. Only by the wooden gate did he answer my question.

'Then we'll have a celebration mass,' he said. 'And a glass or two afterwards.'

Andrea was in the kitchen when I got back to Mapledurcombe. I could see her as I got out of the car. She was in jeans and a check blouse, busy in front of the Aga, and the moment I opened the front door there was a smell of olive oil and rosemary and garlic, indescribably wonderful. I ran down the hall. The doors were open everywhere, and the rooms on the south side of the house were flooded with sunshine. Andrea had the radio on and I could hear her chasing the lyrics. She'd had a passion for Queen ever since I could remember. '*Is this the real life?*' she sang. '*Is this just fantasy?*'

I stepped into the kitchen. Andrea was laying the table now, wiping a handful of knives and forks with a dishcloth. She'd conjured up a huge bowl of salad from somewhere or other, and there was an open bottle of red wine beside it. I glanced at the label, grinning. Marques de Riscal. A lovely Rioja. Perfect.

I began to tell her about my morning in church, how gloomy the first place had been, how I'd more or less abandoned any notion of a memorial service, then about my little conversation with the vicar, and our long trudge up the path, and how guilty I'd felt about his lunch, and then this old stone wall, and this lovely wooden gate, and best of all the half-hour or so that lay beyond it.

Andrea, for once, was listening.

'Brilliant,' she kept saying. 'Wonderful.'

I explained about the little terraced graveyard, and how many guests we could have, and how the down overlooked the church, and how you could smell the sea, and I'd got to the bit about the Mustang and the fly-past when Andrea handed me a wine glass and began to fill it. I was standing by the window, looking out. The kitchen ran the whole depth of the house and on the south side the views were beautiful.

'Flaps down, the Mustang stalls at eighty-five knots,' I mused. 'That's the only problem.'

'Why problem?'

'It would be nice if it was slower.' I was visualising the moment when the aircraft suddenly dropped over the ridgeline behind the church. 'It's a memory you want to hang on to. The Moth would be perfect. You can take her down to forty knots.'

'Use the Moth then.'

'I couldn't. It's mine. This is going to be Adam's day. He'd die if I used the Moth.' I began to giggle, knowing that Adam would be laughing too. My little joke wasn't black at all. Not today. Not the way I was feeling. I lifted the glass to my lips, anticipating the soft, oaky kiss of the wine. Then a hand came into view. I stared at it. It was a man's hand, brown, sinewy, mottled with liver spots. I turned round. Harald was standing behind me, smiling. God knows where he'd been hiding.

'Your sister's invited me to lunch,' he said. 'I called up from the airfield.'

For the first time I took a proper look at the table. Harald was right. Andrea was laying up for three.

'Lovely,' I said. 'Do you mind if I have my wine?'

'I think not.'

'No?'

'No.' He reached for my glass and replaced it with a tumbler of sparkling Badoit. 'Busy afternoon. Things to do.'

'Like?'

Harald studied me a moment, then reached for his own glass of mineral water.

'Remember us talking about you flying the Mustang?' He touched his glass to mine. 'No time like the present.'

All three of us drove over to Sandown after lunch. I'd eaten barely anything, partly excitement, partly anticipation, and partly something else more difficult to define. After the worst week of my life, I'd finally won a little peace for myself, and Harald – whether he knew it or not – was putting it in jeopardy.

I'd walked him into the study before we'd left and shut the door behind me.

'I'm not altogether sure this is such a great idea.'

'Why not?'

'Don't you think it's a bit hasty? A bit soon?'

Harald had shaken his head. The one accusation I could never lay at his door was indecision. He always knew exactly what he wanted to do. And why.

'The weather's perfect,' he pointed out, 'but it ain't gonna last. They're calling a front for late this afternoon and after that it's anyone's guess.'

'But what about next week? Or the week after?'

'I'm away. Back in the States for a coupla days. Then Australia and the Far East.' He nodded at the door. 'Andrea's been telling me what you've decided. I think it's a great plan.'

'Decided?'

'The business. Who does what. As I read it, Andrea's the home body while you do the flying. Isn't that the way it shakes down?'

I frowned, trying to fight a feeling of mild irritation. Harald had a way of accelerating events, of taking the merest hint of a decision and turning it into a *fait accompli*. Andrea and I had certainly discussed how we might organise ourselves over the coming season but I wasn't aware that anything was set in stone.

'I might not be in the mood,' I said, changing tack. 'Have you thought about that?'

Harald laughed.

'Mood? This is flying, Ellie. Not sex.'

'I didn't mean it that way.'

'Sure you didn't. Hey –' He reached forward, touching me lightly on the arm. 'No offence but I really think you should try and hack this thing. I've talked to Dave. He'll have the ship ready for two thirty. Like I say, perfect weather.'

'Dave Jeffries?' I was getting annoyed now. What right did this man have to part my mechanic from his Sunday off?

'Sure. And he's happy to oblige, since you ask. In fact he thinks it's long overdue.'

'Really?'

'Yeah. Talk to Dave and he'll tell you Adam should have been taking you up round the back end of last year.'

'He did. Twice.'

'To learn to fly. Not to cab you to some fancy restaurant.'

Harald stared me out. You could almost feel his contempt for the nicer things in life. Like surprise trips across the Channel. And intimate *à deux* lunches. In Harald's world there were lists of things to do, and a schedule to make sure they got done. Very seldom, it seemed to me, did he draw anything but the straightest of lines between two points.

'Be careful, Harald,' I said quietly. 'I'd like us to stay friends.'

He looked at me a moment longer, his eyes very black, then – abruptly – he softened. There was a folded slip of paper on the desk. He picked it up and gave it to me.

'I saw Dennis last night,' he said. 'I was staying over.'

'Dennis Wetherall? In St Helier?'

'Sure. I deposited the money. He gave me a receipt.'

'What money?'

'The payment for the Harvard. We discussed it. Remember?'

I was looking at the receipt. Old Glory's bank balance was healthier to the tune of £160,000. I glanced up. Harald was opening the door.

'Mind if we take your car?' he asked. 'I came over by cab.'

Dave Jeffries was waiting for us at the airfield. The Mustang was out on the ancient rectangle of hardstanding in front of our hangar, parked beside Harald's Yak, and Dave was perched on one wing, his head buried in the cockpit. Hearing the estate car, he slid down the wing and walked across to meet us.

Andrea was second out of the car after Harald. She'd changed into a rather striking trouser suit – bright yellow with big, fabric-covered buttons – and she was wearing a huge pair of sunglasses. Sandown airfield isn't the centre of the fashion world and I think she was a bit disappointed at the boxy little control tower and the nearby wooden shack – the Touchdown Café – that served hot drinks and a variety of filled rolls. There were a couple of local flyers sitting at one of the tables outside, men I knew well, and they lifted their mugs in salute when I waved.

Harald was already circling the Mustang, pausing beside the nose and reaching up to run his fingers across the spinner. Last year, Adam had commissioned Ralph to research the original paint scheme for our Mustang, and after some debate the pair of them had settled on leaving the fuselage and wings a bare metal silver. The rudder and the spinner were painted in bright red, while the panel on top of the long nose had been finished in matt green. The panel extended from the propeller to the front of the cockpit, shielding the pilot from the lethal effects of dazzle. In its very restraint, the colour scheme looked impressive, and I especially liked the way that most of the aircraft had stayed unpainted. A silver fish, I thought. Sleek. Agile. And almost impossible to catch.

Dave joined Harald and the pair of them completed a circuit of the aeroplane before pausing again, this time to stoop beneath one wing and peer up into the wheel well. I hung back a little, fiddling with the zip on my flying suit, trying to ignore the churning in my stomach. Now that the time had arrived for me to actually fly the plane, every other consideration had fallen away. I'd forgiven Harald for barging into a very special Sunday and being so bossy. I no longer cared whether or not I was in the mood. It didn't even bother me that I'd left most of Andrea's wonderful roast and forgone a bottle of my favourite wine. All that mattered now was doing myself, and Adam, justice. The Mustang would ask everything of me. I was determined not to fail.

Harald and Dave were back within earshot. As ever it was technical chatter, boys' talk about some stage or other in Dave's rebuild. Harald wanted to know how Dave had come up with the pipe runs in the wheel wells, the big bays beneath the wings they'd just been inspecting. I dimly remembered Dave once having a similar conversation with Adam. Adam's grasp of technical detail had been sketchy, to say the least, but Harald was word-perfect, and I listened to the two men talking about B nuts, and sleeves, and the hydraulic advantages of right-angled bends. For this very reason, Harald had won Dave's respect from the moment they first met, and they barely acknowledged my presence as I joined them beside the cockpit.

They were talking about the dual conversion now, Adam's decision to ask Dave to make room for another body in the cockpit. This had meant, amongst a million other things, extending the bubble canopy backwards.

Harald was running his fingers along the groove where the retractable canopy seated on to the fuselage.

'We had some problems,' he said, 'back in the States.'

'You did?' I'd rarely seen Dave so animated.

'Yep, some guys said we'd foul up the airflow back over the rudder, especially when we rigged for landing. Thought so myself, as a matter of fact.'

'So what happened?'

'Nothing.' Harald threw him a grin. 'The tail comes down easy, same as ever. Maybe you have to work a little harder keeping her in a straight line, but nothing fancy, no real heroics.' Harald at last turned to me. 'Dave's been filling me in on the maintenance side. He was working on the engine last week and he found a bit of stem wear on a couple of the valves. He's replaced the head and bank assemblies so there shouldn't be a problem. Give her sixty-one inches boost and auto-rich for take-off. You'll need three thousand r.p.m. on the dial. Climb is forty-six inches. Cruise, twenty-two hundred and thirty-two in auto-lean. Rein her that tight, and we'll still be looking at two eighty true up at twelve thou.'

Dave nodded in approval. I studied my nails. I'd been through scenes like this before, bludgeoned and bullied by men determined to show off their technical prowess. As a prelude to one of the most important take-offs in my flying career, it was deeply unpromising.

Harald was looking at me, waiting for a response.

'You copy that?'

'No,' I said, 'I didn't. But twelve thousand feet sounds optimistic.'

'Why?'

'Above ten and a half thousand, you're in airways.'

The two men exchanged glances, and Dave, at least, had the grace to look rueful. I knew they couldn't argue with the facts. One of the big attractions of the Isle of Wight for private pilots is the amount of unrestricted airspace. To be able to fly where you like, up to 10,500 feet, is pretty rare in the south of England but above this altitude a different set of rules applies. The major commercial north-south airway was no place for a Mustang with a first-time pilot at the controls.

Feeling a little better, I followed Harald up on to the wing. Before I strapped myself to my parachute and harnessed up, he wanted to talk me through the controls. I stepped carefully over the combing around the front cockpit and settled myself into the bucket seat. Wherever possible, Adam had wanted to maintain the original military feel of the aircraft – an obvious attraction for our overseas veterans – and with one or two modifications Dave had left everything the way the Americans had designed it. There was no padding, no upholstery, no fancy touches. Under my feet, the floor was of plain wood, with steel scuff plates beneath the rudder pedals, and the instrument panel still had the heavy yellow band that separated the key blind-flying instruments from the other dials that registered r.p.m., and oil pressure, and all the other read-outs from the engine.

I flexed my arms sideways and wriggled my bottom into the seat. Ralph had always told me how spoilt the Mustang pilots had been for space, and now – on the verge of flying the thing – I knew exactly what he meant. Harald was beside me, squatting on the wing. About a hundred metres away, beyond the Touchdown Café, I could see Andrea talking to the driver of a blue BMW.

'Wing flap lever . . . carb air controls . . . rudder trim tab . . . aileron trim tabs . . . throttle quadrant . . . friction nut . . . prop control . . . landing gear handle . . .' I followed Harald's hand up the left side of the cockpit. When he got to the end, I made him repeat it all over again, then a third time while I followed his hand with mine, back and forth, up and down, touch for touch. He reached across and we did the same down the starboard side of the cockpit, my right hand memorising the shape of each control while I kept my eyes fixed on the instruments, just the way Adam had taught me on the Moth and the Harvard.

After a while, at my insistence, Harald would name a particular control and I'd find it, my eyes shut this time, totally blind. We played this game until I was touch-perfect. With Dave back in the hangar, Harald was infinitely more patient and I think my thoroughness, my determination not to cut corners, must have impressed him, because at the end of it he gave me a little peck on the cheek.

'You did fine,' he said softly, 'just fine. Sorry if I frightened you before.'

'You didn't frighten me.' It was my turn to smile. 'Bored, yes. Not frightened.'

Dave came out with the parachutes. We jumped down and struggled into the harnesses, taking it in turns to check for adjustments. Andrea was back with her camera and she insisted on taking a shot of the two of us with the Mustang in the background. Harald hated having his photo taken – I'd noticed this before – and Andrea had used up half the reel before he consented to put his arm round me. Close to, he felt stiff and a little bit embarrassed, though when I told him to relax, he laughed.

'That's my line, Ellie,' he said, shepherding me back towards the aircraft.

Harald stood on the wing again while I strapped in. Once the harness was tight and he'd checked it, he did a final walk-round, paying special attention to the control surfaces, the big flaps and ailerons on the main wing and then the smaller elevators on the tailplane. From up in the cockpit, I tried to follow his progress but the shoulder straps constrained me and I couldn't help wondering what it must have been like in combat. Just looking ahead was enough of a problem. With the fuselage resting on the tail wheel, and the long, long nose stretching away to the propeller, I hadn't a clue what lay in front of us. The smell was familiar, though, from my trips with Adam. It was a curious smell, the scent of the happiest bits of my marriage, a gleefully abandoned mix of hot oil, sweat and all the nervous anticipation that goes with a 1,500 horsepower Merlin engine and that wonderfully blunt defiance of gravity.

I felt the aircraft sink a little as Harald and Dave clambered up to the rear cockpit. Like Adam, that first time he took me up in the Moth, Harald was insisting that I ride in the front. Not only would this offer me a seat in the dress circle but it would give me my first taste of going through the start-up procedures. Only from the front could the engine be primed and fired.

Harald was making himself comfortable behind me while Dave checked his harness. Seconds later, I was listening to Harald's voice in my earphones.

'I'm gonna talk you through the pre-start,' he said, 'just the way they did it during the war. Pretend you're a rookie out of elementary training. No need to memorise anything. We'll go through it again later.'

I muttered assent and followed him as he took me through the checks. Battery on. Flaps up. Carb heat to Cold Air. Aileron trim zero degrees. Elevator trim zero degrees. Rudder trim six degrees right. The list went on and on and as my hands flew round the cockpit I couldn't help thinking about Adam. He used to do this too. The same mantra. The same invocation. Mixture. Prop. Throttle. Gear. Oh Lord, be good to us. Finally, Harald broke off.

'OK,' he murmured. 'So now you light the fire.'

I heard him calling, 'Clear prop,' and I saw Dave raise his thumb. On Harald's cue, my finger found the priming pump and then the starter switch. The big four-bladed propeller began to turn very slowly, no coughs, no splutters, no smoke. I'd been here before, with the Moth and the Harvard. Probably underprimed, I thought.

Harald came through on the intercom.

'Fuel and mags are on,' he said. 'Fuel pressure's good so try a coupla extra seconds priming. Watch out for flooding, though.'

He called, 'Clear prop' again, and I went through the start-up procedure for a second time. The propeller began to revolve, rocking the aircraft on its undercarriage. Suddenly there was a puff of smoke, and then another, and then the engine burst into life and the propeller blurred in front of me. Harald guided me to the lever beneath the throttle quadrant. I moved it from Idle Cut-Off to Rich and then settled deeper into my seat, scanning the instruments, shutting away the ghost of Adam. The oil pressure began to rise; r.p.m. flickered a fraction over 900, then slowly increased to 1,300.

'Ready to taxi?'

'Fine by me,' I said. 'Just take care of my baby.'

I heard Harald talking to the tower. They gave him permission to taxi and I watched Dave ducking beneath the wing to pull the chocks away. The throaty beat of the engine rose, then Harald released the brakes and we began to move forward, bumping off the ridged concrete on to the cropped grass. Andrea was standing beside Dave. She had both hands over her ears and when I waved she grinned back, shouting something I couldn't hear.

Harald's voice again, giving me control.

'I'll talk you through,' he said. 'You set?'

'I'm fine.'

'OK, first off, just check the brakes.'

I did what I was told. The lightest pressure on the tips of the rudder pedals brought the Mustang to a near-halt.

'Gently.' I could hear the smile in Harald's voice. 'Now push the stick forward. That unlocks the tail wheel. You're steering with the brakes, just like always.'

I eased the control stick forward through the neutral position and I felt the wheel lock disengage. The technique was just like the Harvard and the thought comforted me. Harald was right. I was no different, in essence, to the hundreds of young Americans who'd trodden exactly the same path, graduating from a biplane, through the sturdy old Harvard, to this sleek thoroughbred. They, like me, would doubtless have been sweating, though in their case the immediate future was infinitely bleaker. No matter what happened over the next hour or so, at least I'd never have to face an Me109.

We were abreast of the control tower now, and behind the tinted glass I could see a couple of figures silhouetted against the light. One raised a hand and I abandoned the throttle long enough to wave back. There was nothing around us and I began to weave the aircraft left and right, scrolling big fat S shapes across the grass. With so much engine in front of me it was the only way to be sure about hidden obstacles.

I loosened my grip on the control stick and flexed my fingers. I was wearing skintight leather gloves, a lovely deep-green colour and deliciously sensitive. The gloves had been a Christmas present from Adam, years back, and I'd treasured them ever since.

'Ts and Ps?' It was Harald again.

Ts and Ps stands for temperatures and pressures. I quickly scanned the instruments, knowing how vital it was to keep an eye on the oil and coolant temperatures.

'Oil's fifty-five degrees,' I sang out. 'Coolant eighty.' Harald, of course, had a perfectly good set of duplicate instruments in the back but that wasn't the point. This was a pupil–teacher relationship and it was my job to come up with the right answers. 'Oil pressure's seventy-five p.s.i.,' I went on. 'Hydraulic pressure a thousand.'

'Rad flap open?'

'Affirmative.'

'Fuel?'

'Left tank boost pump on.'

'OK, stop at the holding point.'

I leaned out of the canopy, feeling the hot breath of the exhaust against my cheek. The holding point was down the far end of the airfield, twenty metres or so from the threshold of the marked grass strip. As we zigzagged towards it, I realised that I was beginning to enjoy myself.

Earlier, before driving across to the hangar, Harald and I had confirmed the wind with the tower. This afternoon, as Harald had promised, it was nearly perfect, a gentle five knots a couple of degrees off due west. The runway at Sandown runs 05/23, a heading which gave us a whisper of crosswind but nothing to worry about. Cross-winds can be a problem for all aircraft, but in a taildragger like the Mustang, they can actually help. The Mustang swings to the left on take-off, a consequence of the clockwise rotation of the prop, so firm pressure on the right rudder pedal, slightly diluted to take account of the cross-wind, should do the trick.

We reached the holding point and I turned the Mustang into wind. Before take-off we always do an engine run-up, and today was no exception. I quickly checked the instruments again, following Harald's quiet instructions. For the second time in five minutes it occurred to me that there was something almost religious about our little duet, a pattern of prompt and response that wouldn't have been out of place in a church service. The Old Church at St Lawrence, I thought. The stone wall, and the wooden gate, and the jumble of ancient headstones beyond.

'Ts and Ps?'
'Fine.'
'Fuel?'
'OK.'
'R.p.m.?'
'Thirteen hundred set.'
'Prop lever?'
'Fully forward.'
'Feet on brakes?'
'Check.'
'Canopy closed?'
'Give me a moment.'

I wound the canopy forward and locked it shut, softening the cackle of the engine. The workload was heavier now and I was glad. No time for nerves. No time for fretting about what might go wrong.

'OK,' I heard Harald say, 'stick hard back. Now open the throttle. We're looking for thirty inches' boost.'

Inches are a measure of air pressure. Thirty inches happens to be the ambient – or atmospheric – pressure. For take-off, with the engine on full power, we'd need twice this, the extra pressure forcing the fuel into the hungry Merlin.

My left hand eased the throttle forward. The beat of the engine quickened and I felt the tail twitching around behind me. The r.p.m. climbed to 2,300 and I pushed a little harder on the brakes. Unrestrained, the aircraft would be off.

'Mags?'

I reached for the mag switches and cut them, one after the other, watching for the drop as I did so. Magnetos are a key link in the ignition chain. Without at least one, the engine won't fire. I watched the needle sink on each of the mag dials. Left mag 50 r.p.m. drop, on again. Right mag 70 r.p.m. drop, on again. Exercise the prop; 2,300 to 2,000 r.p.m., twice.

'Good.' I had Harald's approval. 'Throttle back to idle.'

The r.p.m. dropped to 800 and I opened the canopy again. One last lungful of God's good air. Then we'll go for it. With the engine idling, I thought I could hear birdsong. I looked sideways, down the line of the runway. Half a mile away, beside the cluster of parked aircraft in front of the tower, I saw a splash of yellow. Andrea was waiting. She'd have her camera raised, and maybe an admirer or two in tow, and later – sitting on the kitchen table back at Mapledurcombe – she'd doubtless tell me about her afternoon's adventures. The image made me smile and I felt a sudden gust of affection, totally unexpected. This one was for her too. Not just for Adam.

Harald was calling for departure. The tower replied with an affirmative. We were to climb to five hundred feet, make a right turn out. No conflicting traffic. I closed my eyes a moment. I'd flown from this strip dozens and dozens of times, but never this tense, never this aware, never with this absolute sense of focus. In my earphones, there was a new noise, slightly tinny, and for a moment I thought we had a mechanical problem, then I realised it was Harald. He was whistling. I bent my head, trying to make out the tune, and abruptly he stopped.

' "Battle Hymn of the Republic",' he murmured. 'In case you were wondering.'

I grinned and thought of telling him to stick to the day job, but already he was running through the final check list. Twenty-degree flap. Mixture auto-rich. Cooling doors open. Hydraulic pressure 1,000 p.s.i. Harness tight and locked. Hood closed.

I reached up for the canopy one last time and wound it forward.

'Happy?'

'Delirious.'

'Good. Two on board, short field, you're looking for sixty-one inches boost. Lift the tail at sixty m.p.h. Keep right rudder in. A hundred and five and she'll fly.' He paused. 'I'm on the controls with you, Ellie. Make it a good one. And trust me.'

There was something almost plaintive in that last remark, something odd I couldn't quite pin down, but I drove the thought into the very back of my mind, slipping the brakes again and hauling the Mustang on to the grass strip. With the nose occupying most of my forward vision I couldn't see the white markers down the centre-line of the runway, but the tower and the Touchdown Café were exactly where they should be, and experience told me to trust my judgement.

I gave my harness one final tug, kissed the top of my left index finger (one of Adam's superstitions), and then eased the throttle smoothly forward. The Mustang began to move, slowly at first, then faster and faster. Within seconds, I could feel the rudder biting on the airstream, correcting the left yaw. At 60 m.p.h., as instructed, I pushed the stick slowly forward and the tail began to rise. Suddenly, in front of me, I could see what was left of the runway, and the road beyond, and away in the distance the long, dark hump of St Boniface Down.

The bumping was beginning to ease now, cushioned by lift, and as the airspeed needle wound past 100 m.p.h., I eased the stick back, aware of the road flashing beneath us. Off the leash, the Mustang began to accelerate quickly and I maintained a modest rate of climb as the fields beneath began to form the jigsaw I knew so well.

'Gear,' Harald prompted.

I reached for the undercarriage retract and heard the happy clunk of the wheels seating in the under-wing bays.

'Forty-six inches. Two thousand seven hundred r.p.m.'

My left hand returned to the throttle. I cut the boost back as smoothly as I could, and then retracted the flaps.

'Altitude?'

My eyes went to the altimeter. Nine hundred feet already. Shit. I glanced to my right, sweating again, only too aware of how quickly everything happened in this glorious aircraft. Five hundred feet was standard for the right-hand turn-out. Already we'd made twice that height. I nudged the stick to starboard, balancing the turn with a little right rudder. The Mustang responded like the horse of my dreams, dipping a wing, maintaining the climb. I increased the boost an inch or two, nervous of losing power in the turn, and drew a round of applause from Harald.

'Ts and Ps?' he murmured.

I scanned the instrument panel. Temperatures and pressures were fine. I looked out. We were over the middle of the island now. The visibility was crystal clear, a sure sign of an approaching front, and away to the north I could see the long finger of water that reached up to Southampton. We levelled off at 2,500 feet and I cut the power back to 2,200 r.p.m., making a gentle turn towards the west. Our airspeed had settled at 250 m.p.h. and I watched Tennyson Down slip by on the port side as we headed out across the Needles.

The one thing that Harald and I hadn't discussed was where, exactly, we were going. We had fuel for at least an hour's flying but if I was to stay in control I wasn't keen to complicate my first outing with anything as ambitious as navigation. There was a full set of airways maps tucked into the pocket by my right hip. Adam always carried them, but it was all I could do at the moment to keep the aircraft trimmed and flying sweetly.

Way ahead, I could see the blue shadow of the Purbeck Hills and the startling white of the chalk cliffs beyond. The airspace south of this lovely corner of Dorset is a danger area, reserved for military use.

'Make a left,' I heard Harald say. 'One nine zero.'

I eased the stick to the left and then steadied the aircraft on the new heading, aware of how precise, how accurate my flying had to be. Fighter pilots stay alive by getting it exactly right, one hundred per cent of the time.

One nine zero was almost due south. We were en route to France.

'Take her up to three seventy.'

'You mean speed-wise?'

'Sure.'

Three hundred and seventy m.p.h.? I inched the prop and the throttle forward and – on Harald's cue – adjusted the mixture to auto-rich. The needle on the airspeed indicator wound up past 350. At 370 m.p.h., as requested, I cut back. I'd never been so fast in my life, not in my own aircraft, yet there was absolutely no sensation of speed apart from the deafening clatter of the engine.

'New heading,' Harald grunted. 'Two seven zero.'

West again. I checked right. Way below us I could see one of the big oil tankers, inward bound for the refinery at Fawley, and for a moment I wondered if there was anyone on deck, anyone looking up, anyone who might be watching this little silver fish flashing overhead.

'See those clouds, Ellie? On the nose?'

I looked forward. Through the blur of the prop, I recognised the beginnings of the incoming front, a grey smudge on the horizon that signified a skirt of high cirrus. It looked an awfully long way away.

Harald again.

'OK, Ellie, here's the plan. You climb above the cloud. I'm estimating eight thousand max. We'll try a couple of landings. I'll call the moves. Then we'll go home.'

'Landings?' I hadn't a clue what he was talking about.

'Sure.' I could hear him chuckling. 'You've never tried this before? Landing on the tops of clouds? Hey . . .'

The front grew bigger in the windshield. I began to climb, maintaining speed. The power of the Mustang was awesome. You just turned it on. Like water from a tap, it seemed limitless.

All at once, the sea disappeared beneath us and I found myself amongst the tops of the clouds, shreds of thin grey vapour flashing past. I'd been right about 370 m.p.h. Once you got close to anything, it was incredibly fast.

At Harald's prompting, I levelled out at 10,000 feet. The cloud rippled beneath us, like a newly laid carpet.

'Take the boost back to forty-six. You want the cooling flap on auto. Fuel-wise, go for the fullest tank.'

I did as I was told. Looking down, I estimated we had almost 2,000 feet between us and the top of the cloud.

'OK, bring her round till we're downwind. You're looking for zero one five.'

I banked the Mustang, harder this time, feeling the faintest shiver in the airframe.

'Good. Now chop the speed. Below two seventy-five you can take twenty degrees of flap.'

I eased the throttle back. The aircraft began to slow. When the airspeed hit 260, I selected twenty degrees of flap. I felt the airflow roughen and watched the speed fall off. At 160 m.p.h. Harald told me to lower the gear. I reached for the undercarriage lever and tried to push it out of the restraining gate. It felt very stiff. When I pushed harder, it refused to budge. I gave up.

'It won't move,' I told him.

Harald didn't say a word. I told him again. Still nothing. I sought his face in the rearview mirror bolted to the apex of the windshield but all I could see was the top of his head. I couldn't believe it. The bastard was hiding from me. Adam would never have done this. We'd have been down on the ground by now, settling into *omelettes fines herbes* and a decent helping of chips.

'Harald?'

'Sort it out, Ellie. Take your time.'

I hesitated. He sounded like he meant it, like it was some kind of test, and for a moment I wondered whether he'd planned it this way, something he and Dave might have cooked up, a deliberate glitch to stretch me to the limit. The clouds were getting closer. Miles ahead, beyond the front's leading edge, I could see the long, low swell of the Isle of Wight.

I looked down at the undercarriage lever, wondering whether the lowering sequence had even begun. Just in case, I re-selected up, then I edged the lever out of the gate and pushed down again. The resistance was still there and it got stiffer and stiffer but I kept pushing, all the way down, until I heard two clunks and saw three little green lights winking at me. I'd done it. I'd passed the test. The undercarriage was down.

'Atta girl.' Harald had come to life. 'Left to base, full flap, speed one four zero.'

My breath was coming in shallow gasps. I was wet with sweat. I dipped a wing, shedding more speed, positioning the Mustang for the final turn on to our pretend runway. The cloud had become a blurry grey, racing past beneath us. Harald called finals. Over the make-believe perimeter fence, he wanted 110 m.p.h. My eyes were glued to the onrushing cloud. We were losing height nicely. I risked a quick look at the airspeed indicator. I'd never worked so hard in my life. 110 m.p.h. Perfect.

Suddenly we plunged into the cloud. All I could see was grey. Moisture was beading for an instant on the outside of the canopy before it shredded, torn sideways by the airflow. I fought the temptation to pull the stick back, to push the throttle forward, to claw our way back to the sunshine above.

Harald was pleased.

'Pretty nice, Ellie,' he murmured. 'Pretty damn nice.'

Seconds later, the aircraft still sinking, he took control. I heard the undercarriage retract and felt the aircraft respond as the power came back on. He flew the Mustang beautifully, instinctively, the way that Adam had flown it, and I sat back in the front seat, physically exhausted, happy to be a passenger for the rest of the flight.

South of the Isle of Wight, we did a brief series of aerobatics, nothing outrageous, a couple of loops, a single lazy roll, and a manoeuvre called a Cuban Eight that brought us racing in towards Ventnor at less than a thousand feet. I watched the little resort grow rapidly bigger, then Harald hauled back on the stick as the beach and the promenade flashed beneath us. I watched our shadow racing across the top of St Boniface Down, still dazed, and I braced myself for entry into the landing circuit for the airfield beyond, but Harald seemed to change his mind.

He banked the Mustang savagely to port, standing the aircraft on one wing. The force of the turn pulled at my face and limbs, and as the aircraft steadied I looked down again. Harald was slowing the plane, applying flap, and we began to lose height, stately now, all passion spent. I saw a road snaking through a village, then a valley shadowed by the late-afternoon sun, and a stand of trees greening the shoulder of a down. I tried to orientate myself, to visualise where we might be on the map.

Below us was a pond, and a scatter of farm buildings, then the ground seemed to come up to meet us and I braced myself a second time, thinking Harald must have got it wrong. He hadn't. The ground fell away again, just as suddenly, and I found myself looking at a tiny church, half-hidden by trees, and a line of white headstones beside a hedge. I stared down at it, transfixed. The Old Church at St Lawrence. The secret I'd brought back at lunchtime.

'You mentioned it this morning,' Harald murmured. 'What a great, great way to say goodbye.'

After we'd landed, back at Sandown, we all shared a pot of tea at one of the tables outside the Touchdown Café. Andrea was burbling about her afternoon – the friends she'd made, the pictures she'd taken – and when she remembered to ask whether our little trip had gone well, I barely had the energy to nod.

'It was good,' I told her. 'It was very, very good.'

Later, before Harald helped Dave push the Mustang back inside our hangar, I had a chance to corner him alone. He was taking the Yak back to Jersey. He'd be leaving within the hour.

'I just want to say thank you.' I looked him in the eye. 'You'll never know how much that meant to me.'

Harald nodded towards the Mustang.

'She's a beauty,' he said. 'The sweetest ship I've ever flown.'

We said nothing for a moment or two. Then I reached out and touched his hand. He glanced round at me, surprised.

'I'd like you to fly her at the memorial service,' I said. 'Would you do that for me?'

He didn't answer but looked away, across the airfield. Then he excused himself and walked across to the Yak, parked beside the Mustang. I watched him rummaging in the luggage compartment behind the rear seat. When he returned, he was carrying a black dustbin liner. He reached inside and pulled out an old green sports holdall. He offered it to me. It had the legend *Jaguar* on one side.

'My boys in the Channel picked it up yesterday,' he said tonelessly. 'There's never gonna be a good time to give you this but I guess . . .' He shook his head, visibly distressed, avoiding my eyes.

I took the sodden bag, holding it at arm's length. It was still dripping.

'There was nothing else?'

'Nothing.'

'No wreckage?'

'Like I say, nothing.'

I nodded. The last time I'd seen the bag had been a couple of weeks ago when Adam had given it to me to mend. The zip had gone. I'd tried to fix it and failed.

'Look in the side pocket,' Harald muttered. 'Get it over with.'

Trembling now, I inserted my fingers in the wet lining. There was something plastic inside, a card of some kind. I pulled it out and turned it over. The card was American Express. The signature was Adam's.

I looked up, offering Harald the bag. I wanted him to take it. I never wanted to see it again.

'Keep it,' he said. 'It's yours, Ellie.'

We didn't say anything for a long moment. Beside the Mustang, Dave was looking at us, curious. Harald came close and put his arms around me.

'Of course I'll fly at the memorial service,' he said gently. 'It's the least I can do.'

Chapter eight

We held the memorial service three weeks later. My mother, as Andrea had predicted, flew up from the Falklands and Adam's parents came over from Canada. We contacted as many friends and other relatives as we could and in the end there was just enough room in the tiny church to squash everybody in.

The service was simplicity itself. There were prayers, of course, and one of Adam's fellow pilots from his Sea King days gave us a very funny account of his service career. We all recited the 23rd Psalm and Adam's sister, who has a lovely voice, sang a French folk song that had never failed to move Adam to tears.

At the end of the service, the vicar – whose name, I now knew, was Douglas – gave a very brief address. He'd obviously done his homework, contacting various buddies whose phone numbers I'd supplied, and his tribute to Adam – warm, heartfelt, astonishingly accurate – was a memory that will stay with me for ever. For someone who'd never even met my husband, he seemed to have established an extraordinary rapport, and as he commended Adam's soul to God, briefly turning to touch the parachute I'd laid on the altar, I wondered whether there wasn't, after all, something in the phrase 'life everlasting'. Adam, bless him, hadn't gone. He was there, in that church; there, in that wonderful man's closing address.

After the service came the fly-past. Harald brought the Mustang low over the fold of chalk downland behind the church, dipped a wing, and then set course for mid-Channel. Mr Grover, the AAIB investigator, had given me a set of co-ordinates that put Adam a mile or so shy of the fifty-degree north reporting line, and Harald was carrying his SatNav to get the location exactly right.

When he got there, he circled low and dropped a bouquet I'd prepared the previous evening. My mother had been unhappy about a bouquet. A wreath, she insisted, would be more seemly. For once in my life, I ignored her. A wreath was exactly what Adam wouldn't have wanted. My bouquet, on the other hand, an extravagant confection of roses, interlaced with woodland bluebells, snowdrops, spring crocus and angel's tears, would doubtless raise a very big smile indeed. My mother, surprised and a little hurt by my refusal to concede her point, had tried to make an issue of it, but I headed off the inevitable argument by playing the overstressed widow.

'You're lucky I'm coming to the service at all', I told her. 'I should be the one dropping the flowers.'

From St Lawrence, we all drove back to Mapledurcombe. Andrea had worked nonstop for the best part of a week getting the eats and drinks exactly right. Taking charge of what she called 'the practicals' was, she insisted, the least she could do. My own time would be far better spent in trying to come to terms with my loss, and all the other stuff – the preparation, the transport, the accommodations – I was to leave to her.

I protested, of course, but to be honest I was only too grateful to fall in with her plans. Harald's return of Adam's sports bag had shaken me infinitely more than I'd expected and the wet, clammy feeling of the sodden leather had stayed with me for days. While I was on the phone to Mr Grover about the Channel co-ordinates I'd naturally mentioned the bag, and when he asked whether I might send it over to him, I'd been only too happy to oblige. I had many glorious memories of my dead husband but his tatty old sports bag wasn't one of them. Its very familiarity, the fact that it and Adam had been practically inseparable, made it – oddly enough – all the more repugnant. It had travelled with him in the Cessna. It had been there, probably lodged under the passenger seat, when he'd died. Far from being a small, intimate, domestic object, part of the warp and weft of our shared life, it had become something sinister, a mute witness of an event I'd infinitely prefer never to think about. It had to go, and when I wrapped it in a brand-new dustbin liner, and squeezed it into a huge Jiffy bag, I was glad to see the back of it. *Yours for keeps*, I scribbled to Mr Grover. *When you've finished with it, throw the thing away.*

Back at Mapledurcombe, after the memorial service, you could practically hear the collective sigh of relief. All of us, I think, had been apprehensive about the service, partly because the English are pretty hopeless at grieving, and partly because people of our age and inclination – still young, still active, still taking risks – hate being reminded of the consequences of getting it wrong. Back home though, refuelling on endless bottles of Chenin Blanc and Cape Chardonnay, the gathering quickly had the makings of a party. By the time dusk fell, even Adam's father was managing to raise a smile, not so much – I suspect – in solidarity with the mood of the rest of us, but at Andrea's determination to impress a wayward French display pilot who'd been a particular favourite of Adam's.

Jean-Luc, who never bothered much with words, had truly appalling English and Andrea was doing her best to translate her feelings about the funeral into what little schoolgirl French she could remember. She, like the rest of us, couldn't stop talking about the swans. They'd appeared after the memorial service in the wake of the Mustang, holding a perfect V formation, and the drunker Andrea got, the more graphic her arm movements became. She'd long ago given up on the French for 'swan' and instead kept circling poor Jean-Luc, dipping her head, arching her neck and flapping her arms around. It looked more like charades than seduction and when one of Jean-Luc's mates stepped in and acted as translator, the expression on his face brought the house down.

'Ah, *les cygnes*.' Jean-Luc backed towards the windows. '*Je comprends*.'

I was at the other end of the room, doing circuits and bumps with a tray of hot-cross buns, watching Andrea through a forest of heads. At first I thought the pressure on my elbow was accidental, someone jostling for space. I glanced round. It was Steve Liddell. I'd never seen him in a suit before.

'Steve,' I said. 'You made it.'

'Yeah.' He ducked his head. 'I'm sorry. I got . . . lost.'

At first, unlike the rest of us, I thought he was stone-cold sober. Then, with a shock, I realised he was very drunk indeed. I'd invited him over for the service, of course, and I'd even put in a phone call a couple of days ago to check whether he'd be coming, but when I'd got no answer and he hadn't turned up at the church, I'd assumed he must be away.

'When did you get here?'

Steve was looking round, searching – I thought – for faces he recognised. I don't think I've ever seen anyone looking so lost. Harald was over by the fireplace, deep in conversation with Ralph Pierson. Steve caught his eye but Harald barely acknowledged him.

I tried again.

'Did you fly over?'

Steve turned back to me. When I repeated the question, he shook his head. Then said yes.

'This morning,' he added thickly.

'Southampton?'

'Yes.'

'And you got the ferry over?'

'Yes. Red thing.'

'So why didn't you join us?' I gestured around. 'Couldn't you find the church?'

He looked at me. He seemed to be brooding over the answer, sorting something out in his head. Finally, he beckoned me closer.

'I came to say sorry,' he mumbled.

'What for?'

'Adam.' He nodded, 'Adam.'

He laid his hand on my arm. He had big, broad, heavy hands, the nails rimmed with ingrained black. Jean-Luc was calling for more wine. Andrea was still pursuing him. It was the perfect time to leave the room. I took Steve's hand and tugged him towards the door. He came willingly, bumping into me then apologising to someone about a spilled drink. Adam's study was mercifully empty. I shut the door.

'Why the apology?' I turned to Steve. 'I don't understand.'

Steve sank into Adam's revolving chair and buried his face in his hands. As a gesture of guilt, it seemed pretty unambiguous. I perched myself on the corner of the desk. Time for some home truths, I thought. Time for some answers.

'What happened?' I asked quietly.

Steve raised his head and tried to look at me. His eyes were glassy.

'When?' He sounded defensive.

'Over in Jersey.'

'You mean the aircraft? The Cessna?'

I shook my head very slowly. I didn't mean that, and he knew I didn't. The Cessna, in a way, was now immaterial, mere history. Much more important was my marriage, and what this man had done to it.

'Not the aircraft, Steve,' I said.

'No?'

'No. Tell me about Michelle. Tell me about your little girl Minette. Tell me what happened.'

Steve tipped back his head and closed his eyes, a gesture of infinite weariness. One leg reached for the carpet. The chair began to spin, very slowly. I stopped it.

'You came to say sorry,' I prompted. 'Sorry means you must have done something wrong.'

Steve eyed me, watchful now, and I wondered whether the police had been on to him. After DC Perry's visit I'd heard nothing more, but that didn't mean that Steve was off the book.

'I didn't do anything,' Steve said. 'It wasn't me.'

'Then why the guilt?'

'I liked him. I liked him a lot.'

'Who?'

'Adam. Your old man. Your husband. He was lovely, a lovely bloke.' He shook his head hopelessly and then muttered something I didn't catch.

'What? What did you say?'

I leaned forward. I wanted to shake him, to prise the truth out of him, to reach down through the syrup of alcohol and retrieve whatever it was he'd come to tell me. Had Adam stolen his partner? Gone off with Michelle? Lured her away with his big innocent grin and £70,000 of our money? Or, please God, did I have it all wrong?

'Tell me, Steve,' I said. 'Tell me about Michelle.'

'She left me.'

'I know that. Tell me why.'

'You *know* that?'

Steve was fighting to focus his eyes. I told him about Dennis.

'Dennis is away,' he muttered. 'Gone away. Gone to Barbados.'

It was true. Dennis Wetherall had indeed departed to the West Indies, one of the periodic breaks he fitted in, a mix of business and pleasure with the emphasis very definitely on the latter. I'd been phoning him for the best part of three weeks, desperate to find out more about our missing £70,000. Now it occurred to me that there were easier ways of nailing down the money. Maybe I should be asking Steve.

'My husband gave you seventy thousand pounds,' I said slowly. 'I'd like you to tell me why.'

'Lent.' Steve gave the word a lot of emphasis. 'He lent me it.'

'Lent, then. But why?'

'Surprise.'

'*Surprise?*' I was getting angry now. 'Steve, he's dead. He's gone. One of the last things he did was give you a whole pile of money. Our money. My money. I want to know what's happened to it. And why he just lent it to you like that.'

Steve followed my outburst with nods of his head. One hand crabbed up his jacket and slipped inside. I found myself looking at a cheque for £70,000.

'You're supposed to be broke,' I said. 'Where did this come from?'

Steve ignored my question.

'I came to say sorry,' he repeated, trying to get up.

I put the cheque on the desk and gave the chair a kick. Steve slipped helplessly back as it began to spin. Outside, in the corridor, I heard a sudden peal of laughter, the way it happens when someone opens a door.

I spun the chair another half-turn. Steve was starting to look ill.

'Tell me about Michelle,' I said savagely. 'That's the least you owe me.'

'She went off,' he protested. 'Not my fault.'

'Yes, but who with?'

Steve gaped up at me.

'Who *with*?'

He closed his eyes and shook his head. Then I heard a door opening and I looked up to find Harald standing on the threshold. He had a glass of orange juice in one hand and seemed surprised to find me talking to Steve.

'Hey,' he said, 'I'm sorry.'

'It's no problem.'

'It's just –' He was looking at Steve. 'He OK?'

'He's fine.' I waited for Harald to say his piece. Harald was still studying Steve. Steve, at last, seemed to recognise him. Then he bent forward, vomiting noisily on the carpet. I tried to step past Harald, en route to fetch a bucket and a cloth from the kitchen. Harald stopped me, the gentlest pressure.

'I'll fix Steve up,' he said. 'I think you should go see your sister.'

'Why?'

'She's making a bit of a scene. It's your mother I worry about, and the other older folks. Maybe . . .' he shrugged, '. . . you could do something.'

When I got back to the lounge, Andrea was on the sofa with Jamie Pierson. Jamie had been helping us pass round the food and drink, eternally cheerful, but Andrea had clearly told him it was time for a break. There was a bottle of Chenin Blanc on the carpet between her feet and as I watched she poured what was left into her glass. She seemed no drunker than when I'd left, though the way she slipped her arm around Jamie's shoulders, and gave him a little hug, undoubtedly signalled intent. She'd been fantasising about Jamie for weeks but so far I'd seen no signs of reciprocation.

I looked for my mother. She was locked in conversation with Douglas, the vicar, on the other side of the room. I picked my way towards her. She looked far from perturbed.

'My darling.' She grabbed my hand. 'Tell me how I smuggle this delightful man back home.'

'Home?' I was looking at Andrea again. She was telling Jamie some story or other, her eyes hooded, her head cocked at her favourite angle. Maybe Harald was right. Maybe we were in for the full number.

'Yes, I keep telling him we need someone with a bit of . . . I don't know . . . vim.' My mother turned back to the vicar. 'Douglas, you still haven't told me how you did it, getting Adam off like that. It was remarkable. He could have been standing there with you. Don't you agree? Ellie?'

I stayed with them for the next twenty minutes or so, buffering the poor vicar from the worst of my mother. One of the many things she missed on the Falklands was the chance to play the landed gentry. Running six hundred head of sheep on several thousand acres of bog and tussock cuts very little ice in Stanley but here, to my mother's delight, the numbers had an altogether different impact.

Eventually, as gracefully as I could, I disentangled myself and made for the door. Across the hall, the study door was shut. When I opened it, I could smell bleach and a ghastly pine-fresh airspray Andrea had picked up in the village. There was a damp patch on the carpet in front of the chair, but of Harald and Steve there was no sign.

I went through to the kitchen. One of Adam's Fleet Air Arm chums was on his hands and knees, mopping up a pool of liquid by the fridge. When I asked about Steve he peered up at me.

'Tall bloke?' he queried. 'Quite young? Baggy suit?'

'Yes?'

'With another guy? Older? American? Bit of a tan?'

'That's him.'

Adam's chum rocked back on his heels.

'They were in here a couple of minutes ago. The young guy was pissed out of his head. The American was taking care of him. Said he'd give you a ring.'

'He's *gone*?'

'Yeah, said it was for the best. And you know what?'

'What?'

Adam's chum gave the floor a last wipe and got to his feet.

'He was right.'

Two days later, Dennis Wetherall phoned. He said he was sorry to have missed the memorial service but business had delayed him in Barbados. We had the usual exchange about his particular brand of bullshit and after I'd told him what an amazing wake he'd missed, he sounded almost regretful.

'*How* long?'

'Six in the morning. I kid you not. Bodies everywhere. Dennis, it was like a battlefield.'

Our accountant's appetite for parties was legendary, but there was a quirkier side to him that I was only just beginning to recognise. He had a taste for the surreal, for the bizarre, territory that came with one or two of his clients from the music business. Mixing grief with abandon, the way the English so rarely do, would have been a gig worth treasuring.

He was trying to put the thought into words but I spared him the effort. The memory of my unfinished conversation with Steve Liddell wouldn't let me go. I'd got so close to finding out, to confirming my worst nightmare, and regardless of the pain that lay beyond it, I was determined to complete our little exchange. As I'd tried to say at the time, the least Steve owed me was the truth. What happened after that would be my responsibility.

Dennis was still musing about the party.

'Was it really wild?' he asked plaintively.

'Very. I'm coming over tomorow. I'll tell you all about it.'

Dennis, ever the gentleman, met me at Jersey airport. With his Barbados tan, his Lacoste shorts and his bougainvillea-print cotton shirt he looked like one of his clients. Crossing the car park, I asked him whether he wasn't cold.

'Freezing,' he snorted. 'But a suntan's like any other asset. The last thing you bloody do is waste it.'

We had lunch at a new place he'd found, a sushi bar in one of the little back streets near the covered market. Only when we were tackling the second course did I make the connection with Adam.

'This is where he came that last night,' I said, 'with Harald.'

'Yeah?' Dennis had a mouthful of raw squid.

'Yes, Harald mentioned it. That first day he flew over. When it had just happened.'

I looked round. The realisation that Adam had been here invested the little restaurant with a new luminance. What had he eaten? Where had he sat? Had he looked at the waitress? The local girl with the purple nails and the big chest?

Mention of Harald had finally tugged Dennis away from Barbados.

'Interesting bloke,' he grunted, 'your friend Meyler.'

'You think so?'

'Definitely. He's well-connected, too. Shrewd of you to stick so close.'

'You think I'm interested in all that?'

'Of course you are. No point otherwise, is there?' He eyed me over his napkin. The notion of friendship, of a loyalty untainted by anything remotely commercial, was utterly alien to Dennis. Whatever you did in life, whoever it touched, there was always a deal.

'He's a friend,' I protested. 'Adam's friend first. Mine now.'

'You don't know about the rest of it?'

'No.'

'He's never told you?'

'Never. He doesn't tell me anything. Except how to cope with my problems. And at that, I have to tell you, he's brilliant.'

I was thinking about Steve Liddell throwing up all over the house. Only Harald would have had the quiet presence of mind to clear it up and remove Steve before it happened again. As a small act of friendship – unfussy, unsung – it was altogether typical.

Dennis was still having trouble fitting Harald into the right box. Money and connections, in his world, equalled power. And powerful men always, *always*, talked about themselves.

'Not this one,' I said.

Dennis sat back, openly incredulous.

'So here's a guy, brings you a hundred and sixty grand for some beaten-up old aeroplane, and you know sod-all about him?'

'You banked the cheque?'

'Of course I did. What else would I do with it?' He looked round the restaurant, glowering. 'But that's not the point. The point is, what's he up to?'

'He's a friend. He helps me out.'

'Sure, but why? What's the angle?'

'There isn't one.'

'Are you dreaming? There's always an angle.'

'Not this time.'

'Bullshit.' He paused, bunching and unbunching the napkin in his hands. 'Is he in love with you?'

I'd once or twice asked myself the same question – not love, exactly, but maybe some passing fancy – but the longer I'd thought about it, the less likely it seemed. Men who are in love with you drop hints, act out of character, make moves, give themselves away. Not once had Harald done any of these things. No, Harald – as far as I was concerned – was exactly what he seemed. Steady. Dependable. A good, good friend.

Dennis was unconvinced.

'He's an arms dealer,' he said. 'Merchant of death.'

The phrase, heavy with moral outrage, made me smile. Dennis's clients included a couple of businessmen on the fringes of the rock scene who Adam had been sure were major drug-dealers. To be frank, I'd no idea how Harald made his money, but heroin, I suggested quietly, was just as lethal as anything in Harald's armoury.

Dennis feigned indignation. He never touched drugs. Never touched people who dealt in drugs. Harald, on the other hand, bought and sold pretty much anything that would make a hole in you.

'How do you know?'

'Because I do,' he said belligerently. 'Because it's my business to know.'

'But who told you?'

Dennis suddenly grinned at me and touched the side of his nose. One of his favourite hobbies was withholding information. It gave him an enormous kick. Information, after all, was power. And power, for Dennis, was the only currency that really mattered.

'Arms.' He nodded. 'All over the bloody world.'

'What sort of arms?'

'Planes, mainly, and all that fancy stuff that goes with them. The radar set-ups, the fuelling gizmos, plus all the hardware you can strap on. Rockets. Cannons. Bombs. He's a trader, Ellie. He's the guy in the middle. He finds a market, meets needs, and from what I hear he's bloody good at it, too. Mind you, arms dealing?' He spread his arms wide. 'You'd be stupid *not* to get rich.'

'How come?'

'How come? You really want to know? One, it's non-cyclical. One half of the world's always trying to kick the shit out of the other half. Two – you listening to me?'

I'd remembered something Adam had told me a while back, when he first met Harald. He'd said he was a player, a real pro, and that – in Adam's terms – was praise indeed.

'Go on,' I said.

'OK, so two, the world's awash with weapons, good solid stuff, most of it Russian, or East German, or Czech, or whatever. These guys, they've lost a war, they don't need it any more. Plus they're flat broke, most of them. So along comes someone like your friend Harald and offers them hard currency, and bingo, it's party time. For dollars, they don't mind who screws them. He can name his price. Literally.'

'You're still talking about aircraft?' I was thinking about the Yak and Harald's connections in Romania. It certainly fitted the story.

Dennis nodded.

'Aeroplanes, sure. And more or less anything else you'd want. Armour. Small arms. Mines. The whole gig.'

'But Harald specialises in planes?'

'That's what I hear.'

'So who does he sell all this stuff to?'

'Central America, right on his doorstep. Contras. Guatemalans. Salvadoreans. Then you go further south. Venezuela. Colombia. Ecuador. Anyone with an insurgency problem. Anyone with bank facilities in Miami. It's money, Ellie. Money has no smell. Guys want to buy aeroplanes, something rugged, something not too fancy, Harald Meyler's the guy they phone.'

I gazed down at my plate of sea bass, still wondering where Dennis had picked up this information. Maybe he'd met someone in Barbados. Maybe he really had been there on business, in between the lazy days at the poolside. Then I had another thought, much closer to home.

'That bank manager we met,' I said slowly, 'the one with the funny name.'

Dennis pretended he'd lost the plot. Finally I coaxed the name from him.

'You mean Ozilio?' He frowned. 'Ozilio Sant'Ana?'

'Yes. Does he know Harald?'

The momentary hesitation gave Dennis away. I tried to stifle a grin. At heart, like Adam, Dennis was just a kid.

'Meyler does a lot through Tony's bank,' he conceded. 'Since you ask.'

'Sant'Ana told you that?'

'No, someone else did.'

I nodded, struck by another connection, another name.

'Steve Liddell,' I said. 'Is that why he went to Sant'Ana's bank for the loan? Because Harald fixed it up for him? Was that the way it was?'

Dennis was getting in deeper than he'd anticipated and I took the grudging nod as a kind of compliment. I was Adam Bruce's pretty little wife. I wasn't supposed to ask questions like this. I wasn't even supposed to be interested. Amazing what a month of widowhood can achieve.

Dennis was leaning forward, eager now to qualify what little I'd managed to tease out of him.

'Your friend Meyler's a class operator. He's made sackfuls of money in a very competitive business. He knows the moves. He's very sharp. He can handle himself. That's all I'm saying.'

'You make him sound like a gangster.'

'He's not a gangster. Loner, yes. Gangster, no.'

'So are you telling me to be careful? Is that it?'

Dennis gave the question some thought. Then he shook his head and barked with laughter.

'No,' he said. 'I'm just really proud of you for chiselling out that hundred and sixty grand.'

It was at this point that I gave him Steve Liddell's cheque for £70,000. Dennis looked at it in disbelief, held it up to the light, then voiced the obvious question. Just where had Steve Liddell got his hands on a sum like this? I said I didn't know and didn't – to be honest – much care. Far more important to me were the questions that preceded it. How had Adam acquired the money in the first place? And why hadn't he shared news of this little windfall with me?

On the phone, Dennis had used the word 'laundered' and I quoted it back to him, toying with the remains of my fish while he explained exactly what Adam had done.

A group of international businessmen, it seemed, wanted to re-stage a famous wartime operation involving Mustangs and B-17s, the hefty four-engine bombers known to the Mustang pilots as 'Big Friends'. The mission, made possible by the range of both aircraft, centred on a bombing raid against German targets around a town called Ruhland. Bombs gone, the B-17s and their escorting Mustangs headed east to an airfield in friendly Russia. A couple of days later, refuelled and rebombed, the task force hit Poland, then flew on to Italy. A week later, after excursions into Hungary and Romania, the Mustangs returned to the UK, completing the triangle. Within days, the American PR people had turned the operation into a legend. Hunting for a headline, they dubbed it 'The Russian Shuttle'.

I followed Dennis's account, trying to fit our own Mustang into the story, trying to visualise our little silver fish swimming in the clear, cold air over Russia.

'But why the businessmen?' I queried. 'Why their interest?'

'It's a gimmick,' he said at once. 'It's a deal dressed up as history. Just now, Russia's hot, really hot. That's where the opportunities are. That's where the sharp guys make the real killings. What they're after is an angle, a way in. The Soviets are still obsessed by the war. Stage a re-enactment, make an anniversary of it, throw in a couple of gallons of vodka, and you'll have them queuing round the block.'

'And this was Adam's idea?'

'The Shuttle?' Dennis shook his head. 'Came from another guy, very well-connected, good footwork, big player in the warbird market. You may have come across him.' Dennis tore at the remains of his bread roll, waiting for me to catch up.

'You mean Harald?'

'The very same.'

'Harald asked Adam?'

'Yeah. To organise the Shuttle. Get some Mustangs together. Talk to the people with the refurbished B-17s. Plot a route. Shake down the logistics. All that shit.'

'And the seventy thousand?'

'A down-payment on his fee.'

I blinked, watching Dennis brush breadcrumbs into his cupped hand and toss them over his shoulder. So why did Adam pass the money on to Steve Liddell? I wondered. And why had he never mentioned this Shuttle operation to me? I began to put the questions into words but thought better of it. If Dennis was so well-informed, there was a more important issue to resolve.

'Tell me about Steve Liddell,' I said, 'and this woman Michelle. Why did she leave him?'

'I've no idea.'

'Was it someone else?'

'Yeah. But I don't know who.'

I spotted the waitress approaching with the brandies.

'You mentioned some windsurfing school.'

'That's right. Place out on the west coast. St Ouen's Bay. Somewhere near L'Etacq.'

'Is it hers?'

'As far as I know. She started up last year. Did well, the way I hear it.'

The waitress deposited the drinks between us. The huge balloons of Courvoisier brought a smile to Dennis's face. He reached for his glass and proposed a toast. I ignored him.

'How much does it cost to start a windsurfing school?'

'No idea. Starting anything ain't cheap.'

'Seventy thousand?'

I looked him in the eye, waiting for an answer. He took a mouthful of the brandy, then wiped his mouth.

'You're crazy,' he said at length. 'You think Adam funded that? Is that where you're coming from?'

'It's a question,' I said. 'That's all.'

'But you think she needed someone else's money? Michelle La Page?'

This was the first time I'd heard the girl's surname. The inflection in Dennis's question suggested I was being woefully naïve.

'Tell me about the La Page family,' I said evenly. 'What have I missed here?'

'You've never heard of Bernard La Page?'

'Never. Should I have done?'

Dennis gave me one of his despairing shrugs. Bernard La Page, it seemed, was a major, major player on the island. Amongst his many business interests was a clutch of engineering firms in the West Midlands, and sole ownership of a small commercial airline, ChannelAir.

ChannelAir I'd come across. Short Skyvans in a rather fetching shade of green.

'Don't they fly to Heathrow?'

'Twice daily. The Heathrow slots are worth a fortune. Just one reason the guy's got money to burn.'

'And Michelle?'

'Is his daughter.' Dennis nodded. 'Seventy grand to her would be a birthday present.'

'So Adam wouldn't . . . ?' I could feel the relief flooding through me.

'No way. If Michelle went into business, Daddy would have footed the bills.'

'You're sure about that?'

'Of course I'm sure. Stands to reason. That's what families are for, isn't it? Sticking together? One for all? All for one?'

He gave me a rather sharp look, and seconds later I realised why. He'd liked Adam. And, more importantly, he'd thought that Adam had rather liked me.

'He could be very stupid sometimes,' I said defensively. 'Very silly. You know how headstrong he was. How he always wanted his own way.'

'But you think him and this . . . Michelle chick? You really think that?'

In my mind's eye, I could see the creased photo in Adam's drawer, the rolled-down wetsuit, the expression on her face, the adolescent message scrawled across the back. *For you, my darling*, she'd written. *From all of me.*

Dennis was still waiting for an answer.

'Yes,' I said quietly. 'I think it's a real possibility.'

'You're nuts.' He frowned at me. 'You've got evidence?'

I didn't answer him. Not directly. At length, I took a sip of brandy. It burned my throat and made my eyes water.

'You haven't told me what happened to the seventy thousand,' I reminded him. 'You haven't told me why Adam give it to Steve in the first place.'

'That's because I don't know.'

'Then it could have been . . .' I shrugged hopelessly, '. . . something to do with her, couldn't it?'

Dennis, never patient, was beginning to get irritable. He picked up Steve's cheque, still lying on the table between us.

'It's back,' he said gruffly. 'The money's back. What the hell does it matter why Adam parted with it?'

'Is that a serious question?'

'Of course it is. You're paranoid, Ellie. The last thing you need just now are more problems. Christ knows what Adam was up to. You know what he was like. He could be a real lunatic sometimes, a complete dickhead. He'd get some idea, some bee in his bonnet, and off he'd go. The unguided bloody missile. Completely out of control.'

I looked at him for a moment, looked at the exasperation in his face. Then I pushed back my chair and stood up.

'You're right,' I said coldly. 'I couldn't have put it better myself.'

I found Steve Liddell in his hangar on the far side of Jersey airport. He was perched on a pair of wooden steps, working on the engine of one of Harald's latest batch of Yaks. The driver of my taxi was eager to get back to St Helier. I asked him to wait.

'This won't take long,' I said grimly.

Steve watched me walking into the hangar. With the greatest reluctance, he abandoned his spanner and clambered down the steps to meet me. He looked wary and ill-at-ease. We didn't shake hands.

'We were having a chat,' I said. 'Over at Mapledurcombe. I don't suppose you remember.'

Steve wiped his face with the back of his hand.

'Yeah,' he grunted, totally noncommittal.

'I was asking you why Michelle left. You told me it wasn't your fault.'

'That's right.'

'Then whose fault was it?'

Steve bowed his head. He was wearing overalls and his old peaked Timberland cap, and when he looked up again his eyes were shadowed.

'I can't tell you,' he said.

'*Can't* tell me?'

'No.'

'Why on earth not?'

He shrugged, and the way he glanced up at the exposed engine said it all. I'm in the middle of a job. I need the money. What I don't need, just now, are questions like these.

'Was it Adam?'

'I don't know what you mean.'

'Nonsense. Of course you know what I mean. Michelle left you.

139

She left you for someone else. I'm asking you again, Steve. It's a really simple question, a yes or a no. Was it Adam?'

Steve began to frame an answer, then had second thoughts. Instead, he rolled his head on his shoulders, round and round, the way you do when the muscles get tight.

'I'm sorry about throwing up,' he muttered at length. 'Across at your place. That was out of order.'

'It's not a problem.' I stepped closer. 'Yes or no. Then I'll go.'

He looked down at me. Then, very slowly, he shook his head.

'Is that a no?'

He shook his head again. For a moment, I wanted to hit him. It was a quick, hot gust of anger, almost a reflex. I linked my fingers, squeezing very hard, fighting for control. Violence would solve nothing. Violence would simply get Steve off the hook. Adam's missus. Just another hysteric.

I changed tack.

'Adam lent you seventy thousand pounds,' I pointed out.

'I gave it you back.'

'I know, but why? Why did he give you that money in the first place?'

This time Steve obliged me with an answer, gesturing round at the half-empty hangar.

'Debts,' he said. 'Running costs. He bailed me out of the shit.'

'Because he felt guilty? About Michelle?'

Steve thought about the proposition. For some reason it seemed to amuse him, a ghost of a smile that came and went.

'She's gone,' he said bleakly. 'It's over and that's that.'

'You don't feel bitter?'

'Of course I feel bitter.'

'About Adam, I mean.'

For a moment I thought he was going to fall into the trap, but then his eyes closed and he shook his head and shifted his weight from one foot to the other.

'This isn't helping. I know what you want but I can't –' He shrugged. 'There'd be no point.'

'There's every point. He was my husband.'

'Yes, I know. And I'm sorry.'

'That's what you said before. Sorry's not enough, Steve. Sorry's too easy. What I want from you might sound like the earth but actually it's very simple. In fact it couldn't be simpler. Did Adam have an affair with Michelle? Yes or no?'

'The money's safe,' he repeated. 'I gave you a cheque.'

'Fuck the money. Just yes or no.'

140

I thought my language might shake the truth out of him but I was wrong. He just looked down at me, unyielding, and it was then that I realised that the conversation wasn't going any further. We'd hit a wall. For whatever reason, Steve Liddell wasn't going to tell me about Adam and his precious ex-partner.

I glanced over my shoulder. The taxi-driver lifted his wrist and tapped his watch. Across the other side of the hangar, muffled by a thin partition wall, I heard a phone start to trill. The summons made Steve physically flinch. I saw the uncertainty in his eyes, the overwhelming urge to turn his back and run. I reached forward, picking a curl of metal from the sleeve of his overall.

'Answer it, Steve,' I said bitterly. 'It might be something important.'

Back in the taxi, the driver had started the engine.

'St Ouen's Bay,' I told him. 'I'm looking for some kind of windsurfing school.'

Nearly an hour later, the taxi delivered me to a couple of deserted Portakabins on a patch of scrubby ground beside the long sweep of St Ouen's Bay. Beyond the Portakabins, crudely gravelled, was half an acre or so of empty car park, buttressed at the far end by a line of three rusting freight containers.

I got out of the taxi and paid the fare. This time, come what may, I wanted to be alone. Whoever I talked to, however direct my questions, I was getting absolutely nowhere. I'd never felt so angry in my life and I needed time to cope with the consequences.

The taxi driver pocketed the £20 I'd given him and pulled the dented Renault into an untidy U-turn. I was glad when he'd gone. The silence, broken only by the cries of the gulls and the distant rasp of surf, was an immense relief.

I circled the two Portakabins. They were chocked up on concrete blocks and I had to stand on tiptoe to peer in through the windows. One room was evidently an office. It looked neat and businesslike and the calendar on the wall behind the desk was already showing April. On a chair beneath the window I could see a pile of clothes, but when I tried the nearby door it was locked.

Next along from the office was a classroom of some kind, cheap folding chairs drawn up in a semicircle around one of those big prop-up easels sales reps use in meetings. There was a triangular diagram on the plastic wipe-board, bold lines in blue Pentel, and I studied it a moment, trying to make sense of the thicket of little symbols. It was obviously something to do with windsurfing, how best to steer around three fixed buoys. Me, and Adam, and the bitch-queen

Michelle, I thought. Wind force eight and rising. Hurricanes expected within the hour.

I quickly circled the other Portakabin then crossed the car park and checked out the containers. The big padlocks looked brand new. I tried each in turn, not knowing quite why, but none of them budged. I looked back across the car park again. There was a nicely painted sign across the width of the two Portakabins. *Ultra-Max*, it read. *Windsurfing for Girls, Guys, and Gods.* The turn of phrase made me shudder. Ultra-Max? Gods? What had Adam got himself into?

I leaned back against the container. In the early spring sunshine, the metal was already warm to the touch. I closed my eyes a moment, trying to think things through. Should I wait until someone turned up? Or should I find a phone box? And say I did, say I found a number for Michelle La Page, what would I do then? What would I say when a woman's voice answered and I had to introduce myself and explain why I'd made the call? Should I be frank? Insist on a meeting? Somewhere nice and quiet, somewhere a bit like this, somewhere I could indulge my anger and circle this woman's neck with my bare hands, and take a little modest revenge for all the grief she'd given me?

I smiled grimly, content to let this nonsense swirl around my fevered brain. Normally, I'm never this self-indulgent. On the contrary, I normally keep my emotions firmly in check. Letting go is strictly for people like Andrea, or – as I was beginning to recognise – Adam. One emotional basket case in the family was quite enough.

After a while, I had the urge to take a pee. I squeezed down the gap between two of the containers, looking for the shelter they'd give me at the far end. Squatting in the sunshine, I saw the mountain bike. It was red and shiny and brand new. Like the containers, it was padlocked.

Someone was here. Maybe it was Michelle. Maybe she was on site somewhere, watching me, wondering who the hell I was. Then I remembered the pile of clothes in the office. Jeans. A T-shirt. An anorak of some kind. I ran back across the car park. From the Portakabins, a line of paving stones led across to a gap in the sea wall. I looked down at the sand, gleaming wetly in the sunshine. Footsteps tracked away towards the distant line of breaking surf. I jumped from the sea wall and slipped off my shoes. Her feet were a size bigger than mine. Tall, I thought. Taller than me. Younger than me. More beautiful than me. But mine, now. There for the taking. I shook my head, gritted my teeth. Try as I would, the anger kept returning.

I peered seawards, shading my eyes from the sun. At first I saw nothing. Then came a flicker of movement, a tiny blob of colour, yellow and mauve, a child's version of a sail, daubed on the gleaming silver sea. Even at a distance, the sail was moving fast, left to right, lifting from time to time, then slamming down again.

I followed the footprints towards the water's edge. It must have been a couple of hundred yards at least. My mouth had gone dry. Adam had been here, I kept telling myself. I had rights, obligations even.

The sea was less rough than I'd expected, a boisterous little chop that broke in spumy bubbles at my feet. The windsurfer was closer now, a figure in a wetsuit clearly visible. The wetsuit, like the sail, was yellow and mauve, and her body was hanging out over the water, her back inches from the racing waves. The way she controlled the board, freeing it one moment, reining it in the next, reminded me of Smoko, my horse at Gander Creek, and the longer I watched her, the more obvious the parallels became. She and the board were indivisible, a single entity, just the way that Smoko and I had been, and as I followed her wild progress from wave top to wave top it became all too obvious what Adam must have seen in her. The same eagerness. The same athletic abandon. Except that she was younger, and sleeker, and altogether more ruthless.

I must have waited at the water's edge for the best part of half an hour. I knew she'd seen me because she began to stitch a course closer and closer to the beach, taking little glances as she hauled the board round at the end of each run. Eventually she cruised to a halt in the shallows and hopped off. I recognised the hair, the way it lay over her shoulders, long, dark curls. And I recognised the expression, playful, anticipatory, curious. Close to, she had lovely skin, smooth, olive, a hint of foreign blood.

'Hi? Come down for a booking?' She bent to the board and fiddled with something. The mast and sail came away in her hand.

'My name's Ellie Bruce,' I said tonelessly. 'Adam was my husband.'

'Who?'

'Adam.'

Standing upright again, she wiped the wet sand from her hands. The name had taken the smile off her face.

'Shit,' she said quietly.

We stood there looking at each other for what seemed an age. Finally, she picked up the board and held it out.

'Do me a favour?'

The question threw me completely. I wanted to hit her. I wanted to throw myself at her and wrestle her into the water and push her face way down into the sand until she stopped struggling and quietly died. Instead, she showed me how to carry the board, one hand hooked into a footstrap.

'I'll take the rig,' she said. 'The wind gets in the sail. It can be tricky.'

The board was lighter than I'd thought. We walked together up the beach, the situation more surreal by the second. Little Ellie Bruce. Sherpa to her husband's lover. Where the sand began to dry out, I stopped.

'Here's far enough,' I said.

Michelle kept walking. From where I was standing, the attraction was obvious. The long legs. The lovely body. How fit she must be. How supple. I caught her up, empty-handed, and hauled her to a stop. She was holding the rig by the mast and the boom. The wind began to fill the sail. She laid it carefully on the sand.

'We don't need to do this,' she said.

'I do.'

'Yeah, but I don't.' She sniffed, then sealed one nostril with her forefinger and blew hard. The gesture caught me by surprise. So male. So aggressive.

'So how long was it going on?' I'd stepped around the sail, blocking her path up the beach. No escape, I wanted to say. Time to straighten one or two things out.

'How long was what going on?' She sounded careless, almost bored, as if she'd dealt with the same question a million times.

'You and Adam. You and my husband.'

She shook the water from her hair and then unzipped the top of her wetsuit. It was a wholly ambiguous gesture, at once natural and provocative.

'That's ridiculous,' she said. 'I don't have to answer that.'

'You do.'

'Why?'

'Because I'm here. Because he was my husband. Because I want to know.'

Her fingers were still on the big plastic zipper. She was playing with it, sliding it up and down, studying my face with an expression I couldn't quite place. Curiosity? Pity? Apprehension? I didn't know.

'Who chased who?' I said. 'Tell me that.'

'No one chased anyone. There wasn't any chasing. This is pathetic.'

'Was it the money, then?'

'What money?'

'The seventy thousand pounds.' I gestured towards the Portakabins, up beyond the sea wall. 'I don't suppose he knew about your father. All that ready cash.'

This time there was no mistaking her expression. She was outraged.

'What are you talking about? Father?'

I told her what I knew about Bernard La Page. He was immensely rich. He'd staked the windsurfing school. So in the end, Adam hadn't needed our chequebook.

'Who told you that?'

'What?'

'About my father? Paying for all this?' She kicked the mast of the rig. She was pale with anger.

I stared at her, beginning – for the first time – to doubt myself. Had Dennis got it wrong? Had she raised the money some other way?

'Your father's rolling in it,' I insisted. 'Are you telling me he didn't help you?'

'*Help* me? He kicked me out, disinherited me. Not that I care.'

'Why? Why would he do that?'

Like Steve Liddell, Michelle obviously wasn't in the business of giving me straight answers. I began to rephrase the question but she stepped towards me and came very close, her voice almost a whisper.

'I'm adopted,' she said. 'Did your accountant tell you that?'

'No,' I admitted.

'OK, so that's number one. Bernard adopted me at birth – and you're quite right, I had a big fat legacy coming. But number two, I blew it by going to live with Steve. Not only did I live with the guy, I had his child. On this island, believe it or not, class matters. And the one thing that buys you class is money. OK, my father has lots of money. Lots of money buys him lots of class. Steve was skint. Steve was the bottom of the heap. My father thought he was dirt. Told me so.'

I nodded. Her passion was unfeigned. I believed her.

'So what happened?'

'He cut me off.'

'And the child? Minette?'

'Her, too, when she arrived.' She sniffed again and then tossed back her hair. 'There's a trust fund or something for when she's older. But that's not much use, is it? Not when you can't scrape together the price of a packet of nappies?'

I was looking down at the sail.

'I don't understand,' I said. 'If he's cut you off, and you're not living with Steve . . . who paid for the school?'

She laughed, a short, mirthless snort that told me to mind my own business.

'Does that matter?' she said.

'Of course it matters.'

'Why?'

'Because it might have been my husband.'

She shook her head, more in sorrow than anger, and bent to retrieve the sail. The board lay where I'd left it, twenty metres down the beach. She walked down with the sail, reseated the mast in the board, then began to haul the whole thing up towards the sea wall. The way she did it was dismissive. Tired of my questions, this sudden intrusion into her private life, she'd decided that enough was enough.

I caught her by the sea wall. Blocking the steps to the car park, I stopped her.

'If you want to fight about it,' she said simply, 'nothing would please me more.'

'You haven't told me,' I insisted.

'Told you what?'

'What happened between you and my husband. You and Adam.'

'I never took a penny off him.'

I nodded. I'd seen Steve's cheque. Unless there were other holes in our accounts, she was probably telling the truth.

'Forget the money,' I said. 'What about the rest of it?'

'What rest of it?'

'The photo you sent him, gave him, whatever you did.'

'Photo?' She looked totally blank.

'It was taken here,' I said, nodding past her at the beach. 'You were wearing a wetsuit. It was obviously last summer.' I quoted the inscription back at her, word for word.

'And you've seen it? This photo?'

'*Seen* it? I've got it.'

She hesitated a moment, made to say something, then shook her head.

'For fuck's sake,' she said wearily.

She pushed past me. I didn't stop her.

'Why don't you tell me?' I shouted. 'Why don't you just admit it?'

She ignored the question, mounting the steps, upright, graceful, shadowed by the flapping sail. Only when she was back beside the Portakabins, screwing a length of hose to a standpipe, did we bring the conversation to an end.

'Tell me about Adam,' I demanded. 'Tell me why you did it.'

'I can't.'

'But why not? Tell me why not.'

She looked at me anew, as if I'd only just appeared, then she shook her head again, a gesture of resignation.

'I'm sorry about your husband,' she said quietly, 'but I'm the last person you should blame.'

Chapter nine

There was a long fax waiting for me back at Mapledurcombe. It was from Harald. I sat in Adam's study, exhausted after a night without sleep, reading it.

Harald was back in Florida. He'd made a six-week hole in his schedule and he wanted, he said, to use it to my advantage. A proper conversion course on the Mustang needed concentrated flying. The odd hour over the Isle of Wight, weather permitting, offered no real basis for anything, Far better to have him buy me a ticket to the States and put me through the real thing. The late spring would be perfect. He had access to a dual Mustang. Minimum, we'd be talking thirty-five hours in the air. After maybe ten, I'd be going solo. After another ten, I'd be first-stage aerobatic. There might even be scope for some formation work.

In a brisk postscript, he added that he'd been talking to Ralph Pierson. The old man's archival researches had impressed him. Ditto his affection for me. Here was a guy whose judgement he could respect. And in Ralph's view Old Glory would truly thrive with a female pilot at the controls.

I sat back, revolving Adam's chair from side to side, the fax in my lap. The offer was hugely tempting. My encounters with Steve Liddell and Michelle in Jersey had, once again, knocked the bottom out of my world. I felt bewildered and betrayed, the ugliest possible combination, and the longer I thought about it, the more claustrophobic my sense of despair became.

As Dennis had pointed out when I'd arrived on his doorstep, tearful and frustrated, there was no hard evidence, nothing solid to corroborate my inner conviction that Adam had indeed been having an affair. But that wasn't the point. I'd been there. I'd talked to Steve and Michelle, looked them in the eye, and the fact that neither of them had denied my allegations was all the proof I needed. Two days ago, I'd said goodbye to the man I loved. Standing in the churchyard, watching the Mustang bank away to the south, I'd assumed sole ownership. Now, regardless of what Dennis said, I knew that I'd been nothing but a shareholder, entitled – at best – to only part of him.

Harald's fax and phone number were on the top of the first sheet. It was all I could do not to lift the telephone, and dial his number, and simply say yes. Dennis, I sensed, didn't quite approve of Harald, but all his talk of arms dealing and merchants of death seemed to me to be irrelevant. Not once had Harald let me down. Not once had he been anything but steadfast. He could be pretty pushy sometimes, and he certainly wasn't one for shared decisions, but that – I now suspected – came with the territory, a price worth paying for the knowledge that he'd always be there.

I could hear Andrea cruising up and down the hall with the Hoover. In all fairness, the decision to go would be as much hers as mine. Leaving her on her own to cope with the first couple of weeks of our American guests, especially when she'd never done it before, was a big imposition.

I caught her at the end of the hall, respooling the flex. I sensed at once that she'd already read the fax.

'I thought it was a booking,' she admitted. 'Sorry.'

I let it pass. Andrea had always been nosy about my private life.

'So what do you think?'

'Go,' she said at once. 'It sounds marvellous.'

'I know, but what about the first lot of guests?'

She flicked her hair back and shrugged, a typical piece of theatrical indifference. That she could cope, I didn't doubt. But did she *want* to take it on single-handed?

'No problem,' she said. 'Six weeks isn't forever. And anyway, I'm sure you'll be back for your birthday.'

My birthday falls on 10 June. Back home, my parents had always made the point of celebrating family occasions with some style, and knowing that Adam had continued the tradition, Andrea was equally keen to do her bit. Only a couple of days ago, she'd told me that she'd been laying plans. I'd had a bloody awful time of it. A slap-up birthday would put me back on the rails. This gesture, wholly unexpected, had touched me deeply and now I reached up and gave her a peck on the cheek.

'You'll go?'

'I'll certainly think about it.' I looked at the fax again. 'He wants an answer within twenty-four hours.'

I tussled with the decision for the rest of the evening. In some respects, so soon after the memorial service and all the other traumas, it felt hopelessly premature, even irresponsible, yet another part of me ached to get on a big fat jet and wake up in another continent.

Distance solves nothing, of course, but learning to fly a Mustang was something else entirely, and by next morning I'd made up my mind to go. When I phoned Harald, it must have been in the middle of the Florida night. For once, he sounded groggy.

'Thanks for the fax,' I said. 'I'd love to come.'

'Great.'

He told me he'd look into booking some flights. Tomorrow he was off to Bogotá. It might be a while before he'd be back in touch.

'But it's still on? The Mustang?'

I must have sounded more anxious than I'd intended, because he laughed.

'It's a definite go, Ellie. No turning back.'

The decision galvanised me. Suddenly there was a huge list of things to do, loose ends to tie up, pilots to contract for the first month's excursions in the Harvard and the Mustang. I worked through the morning in Adam's study, trying not to day-dream too much about Florida, and by lunchtime – to my delight – I'd managed to produce a first rough flight schedule.

Andrea had been going through Jamie's plans for the terraces at the back of the house and all three of us shared a salad in the kitchen before I slipped away with my calculator and my aviation files to make a start on the maintenance logs.

It was a glorious afternoon, our first spell of warm weather, and I settled myself in the gazebo at the foot of the garden, checking through a list of spares that Dave Jeffries wanted to order for the Harvard. Strictly speaking, the bill was now Harald's responsibility, but the total was less than £500 and given his generosity over the Florida trip I was loath to keep knocking on his door for yet more cash. With his £160,000, plus the windfall cheque from Steve Liddell, Old Glory was very definitely off the casualty list and Dennis Wetherall's news that Steve himself was beginning to trade his way out of trouble was even more cheering. Adam's reckless loan guarantee wouldn't, after all, be called in by the bank, an enormous weight off my mind, and when I totted up the pile of cash in hand, I realised that financially we were in rude health. The building work we'd commissioned at the end of last year had gone a couple of thousand over budget, but even so we had a big fat buffer against whatever turbulence lay ahead.

I scribbled a note authorising Dave to go ahead with the order for the spares and then sat back, enjoying the sunshine. It was lovely and warm in the gazebo and the sun's heat was releasing all the rich, sharp, resiny smells that had been locked away by the winter. I must have gone to sleep because the next thing I remember was a shadow drifting across my face. I opened one eye. It took me a moment or two to recognise the silhouette standing over me.

'Jamie,' I said.

I obviously sounded startled, because he put a hand on my arm.

'Sorry,' he said. 'I didn't think you'd be asleep.'

'Neither did I. Thank God you woke me up.' I hooked an old cane chair towards me with my foot. 'Sit down.'

Jamie hesitated and then shrugged. He was in shorts and an old rugby shirt, green and pink hoops and the beginnings of a rip under one armpit. The way he moved reminded me a little of Adam. He had the same grace, the same easy athleticism. Nothing ever seemed to bother him. Like Adam, he obviously had very low blood pressure.

'The boss wants some azaleas,' he grinned. 'Apparently you know the place to go.'

He'd taken to calling Andrea the boss over the last couple of weeks. He was working for us nearly full time now and I suspected that this was his way of keeping my sister at arm's length. Andrea hasn't got a lot of finesse when it comes to getting something she wants badly, though she kids herself all the time that she's being subtle and immensely sophisticated. Jamie, to my amusement, could read her like a book.

'What's this place called?'

Jamie named a nursery up near Newport. I had an account there, though we hadn't bought anything for months.

'Boss says you ought to come with me.'

'Why can't she go?'

'You'll need to sign. Plus she's expecting a delivery. Beds or something.'

I smiled, stretching on the full-length chaise. Andrea had seen a couple of antique beds in a gallery in Cowes. It spoke volumes about the new balance of power at Mapledurcombe that she'd bought them without even consulting me.

'I hope they're OK,' I said. 'Otherwise, they're going back.'

I drove Jamie to the nursery. The azaleas were part of a big display in a cavernous growing house around the back, and he left me to make my choice while he inspected a stand of young saplings in the yard outside. Having a tree surgeon at Mapledurcombe was already proving an unexpected bonus. Not only had Jamie pruned our modest stock of fruit trees but he also had plans for something exotic to soften the view as our guests turned in at the front gate. In this respect, Jamie was an odd mixture – enormously capable, fearlessly hands-on, yet sensitive as well, with an almost feminine eye for colour and texture. To find such delicacy in someone so young was, in my experience, practically unheard of, though Andrea – as usual – had a blunter way of putting it. 'He's a hunk,' she said. 'He's practically bloody edible.'

While I signed the bill and gossiped with the woman who ran the nursery, Jamie carried the trays of azaleas to the estate car. It was lunchtime, still gloriously sunny, and I was starving.

'Let's have a pub lunch,' I suggested. 'My treat.'

We went to a place I knew near Arreton. We ordered salads at the bar and sat outside at one of the garden tables. The tables were hard up against the back wall of the pub and I could feel the warmth of the bricks through my T-shirt. We talked about Mapledurcombe for a bit and Jamie told me how much he was enjoying it. Early on, he'd tested the relationship between myself and Andrea and he knew he could trust me with the odd indiscretion. Like the afternoon Andrea had suggested they both try out the newly filled swimming pool, only to insist on a lengthy back rub in the gazebo afterwards. Given that Andrea was nearly twice his age, Jamie could easily have been quite unkind about her but he brought a wry sense of affection to the telling of each tale, and I liked that. He had immense patience, as well as a thousand and one other virtues, and when he departed for another round of drinks I found myself marvelling at how much he resembled his grandfather.

Ralph, oddly enough, was the name on his lips when he came back. He passed me my orange split. He was on Stella.

'He asked me to give you a message,' he said. 'I think it's to do with that money he sent you.'

I felt a rush of instant guilt. I'd been meaning to return the cheque he'd sent over. I was eternally grateful for the gesture but just now money was the least of my problems. He must have the £5,000 back.

'He won't take it.' Jamie shook his head. 'I know he won't.'

'Why not?'

'Well, that's the point really. I don't quite know how to put this.'

For once, he looked embarrassed. I sipped my drink, letting him take his time, only too aware of how little I'd seen of Ralph recently. He'd come to the memorial service, of course, and back to the house afterwards, but most of the time he'd been locked in conversation with Harald and I hadn't had the chance for a proper chat. One of the things I badly wanted to say was thank you. His introduction to Douglas, the miracle vicar, had been invaluable.

'It's about flying,' Jamie ventured at last. 'He seems to think it might interest me.'

I looked at Jamie. We were sitting side by side on the wooden bench.

'And is he right?'

'Yes, definitely.'

'And?'

Jamie was blushing now, or at least I think he was. He had a wonderful complexion, weather-roughened, bursting with vitality, and it was hard to tell.

'Well . . .' he began to trace the grain of the table with his forefinger, '. . . he thought that if you had no better use for the money, then maybe . . .' he glanced sideways, '. . . you might teach me how to fly. He seemed to think that might make it easier for you. You know, tendering a service and all that.'

I nodded. Why hadn't I thought of it before? Why had it taken this gentle, unassuming youth to voice something that – God knows – Ralph might have intended all along?

'I'm thick,' I said. 'I'm really stupid. Of course I'll teach you to fly.'

'You will?'

'Yes, it'll be a pleasure. Strictly speaking, I'm not supposed to, but no one need know. My first pupil. When do you want to start?'

Jamie was grinning now. I could see the child in him, the young kid waking up on Christmas Day to a sackful of presents.

'You mean that?'

'Of course I do. We'll have to use the Moth but that's no problem. In fact it's a bonus. Real pilots learn on tail-draggers. Spam cans are for wimps.'

'Spam cans?'

'Modern planes. Nose-wheel jobs. Tomahawks. Cessnas. I picked up the phrase from Adam, actually. He's the one who taught me.'

'To fly?'

'Yes. And we used the Moth. Not mine. That came later. He borrowed one from someone or other, and just told me to get on with it.'

'And what was it like?'

'Brilliant. Wonderful. Life wasn't so great at the time and it was just what I needed. Clever man, my husband.'

I found myself telling Jamie about our time up in Aberdeen, and those dark, cold, everlasting months when Adam flew away to Africa. He was a good listener, one of Ralph's gifts again, and at his prompting I carried the story forward to our early days on the Isle of Wight and the tumbledown manor house that was to become Mapledurcombe. The list of things we'd had to do, first to the house and then to Adam's precious aeroplanes, fascinated Jamie. He wanted to know more. He wanted details. How had we fixed the roof? Why hadn't we gone for solar heating? Whose idea had it been to terrace the garden? I fed his curiosity as best I could, salting the raw information with little anecdotes, and the longer the conversation went on, the stranger the experience became.

It was like opening the door to a long-forgotten boxroom, somewhere way up in the eaves, somewhere remote and unvisited and somehow no longer part of me. One or two of the memories I was sharing with Jamie were – at most – a couple of years old, but already they seemed to belong to another life. The events of the last month or so – Adam's death, the visits to Jersey, Steve Liddell and Michelle La Page – had fenced me off from the marriage that had kept me so secure. I was someone else now. I was out on my own. The past, though busy and colourful and full of incident, was no longer of the slightest relevance.

It was late afternoon by the time we left the pub. On the long valley road down to Shorwell, Jamie touched me lightly on the arm. He'd had at least four pints of Stella.

'Do you mind me asking you something?' he said.

'Not at all.'

'Do you regret not having children, you know, now Adam's gone?'

I thought hard about the question. In reality, of course, having kids was a non-starter. But say I hadn't had a problem? Say I was as fertile as the next woman? What then?

'I'd have loved children,' I said. 'And so would Adam.'

'But it never happened?'

'No.' I glanced across at him. 'We tried and tried but you're right. It never happened. There was a reason. I won't bore you.'

Jamie shook his head.

'I'm sorry,' he said. 'It was none of my business.'

'That's OK.' I was still thinking of the countless monthly waits, the endless disappointments. 'We might have adopted but I don't think it would have been the same somehow. Adam wasn't the adopting kind. Neither was I. We were too selfish, I suppose. And in too deep.'

'Into what?'

'The house. The business. Each other. And the planes, of course. They all take time. And energy . . .' I trailed off. Jamie was still looking at me, still waiting.

'But you loved him,' he said at last.

It was more a statement than a question. I sensed he wanted me to say yes. I sensed he wanted whatever image he had of us as a couple to be confirmed. It seemed to matter to him. A lot.

'Adam's dead,' I said simply.

'But you loved him.'

'Yes, I loved him.'

'And he loved you back.'

The phrase made me smile. It was so sweet, so innocent. Who knows, I thought, maybe he's right. Maybe Adam really had loved me back. Maybe the other adventures – Michelle, God knows who else – belonged in some other bit of his body, not in his heart at all. Maybe he was one of those emotional junkies you read about in magazines, addicted to risk, determined to pile all their chips ever so briefly on a single number. Not because it matters, or because there's any real affection, but simply for the thrill of it. Thrills had certainly figured near the top of Adam's list of priorities. Of that, I was absolutely certain.

Jamie was talking about his own mother. Her name was Ruth. His father's name was Gordon. He'd been the only child. The marriage, superficially so calm, so stable, had been shattered one winter afternoon by the arrival at the front door of another woman, a gypsy-looking creature, dark-skinned, vivacious and very, very angry. With her was a child, a little girl. She'd had long blonde curls, Jamie said, and he remembered the badge pinned to the chest of her dungarees. Comic Relief.

'So who was she? This child?' I was still thinking about Adam.

'My sister.' He corrected himself. 'My half-sister. Her name was Angelika.'

'And the woman?'

'My father's mistress. They lived about a mile away. I must have passed the house a million times on my way to school. My dad was a travelling salesman. He repped for a pharmaceuticals company. He was always on the road.'

'And you never knew?'

'Never had a clue. He'd been leading two lives all the time. One with us. One with them.'

'So how old were you? When all this happened?'

'Sixteen.'

'*Sixteen*? As recent as that?'

Jamie forced a smile.

'It seems yonks ago,' he said. 'Some other life. Do you know what I mean?'

He looked across at me, plaintive, and I nodded, only too aware of the tricks a sudden shock like this can play with time. Then I thought about Ralph and the story he'd told me about his own wife. The American flyer she'd lost in the B-17 crash and the affair she'd had with another American much later. Betrayal's a gene, I thought, passed down from generation to generation.

I could see the turning for Mapledurcombe way up ahead. I slowed the car.

'What happened to your mother?' I asked.

'She committed suicide.'

'She *killed* herself?'

'Yes. She said she was going to London. I remember her leaving for the station. It was raining that morning. Tipping it down.'

He shuddered and I pulled the car to a halt. Minutes later, in my arms, he was still crying. At length, I gave him a tissue and he dried his eyes. I was half-expecting embarrassment, some kind of apology, but he just sat bolt upright in the passenger seat, staring ahead.

'Funny,' he said at last, 'I half-thought Grandad might have told you.'

'He didn't.' I took his hand, squeezing it softly.

Jamie cleared his throat and then shook his head several times as if he was trying to dislodge the memories.

'She jumped in front of the train,' he said, 'She was in pieces.'

'You had to identify her?'

'Yes.'

'Where was your father?'

'He'd left. He'd run away. He couldn't cope.' I could hear the bitterness, the raw anger, in his voice. 'Bastard sneaked back months later for his suits and his pipe. Can you believe that?'

'What about the other woman? And the little girl?'

'He left them, too.' He nodded slowly, his mouth a thin, tight line across his face.

I wound down the window. I could hear skylarks and – much further away – the drone of a circling aircraft.

'And you were sixteen,' I said quietly.

'Yeah, going on six.' He looked at me at last, then down at his hand as if it didn't belong to him. His fingers tightened between mine.

'I've never told anyone that. That's a first. I'm sorry.'

'Don't be.'

'No?'

'No.' I reached up and cupped his face in my hands. 'You're a lovely boy. We're lucky to have you. I'm sorry about your mother. Truly. I think I know how much it hurts, if that's any consolation, and I think I know how other people saying they're sorry isn't any use at all. You're the one who has to work it out, Jamie. There's no other way.'

He nodded. He'd obviously got this far, and probably a good deal further, all by himself, but now he sensed he'd found a friend. I reached for the ignition key and started the engine. Minutes later, we were pulling up outside Mapledurcombe.

'That was nice,' I said lightly.

'*Nice?*' The word made him smile. He found a shred of tissue in his jeans pocket and blew his nose. Then he looked at me. 'You didn't mind?'

'Not in the least. I did most of the talking. Thanks to you.'

'That was easy. I like listening to you. The things you both did. The ways you got it together. It's been brilliant.'

I was looking up at the house.

'We did our best.'

'I meant this afternoon.'

'Oh.' My hand found his again and I gave it a little squeeze. 'It was a pleasure.'

I made to withdraw my hand but he wouldn't let me.

'About the flying,' he said. 'Were you serious?'

'Absolutely. Tell Ralph. Tell him it's on. And tell him there's no question of him paying.'

'He won't stand for it. I know he won't.'

'Too bad. Men can't have it all their own way.' I gave his hand a last squeeze, then reached for the door. 'Just remember that.'

When we got inside the house, Andrea was less than pleased to see us. She wanted to know why we'd been so long, what had kept us. I told her we'd stopped for lunch and that neither of us had been watching the time.

'It's nearly five,' she said pointedly. 'Just how hungry were you?'

The question made Jamie giggle. Aware that he'd been drinking, Andrea's scowl became blacker.

We stared at each other, then Jamie made a move towards the back door. We both watched him leave.

'Congratulations,' Andrea said coldly. 'Ten pints of lager. Never fails.'

'You're out of your mind.'

'Hardly. Have you seen the expression on his face? The way he looks at you? Follows you around? It's puppy love, Ellie. You ought to buy him a collar and a lead.'

I ignored the sarcasm. I'd certainly been aware that Jamie liked me, liked talking to me, but the rest of it was fantasy. Andrea had never quite got the hang of men. One of the reasons, I suppose, that her marriage had collapsed.

157

Through the kitchen window, we could both see Jamie clearing up. He piled his gardening tools into the wheelbarrow and disappeared.

'I suppose he'll need a lift home,' Andrea said resignedly. 'I was planning to put the supper on.'

'He's got a bike,' I pointed out.

'Yes, but he's pissed, Ellie, and I expect you've been drinking too. I can't just let him ride home. He'll kill himself.'

The image made me wince. The sight of your mother pulped by a train would stay with you forever.

'So what happened?' she said. 'You might as well tell me.'

'Nothing happened.'

'So why do the pair of you look so . . .' she scowled, '. . . happy?'

'Do we?'

'Yes, it's all over your face. I know you, Ellie. You can't hide it.'

There was a noise outside. Jamie stamping the mud off his boots. Then his face appeared round the door. He'd doused his head in cold water. His hair clung wetly to his scalp.

'I'm off,' he said, perfectly normal. 'See you tomorrow.'

Andrea stepped forward. I'd left the car keys on the table. By the time she'd picked them up Jamie had gone. She looked at his departing back through the kitchen window. When he got on his bike and rode off, there wasn't the trace of a wobble.

'Cow,' she said softly. 'You know the way I feel about him.'

I finished filling the kettle. When I'd found the teapot and sorted out a spoonful of Earl Grey, I sat down at the table. Andrea's copy of *Cosmopolitan* was open at an article about the unsung glories of monogamy.

'I don't know what you're worried about.' I turned the page. 'I'm off to America, aren't I?'

Ralph invited me to lunch at the end of that same week. We were to meet at a hotel in Bonchurch called The Peacock Vane, and I was twenty minutes late because I'd been talking to Mr Grover. He'd phoned me from the AAIB with news of the bag I'd sent him. After exhaustive tests, he'd said, the technical boys had been able to confirm that Adam's sports holdall had indeed been immersed in seawater for a period of time. This seemed to me to be a statement of the blindingly obvious, but he went on to explain that the real significance of the tests was what they *didn't* confirm.

'I don't understand,' I'd told him.

'They found no evidence of heat damage.'

'Meaning?'

'There's a pretty low likelihood of fire. There was no foreign object

158

damage, either, nothing impacting on the body of the bag. Tiny bits of metal. Anything you'd associate with a catastrophic event.'

'Like?'

'Like an explosion.'

'An *explosion*?' I hadn't thought about this possibility before, though in his wilder moments I'd often expected Adam to go bang. 'You really think the plane might have blown up?'

'Frankly, no. Though it's something we have to rule out.'

'And the bag lets you do that?'

'The state of the bag suggests it's unlikely.' Mr Grover had sounded extremely careful. 'Though naturally we're keeping an open mind.'

I'd brought the conversation to an end a minute or so later, telling Mr Grover I had an appointment to keep. The impression he'd given me was that the inquiry was winding down. In the absence of any other wreckage, arriving at a firm conclusion was out of the question. The reason for Adam spearing in was a mystery and likely to remain so.

I told Ralph about the conversation. We were sitting in the hotel dining room, an exquisite confection of Victorian furniture, sumptuous food and big double doors opening on to a sweep of ornamental garden. Ralph, as ever, was worried about me.

'Doesn't it disturb you? Not knowing?'

'No.' I shook my head more forcefully than I'd intended. 'Not in the least. I've drawn a line, Ralph. I've got a life to lead. I have to get on.' I paused, wanting to soften what I'd said. 'Your friend the vicar was right. Knowing why isn't important. Knowing how doesn't matter. It's being thankful, being able to celebrate the best bits, that counts.'

'And you can do that?'

I looked him in the eye.

'Not at the moment,' I said. 'But one day I might.'

He nodded in sympathy, giving me the chance to explain further, and when I didn't he ducked his head and reached for the menu. Driving across, I'd promised myself I wouldn't burden him any further with the wreckage of my private life. What had happened over in Jersey was for me to sort out.

'Your American chap, Meyler.' Ralph had his finger anchored halfway down the list of starters. 'Fascinating man.'

The word 'your' threw me for a moment. What had Harald been telling him?

'He's been a good friend,' I said carefully. 'I owe him a lot.'

'I'm sure. He was quizzing me about my little project, you know, the research. Wanted to know how far I'd got. I told him what I could, of course. He was really interested, knowledgeable too. He seems to have the aircraft pretty well taped.'

I explained about Harald's passion for our Mustang. Ever since he'd first set eyes on it, way back when Dave Jeffries was still doing the rebuild, it seemed to have held a special fascination for him.

'That's what he was telling me, just exactly that. Seems he's got a couple back home.'

'Yes, and a squadron or two of other stuff.' I ran through the warbirds in Harald's private air force. Ralph couldn't hide his admiration.

'Rich man,' he murmured when I'd finished. 'Has to be.'

I drew the line at passing on Dennis Wetherall's gossip about the sources of Harald's fortune. It was enough, as far as Old Glory was concerned, that Harald had returned us to solvency. I told Ralph about the latest surprise, Harald's offer of thirty-five-plus hours at the controls of a Mustang.

'Thirty-five? That's serious flying, my dear. With thirty-five hours, you'd have been in a front-line squadron. Probably have had time to win a medal or two.'

'Yes, or die.'

'Quite. But with your talents? I rather doubt it.'

I grinned at him. Only yesterday I'd been on the phone to one of the pilots I intended to use for Old Glory during the summer. He'd been a good friend of Adam's. He flew commercial 747s for a living but spent summer weekends displaying Spitfires, Mustangs and Lightnings on the airshow circuit. I'd mentioned Harald's offer in passing and he – like Ralph – had been impressed. With little more than thirty-five hours, under CAA regulations, I could be checked out on simple manoeuvres. That meant not only fly-pasts but also a modest repertoire of aerobatics. The thought of doing loops and upward rolls in our Mustang in front of a paying crowd filled me with a very special kind of glee, though I'd laughed when he'd suggested I might even get as far as formation flying.

'You can join us at the Fighter Meet,' he'd joked. 'Fly as my number two.'

Now, Ralph indulged me even further.

'He's right,' he said. 'A woman in a man's world, it'd be a tremendous attraction.'

I reminded him about the women who'd ferried aircraft around during the war. Not only single-seat fighters but big four-engined bombers like the Lancaster and the Halifax. Wasn't it logical that a woman could be at the controls? Didn't flying demand sensitivity, and judgement, and all those other female virtues? Wasn't it a very male delusion that only blokes could fly high-performance warbirds?

Ralph wasn't having it.

'That's not the point,' he insisted. 'Of course women make wonderful pilots. Of course they can handle planes every bit as well as men. But it simply doesn't happen. Not to the extent it should.' He covered my hand with his. 'All I'm saying, my dear, is good luck. You'll be a natural, I know you will.'

Later, over the most delicious Dover sole I think I've ever tasted, Ralph talked me through his latest progress on the book. His conversation with Harald after the memorial service had obviously fired him up because he'd phoned his contact in the German archives in Berlin and asked her to chivvy up the search for the identity of Karl Brokenka's downed Me109 pilot. The Berlin people, he said, were as bogged down in paperwork as all the other folk he'd had to deal with, and while he sympathised with the pressures they were under, Harald had been right to point out the importance of imposing some kind of deadline. The longer the book was delayed, the greater the risk that another season would slip by. More sales lost. More veterans leaving Mapledurcombe empty-handed.

I coaxed the last sliver of flesh on to my fork.

'Is this German that important?' I wondered.

'That's exactly what your friend said, Harald. I must say I'm beginning to agree with him, though now we've got the photo, it would be nice to have a name to go with it.'

'Photo?' I reached for my napkin.

'Didn't I tell you? It's the one of the Me109 going down. The one from Karel's camera gun.'

'You've got a *photo*?'

'Yes, my dear. I thought I'd told you. It arrived a couple of days ago. Didn't Jamie mention it?'

I shook my head. Since our afternoon at the pub, Jamie and I had seen very little of each other, partly – I think – because he was embarrassed. Across the table, Ralph was folding his own napkin. I could see the excitement in his eyes.

'Just pop home with me before you go back,' he said. 'I'll show it to you.'

After dessert and coffee we drove back in convoy to Ralph's bungalow. It was another glorious day and I opened his french windows and breathed in the scents from the garden while he rummaged through his growing pile of research material. The photo, when he finally laid hands on it, was a slight disappointment, a small black-and-white shot, badly out of focus. In the upper half of the frame was the familiar silhouette of a Messerschmidt 109. Smoke was feathering back across the half-open cockpit canopy and part of the tailplane had been shot away. Beneath the aircraft was a small black blob. On close inspection I suppose it might have been the pilot but I wasn't sure that giving him a name would make that much difference.

Ralph was waiting for a reaction. The last thing I wanted to do was let him down.

'It's great,' I said. 'The real thing.'

'Exactly.' He reached for the photo. 'So maybe we ought to wait just a little bit longer. The woman at Berlin thought it was only a matter of time. Mind you, that's what she said before.'

He studied the photo again. He seemed to treat it with extraordinary respect and I wondered just how much difference his own war experience made. To me, it was a blur. To Ralph, without question, it was flesh and blood.

He looked up at me, struck by another thought.

'Good Lord,' he said. 'We havn't talked about young Jamie. All this time, I've been meaning to bring it up. See what you do to me?'

I grinned at him. I had his cheque for £5,000 in my pocket. I gave it to him.

'This is yours. Jamie mentioned the flying. I'd be delighted to teach him what I can. But only on one condition.'

'What's that?'

'I pay for it. You've been more than kind. It's the least Old Glory owes you, all that research you've done.'

'Nonsense.' He thrust the cheque back at me. 'Flying costs a fortune, even in that old Moth of yours. Here. Take it.'

We tussled over the cheque for a minute or so. I told him we were paying Jamie a pittance and that the flying lessons would help make up. At length, I suggested that he give the money to Jamie and – to my slight surprise – he agreed.

'He's had a tough time,' he sighed. 'I gather he may have told you.'

'He did.' I nodded. 'It must have been ghastly.'

'Yes, well . . .' Ralph looked away, '. . . it certainly wasn't a picnic.' He walked stiffly to the open french windows and gazed out, his hands clasped behind his back. 'Jamie thinks the world of you,' he said quietly. 'As you've probably realised.'

'We get on fine,' I said lightly. 'He's a terrific lad. God knows what we'd do without him.'

'Yes.' Ralph's back was still turned to me. 'But as I say, he's certainly been through it. Be gentle with him, eh? I'd hate to see him hurt again.'

I stared at him for a moment, not knowing quite how to take what he'd said, then he turned round, a bright smile on his face. The time had come to change the subject. He'd said what he wanted to say and it was obviously up to me to make what I would of it.

He went across to the desk and began to scribble on a pad. Then he tore off the sheet of paper and gave it to me.

'Karel Brokenka's address,' he explained. 'He lives near Chicago.' I looked at the address. Shoreview, 2312 Lakeside Drive. The bewilderment must have shown on my face. I heard Ralph chuckling. 'Your friend Harald asked for it.' He began to shepherd me towards the door. 'I told him you'd take it over.'

A couple of days later, a Sunday, I gave Jamie his first lesson. I suspect I should have started with a big fat wedge of theory, classroom stuff about centres of gravity, and angles of attack, and the theory of lift, but Adam hadn't tackled it that way and neither did I. In any case, the weather was still perfect – a huge high-pressure zone anchored over the south of England – and it seemed a shame to waste it.

I met Jamie at the airfield. He was already there when I arrived, sitting outside the Touchdown Café, sipping from a can of Seven-Up. He'd brought a pullover and a quilted, heavy-duty anorak for the Moth's open cockpit, and as we walked across to the hangar where I stabled our three planes, he quizzed me about what, exactly, we'd be doing. In my mind, I'd drawn up the simplest of plans – a walk-round the aircraft, a pretty thorough session with the controls, a couple of take-offs and landings, followed by a full lap of the island, flying just off the coast. In all, I guessed it would fill the best part of two hours, and if my own experience was any guide it would certainly tell us both whether Jamie was in any serious danger of becoming a pilot.

He helped me get the Moth out of the hangar, surprised – as everyone is – by how easy it is to push. I talked him around the aircraft, explaining the way that the elevators and the ailerons controlled pitch and bank and how you could kick the aircraft sideways with the rudder. Beyond that, to be frank, the Moth doesn't ask too many questions. At the sharp end, there's an engine. In the middle, a couple of seats. Do the right things in the right order, and the bird should fly.

'That easy?' He was grinning at me, plainly excited.

'Absolutely.' I grinned back. 'Piece of cake.'

After I'd fuelled up, we bumped to the far end of the runway and paused at the holding point while I did my engine checks. I was in the rear cockpit and I could see Jamie's head in front of me. I'd lent him Adam's leather helmet with the built-in earphones and he was wearing Adam's yellow silk scarf as well because he'd forgotten to bring one of his own, and as I pushed the throttle forward I saw Adam's scarf twitching in the backwash from the prop. Jamie, as it happens, has the same build as Adam and I stared at the back of his head for several seconds, half-convinced I was flying with a ghost.

I got clearance for take-off and turned on to the grass strip. This was the first time I'd flown from Sandown since my outing with Harald in the Mustang and the feeling couldn't have been more different. Being in the Moth was second nature to me. It was so familiar, it was almost part of the family. We had no secrets from each other. Whatever happened, we'd cope. In the Mustang, on the other hand, I'd been apprehensive to the point of real fear. Anything could have gone wrong. And without Harald in the back I'd have been helpless.

I shared the thought with Jamie while we waited for a car to clear the road at the far end of the strip. I'd shown him the Mustang in the hangar and I'd seen the impression it had made on him. At the time, I hadn't mentioned Sunday's little outing. Now it dawned on him that I'd actually flown the thing.

'Hands-on?' he queried. 'You did the take-off?'

'Take-off, climb-out, straight and level, one practice landing, the whole caboodle.' I didn't mention the fact that I'd landed on a cloud. It sounded far too ladylike.

'And what was it like?'

'The Mustang?' I grinned. 'Terrifying. And brilliant.'

I heard him laughing in the front. Like Adam, and I suppose like me, he obviously loved the way the two words sat so naturally together. Without fear, as Adam used to say, there's no fulfilment. Without really crapping yourself, you'll never make it to the stars.

The car had gone now and I started the take-off run. In this kind of wind – barely a couple of knots – I could gauge the lift-off practically to the metre, and we were airborne halfway down the strip. The Moth yawed for a second or two before I kicked it straight, then we were climbing over the road and the rows of shimmering polytunnels in the field beyond as I banked gently to the right. At 1,500 feet, I levelled off, easing the throttle back to 1,950 r.p.m. In the cruise, the Moth will clatter along at eighty m.p.h. Already, we could see St Lawrence, tucked between the undercliff and the sea.

Jamie was peering over the edge of the cockpit combing.

'I thought we were doing circuits?'

'Change of plan.'

'Is that allowed?'

'Of course it is. Why fly otherwise?'

In fact, the tower had already alerted me to conflicting traffic and it seemed saner to get away from the airfield. All the same, I'd meant what I'd said. Flying, for me, had always been a release and there was absolutely no reason, I told myself, why it shouldn't work the same magic on Jamie.

Beyond St Catherine's, the southernmost point of the island, I brought the Moth on to a north-westerly course, parallel to the coast. Below us, two thousand feet of clear airspace. Ahead, the long, low stretch of beach adjoining the Military Road, and then the soaring chalk cliffs of Tennyson Down and the bared white teeth of the Needles beyond.

'You have control,' I said. 'Fly north-west. That's three one five on the compass.'

Jamie grunted an acknowledgement. I felt the tiniest lurch as his hand found the control stick, then we were flying as before, straight and level, the drumming of the engine muffling the rush of the wind past the open cockpit. For a while I kept checking the instruments, monitoring Jamie's progress, making sure he kept to the heading, then – muscle by muscle – I began to relax.

Ralph's boy – I'd begun to think of him as Ralph's boy – flew beautifully. From time to time I'd give him a change of course – twenty degrees here, thirty degrees there – and he'd ease the aircraft around while I watched the needle on the compass settle on the new heading. Very rarely did he lose any altitude, and when he did he'd win it back again without any prompting from me. He had lovely hands, perfect manners. There was no drama, no fuss, just the lightest of touches on the control stick, the deftest of inputs on the rudder pedals. By the time we'd completed our first lap of the island, I was practically asleep.

'This is novel,' I told him.

'What?'

'Being a passenger in my own plane.'

Later, after a brief excursion over the Solent and into Portsmouth Harbour, I took control again. We were heading towards the island. I could see the long wooden finger of Ryde Pier on the starboard quarter. I began to climb.

'You fancy some aerobatics?'

There was a chuckle in my earphones. Ralph again.

'Is that a serious question?'

We played for the best part of half an hour. Loops. Stall turns.

Barrel rolls. Half-rolls off the top of a loop. And finally a long inverted glide that sent the blood pounding through my head. Rolling level again I checked to see that Jamie was in one piece. Not once had he protested, or yelped, or given any indication that life was anything but normal, and deep in my heart I think I was just a little bit disappointed. I wanted to impress him. I wanted to show him what I could do.

'You OK?'

'No problem.'

'Enjoy it?'

'Loved it.'

Back at the airfield, we did a couple of touch-and-goes, one final circuit, and then a landing. On the landing, I gave Jamie control until we were slipping over the perimeter fence with less than fifty feet to go. At this point, for the first time, he got into a muddle with the rudder and we began to yaw away from the landing line. Hearing me on the intercom, he surrendered control with a regretful sigh and we were down in one piece seconds later.

Neither of us spoke as we taxied back to the hangar. After I'd turned the aircraft into the wind and cut the engine, I helped Jamie out of the front cockpit. He looked like a child again, full tummy, soft eyes.

'That thing we did on one of the touch-and-goes . . .'

'Sideslipping?'

'Yes.' He shook his head in wonderment. 'Incredible.'

Sideslipping is one of the tricks you use to lose height in the final turn before landing. First time round it can be an alarming feeling, the aircraft slipping sideways out of the sky.

'You liked that?'

'Loved it.' He took my outstretched hand. 'More, please.'

Chapter ten

Jamie had his way. For most of the following three weeks, to Andrea's intense annoyance, we went up in the Moth while I piled lesson on lesson.

We did endless flying in the circuit at Sandown, crosswind legs, downwind legs, base legs, finals. We did high approaches, low approaches, and glide approaches with the engine throttled back. We practised crosswind landings, soft-field landings, and landings that were so laden with problems that they barely qualified as landings at all.

We did overshoots and touch-and-goes. We did steep climbing turns, steep descending turns and recoveries from a spiral dive. We practised engine failures, mid-air restarts and bits and pieces of elementary navigation. Jamie was as comfortable with reciprocal courses and the problems of magnetic variation as he was with practically everything else I could throw at him. He read maps as if he'd been doing it all his life. The allowances he made for track error and lateral drift were seldom more than a mile or so out. Yet with each successive flight, it became more and more obvious to both of us that the direction we'd taken wasn't simply a matter of pre-flight planning and headings on the compass.

One day we set out for Wales, stopping for lunch and half a tank of fuel at a tiny airfield in North Dorset. The weather, miraculously, was still holding and we sat in the sunshine outside a rusting 1940s Nissen hut, peeling the shells off freshly cooked prawns and dipping them into an open jar of mayonnaise. It was a moment of time I'll treasure forever, untainted by anything more complicated than agreeing that life, for both of us, was wonderful. The cherry trees beyond the tumbledown control tower were in full bloom. The wind tasted of early summer. We barely needed to talk. Just being there was enough.

Jamie was high on flying. I was stratospheric on something even simpler. I didn't give it a name then, and even now, looking back, I'm still stuck for the right word. Was I falling in love with him? Yes, I think I probably was. Did I ever stop to wonder where that might lead? No, I don't think I did. For the first time since Adam's death – six weeks? ten years? several aeons of geological time? – I'd stopped thinking about the wreckage he'd left behind. Jamie, whether he knew it or not, had released me, and for that I was more glad and more grateful than he could possibly have known.

At the end of that third week, I found Andrea waiting for me back at Mapledurcombe. Relations had sunk to an all-time low. In fact we were barely talking.

She was sitting in Adam's study. She nodded at the phone.

'Harald,' she muttered.

'What about him?'

'He's in Jersey. He wants to come over. Says he needs to talk about the States.'

'When?'

'Tomorrow.'

Tomorrow was Sunday. Jersey was just over an hour in the Moth. Good practice, I thought. Excellent chance to put Jamie's navigation to the test.

'Fine.' I smiled at Andrea. 'I'll tell him I'll pop over. Save him the trip.'

Next day there were signs that the weather was about to break. A nasty wind had blown up and high cloud was streaming in from the south-west. I'd met Jamie at the airfield. I was on the point of cancelling the trip but a couple of minutes on the phone to the Met people persuaded me to change my mind. The weather was indeed expected to worsen but nothing dramatic was predicted until early evening.

'Don't look so disappointed,' I told Jamie as I replaced the pay phone. 'As long as we're back by four it'll be fine.'

Jamie handled the take-off and flew the Moth on the way across. He had a map flattened on his knee, and after we'd passed Alderney and Sark on the starboard beam, Jersey came up bang on the nose. I gave him a round of applause and told him to talk to the tower on the way in. Jersey is a busy commercial airport and the workload was much heavier than we'd been used to. We had a British Midland jet five minutes behind us, and this was very definitely one landing we couldn't afford to get wrong. The Moth is designed to land on grass, and putting her down on a hardened runway can be a pain. Just the grinding of the tail skid is enough to put most pilots off.

I was on the point of taking control when Jamie came through on the intercom.

'Do you mind?' he said.

'Mind what?'

'Me doing the landing.'

I could see Jersey airport down to the side of us. The wind was perfect, if a little blustery, straight down the runway. We were on the point of calling finals. This was no time for indecision.

'You think you can handle it?'

'Yes.'

That one word was typical. It was what Adam would have said. What Harald would have said. Maybe, even, what I would have said. It meant that Jamie had self-belief. It meant that he could hack it. No wonder he was going to make such a good pilot.

'OK,' I said. 'Go for it.'

He turned on to base leg. We were slightly high and he began to sideslip, shedding altitude. Unlike the big jets, we didn't need to hit the glidepath miles out and we were already over the perimeter fence when he levelled the aircraft and hauled back on the trim wheel. The flare-out was perfect. The Moth settled on to the centre-line, the slightest bump as the main undercarriage made contact, then a metallic tearing noise as the tail skid grounded.

For the first time, Jamie let out a whoop.

'How about that?' he yelled.

I gave myself a moment to unwind.

'Terrifying,' I told him, 'but brilliant.'

Harald was waiting for me inside the Aero Club. At first I don't think he realised that Jamie and I had flown over together because after he'd kissed me and asked how I'd been, he just gave Jamie a long, blank look as if he was passing through.

'Jamie Pierson. You two met at Mapledurcombe.'

Slowly Harald put the name to the face.

'You came over on the bike?'

'That's right.'

'With a little diecast model? In a Jiffy bag?'

'Yes. That was my grandfather's idea. Ralph.'

'Ralph. Yes, of course, dumb of me.' He shook Jamie briefly by the hand. I told him about Jamie's landing. Jamie looked delighted. 'You landed the Moth? Just now?' Harald was frowning.

'Yep. And flew over.'

'And you're happy about the weather?' Harald was talking to me. 'You're expecting to turn right around and go back home?'

I was looking out of the window. The cloud base was much lower now and the last of the sunshine – livid and sinister – had gone. I began to tell him about the Met people I'd phoned from Sandown. Three o'clock was my deadline. As long as I was back by then, we'd outrun the forecast storm.

I stole a look at my watch. Harald extended a hand, covering it.

'You're kidding,' he said. 'We need to talk. By the time we're through, you'll be weathered in.'

'How long do we need?'

'An hour minimum.' He nodded at the window. 'Believe me, Ellie, even now it's fifty-fifty.'

I could feel the pressure of his hand. As gently as I could, I retrieved my wrist. Then Jamie touched me lightly on the arm.

'He's right. Look.'

I looked. Rain was dimpling the big plate-glass windows.

'OK?' Harald put a patient, slightly fatherly arm around my shoulders. 'Believe me now?'

After I'd hangared the Moth, we drove across to St Helier in Harald's hired Mercedes. Harald was staying in the hotel where he'd taken me before, and in daylight the setting was even more impressive. As we walked from the car to the gabled entrance, I paused to admire the peacocks on the lawn. I turned to point them out to Jamie. Typically, he only had eyes for the trees.

'Wonderful.' He shook his head. 'Just look at that cedar.'

Harald was a couple of paces ahead of us. It was still spotting with rain and he was impatient to get into the hotel. Hearing our voices, his footsteps faltered a moment, then he changed his mind and disappeared through the big panelled front door without a backward glance.

Jamie and I exchanged looks. We felt like kids, both of us, and Jamie mimed a slap on the wrist. In practical terms, he was just as businesslike and focused as Harald, but the older man's brusqueness, his refusal to waste time on the smaller pleasures of life, was lost on him. One of the delights of being with Jamie was his sense of humour. We laughed at the same things, the same little absurdities, and it was already obvious that Harald, in some indefinable way, construed this kinship as a threat.

He was waiting for us in the lobby. His suite was on the first floor, an expanse of heavy oriental carpet dotted with exquisite antique furniture. Jamie and I sat side by side on a beautifully preserved Regency sofa. The low table in front of us was covered in maps. Even upside down I recognised the long, gangly shape of Florida.

'Here's where we start.' Harald beckoned me closer. 'You'll be flying into Orlando. I'll pick you up there. The field's down here.

We've got thirteen hundred metres in three directions. Most days, this time of year, we're flying dawn till dusk.'

I got off the sofa and knelt on the carpet beside Harald. His finger was indicating an area inland from the Gulf coast. I squinted at the name of the nearest city. Fort Myers.

'This is your airfield?'

'Yes.'

'And your planes are there?'

'Most of them, sure. The dual Mustang will be coming from a field up in North Carolina. Guy owes me several favours.'

I nodded, aware of Jamie's interest in our conversation. To date, I'd said nothing about Harald's plans beyond his determination to turn me into a fighter jock. This was the first time, I think, that it had dawned on Jamie that his own flying lessons might be in for some kind of intermission.

'Dates.' Harald had produced a diary. 'We're mid-April right now. The weather over there's looking pretty good. I've got a clear run until early June. Lady at the travel agency I use has a Delta reservation out of Heathrow on Wednesday. How does that sound?'

'*This* Wednesday?'

'Sure.'

I stole a look at Jamie. He was clenching and unclenching his left hand, as if he had cramp, something I'd seen him do a couple of times before. It signalled impatience, even anger.

Harald was still waiting for a decision. I summoned a smile and said I'd have to check with Andrea. I couldn't just walk out. Not at a couple of days' notice. Not without talking to her first.

'But we've discussed it,' I added quickly, 'and in principle it's fine. She can cope.'

'I know. We talked already.'

'Talked about coping?'

'Talked about Wednesday. There isn't a problem. She'll be driving you to the airport.'

'Fine,' I said evenly. 'And does she have my bags packed?'

Harald was still on the floor beside me. He could hear the irritation in my voice, the feeling that once again – uninvited – he'd stepped into my life and determined the way things would be, and when he patted me on the shoulder, and told me to relax, I got to my feet and rejoined Jamie on the sofa. Being rude to someone who's about to present you with thirty-five hours in a Mustang isn't something I do readily, but Harald had swamped me – on this occasion – once too often.

'I'll phone you,' I said. 'Until then, I suggest you hang on to the reservation.'

Harald looked across at Jamie and winked. The wink, to my intense annoyance, said it all. Neurotic woman. Can't read a calendar. Can't make her mind up. Can't, godammit, even get the weather right.

I stood up, smoothing the wrinkles out of my flying suit. Jamie was looking startled.

'Do you have a bathroom?' I enquired. 'Only I'd like a little wash before we head back.'

We didn't, of course, leave. The rain was already lashing at the mullioned windows and there was absolutely no question of getting the Moth airborne, let alone finding our way back across the Channel. Instead, at Harald's insistence, we folded up the maps and trooped downstairs for tea.

Over scones and clotted cream, Harald was infinitely better behaved, filling me in with details about the kind of schedule he'd planned with the Mustang, baiting each successive week with some new enticement. How I'd learn to cope with abrupt or radical stall departures. How I'd be able to interpret the merest tremor in the airframe. How I'd be flying deeper and deeper into the very corners of the Mustang's performance envelope and be able to come out with a smile on my face.

'You fight like you train.' Harald was talking to Jamie. 'You ever hear that?' Jamie said he hadn't. Harald shook his head. 'Too bad. It's what the old-time fighter pilots used to say. Stretch yourself and stretch the airplane. Do it till it's second nature. Do it until you're *wearing* the goddamn ship. Then, when it matters, it'll look after you. Hey . . .' he leaned forward, '. . . I'll give you an example. Peacetime. Not wartime.' He looked in my direction, gesturing me closer to the table, holding both hands flat, palms down over the china pots of strawberry jam. 'You're flying some display with your wingman. You both lay down one of those dazzling airshow strafing passes. Then you want to bring her around in a pretty big hurry so you pull hard in the break and there's just a flicker of airframe buffet and then – wham – you're snap inverted and everything's upside down because – hey – you're pointing at the ground. Well?' He sat back and favoured me with one of his rare smiles. 'What do you do?'

Jamie was open-mouthed. I shook my head and said I didn't know. I was still staring at his hands as he went through the manoeuvre again, determined to milk the story of the last drop of tension. Where had I seen this body language before? The hands? The smile? The face tilted up in triumph as the Mustang plunged earthwards?

'Pass,' I said for a second time when he asked me what I'd do. 'Just listening to you terrifies me.'

'But that's the point, Ellie, that's the point exactly. It needn't terrify you. Not if you do it the way I'll be showing you. Not if you *train* right.'

I nodded, only half-hearing him, sitting back in my chair while he went through some other manoeuvre with Jamie, weaving his hands left and right, posing fresh problems for himself and his wingman. The image had come back to me now, the memory of where I'd seen these gestures before.

It had been at Ralph's place, the night he'd shown me the photos of Karel Brokenka, the Czech pilot who'd downed the Me109. Brokenka had been standing on the tarmac beside his Mustang, newly returned from some sortie or other, and he'd been telling the story precisely the same way, hands outstretched, one flattened palm chasing the other.

Now I looked at Harald afresh, wondering for the first time exactly how far his flying experience extended. As a businessman, according to Dennis Wetherall, he kept dangerous company. Arms-dealers, I assumed, could scarcely do otherwise. But what if Harald was infinitely more hands-on than even Dennis had imagined? What if he'd been up there, at the cutting edge, doing what Ralph had done? What Karel Brokenka had done? What if all this hot flying wasn't entirely for the benefit of umpteen thousand punters at some Florida airshow? What then?

In truth, I didn't know the answer, and there was no way I was going to find out over tea and scones, but the question continued to haunt me and the more I listened to Harald impressing Jamie with his Mustang stories, the more I remembered Ralph musing about what it took to become a top-scoring fighter ace.

These men were ruthless, he'd said, and even a little mad. They suffered tunnel vision. They thought of nothing but the next kill. It wasn't a question of flesh and blood, of inflicting anything as mundane as pain. It was just an overwhelming determination to engage your opponent, to out-fly him, and out-turn him, and out-dive him, and then come in so close, so tight, so intimate, that there was absolutely no possibility of squeezing the trigger and missing. What happened next – whether he lived or died, got horribly burned or survived intact – was of absolutely no consequence. The point of that glorious moment was getting back, and shedding the parachute harness, and standing beside your aeroplane while your buddies gathered round and you extended each hand, explaining – second by second – exactly the way it had been. Another kill. Another downed Me109 to join the little frieze of swastikas below the cockpit hood.

Impressive? Compelling? Brave? I didn't know. But listening to Harald, that stormy afternoon in the hotel outside St Helier, I recognised all too clearly the authentic voice of the real Mustang pilots and for the first time the thought of the aircraft – its shape, its sound, its silhouette – froze my blood. Not, after all, a plaything, a pretty relic of some half-forgotten war, but a killing machine, a predator, as effective now as the day Karel Brokenka bloodied her. Last year, some time, Adam had taped a warning to himself on the dashboard in the front cockpit. The warning read PERMISSIBLE LIMITS. Was this what he'd meant? Had he, like me, listened to Harald Meyler?

I tried to explore these thoughts with Jamie in the taxi back to the airport but, unusually, he didn't seem in the mood to listen. He was sitting in the front alongside the driver and when I leaned forward, telling him about the photos Ralph had shown me, he simply nodded, staring out through the blurry windscreen. The weather, if anything, had got worse, and the wind was lashing at the stands of elm and oak beside the road. On the phone, from the hotel, I'd booked a couple of seats on the early-evening Air UK flight back to Southampton, accepting Harald's offer to return the Moth when the weather cheered up, but now I was beginning to wonder whether even the big turbo-prop would be able to cope.

When we got to the airport, it turned out I was right. There was a small crowd of passengers around the Air UK desk. Most of them looked relieved.

'Delayed or cancelled?' I asked the ticketing girl.

'Delayed for now,' she said. 'But to be honest I think you've had it. The next three or four hours are going to be awful and tomorrow's not looking much better.'

I glanced at Jamie. He hadn't been listening.

'We're marooned,' I told him. 'Harald was right. We should have stayed at home.'

The girl behind the desk had some accommodation vouchers. The airline had a discount deal with a nearby hotel and we were welcome to take advantage of it. When I asked Jamie what he wanted to do, he shrugged.

'Looks like we're stuck,' he muttered.

I agreed there was no option. While the girl hunted for the vouchers, Jamie wandered off.

'You're lucky.' The girl had found the last of the vouchers. 'We've had a bit of a run.'

'Should I phone up? Make sure they've got a room?'

'Good idea.' She glanced at my ticket and made a note of my name. 'They do good seafood. Lovely mussels.'

I phoned from a call box across from the ticketing desk. When I got through to the hotel, the receptionist had one room left.

'It's a twin,' she said. 'En suite.'

I was watching Jamie. He was standing in the airport bookshop, thumbing his way through a cycling magazine. There was something about him that told me he'd speared in. The smile had gone. The spark. When he looked up and caught my eye across the concourse he ducked his head again, as if he didn't want the attention.

The receptionist was asking for a decision about the room. She had some more calls waiting.

'I'll take it,' I said. 'Expect us in a couple of hours.'

We took another taxi and let the driver drop us at a pub he'd recommended. It was nearly seven o'clock. The pub was empty, a dispiriting roadhouse with appalling décor that must have been run by the taxi-driver's brother. Jamie drank Guinness. I had a glass of lukewarm white wine. We shared a couple of packets of crisps, not saying very much. At length I reached for a beer mat and slipped it gently over the top of Jamie's pint. The last month or so had earned me the right to be candid.

'What's the matter?' I asked him. 'Tell me.'

Jamie's a tall lad, well over six foot, but the last couple of hours seemed to have physically diminished him. He was almost slumped over his Guinness. He didn't look up.

'Nothing,' he muttered.

'Come on. There is. I can tell.'

Jamie shook his head. Whatever had upset him, whatever had happened, he was in no mood to talk about it.

'Hey.' I grinned at him, a gesture of solidarity. We were buddies, partners in a wild adventure. I'd already told him how well he'd done on the way over, but even this hadn't lifted his spirits. Now I tried again. 'It was a wonderful landing,' I told him for the umpteenth time. 'The Moth's a swine on hardened runways.'

'I was lucky,' he grunted. 'Any other day I'd have messed it up.'

'Why do you say that?'

'I dunno.' he shrugged. 'It just felt right, that's all.'

'This morning?'

'Yes.' He began to stir, a flicker of the old Jamie. 'I was really looking forward to the flight back. Next week. All that.'

He sat back on the banquette, looking me in the eye, the rest of it unsaid. This morning, back at Sandown, we'd mapped out the next steps in his flying education. Soon, if he was to head for a Private Pilot's Licence, I'd have to hand him over to a qualified instructor. Before that, though, I wanted to see him take the Moth up by himself. Wednesday happened to be the day we'd ringed for his first solo flight. Now, thanks to Harald, Wednesday was off.

'It's Florida, isn't it? Me doing my thing?'

'No.' He shook his head again. 'Not at all.'

'You don't mind?'

'How can I? You said it yourself. It's the chance of a lifetime. Thirty-five hours in someone else's Mustang? You'd be daft to turn it down.'

'So it's not a problem?'

'Not Florida, no. Not the Mustang, either.'

One of the things I loved about Jamie wasn't simply his honesty but the gift he had for softening the more brutal truths. Now he could scarcely have been more direct, yet even so he was leaving it to me to draw the obvious conclusion.

'It's Harald? You're upset about Harald?'

'Yes.'

'Why?'

'*Why?*' His face twisted into what might have been a smile. 'Why am I pissed off that you're spending six weeks with another man? Why am I pissed off that he's wealthy? And unattached? And owns half the warbirds in the world? Why am I pissed off that he obviously fancies you? Can't wait to get you out there? And why, most of all, am I pissed off that I haven't got any rights here? Not one?'

Jamie very rarely made speeches. I fought the temptation to applaud.

'Rights?' Deep down I felt immensely pleased. 'I don't understand.'

'No, you don't. And the really sick thing is I haven't even got the right to explain.'

I leaned forward over the table. I'd mistaken anger for something else, something far gentler, and I'd got it badly wrong. Jamie was seriously upset.

'Why not try?' I suggested. 'Why not try and explain?'

I touched him lightly on the hand. He withdrew it at once, an instinctive reflex action, as if I'd scalded him.

'Don't,' he said. 'Please.'

'I'm sorry. I was only –'

'It doesn't matter.' He tipped the beer mat off the Guinness and took a long, deep pull, avoiding my eyes. Ralph, I thought. His murmured plea when we'd been talking a week or so back. Be gentle with the boy. Don't add to the hurt.

'For the record,' I said quietly, 'there's nothing between Harald and me. We're good friends. He's been more than kind. Without him, I'd have been in a terrible mess. But that's where it ends. He knows it and I know it.'

'I don't believe you.'

'It's true. He's fifty-five, Jamie. At that age you get wiser. You accept things. You know what's possible and what's not.'

'And you really think that applies to him?'

'I know it does.'

'Then you're mad. He's all over you. I can see it. You just have to be there. You just have to watch.'

A shudder ran through him, a sense of deep physical revulsion, and I began to wonder whether booking the hotel room was such a great idea. I'd done it on the spur of the moment. It had been impulsive, and a bit naughty, and altogether in keeping with the way our relationship had developed. Quite what would happen, I didn't know, but we were good friends, good mates, and wherever the evening led, I couldn't foresee a moment's regret. I was older than him, quite a lot older, but the age difference had never mattered. Until now.

'You're jealous,' I said, 'and you needn't be.'

'Why not?'

I didn't answer him. His glass was nearly empty. I went to the bar and ordered refills for both of us, carrying the drinks back to the table.

'This hotel I mentioned,' I murmured. 'There's only one room left.'

'And it's a double?'

'A twin.'

'Same thing, isn't it?'

'Yes.' I looked up at him. 'It's all they had. There wasn't a choice.'

'You're telling me there aren't other hotels in Jersey?'

'No, of course not.' Chastened, it was my turn to duck my head. Neither of us said anything for a while. Then I felt the lightest pressure on my arm. Jamie was looking at me. He might even have been smiling.

'I think it's a great idea,' he said. 'I just hope I can handle it.'

'It?'

'Everything else. Florida. Your rich friend. Six bloody weeks.'

I was gazing at him, trying to stay cool, trying to stay in command, trying to play the older woman, the instructress, when all the time I was flooded with something infinitely warmer. All of a sudden, with his smile, and his impulsiveness, and – yes – his vulnerability, Jamie had transformed an evening that was threatening to turn into a disaster. There was a protocol here, rules of engagement, and both of us knew it. Yet the sheer pace of the relationship, our headlong gallop towards each other, was the only thing that really mattered. It had been happening for a while. Smiles. Gestures. Touches. Laughter. Now, in this ghastly pub with its mock-Tudor beams and sticky table tops, we both knew that something profound had happened.

Jamie's big hand had tightened round mine. He'd pushed his Guinness to one side. I pretended to look at my watch.

'They do great seafood,' I murmured, 'if you're hungry.'

He stood up, tugging me after him. He was grinning now, the cloudbase abruptly lifted.

'Bugger the seafood,' he said.

The hotel had once been a farmhouse. Two long barns had been converted into accommodation and the work must have been recent, because the corridors smelt of drying cement and newly sawn timber. Jamie had the room key. The promised twin beds were marooned in an ocean of brand-new carpet.

I went across to the window. Outside there was a paved courtyard that served as a car park. I pulled the curtains. Behind me I could hear Jamie hauling out the bedside unit that separated the two divans.

I helped him push the beds together.

'You've done this before,' I said lightly. 'I can tell.'

Jamie glanced up at me.

'That's a long story,' he said. 'If you've ever got the time.'

I stood upright. My flying suit unzipped down the front. I felt absurdly happy.

'I've got all night.' I kissed him. 'Will that be long enough?'

We made love. It was clumsy and passionate and over far too quickly. Afterwards, the bedside light still on, Jamie hung over me, propped on one elbow. He had a lovely body, his belly taut, his chest dusted with freckles and little whorls of reddish hair. Already, I felt I'd slept with him forever. That intimate. That close.

'Tell me about Adam,' he whispered.

'There's nothing to tell.'

It was the truth. I was amazed.

'You mean that?'

'Yes.'

'No guilt?'

'About what?'

'About us. This.'

'None. Adam and I had a fabulous marriage.' I moistened a finger and ran it around Jamie's nipple. 'And now he's dead.'

'That simple?'

'Yes.'

'No regrets?'

'Don't be silly. I've got every regret. I lost the man I loved. And then he died.'

Jamie gave my answer some thought. Then he was back on one elbow, looking down at me.

'What do you mean? *And then he died?*'

I gazed up at him. Would there ever be a better time to tell him the truth about Adam? That he'd betrayed me? That he'd gone with someone else? Would it comfort Jamie to realise that he wasn't, after all, alone?

'Adam had been having an affair . . .' I began. 'It's something I've only recently found out about.'

I told him about the photo in the desk drawer, about the message on the back. I'd been over to Jersey, I'd talked to Steve Liddell, confronted Michelle.

'And what did she say?'

'She wouldn't talk about it.'

'But she admitted it?'

'No. Not exactly.'

'Then how do you know . . . ?'

Jamie waited for an answer. I was gazing up at the ceiling. How could I get across to him the shock of finding that photo? What other evidence would you ever need?

'It was in his desk drawer,' I repeated. 'Where he knew I'd never look. Are you telling me someone else put it there?'

'No, of course not.'

'Then what's the point of looking for some other explanation? He was having an affair, Jamie. Men do that. Even Adam. If you want the truth, it broke my heart.'

Jamie kissed me. His eyes were big and serious.

'And it's still broken?' he asked gently.

'I . . .' I caught his hand, and held it tight, '. . . don't know.'

'But is that why you're here? Light relief?'

'Don't be silly.'

'I mean it. I want to know.'

'Why?'

I struggled upright, my back against the bedhead. I knew this was a conversation we had to have, me as much as Jamie.

Jamie had draped the sheet around his waist.

'I'm in love with you,' he said quietly. 'You must have known that.'

I didn't answer. Andrea had said exactly the same thing, but I'd chosen to ignore it.

Jamie lay back, pulling a pillow towards him, closing his eyes and making himself comfortable. It was probably what he did every night before he slept, cushioning his head against the perils of the dark. I bent over him, tracing the lines of his face with my fingers, and I thought about what he'd said. Should I tell him how pleased I was? How flattered I was? How much of me had wanted him to say it? Or should I hang on to whatever was left of the old, wise, sensible me?

'Of course I knew,' I whispered at last. 'But knowing it and hearing it are different.'

'Do you mind me saying it?'

'No. Of course not.'

'And you?' One eye was open now. 'How do you feel?'

I hesitated. I knew exactly where we were. I'd been here twice in my life. Once when I was far too young to know what I was doing. And once with Adam. On both occasions, because I'd meant it, I'd cast caution to the winds.

'I love us.' I kissed him again. 'I love the way we are.'

'That's not an answer.'

'Yes it is.'

'No it's not. I asked if you love me. Not us, me.'

I looked down at him for a long moment. There was trust in his face, but there was need as well.

'Do you really think I'd be here if I didn't?' I asked him.

'Say it then.'

'Say what?'

'Tell me you love me.'

I smiled. Was it really that important? Did it really need putting into words? I bent to his ear.

'I love you,' I whispered.

'I love you, too.' He closed his eyes. 'The rest of it is shit.'

'What rest of it?'

'Harald. Florida. All that.'

I reached down for him and stroked his face.

'I'm still going,' I said.

'I know.'

'You don't mind?'

'Not as much. Not now.'

'But a little bit?'

'What do you think?'

He bit me lightly on the little fold of flesh around my hips and said that maybe – in some ways – it was good that I was going away.

'Why?'

'Because otherwise I'd be all over you. Every day.'

'Like Harald?'

'Sod Harald. You're right. Harald's an old man. No. Like this. Like now.'

'You're beautiful.' I kissed his eyelids. 'A beautiful man.'

Jamie didn't say anything. The way he held me, so close, so needful, he might have been a child. After a while, he began to tremble, a series of deep physical shivers. I reached down and pulled the blanket up around us. It made no difference.

'Jamie?' I bent over him, blowing softly on his face the way my mother used to when I was frightened or upset. 'You OK?'

Jamie gazed up at me for a long moment, a strange confessional look on his face.

'I loved you the moment I saw you. Am I allowed to say that?'

I smiled, trying to place exactly when that moment might have been.

'Ralph's? That day I popped down to St Lawrence?'

'Yes. I was going for a run. I ran for you. Every step of the way. I could hear your voice. We even talked.'

'About what?'

'This.'

'You're crazy.' I laughed. 'You didn't know me. You'd never met me. I could have been anyone. I could have been married.'

'You were married.'

'I know, but –'

Jamie was up on one elbow now, his voice low and urgent as if he had a message to deliver, and I realised that it didn't matter what I said. This was no longer a conversation.

'It's in your face.' He reached up for me. 'Your eyes. The way you laugh. The way you make us feel so . . .' he frowned, '. . . good.'

'Us?'

'My grandad. Me. Ralph mentioned you before. He used to talk about you on the phone. He thinks the world of you. You must know that.'

I smiled, touched, remembering the last time I'd been with Ralph. He'd used exactly the same phrase – *he thinks the world of you* – though he'd been referring to Jamie rather than me.

'He's a lovely man,' I said quietly. 'And the feeling's mutual.'

'But he's like me. Don't you see?'

I must have looked confused because Jamie came even closer. I could smell my own perfume on his breath.

'It's about trust,' he whispered. 'We trust you. You make us want to trust you. Don't you realise how important that is? How rare?'

It was hard not to smile. So young. So earnest.

'I know a great deal about trust,' I said. 'And I know what happens when you trust too much.'

'Of course you do.' He reached up and kissed me. 'I'm sorry.'

'Don't be. There's no need.'

'But I am. It must be horrible. Even if it's not true, it must be horrible. Having to live with the thought that . . . you know . . .' He broke off, shaking his head.

I lay back, watching a pair of headlights sweeping across the wall as a car drove into the courtyard below. After the engine died, there was silence.

'If you're talking about Adam, you're right,' I said at length. 'It's worse than losing him really, worse than someone phoning you up and telling you he's dead. Death's easy. You can blame fate, or bad luck, or a million other things, but doing what Adam did . . .' I closed my eyes and turned over in the bed, not wanting to take the thought any further.

After a while, I became aware of Jamie hanging over me. I didn't know quite what I'd had in mind when I'd booked the room, but a couple of hours seemed to have taken us a great deal further than either of us had expected and I wasn't altogether sure that I was keen on Jamie shouldering my burdens. That wasn't his role at all. He was the sunshine in my life. He made me laugh. He made me sing. He made me pleased to be me. He made me forget about Jersey and Steve Liddell and Michelle La Page and all the rest of it. So why did the conversation keep coming back to Adam?

I found Jamie's hand and gave it a squeeze, trying to share the thought. We were best mates. We had a fabulous relationship. He was the new start, the clean sheet, I'd so desperately needed. The last thing I wanted to do was turn the clock backwards.

'Clean sheet?'

I could tell by the tone of his voice that Jamie hated the phrase. Too late, I tried to substitute another.

'A challenge,' I murmured sleepily. 'The flying, watching you hack it. It's wonderful, brilliant, I can't tell you how –'

'And us?' He made no apology for butting in.

'Us? We're here. Isn't that enough?'

He caught my hand, fending me off.

'That's not what I meant. I love you. I care about you. I want you. Christ, if you only knew . . .'

'Knew what?'

He looked at me for a long time and then shook his head, and for that one split second the expression on his face told me everything. My chatter about clean sheets and new starts had touched a nerve. Like it or not, I'd just opened a brand-new chapter in Jamie's young life and the consequences for both of us weren't going to be something I could easily ignore. *Be gentle with him*, Ralph had said.

'Do you mind if I write to you?'

'When?'

'When you're in Florida. While you're over there.'

I saw the anxiety in Jamie's face. He wants to be sure of me, I thought. He wants to rope me down, make me responsible, make me *his*.

'You'll be rushed off your feet as soon as the season starts,' I said lightly. 'Then there's Andrea. Any spare moment, she'll be on your tail, out of the sun, dagga-dagga-dagga.' I mimed the rattle of cannon fire.

Jamie just looked at me. He wasn't smiling.

'There's stuff I need to tell you. Explain to you.'

'About what?'

'Me. The person I really am.'

'I know the kind of person you are.' I brought my hands up from under the sheet, tallying my little list of virtues. 'You're talented, and funny, and strong, and wonderful in bed. You're practical, and sensitive . . .' I ran out of compliments. 'What else could a girl want?'

'You think it ends there?'

'Of course it doesn't. No one ends there. I'm just telling you what I love about you . . . telling you the way I feel . . . What's the matter?'

Jamie had swung his legs out of bed. Sitting on the edge of the mattress, he had his back to me. I got up on one elbow, wondering what on earth had happened, what I'd said, why – so suddenly – the mood between us had changed.

'Jamie?'

I could see him shaking his head. For a moment, I thought he was crying but when he turned back towards me, his eyes were dry.

'This isn't a game,' he was staring at me, 'is it?'

'A *game*?'

'You know what I mean.' He gestured at the rumpled sheets. 'A casual fuck. Therapy. Whatever you want to call it.'

I shook my head, appalled. Then I got up and knelt behind him, my breasts against his back, my arms encircling him.

'Do I make you happy?' I whispered. 'Or was this a mistake?'

'*Mistake?* Christ, no, far from it.'

'OK.' I kissed the back of his neck. 'So tell me.'

'Tell you what?'

'Tell me whether I make you happy or not.'

'You make me very happy, incredibly happy, that's the problem.' His eyes were glistening. I'd been right about the tears. 'Past a certain point, I'm lost. I know it. I know the feeling, the way it happens. Past a certain point I just . . . cave in.'

'It's happened before?'

'Yes. Once.'

'And here? Now?'

'Lost' he mumbled, 'Completely lost.'

'And you think I'm playing games? You really think that?'

'No. No, you're not. Of course you're not. I just have to ask, tnat's all. I just have to be sure.'

He turned round again, imploring, and I tugged him gently back to bed. We lay together for a long time, cheek to cheek, belly to belly, not talking. I held him very close. I could feel his heartbeat against my flesh. After a while, it began to slow. I was on the point of reaching for the light when he slipped out of my arms and got up again.

I could hear him in the bathroom, running water into the wash basin. When he reappeared, he was wiping his face with a towel.

'Something's wrong' I said, 'Isn't it?'

He looked down at me, smiling.

'Nothing's wrong. As long as we both mean it.'

I thought about the proposition for a moment, then I sat up in bed and made myself comfortable. We'd never been less than candid with each other.

'Do you think this was a mistake?' I asked him for the second time. 'Only it was my idea, my doing. We could push the beds apart. Pretend it never happened.'

'Pick up tomorrow morning? Where we left off?'

It was a good question. Both of us knew that was impossible. It had happened. Most of it had been wonderful. But what next?

Jamie was sitting on the edge of the bed again, the towel laid over his lap. I gave him my hand and he stroked it softly. Twice he told me he loved me. Then he stood up and went to the window, letting the towel drop to the floor. He parted the curtains and looked down into the courtyard. It was still quite early and I said something grown-up about people getting funny about guests wandering around naked. Jamie didn't seem to have heard me. Something had caught his attention. Slowly, he closed the curtains again. Then he came back to bed.

'What's the matter?'

He just stared at me.

'How many other people know we're here?' he asked at last.

'No one.'

'Are you sure?'

'Absolutely sure. Why? Why do you ask?'

He gestured back towards the window.

'White Mercedes?' he queried. 'With a sunshine roof?'

For a moment I hadn't a clue what he was talking about. Then I remembered the drive from the airport to St Helier.

'Harald?'

Jamie nodded.

'Watching,' he said. 'From down there.'

I got out of bed. There was a big blue towel in the bathroom. I wrapped it round myself and pulled back the curtains, staring down. The courtyard was empty. There was no sign of a car.

Jamie had joined me at the window. I could feel the heat of his body next to mine.

'He must have gone,' he said. 'He must have seen me.'

I looked up at him.

'Are you sure?'

'Yes.' His hand found mine. 'Don't you believe me?'

Chapter eleven

A couple of days later I flew to Florida. The previous evening, Tuesday, Jamie drove me to London. We spent the night at a small hotel near Heathrow. It was wistful, and passionate, and sad, and we were still awake when dawn broke, talking.

At the airport, beside the queue for passport control, we said our goodbyes. We hugged, and kissed, and when the overhead TV screens announced Final Boarding, Jamie whispered a question in my ear.

'Three greens?'

I buried my face in his fleece. Three greens is one of the checks you make before you land. It means all three wheels are down and locked. I looked up at Jamie. He wanted me back in one piece. I couldn't wait.

'Three greens,' I confirmed.

My flight took off late, delayed by a no-show passenger. I cursed the extra time I could have spent with Jamie, watching Windsor Castle disappear beneath a veil of thin cloud. By the time we were over Ireland, I'd written him my first letter, read it, and torn it up. Halfway across the Atlantic, two more were in shreds around my feet. The American woman sitting next to me thought they looked like confetti. The image brought tears to my eyes.

By the time we landed in Orlando, I was more or less back in control. I knew Harald would be waiting to meet me and I was absolutely determined to be the Ellie Bruce he'd always known: level-headed, sane, utterly normal. I no longer cared whether it had really been him in the hotel car park that night. What I did with my private life was none of his business. He was a kind and generous man, and we were the best of friends. End of story.

I spotted him the moment I emerged on to the arrivals concourse. He was standing beside a vending machine, nursing a can of Coke. The sight of me bumping my luggage trolley through a gaggle of kids bound for Disneyworld brought a brief smile to his lips.

'Here.' He took charge of the trolley, kissing me lightly on the cheek. 'Great to see you.'

We took a cab across the airport to the General Aviation Terminal. Nothing had prepared me for the heat and the sheer brightness of the light, and while Harald paid the driver I stood on the tarmac, feeling the first prickles of sweat inside the creased cotton of my shirt. The flight over had been full to bursting, ten hours in a cramped seat with bad food and worse movies, and I was only too aware of the way I must have looked.

'See the flight line?' Harald was indicating a row of parked aircraft. 'Second from the end.'

I followed his pointing finger, half-expecting to find a Mustang. Instead, shimmering in the heat, I thought I recognised the high wing and the gently angled tailplane.

'A *Cessna*?'

'Sure. A 172.'

I glanced at Harald. Adam had been flying a 172 the day he died. Was this part of the training? An early test of character? Or should I blame it on coincidence and my own hyper-sensitivity? Shouldering the lightest of my bags, I decided on the latter: 172s, after all, were ten a penny. You see them everywhere.

There was a fuel bowser beside the little plane and I stole a moment or two with my vanity mirror while Harald checked the tanks. The face that looked back at me – wary and a little bit dazed – exactly matched the way I was feeling, and we were airborne on a long, climbing turn over the Orlando suburbs before Harald asked me about the flight over. When I told him more or less the way it had been he pulled a face.

'I tried for Executive Class.' He sounded apologetic. 'I'm sorry you ended up in Coach.'

I heard myself telling him it didn't matter. The important thing was getting here in one piece. A good night's sleep would sort me out and by tomorrow I'd be fit for anything.

Harald glanced across, his right hand easing back the throttle.

'I was going to talk you through the schedule,' he murmured, 'but maybe we ought to wait.'

The rest of the flight passed in near-silence. Harald was busy juggling radio frequencies most of the time, hopscotching from controller to controller as we droned south-west towards the Gulf Coast. Even at 5,000 feet the heat haze blanketed the ground beneath us, blurring the scatter of townships that dotted the landscape. The terrain was flat here, all of it cultivated, the huge fields parcelled together by long, thin ribbons of road. From time to time, the sun would splinter briefly on stretches of water, and twice I saw big lakes off to the east, a dull gunmetal grey, not at all the way I'd imagined the Sunshine State.

After about half an hour, Harald tapped me on the arm. Exhaustion, and the heat of the sun through the perspex, had made me drowsy.

'Ahead there, look.'

I followed his pointing finger. Through the blur of the propeller I could see the dark mass of an approaching city. The city straddled the mouth of a river and beyond the high-rise office blocks of the downtown area I could just make out the long curl of an offshore island. The water here was very different, a brilliant blue, and Harald began to lose height, dipping a wing to give me a grandstand view as we followed the river into the heart of the city.

'Fort Myers,' Harald grunted. 'I'll give you the tour later.'

'You live near here?'

'Thirty miles inland.' He jerked a thumb over his shoulder. 'I thought we'd take a look at the Gulf first.'

We were over open water now, closing on the offshore island, and I gazed down, marvelling at the whiteness of the sand against the deep blue of the ocean. The coast here had been highly developed, a waterside jigsaw of apartment blocks, marinas and shopping complexes, and I listened to Harald describing just how the area had exploded in recent years. The way he tallied the statistics – highest per capita boat ownership, richest population profile – didn't sound the least bit enthusiastic and I was still wondering exactly why he'd chosen this place as home when he pulled the Cessna into a tight 180-degree turn and headed back inland. Minutes later, much lower, the sprawl of houses and backyard pools had given way once again to an endless expanse of fields. The sight of a line of one of those huge irrigation sprinklers throwing out long ropes of water made me think quite suddenly of Jamie. He'd just installed something infinitely smaller in the garden at Mapledurcombe and only a couple of days ago I'd watched him showing it off to Andrea.

A couple of days ago? Jamie? I shut my eyes a moment, squeezing hard, determined not to be swamped again. I'd thought of him nonstop for most of the way over, but now was the time to concentrate on this new chapter in my life. I'd never before set foot in the States. I'd never before been offered any flying remotely as exciting as the Mustang. Unless I got myself back into some kind of mental shape, I was in danger, in Adam's phrase, of spinning in. Spinning in, very definitely, was not on my agenda. Apart from anything else, it would probably kill me.

A change in the engine note opened my eyes again. We were down below a thousand feet, easing in towards a touchdown on what I assumed was the local municipal airfield. We were landing to the south-west and Harald had put on a pair of battered aviator sunglasses.

'Your place is near here?'

'My place *is* here.'

I looked again. The runway, fully paved, couldn't have been less than a mile long. Taxiways at either end led to a couple of hangars. One of them looked big enough to take a medium-sized jetliner. The doors of the other one, not much smaller, were open and as we got lower and the angle flattened I could see a cluster of familiar shapes inside. At least three Mustangs. A couple of Harvards. A Yak without an engine cowling. And a bigger two-engined transport plane called a Dakota. I'd seen them before at airshows with Adam. The beat of their engines was, according to my late husband, the sweetest sound on God's earth.

Harald was hauling back on the control yoke, juggling the flaps against a modest crosswind. When he finally wheeled the Cessna on to the racing tarmac, I barely felt the bump.

'What do you use those for?'

I'd seen three white lines painted across the runway, the last one a foot or so beyond a tangle of rubber scorch marks from previous landings. Harald was toe-ending the brakes and cleaning up the control surfaces.

'Tell you later,' he said. 'It's a game we sometimes play.'

'Game?'

'Yeah.' For the first time I sensed the grin was spontaneous. 'Welcome to Standfast.'

We taxied to the apron in front of the smaller of the two hangars. An ancient jeep came bouncing across the grass towards us. In the distance, surrounded by palm trees, I could see the long white outline of what looked like a house.

The jeep pulled up beside the Cessna. The man at the wheel was wearing an old army shirt, the sleeves rolled up over a pair of brawny arms. He threw Harald a lazy salute and turned off the engine. Harald opened his door and in the sudden silence I could hear the sharp metallic clang of someone at work with a hammer. It came from inside the hangar, each blow echoing for a second or two.

The driver of the jeep was still looking at Harald. He was a big man, tall, broad-shouldered, with a tight, greying crew cut and a deeply tanned face. Harald had taken his glasses off. The hot wind across the airfield ruffled his hair. He nodded towards the hangar.

'How's it shaping?'

'Fine. Enriqué says he'll have it done by sundown.'

'And the FAA guy? He phoned back?'

'Sure, he's talking mid-May. I told him we'd need a coupla days' notice.'

Harald turned to me.

'You recall that 109 I mentioned?'

I frowned, trying to place the conversation. Then I remembered that Harald was doing some heavy restoration on an old Messerschmitt. As soon as it was airworthy, he planned to ship it to Europe.

'The Fighter Meet,' I said brightly, 'September.'

'That's right. Care to take a look?'

Harald introduced me to the driver of the jeep and all three of us walked over to the hangar. The driver's name was Chuck Beatty. He had a wonderful Southern accent and none of Harald's reserve. By the time we were standing inside the cool of the hangar, I'd practically told him my life history.

'Mapledurcombe?' He was running one huge hand through his grizzled hair. 'What kinda damn name is that?'

Before I had a chance to tell him, Harald was escorting me across to the far corner of the hangar where a couple of mechanics were working on the Messerschmitt. I was struck at once by how small it was, almost dainty. The nearby Mustang, with its broad undercarriage, underslung radiator and long silver snout, looked twice the plane.

Harald was questioning one of the mechanics in Spanish. He and Harald were crouched beneath the exposed engine, Harald nodding while the mechanic's torch mapped the tangle of pipes. At length Harald emerged, standing upright beside the cockpit.

'We had a coolant problem,' he explained. 'Enriqué's fixed it though, so we're back on schedule.'

'For what?'

'Certification. An inspector comes down from Atlanta. These guys show no mercy. The smallest glitch –' He drew a forefinger across his throat.

I raised a dutiful smile, only half-listening. Something on the Messerschmitt had caught my attention. The tape sealing the mouth of the cannon on the nearside wing had been shredded and there were scorch marks on the bare unpainted metal of the wing's upper surface behind it.

'What happened there?'

Harald followed my pointing finger. Harald looked, if anything, embarrassed.

'First coat of primer goes on at the weekend. Second and third coats Tuesday and Thursday. By the time the FAA guy flies in, she'll be back in full camouflage.'

'I meant the black marks. There. You can see them.'

I stepped across and ran my finger over the blemishes. The metal felt faintly greasy to the touch. By the time I turned round again, Harald was bent over an open wooden box. There was a metallic slithering noise and as I watched he pulled out a long belt of ammunition. There must have been hundreds of shells, each one seated in its shiny brass casing, the lead nose tipped in red.

'Twenty-millimetre cannon.' Harald nodded at the Messerschmitt. 'Standard issue on the 109G.'

I was still staring at the ammunition belt. The shells seemed so sleek, so beautiful. I couldn't take my eyes off them.

'And they're real? Live?' My fingers found what was left of the tape over the mouth of the cannon. 'You've used them? Tried them out?'

'Of course.' Harald sounded amused. 'How else do we test the guns?'

'But no one . . .' I shrugged, feeling hopelessly naïve, '. . . minds?'

'Minds?' It was Chuck's turn. He was laughing. 'In the land of the free, ma'am? *Minds?*'

Afterwards, Chuck drove us to the house. I sat in the back of the jeep, hanging on for dear life as we weaved and bumped over the parched grass. I couldn't get the image of the cannon shells out of my head. What were they doing there? Why on earth would anyone want to fly around with belts of live ammunition? Crossing the runway, I thought of asking him but decided against it. Sooner or later, I knew full well that Harald would tell me anyway. One of the reasons he'd got me here, I'd decided, was to put me wise about real flying.

The house was even bigger than I'd thought, a low, white, wooden-framed structure built around three sides of an inner courtyard. A shallow-pitched tiled roof overhung the veranda at the front and the slim fluted pillars that supported the roof lent the place a slightly colonial feel. With a couple of wicker chairs and a servant or two, I might have stepped into an outpost of the Raj.

Chuck was lifting my bags out of the back of the jeep. I joined him on the newly surfaced drive, brushing myself down, still looking at the house. At the end of a line of garages stood a flagpole, and at the top I thought I recognised the limp folds of the Confederate flag.

'Welcome to the Casa Blanca.'

I turned round, shielding my eyes against the sun. Harald was behind the wheel.

'You call it the White House?'

'Sure.' He nodded. 'You speak Spanish?'

'A little. We learned it at school.'

'*De verdad?*'

'*Sí.*'

Harald looked at me for a moment, his face for once betraying his surprise, then he said that he had to fly again. He'd be back before dark. Later, over a meal, we'd all have a proper chance to talk. I nodded and began to thank him for meeting me and flying me down but he waved my little speech away, pumping the accelerator and pulling the jeep into a tight turn. On the back, a line of stencilled white letters read *Standfast Inc.*

'You coming in, ma'am?'

I followed Chuck into the house. After the heat outside, the air-conditioning was a huge relief. Chuck led the way through a maze of rooms, cool parquet floors patterned by sunshine through the half-shuttered windows. There were pictures everywhere, mostly of aeroplanes, and one or two really nice pieces of low-slung bamboo furniture, but the place had a sparse, almost formal look to it, mostly – I think – because of the lack of clutter. Nothing ever seemed to have happened here. No one had half-read a newspaper, or half-finished a snack or a cup of tea, or paused for any one of those little self-indulgences that dot most people's working day. In this respect, the house felt empty and austere and a little bit intimidating, and it was a relief when I saw Chuck come to an abrupt stop, rap lightly on a door and then step aside to let me through.

I found myself in what I assumed to be a living room. The air-conditioning must have been on full blast because it felt even chillier than the hall outside. The window was fully shuttered and the only light came from a standard lamp in the far corner. In a big old armchair beneath it sat a tiny woman in a long black dress. She struggled to her feet the moment I walked in, pushing a blanket aside and supporting herself on an exquisite black ebony cane. We met beside her armchair.

'This is Mrs Meyler.' Chuck towered over both of us. 'Harald's mother.'

'My name's Monica, my dear, and you know something?' She peered up at me, her eyes a filmy blue. 'You're every bit as pretty as Harald promised.'

She held my hand in hers. Her fingers felt as fragile as twigs and her flesh was cold to the touch. In the light from the standard lamp, her face was the palest white, a thick dusting of powder softening the deeper lines, and I could see at once where Harald had got his cheekbones. As a younger woman, she must have been devastating.

She was telling me about the sleeping arrangements. I was to have one of the guest suites away down the hall towards the back of the house. The room faced east, she said, and if I was brave enough to sleep with the shutters open, then I'd be the luckiest girl alive.

'Why?'

'The dawns, Ellie. They're just spectacular.'

She was still clutching my hand, an intimacy so instant it made me feel slightly uncomfortable. She was acting like she'd known me most of my life and I began to wonder exactly what Harald had been telling her. She was tugging me over to the window now, pausing every step or two to catch her breath.

Chuck opened the shutters. The room was suddenly flooded with sunshine.

'There. I show everyone.'

I found myself looking out at a towering wall of green. It began the other side of a sturdy chain-link fence. There was a padlocked gate set into the fence and a paved path curled away into the dense vegetation.

'When you're rested, Ellie, we'll take a walk, just you and me. Let's see now. I've got black mangrove, white mangrove, wild coffee, cabbage palm, Brazilian pepper. I've got wild orchids, strangler figs, saw palmetto . . .' She was counting them off one by one, exhausting the fingers of both hands. The list sounded like a menu, something to whet my appetite, and when she got to the end of the plants she'd catalogued, she started on the wildlife. Ants excited her. She could find me small black ones that hunted in packs, big black monsters that foraged alone, and a voracious red specimen that would chew me up for breakfast. When I obliged her with a shudder and said I hated all insects, she laughed.

'I'm queen in my kingdom.' She was still gazing out of the window. 'You've nothing to fear.'

For the first time, I detected something snagging in her accent, the slightest displacement of the normal stress, and I looked down at her again wondering where life had taken her before she'd settled down in Florida. Was she American born and bred, like Harald? Or had she come from somewhere infinitely more exotic?

'Help me back to my chair, my dear. Take my arm.' I began to guide her across the room by her elbow but she shook me free. 'My arm, dear, don't be frightened, it won't fall off.' I did what I was told. My hands aren't that big but I could circle her upper arm without difficulty.

We paused by the chair while she stooped to rearrange the blanket. On a shelf behind the chair was a line of photographs, most of them sepia, mounted in tiny silver frames. The same face peered out from at least three of the photos, a man in his twenties, heavy-featured, with slicked-back hair and a wary smile.

Mrs Meyler had sunk back into the armchair, tucking the blanket around her knees as if she was expecting a journey of some kind. She peered up at me.

'Well?'

Nonplussed, I tried to smile.

'It looks intriguing,' I said, 'that kingdom of yours. Does it go back a long way?'

'Ten acres, my dear. Harald hates it, always has. That's why I never leave, of course, never go anywhere. The moment I went, he'd put the bulldozers in. Men are all the same, you know. They hate letting nature have its way.'

I heard Chuck's soft laugh behind me.

'It's a wilderness, Mrs Meyler. Harald just likes to tidy things up a little.'

'Exactly, *exactly*.' I felt fingers reaching for my hand again, and then a little squeeze. 'What did I tell you, Ellie? Men do so like to *interfere*.'

Chuck took me down the corridor to my room. It was grander than I'd expected, with beautiful Aztec-patterned rugs on the floor and a small en suite bathroom attached. There were lots of hangers in the built-in wardrobe, and a little fridge in one corner was stocked with cartons of mango and guava juice. A china vase on the chest of drawers held a single purple orchid, and someone – Harald presumably – had mounted a photo of a Mustang and positioned it on the little table beside the bed.

I lay there looking at it, and it was several minutes before I realised that it was our Mustang. I recognised the hangar behind, and the big dual cockpit, and the paint scheme that Ralph had so carefully researched, and the knowledge that Harald must have been poking around with his camera wasn't altogether welcome. How many other shots did he have? What gave him the right to decorate this room of his with shots of Adam's pride and joy?

It was, of course, a daft question. Harald, after all, had bought forty five per cent of the plane and it was therefore entirely natural that he should have taken the odd photo. Putting it beside my bed was simply a thoughtful gesture, a way of cushioning my landing in this strange new world, and I was still smiling at my own ingratitude, and wondering whether or not to take a shower, when I drifted off to sleep. The last thing I remember hearing was the distant cackle of a

Merlin engine. Harald, I thought, readying his own Mustang for take-off.

I awoke hours later to a soft knock at the door. It was dark outside and the wind had dropped. When I opened the door, Harald was standing there. He had a towel in one hand and a thickish-looking book in the other. He was still wearing his leather flying jacket.

'Take your choice.' He held out the book and the towel. He was smiling.

I took the towel. He looked disappointed. I nodded at the book. 'What's that?'

'A little light reading. There's no hurry. Tomorrow will be fine.' He gave me the book, then glanced at his watch. 'We're eating around eight. That OK by you?'

I rubbed my eyes and nodded. The last thing I wanted was food.

'Sounds lovely,' I said.

The book turned out to be an instruction manual for the Cavalier Mustang, a specially adapted version of the fighter which was, as far as I knew, no longer in production. Adam had talked about them a couple of times, and I stood in the shower, soaping away the grime of the journey, wondering quite what part this particular breed of Mustang would be playing in Harald's plans for the next stage of my flying career. The Cavalier is specially built to carry bombs and rockets. Some of the smaller Third World air forces were still using them.

Towelling myself dry, I slipped back into the bedroom and began to leaf through the diagrams and accompanying text. Why on earth did I need to know about internally mounted munitions and external armament loads? When would I ever need to master the bomb-arming switch? I looked up at the little patch of sky I could see through the window, thinking about the red-tipped cannon shells again, remembering something Dennis Wetherall had once said. Harald had made his money in the arms business. Dennis had called him a merchant of death. At the time the phrase had seemed wildly excessive, Dennis at his most extravagant, but now – for the first time – I began to wonder.

We had supper in a big, airy room at the back of the house. Beyond the insect mesh and the spill of light from the window I could hear cicadas and the stir of wildlife in the hot darkness. The temperature in the dining room was wonderful, dry and cool.

Chuck had joined us for the meal and Monica sat at the head of the table, sipping tiny spoonfuls of soup between flurries of conversation. She'd tied up her hair with a twist of red ribbon and she looked like a child, perched on a tassled velvet cushion to bring her up to the level of the table. It bothered her somewhat, she said, that I'd flown all this way and yet didn't know a soul. Harald, she was quite certain, would have told me nothing about the way things were around the Casa Blanca and so it fell to a woman – as ever – to see to what she termed 'the basic damn courtesies'.

When Harald raised his eyes to me and winked, she reached across to him, flapping her hand to mime a slap on the wrist. A thin red line of gazpacho was dribbling down from the corner of her mouth and I watched Harald attend to it with the tail of his napkin. He did it tenderly, with great deftness, and afterwards he adjusted the spoon in her hand so it was no longer upside-down. Monica appeared not to notice.

'Did he tell you about Chuck, Ellie?'

'No, Mrs Meyler.'

'Monica, dear, you must call me Monica.' She looked over at Chuck, then back to me. 'He saved my boy's life. Did Harald tell you that, I wonder?'

Harald looked at Chuck this time. Both men obviously knew what they were in for but when Chuck tried to change the subject, I intervened. I was interested in this story. I wanted to know what had happened.

'Was this recent?' I asked. 'Something that happened recently?'

Monica threw her head back, a thin, piping laugh.

'You call Vietnam recent?' I watched her hand crabbing towards mine across the table. 'And Harald never mentioned anything *at all*?'

'Never.'

'Well, well, then. It's my pleasure.'

She gave my hand a little squeeze. Harald had been flying with the Marine Corps. Home was an aircraft carrier on the South China Sea. He'd been out there the best part of six months, writing home every week or so. Then the letters stopped.

'And you know why, Ellie?'

I shook my head. Harald had started his third bread roll. Chuck was looking at the ceiling.

'Why?' I asked. 'What happened?'

Monica was looking at her son. Her silence finally stirred a response.

'I was flying A-7s,' he said simply, 'and one night I screwed the pooch.'

'*Harald!*' Monica was outraged.

'It's true, I did.'

I was still staring at Harald. Screw the pooch? Harald caught my eye. He must have seen my bewilderment.

'I got myself shot down,' he said. 'We were way up north, Route Pack Six.'

'What's Route Pack Six?'

'It's an area of North Vietnam. The headquarters people divided the north into seven sectors. Six was the hottest.'

'So what happened?'

Harald looked at me a moment.

'You really want to bother with all this?'

'Yes please.'

'OK.' He shrugged, wetting a finger and retrieving crumbs from the tablecloth, 'The mission was pretty routine, part of the Rolling Thunder programme. We were looking for POL targets, that's petrol, oil, lubricants. The gomers had these flak traps they used to bait. They got to be pretty good at it.'

Chuck intervened with a grin. Gomers, he explained, was service slang for the North Vietnamese. I thanked him, turning back to Harald.

'And flak traps?'

'Chunks of airspace, like so.' I watched his hands shape a box over his soup bowl. 'They're firing blind, of course, but they're pretty much covering all the numbers, five hundred feet up to ten thousand. Pump up enough lead, it becomes a crap shoot. The laws of probability say you won't make it.'

'And you didn't?'

'No.'

'And Chuck? He was with you in the plane?'

Harald and Chuck exchanged another glance. Harald's hands were still poised over the soup bowl. I swear I detected just the slightest tremor.

'Chuck was a rotorhead. He was flying one of the big rescue choppers out of Da Nang. We called them the Jollies. At night they'd come in over the DMZ, settle themselves down, and tune in to the strike freqencies.'

'He pulled you out?'

'Next day, yes.'

'Saved your life?'

'Without question.'

I looked at Chuck. With enormous tact, he converted a yawn into a hollow cough. There was a long silence. After a while, I frowned.

'So how come you screwed the pooch? Why was it your fault? I'm not sure I understand.'

Harald at last met my eyes.

'The Corsair's a single-seater,' he said quietly. 'If you're talking blame, the buck stopped with me.'

After supper, Chuck disappeared. Harald walked his mother back to her room, and before the door closed I heard him kissing her good night. When he came back, he was carrying a cafetière. The coffee smelled wonderful.

'You want to come along to the den? We could talk there.'

If I hesitated, I hoped it didn't show. I was dog-tired, so tired I could barely get up from the table, but the stuff about Vietnam had intrigued me more than I cared to admit and I wanted to find out more.

I followed Harald through the darkened house. I was trying to shape some kind of plan of the place in my head and I sensed we'd turned into the furthest of the two wings I'd seen when I arrived. Harald paused outside a locked door. I held the cafetière while he fumbled for a key.

The den, small and cluttered, reminded me at once of Adam's office beside the hangar on the strip back at Sandown. The desk piled with paperwork. The brimming bookcases. The neatly folded maps. The shadowed pictures jigsawed across the wall. Even the smell was the same, a mixture of old leather, stale coffee and half-smoked cheroots.

Harald waved me on to the low sofa that flanked the desk. When he switched on the little desk lamp beside his laptop, the light pooled on a stack of invoices. Before he tidied them into a drawer, I caught a glimpse of the top one. It came from Steve Liddell Engineering and for a second or two the sight of the familiar letterhead brought a lump to my throat. The last time I'd been over to Jersey was with Jamie. I remembered the landing he'd pulled off with the big commercial jet on his tail, and I remembered as well the night we'd spent together, waiting for the weather to clear up. More smells. More memories.

I sat down on the edge of the sofa, swamped by a great wave of longing and hopelessness. God, how I missed him. I stole a glance at my watch, trying to work out what time it might be back in England.

'Coffee?'

Harald was stooped over me, and looking up at him I sensed that somehow he knew about Jamie. Maybe he really had been down in the hotel car park that night, watching and waiting. Or maybe it was simple intuition.

I took the polystyrene cup.

'Best china,' I said lamely. 'Makes a girl feel quite at home.'

'You're sure you take it black?'

'Black's fine.'

He looked at me a moment longer, then sat down. I forced myself back to the conversation over the dinner table, blotting out Jamie and the times we'd shared since Jersey, and all the other wonderful secrets I'd hauled across the Atlantic.

'You and Chuck must go back a long way,' I said lightly. 'It's nice to keep a relationship like that going.'

Harald nodded.

'We first hooked up at Anapolis.' He indicated a photo on the wall behind my head. 'We were both nuts about the navy and we ended up in the same plebe year.'

I half-turned on the sofa. Plebe year, he explained, was when you got your first taste of service discipline. I nodded, squinting at the photo. There were three rows of cadets in dark-blue uniforms. Chuck was in the back, a tall, skinny youth with a lop-sided grin. Harald was seated in the front row. Even then, his expression – set and unsmiling – gave nothing away.

'How long were you there?'

'Couple of years.'

'And you liked it?'

Harald stretched over me and hooked the photo off the wall. In the light from the desk lamp I watched his finger tracing the lines of eager young faces.

'I loved it,' he murmured at last. 'It changed my life.'

'You mean that?'

'Sure.' He nodded. 'It was pretty brutal to begin with, you know, lots of crazy stuff to try and find your breaking point, but once you understood that, understood what lay behind it . . .' He glanced up, then reached for the cafetière. 'There was a routine called rigging pitchers. This is a pitcher of water. It's full. It's heavy. You're a plebe in your first year. Mealtimes, you stand to attention in the mess hall. Last in the chow line. Last for everything. Then they give you this.'

'Who's they?'

'The upperclass men. The top kicks.' He had the cafetière in his hand now and he slowly extended his arm until it bridged the gap between us.

'And you just had to stay that way? Holding it? At arm's length?'

'Sure.'

'Until when?'

'Until you broke.'

'What does that mean?'

'This.'

Slowly, he let his arm fall. There was a soft clunk as the cafetière reached the desk. I shook my head. It was primitive, I said, and mindless. What could rituals like that possibly teach you?

Harald was still looking at the cafetière.

'Everything,' he said softly. 'Academy dealt in blacks and whites. You either hacked it or you crashed and burned. There were no shades of grey, no room for arguments.'

'And you think real life's like that?'

'I know it is.'

He returned my gaze, recognising the challenge in my eyes. I thought he was talking nonsense and I was exhausted enough to let it show. He got up from the desk. A couple of steps took him across the room. When he came back, he had two more photos for me.

'I was going to talk about flying,' he said, 'but maybe this is better. Here.'

He slid a framed photo across the desk towards me. I found myself looking down at an aircraft carrier alone in a huge expanse of ocean. The steely-grey light threw long shadows across the crowded flight deck and the long spreading V of the carrier's wake gave the shot a wonderful sense of purpose and urgency. I held the photo at arm's length, half-closing my eyes. The aircraft were parked wingtip to wingtip, a pattern repeated the length of the ship, as perfect as marquetry.

'Beautiful,' I said. 'They look like toys.'

'Exactly. So here's another.'

The second photo had been taken on the flight deck at night. Rain had smeared the lens of the camera, giving the shot a strange, blurry, almost surreal look, but the sheer power of the image was astonishing. The big jet fighter that filled the frame was seconds away from touchdown. The shark-like nose was rearing up and one wing was slightly tilted while the long silver legs of the main undercarriage groped for the deck. The way the plane hung there was at once ungainly and beautiful. It defied everything I'd ever learned. No landing should be like this, I thought. So brutal. So hit and miss.

I fingered the glass that covered the print.

'You flew one of these?'

'Sure.' Harald nodded. 'That's an A-7 Corsair. And that's me.'

I peered at the photo, trying to imagine what it must have taken to get a plane like this down in one piece. Admiration is too small a word for what I felt. I could practically smell the fear that must have gone with this kind of flying.

'How fast?' I gestured at the photo.

'Over the ramp?' Harald shrugged. 'Hundred and eighteen knots. Maybe a little more. Depending on the wind.'

'And it was hard? Scary?'

Harald pulled a face.

'Hardest thing I ever did. We had some guys out on the boat once, some medical research guys. They strapped sensors all over us and ran stress tests on some of the missions, and you know what they found? They got readings from guys under fire, guys getting chased around by SAMs, guys pulling Christ knows how much g, all that stuff. And then they got readings at the end of the mission, those five minutes when you're in the groove, and you're coming down the glide slope, flying the meatball, and it's dark as hell, and the wind's all over the place, and it's raining, and the damn boat's heaving around in three dimensions, and you've got bingo fuel, and –'

'Bingo fuel?'

'Dry tanks. Nothing left to divert. One chance to get the baby home.'

I was looking at the photo again. I couldn't take my eyes off the big Corsair, hanging there on the very edge of the stall.

'And these tests were for stress?'

'Too damn right. And you know what they showed? They showed that night landings on to carriers were three times, *three times*, scarier than anything the gomers could throw up at you. Not that any of the guys couldn't have told them that to begin with, saved them a lot of dough.' He stared at the Corsair, brooding. 'Most nights we never saw a missile. But every mission ended with one of these.'

In the light from the desk lamp I could see the sweat beading on his forehead.

'And this landing worked out? This particular landing?'

'Sure.' He sat back. 'They used to rate us on the landings. They had a guy out on the fantail, a pilot, a guy who knew what he was talking about. There were various grades he'd give you. A cut grade was the worst. That meant a dangerous pass, almost an accident. You got to do a lot of explaining after a cut grade.'

I was studying the photo again. I wanted to know more about flare-out speeds, about degrees of flap, angles of attack, throttle settings. What happened if you made a pig's ear of the landing? How long would it take to spool up the engines and go round again?

'Do a bolter, you mean?'

'Is that what you used to call it?'

He nodded, talking me through the overshoot procedure. With the throttle against the stops, and a great deal of luck, the plane would stay airborne. Then it was a question of clawing your way back to altitude, back into the pitch-black sky, then rejoining the queue of planes in the landing circuit, popping the speed brakes, lowering the nose and settling the airplane back into the landing groove. Some guys made as many as eight passes before snagging a wire. The master hooksters, on the other hand, mostly put down first time.

'Hooksters?'

Harald bent over me, his forefinger following the line of the Corsair's belly until he found the long black hook dangling from the rear of the fuselage. Stretched across the flight deck were three arrester wires. You normally went for the third wire, he said, which meant aiming the aeroplane at an eighteen-inch strip of deck coming at you at around 120 knots. Miss it with empty tanks, and you were most probably dead.

I sat back, thinking suddenly of the approach we'd made to the field that very afternoon. There'd been three white lines striped across the runway and an awful lot of rubber around the third. I'd seen the lines again when we'd driven across the airfield in the jeep. I asked Harald about them. Was this what he did in his spare time? Strapped on an aeroplane and pretended he was back at sea?

Harald was pouring more coffee.

'It's a training aid,' he said. 'We rig lines across the runway and feed them into little detonator caps. The guys in the hangar have fixed a hook to one of the Yaks. Snag a wire and the bang says you're on the money.'

'Will I be doing that?'

'Of course.'

My eyes strayed back to the photo. At least the runway wouldn't be moving up and down, I thought, and with luck it wouldn't be dark.

I smiled.

'Can't wait,' I said gamely. 'When do we start?'

'Tomorrow. The forecast is pretty good. I want us airborne by ten.'

'In the dual Mustang?'

'In the Harvard. I know you've got solo time already but I'd like to put you in the back seat and see how it goes. Get the numbers right and we should be in the Mustang by the afternoon. How does that sound?'

I said it sounded fine. I was thinking about the instruction manual for the Cavalier Mustang, the one Harald had given me earlier. Now I'd seen the carrier photos, it was a great deal easier to understand his near-obsession with military hardware and it began to occur to me that his years over Vietnam had probably shaped the rest of his life.

'Tell me more,' I said.

'About what?'

'About the war.'

'Why do you want to know?'

'Because you're a wonderful pilot. And that fascinates me.'

He gave me a look, at once troubled and proud.

'Wonderful?'

I could tell he wanted to believe it. I hunted for other adjectives, then settled for a verb.

'You *feel* it,' I said. 'It just comes naturally. Flying with you, I get the feeling nothing could go wrong.'

'I crashed,' he pointed out. 'I lost a Corsair. I screwed the pooch.'

'You flew into heavy fire. You said it yourself. The odds were against you. There's nothing you could have done.'

'There's everything I could have done. You know what they say about the careful guy?' I shook my head. 'The careful guy who wants to die in bed always *checks*.'

'And you didn't?'

'On this occasion,' he shook his head, 'no.'

There was a long silence. Outside, deep in what I took to be Monica's wilderness, I could hear the hooting of a night owl. Harald, for once in his life, looked almost vulnerable.

'Do you want to talk about it?' I asked softly.

'Not really.'

'Do you mind me asking?'

'Not at all. I like your curiosity. It's ballsy. It suits you.' His eyes found mine again, then he looked away. He was leaning forward now, his hands knotted together, the knuckles white. Recklessly, I asked him for a third time about the accident.

'It wasn't an accident. I got shot down. Partly their doing. Partly mine.'

'Why yours?'

'I'd strayed off track. The POL stuff hadn't materialised and I was looking for targets of opportunity. Our intelligence guys had warned us about this particular flak trap but I guess I didn't take them seriously. In any case, I was a fighter pilot, and that pretty much sums it up. We're not in the business of self-doubt, Ellie. We own the airspace we occupy. It's ours.'

'Until someone shoots you down.'

'Exactly.' He looked up, a strange faraway expression in his eyes. 'You know the sweetest sound in all the world? It goes like this. Da-dee-dah. Three notes. Da-dee-dah. It's the signal you get in your earphones when their tracking radars lock on. It means they've found you. It means they're painting you. It means they're seconds away from loosing the missiles.'

'And that's a *sweet* noise?'

'Sure, because then you get to earn your money. They used to fire those mothers in twos, a salvo, bang-bang. The second fella got you when you thought you'd out-turned the first, but the wilder guys just figured it was twice as exciting. The Corsair was a beautiful ship. Big strong airframe. Plenty of power, plenty of speed. We were the last of the stick-and-rudder men. Yank and bank. Turn and burn. It was a plane you had to *fly*, hands-on. Even the missiles couldn't catch us.'

'But you crashed.'

'Sure, and in the end I figured it out. I must have gone down to small arms. I was under three hundred feet. That low, it couldn't have been anything else. Just goes to show, doesn't it?' He looked up, expectant, almost childlike.

'Show what, Harald?'

'Show that you can't cheat a bullet. Over 'Nam, around that time, flying was getting tricksy. The blue-suiters, the air force guys, were packing Sidewinders and Sparrows, big fancy missiles. That called for all kinds of clever shit. Their Phantoms wouldn't fly without two men, guy at the front to keep the thing airborne, and his buddy down aft to sort out the technology. Those guys in the back never looked out of the window. They had their heads down, eyes glued to the tube. If the computer went squirrelly, you gave up and hauled ass and went home. What the hell kind of flying is that?'

Abruptly, he came to a halt, staring down at his hands, embarrassed and a little ashamed – not of losing his precious Corsair but of talking about it. I reached out and touched his arm. It was a gesture of sympathy, of reassurance, and maybe an apology as well for going too far, but the physical contact made him flinch and I wondered just how many times he'd told this story.

'Do you talk about it a lot?'

'The A-7? 'Nam? Never. My mother, she loves all that stuff. She thinks it was all guts and glory, Burt Lancaster, Charlton Heston, wide-screen, comic-book stuff. It wasn't, Ellie. Good guys got wasted. Put a foot wrong, you bought the farm. And for what?' He looked up again, boxing me in with his questions. 'You know where that war was lost? Here, in the States. In DC. And you know why? Because we were fighting the wrong war with the wrong weapons. We were toting millions of dollars' worth of ordnance and all we ever did was nail the little guys on bicycles, or maybe the odd canal, or – hell – even a truck or two. What we didn't do was go for something that really mattered. Like the dikes. Or some of those downtown

Hanoi ministries. And you know why not? Because all those big fat targets were off-limits. And you know why *that* was? Because the politicians said so. Because the guys in Washington wanted to keep the thing under control. You can't do that, Ellie. Not in war, not in peace. Either you fight to win or you quit. Everything else is conversation.'

He reached for his coffee, apologising for the outburst, and I withdrew my hand, knowing that in some strange, unfathomable way this man was beyond comfort. Showing me the carrier photographs, talking about Vietnam, had unlocked a bit of himself I'd never seen before. Watching him bent over the polystyrene cup, I sensed that he was haunted by ghosts of his own making.

Putting the photos to one side, I tried to change the subject.

'Tell me about your father,' I said. 'What happened to him?'

For the second time in five minutes, I saw him physically flinch.

'My dad?'

'Yes.'

He frowned a moment, steadying himself, then he shook his head, dismissing my question.

'My dad died years ago,' he said. 'Poor bastard.'

Chapter twelve

We went flying, as planned, next morning. A slim, pretty girl with a flat Indian face and a cap of jet-black hair woke me with a cup of tea, and within the hour Chuck was driving me back across the airfield in his jeep. I was in the front seat this time and I had a grandstand view as we slowed beside the runway to let a pair of Mustangs land.

They were both single-seaters, and watching them flare for neat three-point landings I noticed that both of them had underwing pylons that I'd seen earlier in the manual for the Cavalier Mustang. The pylons are fitted to carry bombs and rockets, and the fact that they were both empty made me wonder about a series of distant thumps I'd heard earlier when I was back at the Casa Blanca, pulling on my flying suit. I'm clueless when it comes to high explosives – even in the Falklands, the war had spared Gander Creek – but it occurred to me now that the deep bass rumbles which had taken me to the window might well have had something to do with the fighters that were taxiing towards the hangars. Harald's private air force wasn't, after all, purely for display. Just what was I getting into here?

Harald was waiting for me beside the Harvard. It was incredibly hot already, with a light crosswind barely stirring the orange windsock, and he had forsaken his flying jacket for a light cotton zip-up. He had a pair of skintight leather gloves tucked into the waistband of his jeans and his eyes were invisible behind his aviator sunglasses.

The moment I said hallo I knew something was wrong.

'Sleep OK?' he grunted.

'Fine, thanks.'

'Good. Put that on, then we'll go.'

He stood aside while I strapped on the parachute harness, then he swung himself up on to the wing and gestured for me to follow. The Mustangs had taxied the length of the apron now and were turning to join the flightline of other aircraft nearby. Above the cackle of the

Merlins it was difficult to hear what Harald was saying. The cockpit was already open, the lapstraps of the seat harnesses neatly criss-crossed on the metal seats. I began to clamber into the front cockpit but Harald stopped me. He had a bottle in his hand. He made a tipping gesture then gave it to me. I unscrewed the top and took a couple of mouthfuls. It was deliciously cold and slightly saline. The Mustang pilots killed their engines and in the sudden silence I handed the bottle back.

'You're sure you've had enough?'

'Absolutely. Your mother poured coffee down me. The last thing I need is more liquid.'

I gestured loosely at the waiting cockpit, trying to make a joke of my weak bladder, but Harald didn't smile. After he'd finished the bottle and handed it to a waiting mechanic, he helped me into the rear cockpit. As he bent to tighten the seat straps, I remembered the smell of his aftershave from the last time we'd flown together, back home at Sandown, and I remembered as well how different he'd been on that occasion. Relaxed isn't a word I'd ever associate with Harald, but over the Isle of Wight he'd filled me with nothing but confidence – not in my own abilities but in his willingness to teach me just a little of what he knew. Now, that feeling of kinship seemed to have gone completely. He was brusque and impatient, as if I and this wretched Harvard had come between him and something infinitely more important. When I pressed against the seat harness and tried to turn my head, suggesting it was maybe an inch or so too tight, he just looked at me as if I were some punter at a country fair.

'It's there to restrain you,' he said. 'Or hadn't you noticed?'

I kept my mouth shut, not wanting the argument. Already, the draining heat and a flutter or two of pre-flight nerves were making me feel queasy. With the cockpit canopy shut, I knew I was going to roast. While Harald signalled for the mechanic to strap him into the front seat, I sat back, telling myself to relax.

Compared to yesterday, the airfield was buzzing. A couple more planes had touched down – high-winged twins of a kind I'd never seen before – and they too were taxiing towards the hangar. At the far end of the apron, a big white minibus had just come to a halt, and I watched half a dozen men in combat gear step down on to the tarmac. Here was yet more evidence to justify Dennis Wetherall's brisk analysis of Harald's real business interests. The men from the minibus were carrying short, stubby weapons, machine guns of some kind, and they ambled across towards one of those old Huey helicopters you see in the Vietnam newsreels. The soldiers were dark-skinned, Latin American in appearance, and I was still watching them when I heard a crackle in my headphones and then the rasp of Harald's voice.

'Remind me how many hours you've got.'

'On Harvards?'

'Yes.'

'Thirty-six.'

'Recent?'

'Over the last year or so.'

'OK, we'll see how you do.'

There was a brief silence, then he told me the aircraft was mine. He'd done the external checks already. After the start-up routine, I was to taxi to the hold. We would be taking off to the north-east.

The intercom went dead. I sat rigid in my harness, staring at the back of his head over the top of the cockpit combing. What kind of brief was this? Where were we going? What should I expect in the way of conflicting traffic? How long might the flight last? What about the weather?

My eyes went automatically to the fuel gauges. The Harvard can carry around 120 US gallons in the two wing tanks. If I was careful with the boost, a full load should give us a safe duration of about three hours with a thirty-minute buffer for emergencies.

I fingered the intercom button.

'Where are we going?'

There was no answer. I stared at the instrument panel. The sun was beating down on the top of my head and I was sweating already, but Harald's attitude – close, I thought, to real hostility – was making things much, much worse.

For a second or two I toyed with aborting the flight, blaming a headache or jetlag, but the moment I pictured the expression on his face – contemptuous, or perhaps amused – I dismissed the thought. This was something I had to go through, had to conquer. Harald had doubtless set this up deliberately, a carefully planned ambush, crowding pressure upon pressure until he'd finally make me break. Rigging pitchers, I thought, listening to him working the hand pump to fill the fuel lines and the carburettor prior to ignition. You can only start the Harvard from the front cockpit, and I made the best of this brief respite until the engine fired and Harald's voice was back in my headphones.

'She's yours now. Taxi to the hold.'

'Thanks.'

I tried to keep the sarcasm out of my voice but failed. The heat was getting worse by the minute, but if I felt anything then it was anger. I surely deserved better than this. Humiliation is a crazy way to start a day's flying.

Grim-faced, I determined to press on. The aircraft's call sign was taped across the dashboard, together with a note of the local tower freqency. When I called for permission to taxi, a Spanish-sounding voice gave me immediate clearance.

The Harvard, compared to my beloved Moth, has always felt like a big aeroplane. It taxies with its nose in the air and forward visibility is especially tricky from the back seat. In truth, though I hadn't told Harald, I'd never flown the Harvard from the back before, and it took every ounce of my concentration to weave the aircraft out across the apron and on to the taxiway, eagle-eyed for anything that might be in the way.

Taking off to the north-east meant reversing the landing we'd made coming in from Orlando, and the long taxi to the far end of the runway filled the cockpit with the stench of unburnt Avgas swirling back from the engine. I was half-tempted to pull the canopy back and block out the smell, but I was already dreading what the sun would do to the temperature through the hot perspex, and keeping the thing open seemed – on balance – the lesser of the two evils.

At the end of the runway, I turned and then applied the brakes. The engine run-up and mag tests went without a hitch. I throttled back to 1,000 r.p.m., consulting the Harvard check-list I'd retrieved from Adam's office back in Sandown. Thank God I'd bothered to pack it, I thought. I did my final checks – trim, mixture, prop, fuel, flaps – and then pulled the canopy back until I felt it lock. We'd now reached the point where Harald had to break the silence. The pilot with no idea where she's going is seconds away from a major accident. Harald must have been reading my mind.

'Left hand turn-out at five hundred feet,' he grunted. 'The circuit height's fifteen hundred. I'll talk again on the downwind leg.'

'Thanks.'

'My pleasure.'

The intercom clicked off. I shut my eyes for a second or two, kissed the tip of my left forefinger, took a couple of shallow breaths, then steadied myself for the take-off. My left hand found the throttle and I inched the aircraft forward, making sure the tail wheel was properly aligned before pushing the throttle lever fully forward to the gate. Everything began to shudder around me, and as soon as the aircraft gathered speed, I knew that I was going to make a mess of it.

The cockpit felt like a sauna. I was too hot, too ragged, too confused by the way this so-called proving flight had just acquired a momentum of its own. I must have taken off literally hundreds of times, yet never had I felt so mentally unprepared, so physically uncomfortable. If Harald's plan had been to unnerve me, he'd succeeded beyond his wildest dreams.

At forty knots, I pushed the stick forward, raising the tail. The end of the runway swam into view, a line of green extending either side of Harald's head, and the fact that I couldn't see properly made my stomach heave. If something went seriously wrong, Harald would be closer to the accident than me, but even this thought was oddly unconsoling.

My eye was back on the airspeed indicator. So far, through my feet and even my bottom, I'd felt every bump and groove in the runway, but at seventy knots I eased back on the stick and the moment the Harvard was airborne the juddering began to ease. At 400 feet I raised the wingflaps and seconds later I pulled the aircraft into a gentle left-hand turn, following Harald's instructions. The shadow of the canopy drifted across the dashboard. I swallowed hard and mopped my forehead with the back of my hand, straining against the seat harness in the search for other traffic. Adam had always told me that the Harvard was a bitch to fly – endless re-trimming, lots and lots of things to do – but I think this was the first time I was positively grateful for the workload. Given the chance to think of anything but keeping the bloody thing airborne, and I was certain I'd throw up.

On the downwind leg, Harald came through again.

'You remember those three white lines?'

My heart sank. I heard myself say yes. I was looking down to the left of the aircraft, searching the far end of the runway.

'You want me to hit them?' I asked. 'Go in for a landing?'

'You got it.'

I was still trying to find the lines. Then I remembered the heading we'd flown on yesterday's touchdown.

'They're at the wrong end,' I said quickly. 'The lines are at the wrong end of the runway.'

Harald must have caught the panic in my voice because I could hear him laughing over the howl of the engine. The fact that I'd said something funny was a huge relief.

'OK,' he said. 'I'll pass you on that one.'

'Pass me? What does that mean?'

He didn't answer. I could hear him talking to the tower. Two imminent take-offs were to be put on hold. An aircraft inbound from the coast was to join overhead the circuit at 4,000 feet. By now, we were seconds away from another left-hand turn on to base leg. Base leg would take me back towards the runway and my final turn before landing.

'One eighty degrees right,' I heard Harald say.

'*Right?*'

'Just do it.'

I did what I was told, hauling the big old plane round until the compass told me we were heading back the way we'd just come.

'Watch your needles. Speed's falling off.'

I looked at the airspeed indicator. Harald was right. In my eagerness to find the exact reciprocal of my old course, I'd allowed the nose to rise, shedding speed. The Harvard, in this respect, is unforgiving. Keep the nose up and she'd flick on to her back with precious little altitude to sort the situation out. I was beginning to feel nauseous now, the taste of fear in the back of my throat.

'You still want those bloody lines?' I muttered.

Harald must have heard me. He was laughing again.

'Line,' he said, 'Singular.'

'Which one?'

'The third one. Chuck rigged the detonators this morning. Use the tail wheel as a hook. It's fishing line, minimum breaking strain. There won't be a problem.'

'And I'm cleared to land?'

'Ask. You're the pilot.'

I contacted the tower. The controller was as impassive as ever. The surface wind was still three knots from 130 degrees. I glanced down to the right. I could see the two aircraft waiting to take off, both stationary on the taxiway. Somewhere overhead, another aircraft was orbiting at 4,000 feet. Nothing like an audience, I thought grimly, going through my landing checks before dipping a wing and turning on to base leg.

With twenty degrees of flap, the Harvard began to drop. Out to the right, the runway was slowly coming into line, and I left it another twenty seconds or so before easing the aircraft into the final turn. I was a little high and I crossed the controls a moment, sideslipping down before kicking the aircraft straight and lining up as best I could on the smudge of white which were Harald's precious markers. Snagging the fishing line with the tail wheel meant a three-point landing – all three wheels touching down at exactly the same time – and while I rather prided myself on my three-pointers, it would obviously mean a last-minute flare-out to bring the nose up and the tail wheel down. That in turn would mean losing all sight of the three white lines for the critical part of the landing, hardly ideal for the kind of pinpoint accuracy that Harald was demanding.

I was still trying to configure the landing in my mind when everything – quite suddenly – began to fall apart. I had just under a hundred feet of altitude. My airspeed was a nudge over eighty-five knots, way too fast if I was to touch down at seventy. Worst of all, Harald's head had blacked out my last sure fix on the onrushing blur of white. Like an idiot, I put the nose down, trying to improve the visibility. The speed increased. Go any faster, and I knew I'd damage the flaps.

I hauled back on the stick and it was at this point that I lost what we pilots call 'the picture'. The picture has absolutely nothing to do with what you can see out of the cockpit window. It refers to that inner mental knowledge you retain of exactly where you are, and exactly what happens next.

In both respects, I knew I'd lost it completely. I'd been going way too fast and now – nose up again – I was losing speed at an equally alarming rate. My glide slope, ideally a nice smooth descent on to the runway, was beginning to resemble the Cresta Run. Short of speed and height, the Harvard was beginning to wallow. I knew, with a terrifying certainty, that I'd never been so close to a crash.

My left hand closed on the throttle. The engine missed a beat then responded with a throaty surge of power. Harald, who had a grandstand view of the impending disaster, said absolutely nothing. At thirty feet, I'd recovered control. I knew where I was now. I knew we were going to make it.

Slowly, I eased the power off, letting the aircraft sink. Watching the blur of racing tarmac behind the right wing, I waited until the last moment before lifting the nose and flaring out. The soft nudge of a perfect three-point landing brought a little gasp from my lips, part surprise, part relief, part deliverance. I kept the stick hard back, my knuckles bunched in the pit of my stomach, anchoring the aircraft's tail to the runway. Knowing I still had plenty of tarmac to spare, I applied the brakes in little dabs, watching the speed drop off. Only when we were down to fifteen knots did I open the intercom again. The last thing I wanted to give Harald was the chance to be first with the news.

'Missed,' I said. 'Sorry about that.'

It wasn't a laugh this time, more like a chuckle.

'The wires or the flight deck?' he said.

We flew for the rest of the morning, except for a brief refuelling stop during which we swapped cockpits. After the trauma of that first landing I managed to improve, but Harald spared me another attempt at the white lines. Whether or not my near-miss had unnerved him I never knew, but I think he was pleased that I'd refused to give up, even if he didn't admit it. Up at altitude, away from the airfield, he put me through a series of recovery manoeuvres – some of them reasonably tricky – and although I didn't cover myself in glory, I sensed I'd done enough to bring a slightly lighter note to his brisk interjections from the back.

Once I'd managed to sort out a stream of nice cool air through the ventilator control beside my left foot I felt much better about the world, and I even managed to steal a glance or two at the purple-streaked thunderheads that had been building up all morning. Later on, when I'd done a lot more flying, I came to recognise these massive towers of cloud as a regular feature of the Florida sky. The blackness of the shadows they cast on an otherwise brilliant sea never ceased to fascinate me, but that first morning I was too busy with the Harvard to pay them anything but the briefest attention. As a piece of scenery, they were wildly exotic, full of mystery and threat, a confirmation – if I needed one – that I was an ocean away from lazy circuits around the Isle of Wight.

With forty minutes' flying left in our tanks, Harald gave me a new compass heading. What he called 'the classroom stuff' was evidently over. Before we returned to Standfast, he wanted to show me a little action.

I flew south-east for maybe fifteen minutes. Soon the neat rectangles of citrus fields gave way to an endless tract of swamp dotted with dark-green islands of mangrove. Its flatness and lack of features – no trees, no hills – robbed the landscape of depth and dimension, and looking down it was hard to work out where the water ended and the sky began. These, I knew, were the Everglades – a huge area of humid, knee-deep wilderness teeming with alligators, snakes and mosquitoes – and the rattling cocoon of the noisy old Harvard suddenly seemed an altogether nicer proposition than fighting it out with the reptiles and insects below. I'd heard stories about this place. How a snake called the water moccasin could finish you off in five minutes. How female alligators liked nothing better than the taste of human flesh. Even from three thousand feet I could well believe it, and when Harald directed my attention to a curl of smoke away to port, I was at first reluctant to investigate.

'What is it?' I asked him.

'Some guys from Standfast, part of Chuck's detail. Let's go look.'

I nosed the Harvard down and dipped a wing. For some reason, Harald wanted me to approach from the west.

'You're looking for five hundred feet at the bottom of the run,' he said. 'Give yourself plenty of room for the pull-out.'

Run? Pull-out? I pressed the intercom button.

'Say again?'

'Chuck's leading an infil exercise. He drops in with the Huey and off-loads the guys. It's our job to make it realistic.'

'How?'

'OK, you see the button at the end of the throttle lever?'

My thumb found the button. In our Harvard, it triggered the bomb-release mechanism.

'Got it,' I confirmed.

'OK, now look at the dash. You know where to find the bomb-master and selector switches?'

I did. The bomb-master switch is on the left-hand side of the dashboard, the last in a line of six. The selector switches, four of them, fell to my other hand. Here again, we had the same configuration in the Old Glory Harvard. Keeping the original armament fit, according to Adam, had brought a tear to many a veteran's eye. I glanced up at the rearview mirror. Harald was gazing out to the right, his lips curled in what might have been a smile.

'Which switch?' I asked him.

'Second from the right. Starboard inboard.'

I reached for the master switch and flicked it down, then my right hand found the bomb-selector switch. During our brief refuelling stop back at Standfast, one of the mechanics had taken me across to the hangar for a glass of iced tea, and looking back out at the apron I'd seen a couple of guys attaching something to the underside of the starboard wing, but only now did it occur to me that the sleek olive canister might actually have a purpose.

'What happens when I press the bomb release?' I enquired drily, 'Only I really liked Chuck.'

I could hear Harald laughing again, but this time it sounded real.

'It's only smoke,' he assured me. 'And Chuck knows the routine backwards.'

We were passing a thousand feet in a shallow dive, the airspeed nudging 160 knots. There was a gyro gunsight mounted on top of the dashboard and Harald told me to level the pipper once I'd found the guys in the swamp.

'Where are they?'

'I don't know.'

At 700 feet, seeing nothing but islands of mangrove, I pulled the Harvard out of the dive. Flying the plane from the front cockpit was infinitely easier and I winged it over as we began to climb again, still not knowing quite what I was looking for.

'There! Three o'clock low.'

I looked down to the right, following Harald's instructions. At first I didn't see it. Then a strange, feathery pattern on the water drew my attention, the downdraught from a rotor blade, and I realised I was looking at a helicopter. It was the old Huey I'd seen beside the hangar earlier. The jungle camouflage blended perfectly with the greens and browns of the swamp.

'What now?'

'Go for it again, same heading. He'll be dropping the guys in any time now.'

Checking the compass, I pulled the Harvard into a climb, pushing the throttle forward against the stops and holding it there. Passing 3,000 feet I levelled off, then winged the old plane over, heading back. For the first time in my flying career I felt a thrill of what I can only describe as bloodlust. No one had ever asked me to look for the bomb-release button before. Not in earnest. Not with flesh and blood on the receiving end.

'Promise it's just smoke.'

'Don't you trust me?'

I didn't have time to answer. I was too busy trying to locate the helicopter. From 1,500 feet it looked like an insect. Seconds later, I heard Harald's voice again. He was shouting.

'He'll break to the right. Wait until I say.'

The Huey was fattening in the gunsight. Suddenly it sheared away to the right, leaving tiny figures splashing around in the swamp. They looked hopelessly vulnerable. I could see one or two faces raised skywards, then a man running. I glanced at the altimeter. I was God up here, but I was fast running out of height.

'Tell me when,' I yelled.

'Now!'

I felt the little black button give under my thumb. At the same time I hauled back on the stick as hard as I could. The airframe was juddering around me and for one horrible moment I thought I'd left it too late. Then I caught a blur of faces and bits of green and brown racing past and finally a huge patch of blue, blue sky that filled the gunsight and seemed to spill over the rest of the cockpit. I could hear the thump-thump of my own blood pulsing through my head and I felt a wild exhilaration that even now I find hard to describe. I wanted to share it with Harald but I didn't know how to put it, so in the end I cranked the speed up to 140 knots and barrel-rolled the fat old trainer, my own way of saying thank you for one of the most exciting pieces of flying I'd ever experienced. The fact that I'd just crossed the line between flying for pleasure and flying for some infinitely darker purpose didn't, I think, occur to me. All I could think of was the undeniable fact that I'd hacked it. Harald had set me a task, I'd followed the brief, and – guess what – we were still in one piece.

Horizontal again, I glanced up at the mirror. Harald was half-turned round in his seat, looking back at the guys in the swamp.

'Upwind and on target, Ellie.' He sounded gleeful. 'You really rattled their cage.'

After we'd landed back at Standfast, Harald disappeared without a word. I watched him hurrying across the tarmac towards the hangar, and it was one of the mechanics who finally clambered on to the wing and helped me out. When I asked him where Harald had gone, he said he didn't know, and the longer I stood there in the blazing sun, the more attractive the prospect of the afternoon off became. Only now did I realise how exhausted I was. With no life-and-death decisions left to make, all I wanted to do was sleep.

I hung around in the shade of the hangar for maybe half an hour. Then the mechanic who'd rescued me earlier took pity on me again and ferried me across to the Casa Blanca. The house was empty except for the sound of music from a radio in the kitchen. I let myself into my room. Someone had made the bed and I stepped out of my sweaty flying suit and slipped gratefully between the cool, crisp sheets.

A noise outside the window awoke me hours later. I'd been dreaming about that first landing in the Harvard, the runway this time shoelaced with thick lengths of white nylon tape. It had felt horribly real, like dumping the plane into a cat's cradle, and I was seconds away from certain death when the sound of a woman's voice jerked me awake.

I got up on one elbow, rubbing my eyes. It was the voice of someone old, almost singsong, calling a name I didn't recognise. I went to the window. Along the fence, inside the open gate, a thin black figure was bent over a stick. It was Monica. She was calling into the wilderness, the way you might try and summon a pet cat or dog. Beside her stood the girl who'd brought me my morning tea. She was carrying some kind of metal cage. It was about the size of a shoe box and there was something moving around inside it. As I watched, Monica raised her stick, pointing down the path that led into the dense wall of green, then tugged at the girl's arm. The pair of them ventured forward, disappearing for a minute or so before returning with the cage empty. Monica tapped the girl lightly with her stick, a gesture – I thought – of approval, then both women turned back towards the house.

I stood at the window for a while, staring into the wilderness. The wind had got up a little and it carried a rank, slightly sour smell I'd never come across before. It spoke of fertility and decay and I thought at once of the vast expanse of swamp we'd flown across only hours ago. Monica, it seemed, had returned this little parcel of Florida to its virgin state. Quite why she'd want to do this was beyond me but I kept wondering about the metal cage the girl had been carrying, and what it might contain. The answer of course was to go and have a look and I was debating whether to do just that when I heard a shuffle of footsteps on the bare wooden floor outside.

It was Monica. She stood in the open doorway. She was holding a cordless telephone in one hand and a slip of paper in the other. I took the slip of paper and she peered up at me while I made sense of the figures. The handwriting, I knew at once, was Harald's. He'd scribbled a phone number, underlining the prefix three times. The end of the number was all too familiar. 0860 354876. My own mobile.

I glanced down at Monica. She had a strange twisted smile on her face.

'Nice young man,' she said at last. 'Jamie, I think Harald said his name was.'

I was confused for a moment, then I remembered that I'd left my mobile with Jamie at the airport. I didn't think it would work in the States. There seemed no point taking it.

'He phoned? Jamie phoned?'

'This morning, my dear. Very early.' The smile, if anything, widened. 'Twice.'

'*Twice?*'

'So Harald tells me.'

'Ah . . .'

I looked at the number again. Maybe this was why Harald had been so curt with me, so distant. He'd fielded the calls from Jamie at God knows what hour and drawn the appropriate conclusions. Not that it was any of his business. Not that it should have made the slightest bit of difference.

'Is Harald around? Only I obviously owe him an apology.'

'Harald's gone to Miami, my dear. He'll be back tomorrow.' She offered me the phone. 'Now then, do you want to talk to your young man?'

'Not now.' I almost resented the way she was thrusting the phone at me. 'No thanks.'

I swear Monica looked disappointed. Then she reached forward, taking my hand the way she'd done that first time we met. In a second or two she'd be asking about Jamie, who he was, what he meant to me. We were friends, allies. Whatever secrets I had would be safe with her.

I began to back into my room. I was still only half-dressed. Monica turned to go, then stopped.

'I nearly forgot,' she said. 'Chuck wants you to meet his wife. He says she's been cooking for you all day.' Her eyes strayed to the phone number. 'Be nice to meet new people, my dear. Don't you think so?'

Chuck called for me at seven o'clock. He was wearing civilian clothes this time, a pair of nicely cut chinos and a blue and white striped shirt that really suited him, and as we drove around the airfield perimeter track I was glad I'd made the effort to iron a frock and put on a squirt or two of decent perfume. Whether she'd meant to or not, Monica had hit the mark. The Casa Blanca was already beginning to feel just the slightest bit claustrophobic.

Chuck lived forty minutes away, in a small township called Corkscrew. When I laughed at the name, he looked amazed.

'That Maplewhatever place of yours –'

'– durcombe.'

'Mapledurcombe, yeah. And you think *Corkscrew's* wild?'

I told him how ancient Mapledurcombe was, how it went with the grain of an old, old country, and when he demanded to know more, I found myself turning the last four years inside out, explaining about all the building work we'd done, and Adam's passion for vintage aircraft, and exactly how we'd set about building a bridge to all the USAAF veterans who'd made Old Glory such a success. The idea behind the business fascinated him. His own father had flown against the Japanese and he knew only too well how powerful the tug of those wartime years had become. Something like Old Glory was exactly the kind of dream vacation folks like Chuck's dad were looking for. With proper marketing, he said, we'd make a fortune.

'You're right.' I nodded. 'But I expect we'd need a bigger house.'

'And more airplanes.'

'Exactly.'

'So is he looking?'

'Who?'

'Adam. This husband of yours.'

I stared at Chuck. It was a straight question.

'You haven't heard?'

'Heard what?'

'About my husband, Adam.'

'No.' He was frowning now. 'What am I missing here?'

I told him briefly about the accident. Adam was dead. His Cessna had disappeared in mid-Channel and so far no one knew why. Chuck couldn't believe it.

'And this happened . . . ?'

'Back in February. You're telling me Harald didn't mention it?'

'Not a word.'

'Did he mention I was married?'

'No, but then I guess I never asked. He just said you were a good friend. He said he owed you lots of favours, said you were crazy about Mustangs. I just thought . . .' he shrugged, '. . . you know . . .'

'That we were together? Harald and I?'

'Yeah . . . well . . . kinda. He never actually said it, you know, spelled it out . . . but, I guess, hell . . .' He shook his head, visibly embarrassed. 'I'm sorry, I'd no idea, Jeez.'

The next mile or so passed in silence. I stared out at the gathering darkness, trying to make sense of this little bombshell. How come Harald could lose one friend and not tell another? How come these separate compartments in his life were so bloody watertight?

Chuck was slowing now, and a sign loomed out at me. *Welcome to Corkscrew*, it read, *Gateway to the Everglades*. We turned left, and left again, and then coasted to a halt. The street was lined with low-rise, timber-framed bungalows. With the engine off I could hear the tick-tick-tick of a dozen lawn sprinklers. Chuck muttered that we were home and began to open the door but I reached across, my hand on his arm.

'How well do you know Harald?' I asked him.

Chuck glanced back at me. His face betrayed his bewilderment.

'I know him pretty good,' he said at last. 'Yeah, pretty damn good.'

Chuck's wife met us at the door. She was Costa Rican, at least half his age, with a beautiful smile and a figure most men would kill for. Her name was Esmeralda and she spoke American with barely a trace of an accent. The food was already on the table, a vast selection of exotic-looking salads, and she darted in and out of a nearby bedroom while Chuck busied himself fixing drinks from a huge fridge in the kitchen.

He and Esmeralda had just had their first baby, a little girl called Conchita, and when it was obvious that she wasn't going to sleep I insisted she join us. If anything, she was even more exquisite than her mother – wonderful almond eyes and the most perfect little feet imaginable – and watching her nestled in Chuck's huge arms it was obvious that this marriage, at least, had been a love match. He and Esmeralda had met at an embassy party in San José. She was working for one of the big American oil companies and within six months they'd been married. Chuck never actually spelled it out but I suspected there'd been other wives before Esmeralda. Not that Esmeralda seemed to care.

After the meal she disappeared back into the bedroom with the baby. I offered to help Chuck with the washing-up but he wouldn't hear of it. He had some nice cool Chardonnay. We could take it through to the lounge and relax. Ezzie would join us when junior was finally squared away.

Chuck's lounge reminded me a little of Harald's den. There was a woman's touch in the extravagant stands of scarlet flowers and the bits and pieces of what I took to be Inca pottery, but the biggest picture on the wall featured a huge twin-rotor helicopter half-glimpsed through swirls of rising dust. We all carry baggage from the past and this, I assumed, was Chuck's.

I stood in front of the canvas. The helicopter was hovering on the edge of a paddy field. A nearby copse of spindly trees spat flame while a defensive ring of US Marines sprawled in the short grass were returning fire. Somewhere in the middle of the picture, his back against a dike, slumped a small, broken figure in a flying suit.

I stepped forward and took a closer look. Without doubt, the painting was an original. The colours were pretty dramatic and some of the figurework was a bit uncertain but the feeling of immediacy, of actually being there, was undeniable. This was an important corner of someone's war and it wasn't difficult to work out whose.

'Vietnam?'

Chuck was rummaging in a drawer behind me.

'Yep.'

I pointed at the figure at the foot of the dike.

'And this is Harald?'

'Nope, another guy. Same year, though. Seventy-one.'

'And you rescued him? You pulled this guy out?'

I glanced round. Chuck was looking almost bashful.

'That's right, ma'am. All part of the service.'

I went back to the picture again. The temptation was to ask about medals and citations and what twenty-five years had done to memories like these, but I sensed that Chuck was past all that. I could hear him drawing the cork from the wine. I sat down in one of the big Naugahide chairs.

'Tell me about Standfast,' I said. 'Tell me what happens there.'

'Like this morning?'

'Like any morning. Those guys I saw, the ones in combat kit, the ones you must have taken out to the swamp. What was all that about?'

Chuck was pouring the wine. He passed me a glass, complimenting me on the smoke bomb.

'You pickled it pretty good,' he said. 'Even Harald was impressed.'

'All I did was hit the release. He talked me through it.'

'Yeah, sure, but you were at the sharp end. At least that's the way I heard it.'

I grinned, wanting to agree. The memory of what we'd done would be with me forever. The rich greens of the mangrove filling the gunsight, the flailing bodies of the soldiers, the way the g forces had tightened around my belly, forcing the blood to my legs the moment I hauled the Harvard out of the dive. I wanted to tell Chuck about it, to share the excitement, but to someone with his experience, my little adventure would be pretty small change.

He was telling me about Standfast. The business belonged to Harald. It had developed from stuff he'd been doing in the eighties, helping out the Reagan people down in Central America. The airfield had once belonged to the military, an important staging post on the resupply runs down to Honduras and El Salvador, but Harald had since acquired it on a thirty-year lease.

I frowned, trying to follow the history. The ins and outs of the Contra scandal were largely beyond me.

'What was Harald doing down there?'

'Training, mainly. We were helping out the rebels in Nicaragua. The strategy had to do with rolling back the commies. Same game plan as 'Nam, except that Central America is a helluva lot closer.'

'You were there, too?'

'Sure. I was out of the Corps and bored to hell. Harald called up one day and asked whether I was interested in making a buck or two to help out Uncle Sam.' He shrugged. 'What do you say when a guy makes that kind of offer?'

He sipped at the wine, an infinitely delicate gesture from such a big man, and then he told me the way it had been down in Central America. The ferrying-down of supplies. The endless problems with spares and reliable munitions. The brutal fact that many of the so-called insurgents were simply in it for the money.

'We were flying into a couple of airstrips, Llopango and Santa Elana. As fast as we warehoused the stuff, they just sold it on. In the end we could have been working for Federal Express. Even Harald said so, and he doesn't give up easy.'

'But what about the training?'

'We did what we could. The stuff we had to use was pretty Mickey Mouse. Fixed-wing, you're talking Cessna twins with a couple of five-hundred-pound bombs strapped on. Most of the choppers were hangar queens.'

'Hangar queens?'

'U/S, unserviceable.' He frowned, running his fingertip around the rim of the glass. 'Wars like that, you don't need anything fancy, but you're still talking regular maintenance and proper operational procedures. That was pretty much first base to these guys and most of them didn't make it. Hell, we tried our best. We all knew that without air support the Contras would go down. Turned out we were right, too.'

I was still thinking about Standfast, the kinds of planes I'd seen, good solid propeller technology, nothing complex, nothing too hi-tech. Was this the way it had evolved? Had Harald put his Central American experience to work back home?

Chuck nodded.

'You got it.' He grinned, leaning forward in the armchair. 'Harald figured there had to be a market for all that hardware. Refurbished Mustangs. Ex-combat choppers. Dumb bombs. Rockets that don't cost a million bucks a throw. The name of the game is affordable air power, and believe me, we've got customers lining up all around the block. Harald sells them the package. Flight training. Aircraft. After-care. And any little extras they might care to name.'

'Extras?' The word had a faintly sinister ring. 'What kind of extras?'

'Stuff you pick up en route. Skills, tricks, techniques. You build up a kind of repertoire.' Chuck gazed at me a moment. 'Exactly how well do you know Harald?'

I thought about the question.

'My husband and Harald were good friends,' I said carefully. 'They had lots in common, flying mainly. Since Adam died, Harald has been incredibly helpful. Generous, too.' For a moment I toyed with describing Harald's several bids to buy our Mustang outright but in the end I decided against it. 'He's made a huge difference,' I said instead. 'I don't know what I'd have done without him.'

'Sure.' Chuck nodded. 'So you'll know how hands-on he can be.'

For a split second, I misinterpreted the phrase. Chuck saw the expression on my face and roared with laughter.

'Excuse me, ma'am.' He shook his head. 'I'm talking hardware, nuts-and-bolts stuff. The man eats and sleeps schematics. Show him a wiring diagram, you've made his day.'

I nodded. I was thinking about the times I'd seen Harald and Dave Jeffries together, discussing how to fine-tune our Mustang. Chuck was right. Harald, it occurred to me, even thought like an engineer. Everything in its rightful place. Everything carefully buttoned down.

'So how does that relate to Standfast?' I wondered aloud. 'To what you're up to here?'

'Hell.' Chuck grinned again. 'You're talking business now. We get clients from all over, like I said. Central America, Latin America, the Pacific Rim, even Africa. Those guys you saw today, they're from Honduras. If the shoe fits, we can give them anything, jungle survival, air combat, ground attack, reconnaissance, infil, exfil, deniable violence, you name it.'

'Deniable violence?' I'd never heard the phrase before.

'Sure.' Chuck was looking around now, trying to illustrate a point. 'You're holed up in some hotel room some place. You've got access to soap and maybe a little gasoline. You want to make yourself a bomb but you've no idea how. No problem. Our guys will talk you through it.'

'And Harald?'

'Harald teaches our guys. All that stuff just fascinates him. Always has done, ever since the Academy. Give the guy a screwdriver and a couple of batteries and a metre or so of wire and you've lost him for the rest of the day. I guess that's partly why he's such a good pilot. He thinks his way into it. He becomes the machine.'

I tried not to look shocked. The last twenty-four hours had given Harald Meyler dimensions which even Dennis Wetherall hadn't suspected. Not just a merchant of death but maybe a practitioner, too. Soap? Gasoline? Screwdrivers? A length of wire? Was Chuck serious? Did Harald really specialise in blowing people up?

Another thought crossed my mind.

'Tell me,' I said. 'Was Harald ever married?'

Chuck looked at me a moment, then shook his head.

'Never.'

'Was he ever close to it?'

'Not that I know about.'

'Why not?'

Chuck gave the question some thought. Outside, I could hear the soft clunk of a door closing. Chuck got to his feet, fetching a third glass.

'I guess he never found the right diagram,' he murmured. 'I guess he never figured it out.'

Chapter thirteen

Next morning, I found the letter on the floor outside my room. The airmail envelope was addressed in a thick green Pentel and I knew from the line of kisses on the back that it had come from Jamie.

I retreated back to bed, kicking off my shoes and lying full length on the duvet as I tore the envelope open. I'd been awake half the night, trying to work out when would be the best time to phone home to Mapledurcombe. I was missing Jamie more than I'd ever thought possible and the feeling of emptiness, of being completely alone, was beginning to affect me in ways I didn't like to admit. Abandoned lovers make lousy pilots. Thank God he'd put pen to paper.

The letter was almost incoherent and I wallowed in it. Saying goodbye at the airport had been the hardest thing he'd ever had to do. He remembered nothing about the drive home. He'd had nightmares about the plane crashing and next day the nightmares had got worse. By lunchtime, I'd fallen in love with Harald, chosen a bridal gown, booked a honeymoon cruise and made love in a million and one positions. I dwelt on each phrase, the way you linger over a box of chocolates, enjoying Jamie's wild desperation, picturing him bent over the lined foolscap pad, trying to make me understand just how much I'd changed his life.

He loved me more each passing hour. Real life was a blur, remote and irrelevant, a sad, passionless tableau in which people worried about the weather, and the mortgage rate, and Andrea banged on and on about grass stains on the hall carpet. She'd told him only yesterday that his job was on the line. He'd stopped concentrating. He'd stopped even caring whether the filter had been changed in the swimming pool, or the curtain tracks replaced in the Mitchell Suite, or the taxis booked to meet the first bunch of guests off the hydrofoil from Southampton. None of that stuff, he said, was of the slightest importance. Not compared to me. Not compared to us.

Andrea, of course, must have known only too well what was going on in Jamie's head, and the realisation that I hadn't really gone at all

– that I still haunted Mapledurcombe – was obviously driving her barmy. According to Jamie, she'd totally lost her cool. Only yesterday, he wrote, she'd sneaked into the little garden shed where he stored his bike and kept his tools. He'd pinned a couple of snaps of me to the back of the door and he'd returned to find them torn up and scattered all over the floor. This particular image made me giggle. Andrea had never been able to resist direct action and if I needed proof that Jamie was as dizzy and lost as I was then this was surely it.

I was still halfway through the letter when someone knocked on the door. It was the girl who normally brought me tea. She'd had a phone call from Mr Meyler. He was over on the flight line. He was sending the Jeep for me in ten minutes.

Back in the real world, I pulled on my flying suit, slipping the letter into one of the top button-down pockets. Close to my heart like that, it gave me the warmest feeling, and I was still grinning when the Jeep delivered me to the hangar on the other side of the airfield where Harald stood waiting.

He was standing beside a Mustang I'd never seen before. The metal skin had been burnished until it shone and the only paint on the fuselage had been applied to the anti-dazzle panel that extended from the windshield to the propeller boss. The plane must have been flown in that very morning because I could still feel the heat from the engine.

Harald gestured up at the open cockpit.

'Here she is,' he said. 'Sweetest T-bird in the south.'

T-bird is aviation slang for a trainer. This Mustang, like ours, had dual controls.

'This is yours?'

'Nope. Belongs to a buddy of mine, but there's no limit on the loan.'

I sensed at once from his tone of voice that we were in for a wonderful day's flying. Yesterday's sourness, that feeling of thin-lipped reproach, had disappeared completely. Instead, Harald was back to his usual self, patient, precise, infinitely painstaking. The weather was glorious. We'd be flying most of the day. First, though, I needed a proper brief.

We walked into the hangar together, picking our way between the parked aircraft. At the back, beside the flight of metal stairs that led up to his office, Harald paused beside the Messerschmitt that I'd seen when I first arrived. The last of the certification tests was due in a couple of days and the inspector from the Federal Aviation Agency would be flying down from Atlanta.

Harald beckoned me over to the cockpit. The canopy opened sideways, hinging upwards.

'You want to sit in? Fantasise a little?'

I accepted the invitation. Compared to the Mustang, the cockpit felt small, narrow and cramped. I reached up, pulling the canopy closed. If I was taller, as tall as Adam, I'd have to crouch to fly the thing. The stick felt miles away. I bent forward and waggled it a couple of times, and then glanced over my shoulder. The visibility to the rear was awful.

Harald was looking in at me. I made a face at him, then opened the canopy again.

'Not nice,' I said. 'Or not as nice as the Mustang, anyway.'

Harald laughed, taking my hand as I climbed out of the cockpit and jumped off the wing.

'Damn right,' he said. 'She's a monster on take-off, really nasty torque swing, and there's no rudder trim so you're forever working the pedals. Put her in a dive and the ailerons lock solid. First time I did it I nearly made a hole in the Everglades.'

For Harald, this was quite a speech. Messerschmitts in working order are hard to find, so why had he bothered?

'Nostalgia.' He patted the wing panel. 'The guys who flew these things had a really hard time. See the width of that undercarriage?'

He was squatting now, his arm outstretched. I knelt beside him. The narrower the undercarriage, the easier it is to screw up on landing, and the thin little tyres on the Messerschmitt certainly seemed uncomfortably close together.

'I've got a library of books on the 109. Some months they lost more to landing accidents than combat. Tight fields, you see. And young guys with no experience.' He shook his head fondly. 'She's one helluva bitch. Getting to know her's been a real pleasure.'

We went up the stairs to Harald's office. It was much bigger than I'd expected and he settled me in a comfortable old canvas chair before disppearing to fetch some juice. I looked round. The place had the feeling of one of the ops rooms you see in old black-and-white war movies. A row of grey metal filing cabinets filled the space beneath the long window that looked down on to the hangar floor and the wall opposite was entirely occupied by a huge board charting the deployment of more than a dozen aircraft. The forward schedule took each plane to the end of August, and judging by the lack of empty white spaces, Standfast looked set for a busy summer.

I was still trying to make out the movements of the DC-3, a big two-engined cargo plane on the hangar floor beneath us, when Harald returned with a huge carton of orange juice. He'd already warned me about the draining heat, how easily it could affect concentration in the air, and he poured the juice into polystyrene cups before handing me a couple of salt tablets.

'Pop these,' he said briskly, trying to answer one of the two phones on the desk.

When he'd finished, I pointed at the board. For the Dakota, under June, I'd finally deciphered four destinations. Kiev. Piryatin. Karkov. Moscow. How come?

'The Russian Shuttle,' he said without looking up. 'Commerce dressed up as history.'

The Russian Shuttle. The phrase sounded familiar. Wasn't this what Dennis Wetherall had been telling me about?

'Adam,' I said aloud. 'Wasn't he going to be involved in all that?'

Harald looked up, surprised.

'Yes,' he said, 'he was.'

'Didn't you ask him to organise it?'

'Yes.'

'And didn't you pay him . . .' I frowned, '. . . seventy thousand pounds?'

Harald nodded, saying nothing. Finally he got up and went to the window.

'You weren't supposed to know about that.'

'My accountant told me. It showed up in the figures after Adam went down.' I paused, waiting for an explanation. When none came, I asked him where the money had gone.

'It went to Steve Liddell.'

'Why?'

Harald bent to one of the filing cabinets. I heard the drawer slide out and then the scrape of the metal files as Harald hunted for something inside. At length he handed me a fat airmail envelope. The stamps were Indian. The postmark read *Madras*.

'Open it.'

I shook the contents of the envelope on to my lap. There were perhaps a dozen colour photographs. I recognised the lines of the Spitfire at once. This one was in desert camouflage, yellows and browns. It had definitely seen better days but everything looked more or less intact, and judging by the grin on the face of the pilot kneeling beside one wheel, it may even have been airworthy.

Harald was standing behind me, looking down over my shoulder.

'It was meant to be a birthday present,' he said. 'For you.'

'For me?' I twisted round, staring up at him. 'How come?'

'Adam wasn't keen on the Shuttle business. He thought it would be a distraction, take up too much of his time. It was only the money, plus my promise to find him a Spitfire . . .' he nodded at the photo, '. . . that changed his mind.'

'He was going to buy this for my *birthday?*'

'Sure. Maybe next year's. The engine needed a lot of work. Steve estimated around nine months. Possibly longer.'

I gulped, leafing through the photos again. My birthday falls in June. A year from now, had Adam not died, I'd have been the proud owner of my very own Spitfire. Was this the kind of present a man would buy for a wife he didn't love? For a wife he was about to abandon for some sex goddess on a windsurfer?

I reached for my orange juice. Confusion is too small a word to describe the way I felt. I risked a glance at Harald. He'd have known about this morning's letter from Jamie. God knows, he might even have left it outside my door. And even if he'd have missed the morning's post, he certainly knew about yesterday's calls because it had been Harald who'd answered the phone. So what must he be thinking? Adam barely dead and buried and yours truly involved with a youth nearly half my age?

Harald didn't have to say anything and he knew it. I watched him bent over the filing cabinet. The photo, I thought. The photo I'd found in the drawer in Adam's office. Wasn't that the clinching evidence? Didn't that *prove* I'd been betrayed?

Harald turned round. I was on the point of telling him everything, getting it all off my chest, giving myself just a shred of self-respect, but the moment passed.

'Let's go through the theory first,' he said. 'Get it out of the way.'

'Theory?' I asked blankly.

'The Mustang.' He smiled down at me. 'You need to know what makes it the best fighter in the world.'

Harald talked me through the technical brief for the best part of an hour. We explored areas where even Adam would have been struggling – stuff about laminar air flow, and drag co-efficients – but he had a little plastic model of a Mustang and whenever I looked more stupid than usual, he took care to spell out the real-life consequences of all that aeronautical jargon. How the Mustang would slip into a stall with very little warning. How the stick would go light, how I'd feel just a shiver or two of airframe buffet, and then how the left wing would suddenly drop if I didn't ease off the back pressure and reduce the angle of attack.

The Mustang was a big plane, he said. It was forty per cent heavier than a Spitfire but the design was technically more advanced. It was built, he told me, around a very simple proposition. That it would out-fly, and out-manoeuvre, and out-range anything else in the sky. It was a fighter pilot's mount, a thoroughbred in every conceivable respect, and that meant I had to adopt what he called a very definite mind-set.

'This machine doesn't know you're not a fighter pilot.' He was holding out the little model at arm's length. 'So that's what you've got to become.'

Yesterday's adventure with the Harvard and the smoke bomb suddenly began to make sense.

'You mean that?'

'Absolutely. No question about it. That's what this plane expects. I'll be taking you to the limits. I'll be showing you bits of the envelope you never knew existed. You'll be doing things here that'll seem crazy at the time – high-g accelerated stalls, vertical departures, post-stall shimmies from blown overheads, the whole caboodle. At the time it'll scare the hell out of you and you'll be asking yourself what on earth all this has to do with your kind of flying, but believe me, you'll be grateful.'

He got to his feet, leaving the model on the desk, and went over to the window again. Down on the hangar floor I could hear the phut-phut of a rivet gun. I reached for the Mustang, turning it slowly in my fingers, still listening to Harald.

'We're talking extreme situations, Ellie. You'll get to think like a fighter pilot, fly like a fighter pilot, do everything else like a fighter pilot, and who knows? It may one day save your damn life. That's what we tell the guys here, the ones that come up from the south. We tell them sweat more in peace, bleed less in war.' He turned round. 'Does that make any kind of sense?'

I said it did. We finished the carton of orange juice and went back to the sunshine outside. The light and the heat hit me like a hammer blow. I did the external checks on the Mustang then struggled into the parachute harness and let Harald strap me into the front cockpit. The aircraft had been refuelled already, and within ten minutes we were airborne. Harald had given me a notepad to slip into the thigh pocket on my flying suit, and every time I hit a snag or had a query, he made me scribble a note to myself. These, he said, would take us through the debrief. Not only that, but adding yet another little task to my in-flight list would stretch me the way I needed to be stretched.

He was right. Flying the Mustang imposed an incredibly heavy workload – eyes, ears, fingertips, nerve ends – and paying the aircraft the respect it deserved took every ounce of my concentration. Time and again, over the weeks to come, Harald was to hammer this message home. It was all about detail, he'd insist. It was all about preparation, about getting the smallest things right. The truly successful pilot, the guy who'd die in bed, was the guy who'd get immense satisfaction from the smallest of the small print. A perfectly plotted course. An exquisitely flown instrument approach. Finding the best technique for bringing various aircraft types *smoothly* to a halt. Only by mastering the small things, he said, would I be able to build that faith, that inner confidence, that would enable me to cope with split-second decisions that could otherwise lead to catastrophe. Without that confidence, any pilot might one day be overwhelmed.

'By what?'

'The terror.'

It was our third sortie of the day and I was exhausted. To my shame, and perhaps relief, I'd even forgotten about Jamie.

'The terror?' I repeated blankly.

'Sure. Flying's unnatural. We were never meant to do it. If it's an expression of anything, it's an expression of will.' He paused. 'We all want to play God. Flying tempts you to do just that. You get to think you're all-powerful. There's nothing you can't do, no place you can't go. Then – BAM – something happens, something breaks, something falls off, and hey, you're as mortal as the next guy.'

I checked the mirror. I'd never had Harald down as a philosopher but there was a new tone in his voice, a thoughtfulness I'd never detected before.

'I disagree,' I said. 'I think flying's completely natural. At least, that's the way it feels to me. Maybe I'll come back as a bird.'

'You are a bird. You fly very well.'

'You mean that?'

'I do.'

I felt the warmth flooding through me. Up above 6,000 feet, high above the coast, we'd been practising recoveries from clean stalls. Time and time again, I'd slow the aircraft down, nudging back the stick, waiting for that tiny tremor through the airframe that signalled a loss of control. The wing always dipped to the left and the first couple of times I had my heart in my mouth as we plunged earthwards. But Harald was right about pushing the limits. The more I practised the stalls – even the trickier ones – the more routine, the more familiar, they became. I wasn't, after all, flying a legend. Merely a very powerful aeroplane with imperfect manners and a tendency to bite hard when you weren't paying it the right kind of attention.

This realisation gave me just the beginnings of confidence. I could get on top of this. I could hack it. From the back, Harald said very little, setting me trap after trap, challenge after challenge, but I could tell from his tone of voice that I was doing OK. One of my landings, an absolute greaser, had even drawn a second or two of applause.

I looked down at the ribbon of beach below, smothering a yawn. This was Florida's Gulf shore. Late afternoon, the shadows of the big waterfront condominium blocks were beginning to lengthen and I could see a pair of motor cruisers ploughing up the coast towards the smudge of a distant marina. The Mustang seems to fly nose down. The view forward through the grey disc of the propellor is better than most planes and there's a tendency to think you're forever in a shallow dive. I'd noticed it first on my maiden flight with Harald, back on the Isle of Wight, but already I'd mastered the urge to check the altimeter, another little sign – I realised – that this thing wasn't quite as intimidating as I'd thought.

I got on the intercom to Harald. Fatigue was beginning to get the better of me, though the last thing I'd ever do was admit it.

'What next?'

'Home. Standfast.'

'We're through?'

'For today, yes.'

'You want to give me a heading?'

'No, use the map.'

I slid the map out of the pocket to my right. My own version of dead reckoning put us thirty or so miles south of Fort Myers. The next city along the coast was Naples but I resisted the temptation to do the obvious – hang on until we got there and then fly the radial back. Instead, I dropped the left wing and pulled the aircraft round until we were heading north-east again. On a day like today, with good visibility and no wind to knock me off-course, I knew I'd fly close enough to Standfast to make a visual contact. After that, with my new-found confidence, it would simply be a matter of pulling off another yummy three-pointer.

We droned inland, the sun still hot through the canopy. I could hear Harald singing to himself behind me, an old John Denver song. The heat and the music compounded my fatigue and once or twice I had to fight to keep my eyes open.

Then, very suddenly, I heard a voice in my earphones. It was Harald.

'Five o'clock low,' he said. 'I have control.'

I felt the stick jerk sideways out of my hand. Harald was flying the

Mustang now, standing the aircraft on its starboard wing and hauling it round in a turn so sudden and so tight that I began to pass out. A huge weight was crushing my chest. I could hardly breathe. I tried to reach for the dashboard but my left hand wouldn't move. I began to panic. I'd been in plenty of g turns with Adam but nothing this painful.

Abruptly, the pressure eased. We were near vertical, still diving. I did my best to focus on the altimeter. Two thousand three hundred feet and unwinding fast. The stick moved again, coming back towards me, and I braced myself as the savage pull-out forced the blood into my legs. Colours drained from the cockpit. Everything went grey. And then I heard Harald laughing, not quite a laugh, more a yelp, and I peered forward through the windshield, seeing another Mustang, silver and red this time with a yellow and black chequerboard tail, hanging in the air in front of us.

The pilot must have seen us at this point because he broke hard to the left, diving for the ground. Harald followed him, a slightly tighter turn, gaining all the time. My eyes were swimming. Bits of gleaming swamp were coming up to meet us and I tensed for the inevitable pull-out. When it came it was even more brutal than the last and I think I must have lost consciousness, because the next thing I remember is finding ourselves back at altitude – 3,000 feet at least – with the black and yellow tail of the other Mustang still filling the windshield. There must have been some kind of protocol in these mock dogfights because I could hear Harald exchanging banter with the pilot up ahead. They were talking in Spanish, and when they'd finished Harald came back to me on the intercom.

'Guy's name's Ernesto,' he grunted. 'And right now he's a dead man.'

He muttered something else about the perfect bounce, then gave me back the stick. Every nerve in my body told me to stay a passenger for the rest of the day, but after this morning's little pep talk I knew that simply wasn't an option. What we'd just been through was a little mild horseplay, nothing else. There was one landing left and the privilege was entirely mine.

We were second in the circuit after Ernesto's Mustang. I watched him cranking down his gear and then make the last turn on to long finals. I switched the fuel to the fullest tank, throttled back, and with the speed dropping below 170 knots checked for three greens as I lowered the undercarriage. My temperatures and pressures were good. The tower had given me clearance to land. Glancing down to the left, I pulled on my harness, then selected full flap for the final approach. Trimming and re-trimming, I lined the aircraft up with the approaching runway. At twenty feet, I eased the stick back, letting the aircraft sink, waiting for the soft kick of the landing. With the nose up, I'd lost the horizon. Adam used to talk me through this in the Moth. 'If you can't see the bloody runway,' he'd say, 'then it must be there.'

And it was. I felt a couple of nudges, then the rumble of tyres told me we'd landed. The stick well back, I anchored the tail wheel to the runway and then applied the brakes, gentle dabs at the toe-pedals, nothing too forceful, nothing that might put the aircraft on its nose. The grass beside the runway began to slow. With 600 metres still in hand I went for the first of the two run-off exits, winding back the canopy and letting the hot, moist air sluice in. I put one cheek into the slipstream. My face was bathed in sweat.

'You did great.'

It was Harald. I thanked him. I wanted to sleep for a year.

He came to my room to collect me at half past seven. I'd even been too tired to read the rest of Jamie's letter. Harald was wearing a T-shirt and a pair of black jeans. It shouldn't have suited him – too young, too hip – but somehow it did. For a man of fifty-five he still had an amazing body.

I sat in his car, an imported Jaguar XJS. It smelled of new leather and that special wax they put in the body sections.

'I thought you were joking,' I said. 'You should have saved yourself the trouble.'

'Taking you out?'

'Making the effort. You're the one who's going to have to do the talking. I'm dead from the feet upwards.'

We drove into Fort Myers. All I really remember is an endless avenue of palm trees, miles and miles of them, following the river all the way to the bay. When we got to the ocean, we crossed a bridge on to Sanibel Island. The sidewalks were thick with elderly couples, stooped and nut-brown. Harald drew up outside a restaurant called Clancy's. We got out and he tossed the keys to the uniformed doorman.

'You hungry?'

'Starving.'

The table he'd reserved was at the back. We picked our way across the floor, and when we'd sat down a waiter came for the drinks order. I had a small pitcher of home-made beer. Harald stuck to Diet Coke. Waiting for the food to arrive, we went over the day's flying, instructor and pupil. Again, Harald told me how well I'd done. I said I'd enjoyed it. It had been all the things he'd promised – a wild mix of challenge, terror and exhilaration – but thanks to him, I'd never once let it get on top of me. He liked that. It felt, he said, like the very best kind of compliment. It meant that I'd listened to him. It meant that I was gutsy as well as able. And it meant, above all, that he'd been right.

I didn't quite know how to take the last bit but I was determined to hang on to this new relationship of ours. We respected each other. We trusted each other. We really could be friends.

Over the second helping of baked grouper, I changed the subject.

'Tell me about Adam,' I said quietly, 'How well did you really know him?'

'Pretty well.'

'And you liked him?'

'Very much.'

I nodded. There was no perfect way to approach this, no rules about minimum speeds, flap settings and all the other stuff you had to learn to stay alive. I decided on long finals, nice shallow glide path.

'He was away a lot,' I mused.

'Obviously.'

'And sometimes, you know, I felt I lost touch a bit.'

I went on about Mapledurcombe for a while. The house, I said, had been as demanding as any baby. I'd had to nurse it to keep the business alive. Much to my regret, there'd been absolutely no chance of spending as much time with Adam as he'd deserved.

'He thought you were doing a wonderful job.' Harald was shredding the last of the flesh from the grouper's backbone. 'I know he did.'

'But was that enough, do you think?'

'Enough?'

Harald caught my eye and I knew at once that all my careful preparations for landing had gone pear-shaped. He knew already. He knew exactly what I was talking about.

I leaned forward. Touchdown, I thought. At last, the truth.

'Adam was having an affair, wasn't he?'

Harald wrinkled his nose, as if a bad smell had just wafted in from somewhere or other.

'Adam was crazy about you,' he said softly. 'It was obvious to anyone who knew him. There wasn't anything he wouldn't do for you.'

'Like buy me a Spitfire?'

'Yes.'

'But that's exactly the way he'd play it, don't you see? He was a lovely man, a lovely, lovely man, but he was larger than life, Harald. And he couldn't get enough of it.'

'Enough of what?'

'Life. Mustangs. Spitfires. Women. Whatever. It was all meat and drink to Adam. He was terrible at . . .' I shook my head, staring at the wreckage of the grouper, '. . . drawing the line. He wanted everything, all the time.'

'But he had you.'

'I know he did. Of course he had me. But me wasn't enough. He was an attractive man. He was over there on bloody Jersey all by himself. He had money, time, opportunity. And he got bored really easily. You know he did. You must have seen it.'

Harald might have been smiling.

'Are you making a case for yourself here? Only something doesn't quite fit.'

'Like what?'

'Like all this. It's almost as if you *wanted* him to have an affair. Retrospectively, of course.'

'I *hated* him having an affair. It broke my heart.'

'But you definitely know, do you? There's no doubt in your mind?'

So far I hadn't mentioned Michelle La Page, but I was too exhausted to care any more about withholding bits and pieces of this sordid little story. Either Harald was the friend I wanted him to be, or something else was going on. Briefly, I told him about finding the photograph in Adam's office drawer. Harald was less than impressed.

'Pretty girl. Nice day on the beach.' He shrugged. 'What does that prove? Except he had a camera.'

'There was a message on the back.'

'Oh yeah?'

'It was pretty explicit, Harald. It didn't leave much to the imagination.'

'You want to tell me what it said?'

'Not really.'

Harald leaned back, letting the waiter clear the plates away.

'Maybe the message was for someone else. Have you thought about that?'

'Don't be silly, Harald. Whoever collects other peoples' billets-doux? It just doesn't happen. Especially to someone like Adam. He was as red-blooded as the rest of you. Probably more so.'

This protestation, for some reason, made Harald smile again.

These smiles of his were beginning to get to me. He knew. I knew he knew.

'Listen Harald, you were good friends with Adam, good buddies. Believe it or not, I know how these things work. Men confide in each other, just the way women do. Something was going on and I just don't believe you weren't aware of it.'

'You're right.'

'Something was going on?'

'No, Adam was a really good friend.'

'And that's where this conversation ends? Is it loyalty, Harald? Discretion? All that crap?' I was getting really angry now. 'You're my friend, too, you know. Or isn't that quite the same thing? What should I do, Harald? Wear Chinos? Get myself a deeper voice? Drink more beer?'

His hand came out and covered mine. It was the first time he'd ever touched me like that.

'It's an impossible question, Ellie. There's no way I can answer it.'

'Ever?'

'Ever.' He nodded.

'But you know?'

'That's your assumption.'

'You must know.'

'Not necessarily.'

'So why the games? Why the evasions? Just tell me, for God's sake. Tell me whether you know or not.'

Harald gave my hand a little squeeze and then leaned back.

'What difference would it make?' he asked at last.

'Every difference. Every bloody difference in the world.'

'Why?'

'Because it would prove it one way or the other. And that would put my mind at rest.'

'OK.' He nodded. 'So say it was true. Say he was having an affair. Would that make life easier?'

The final word in that sentence settled heavily between us. Easier. Easier for me. Easier for Jamie. Easier to justify a widow losing her heart to a twenty-one-year-old. Was there any point in trying to complete this conversation? Was there anything left to say?

I lowered my head, sullen, disgruntled. I felt about twelve.

'You know Jamie,' I muttered. 'Or you've met him, at least.'

'And?'

'That's it. He's there. He's been kind to me, more than kind actually. These things make you vulnerable.'

'Someone dying?'

237

'Yes.' I looked up at him. 'Does that surprise you?'

'Not in the least.'

There was a long silence. I felt incredibly tired. Then Harald stirred.

'We've all tried, Ellie. We've all done our best . . .' He frowned, fingering the tablecloth. 'I've never lost a wife . . . you know . . . had a marriage go from under me. It must be tough.'

'It is. It's bloody tough. And I'm grateful, Harald, don't get me wrong. Old Glory, our Harvard, all the time you've spent, all the money, this . . .' I gestured round. 'God knows what I've done to deserve it.'

Harald watched me tallying the help he'd given me since Adam's death. The smile had gone now and there was another expression on his face, infinitely bleaker. He signalled to the waiter, calling for the tab. It was barely half past nine. I couldn't believe it.

'Is that it, then? We just go home now?'

Harald was sorting through a sheaf of credit cards. When he spoke, he didn't bother looking up.

'You're tired, Ellie. We've got a helluva day ahead of us, a helluva week. I want you solo by the end of the month. That's a damn tight schedule.'

'But what about Adam?' I glared at him across the table.

Harald sighed. He'd had enough of this conversation and he wanted me to know it.

'Adam and I had supper that last night. You probably remember me mentioning it.'

'The Japanese place. Adam had sushi.'

'He did. We also talked a lot. Like always.'

'And?'

'He wanted me to do something for him, just in case . . . you know . . . anything ever happened.'

'He had a *premonition?*'

'Absolutely not. You know him. He'd laugh at all that horseshit.'

'You're right.' I nodded vigorously. 'So what exactly did he say?'

The waiter had returned now and Harald scribbled a signature on the credit card slip. Then he looked up.

'He asked me to make sure you'd always be OK,' he said softly. 'He asked me to look after you.'

'*Me?*'

'Yes.'

'Why?'

'Because he loved you. Because he cared. Because he never wanted to see you hurt.' He pushed his chair back and got to his feet. 'Now does that answer your question?'

On the way back to Standfast, confused, exhausted, drained of all anger, I had a major attack of the guilts. This man had been more than kind to me. He'd kept the business afloat. He'd shipped me halfway round the world. And now he was spending his own precious time teaching me to fly one of the world's trickier aircraft. Yet all I could do in return was put him on the spot about Adam. As we sped down the long, dark blacktop, I felt cheap, and adolescent, and ungrateful, and when we finally made it back to the Casa Blanca, I tried to make amends.

The wind had got up, and standing in the warm darkness beside Harald I could hear the slap-slap of the halyard against the metal flagpole.

'Tell me about the flag, Harald.' I gestured up at the ghostly cross and stars rippling in the night wind. 'Why that one?'

'It's the Confederate flag. Dixie. The old South.'

'Were you born round here? Is that where your heart is?'

'No.'

'But you like it?'

'The mind-set, yes.'

I wanted to slip my arm through his, be friends again, but Harald wasn't having it. I followed him into the house. It was barely half past ten but already the place was in darkness. He led the way to the kitchen and turned on the lights.

'Help yourself to anything. Coffee, juice, whatever. There's liquor if you need it. I'll see you in the morning.'

He gave me a thin smile and a peck on the cheek and he was halfway up the hall before I heard his footsteps falter. Then he was back again. The base station for the cordless phone was on top of the dresser. He picked up the phone and gave it to me.

'Take it to bed if you want to. The code for the UK's zero-zero-four-four.'

He left me holding the phone, and seconds later I heard a door opening and closing down the hall. Then came a soft surge of music, something classical, and I sank into a chair at the long pine table, feeling terrible. Adam asked me to make sure you'd always be OK. That's what he'd said. Adam asked me to look after you because he cared.

Cared about what? That I was a child? That I was vulnerable? That I'd fall apart at the first suspicion that the man I'd loved might have had eyes for someone else? I shook my head, confused and bewildered and above all disgusted with myself. I'd seen the look in Harald's eyes. He was disappointed with me. He thought I was worth more than Jamie, worth more than my petulant outburst in the restaurant, worth more than a daily drip-feed of schoolgirl letters. God knows, maybe he was right. Maybe I should try and grow up, be stronger, behave like the woman he so obviously thought I could be.

I hauled myself to my feet and drifted across to the fridge. There was a corked bottle of Chablis in the rack, half full, and I poured myself a generous glass. The wine tasted of oak and apples and I drank it the way you'd drink fruit juice, big, needful swallows. I was thinking of that first night Jamie and I had slept together at the hotel over in Jersey. Maybe it really had been Harald's Mercedes down in the courtyard. Maybe he'd followed us, discharging his pledge to Adam, keeping an eye on the wilful, headstrong widow.

I thought about it some more, trying to work out the way he'd have done it, keeping his distance in the dark, parking up beside the pub where we'd stopped for a drink, and then I suddenly remembered the girl at the check-in desk at the airport. She knew where we'd gone. She'd even given me the hotel's number. So all Harald had to do, like any caring friend, was phone the airport to check we were away safely. The girl, of course, would have said no. They've had to stay overnight. They've gone to this place up the road.

What then? I shut my eyes a moment, knowing full well that it was absolutely in Harald's character to drive across and make sure we were OK. He'd probably had plans to join us for a meal, chat a little more about the States, make us feel at home. But when he got to the hotel he'd have found the restaurant empty, and a double room booked, and the curtains drawn up on the first floor. No wonder he was keeping me at arm's length. No wonder he was so distant.

I returned to the fridge and emptied the remains of the Chablis into my glass. A couple of brief hours had transformed Harald into a kind of father figure – concerned, watchful, occasionally forbidding. He had my best interests at heart. He was trying to nudge me in directions he thought Adam would have wanted. The last thing that I – or Jamie – should do was misinterpret any of that.

I took my glass to my room, feeling better. At least I knew where I was. At least, emotionally, things were a little simpler. I sat on the bed with my legs up, reading the rest of Jamie's letter. After the initial outburst, he'd quietened down – almost as if he, too, had realised the need for a bit of restraint. The next few weeks, he said, would be like one of his longer runs. We had to pace ourselves, save ourselves, be patient. We had to have the faith and the trust to know that the days would roll by, and that May would spill into June, and that this huge, yawning gap in our lives would come to an end.

He said he'd ringed my birthday on the calendar he kept by his bed at Ralph's: 10 June. By then, I'd be back. By then, we could celebrate, maybe even go flying together, just like the old days. In the mean time, I was to promise him that I'd take care, stay in one piece, and make sure I put the bloody undercarriage down *before* I tried to land. At the end of the letter, above the neat row of kisses, he'd written 'Three greens?', a gesture that – to me – touched the very essence of what there was between us. In the air and on the ground we were a wonderful team, but there were rules that applied to even us. Break those rules, ignore gravity, and we'd very definitely come to grief.

I re-read the letter, smiling at Jamie's wilder excesses, and then went back to the kitchen. I wanted to talk to him. I wanted to share this feeling of mine that we'd come to an important moment in our relationship. It wasn't that we needed to rein each other in. It was just that we ought to – in his phrase – pace ourselves.

Tingling with anticipation, I took the phone back to bed. It would be lovely to hear his voice, to compare notes, to agree that – together – we were on track.

I dialled Mapledurcombe. The phone rang for ages. I hadn't bothered to work out the time in England and it was Andrea who spared me the effort.

'It's five o'clock in the morning,' she mumbled. 'What's going on?'

'Nothing.' I was looking at the wine glass. 'How are you?'

'How am I? Bloody tired if you want the truth.'

I said I was sorry for phoning so early. I heard the scrape of a match in the background, then Andrea was back on the phone again. This time she sounded a little more coherent. I asked her how things were going and she said fine. The first week's guests had only arrived a couple of days ago but already she knew she could count on at least three invitations back to the States. They were sweet, the men especially, and they all thought Mapledurcombe was divine.

'Great,' I said. 'How about the flying?'

I'd fixed for a couple of commercial pilots, both friends of Adam's, to be on standby for the Harvard and the Mustang. Our guests would have to fit in with these guys' work schedules but Andrea assured me that it was all sorted.

'It's going to be hard to get them out of the house, though.' I could hear her laughing. 'You won't believe how much they love this place.'

She went off on a long story about some woman or other, a Mrs

Fernstein, and I sipped the wine, waiting for the punchline. When she'd finished laughing, I bent to the phone again.

'How's Jamie?'

'I've no idea.'

'What?' My voice gave me away. Where was he? What was going on?

'He's been in London,' Andrea explained. 'Since the day you left.'

'*Where?*'

'London. He said he needed time off. It's a real pain, Ellie, but I could hardly say no, not after everything he's done.'

Jamie's letter was still open on the duvet. I stared at it, numb with disbelief. What about all the problems he was supposed to be having with my rabid sister? What about those photos she'd found in his precious garden shed? Why tell such extravagant lies when I was bound to be talking like this to Andrea?

I lifted the phone again, determined not to give myself away.

'Any idea when he's back?'

'Tomorrow night. He phoned last night.' She paused. 'Any message?'

I shook my head and mumbled something about sending him my love. Then I put the phone down.

Some time later, I've no idea exactly when, I crept out of the bedroom. I was still fully clothed but I'd slipped off my sandals. I padded through the darkened corridors, following the sound of music. There was a thin strip of light at the bottom of the door to Harald's den. I knocked softly. There was no answer. I knocked again and then, very slowly, pushed the door open.

Harald was lying full-length on the sofa beside his desk, his eyes closed. Light from the desk lamp had pooled around a photo he'd propped against his laptop. The photo was a black-and-white shot in one of those clear plastic stand-up holders. It showed a man in a long black leather coat. It was obviously winter, because there was snow on the ground behind him. The man had a strong, young face, pinched with cold. His eyes were deeply sunken and his cheeks were hollowed with fatigue but he was trying to smile. I looked at the photo a moment longer, certain I'd seen the face before. Then I remembered the shots lined up on the shelf behind Monica's armchair. Same half-smile. Same overwhelming sense of exhaustion.

Harald's eyes opened. He ran a hand over his face and got up on one elbow.

'Something the matter?'

'No.' I shook my head. 'I've just come to say sorry.'

'What for?'

'Tonight. I behaved like a child. Just ignore me. Pretend it never happened.'

Harald gazed up at me. Then his face broke into a grin.

'You're right, it never happened.' His eyes closed again. 'Sleep well.'

Chapter fourteen

Exactly a week later, two days ahead of schedule, I went solo. The moment, when it came, was almost an anticlimax. We'd spent the morning practising aerobatics, Harald leading me through a series of rolls. The rolls led to a wonderful manoeuvre called a Cuban Eight which I'd been doing for years in my Moth. The Cuban is basically a couple of half-loops stitched together in the middle – forming a sideways figure eight – but getting it as right as Harald demanded involved a degree of accuracy that stretched me to the limit.

My fourth or maybe fifth Cuban Eight was the one that drew Harald's applause. We were fifty miles south of Standfast and on the way back he took me through a couple of hesitation rolls. As ever, he was interested in precision – pausing the roll at exactly 90 degrees, exactly 180 degrees, exactly 270 degrees, before flicking it back to the horizontal. My first attempts were pretty woeful and I used up far too much sky, but with the airfield in sight I won my second gold star of the morning.

'Very nice,' he grunted as we joined the circuit and I lowered the undercarriage for the gentlest of landings.

Back on the apron, he did some calculations on the fuel load and organised extra Avgas while I made notes for the inevitable debrief. By the time I'd finished, he was unbuckling his parachute harness. Thinking it was time for lunch, I got out and began to do the same. A hand on my arm told me to stop.

'She's yours,' he said. 'Take her back south. You've got fifty minutes in the wing tanks, plus a reserve.' He grinned at me. 'Enjoy yourself.'

At first I didn't understand the implications of what he was telling me. Then he glanced at his watch and said he had some calls to make, and it dawned on me that I was to go off on my own. As ever with Harald there was no drama, no fuss, just a second or two of eye contact and the question that said it all.

'OK?'

I nodded. I expected a flutter of nerves but somehow it didn't happen. To clamber back into the machine and fly away by myself seemed the most natural thing in the world.

Harald watched me settle in the front cockpit. When I was comfortable, he climbed up and checked the harness. Then he patted me on the shoulder and asked me what I'd like for lunch.

'Tuna on rye,' I said at once. 'And three bottles of champagne.'

Barely five minutes later, I was airborne. I banked away to the south, still climbing. It was a beautiful, cloudless day and for some reason the visibility was much sharper than usual. Up at 7,000 feet I could see the long white line of the coast all the way down beyond Naples. I climbed higher still, the engine drumming away in front of me, and the further south I went the more I sensed that something about my flying was very different.

It wasn't simply that I was alone. It was something else, something so unfamiliar that it began to unsettle me. I double-scanned the instruments, checking my heading and speed against my watch, drawing and redrawing my course in my mind. I looked out to port and starboard, and then over both shoulders, wary for other traffic, ever more anxious to pin down this vague feeling of impending trouble. The aircraft, for once, was trimmed out beautifully. We were alone in the sky. So what was it that kept niggling away at me?

The realisation, when it came, spread a big, fat smile across my face. At last, after nearly a fortnight of nonstop effort, I had time. Time to look out at the view. Time to plot the long left-hand turn that would take me back towards Standfast. Time to realise that the Mustang – in the end – was just another aircraft, a friend as well as a legend. I shook my head in admiration, understanding at last why Harald had been cramming so much into the last ten days' flying.

My log book told the story. With a huge high-pressure zone anchored over the Gulf of Mexico, we'd been up two, sometimes three times a day, each sortie packed with fresh problems, fresh solutions. Scarcely a minute would pass without Harald nudging me from the rear seat. Another abrupt departure from straight-and-level. Another spin. Another chance to watch the flat brown fields below revolving and revolving until I'd stabbed hard at the rudder and lowered the nose and put myself back in control. These traps that Harald would so carefully set seemed never-ending, and after barely a couple of days I'd found myself developing an instinct for trouble that became a kind of sixth sense. The aircraft had become an extension of my own nervous system. It would speak to me, tell me things. The tiny shivers that triggered a stall. The change in the engine note when we flew through cloud. How heavy the controls became when we hit the throttle and explored certain corners of the flight envelope.

At the end of each of these extraordinary days, with my knee pad full of despairing notes, Harald would debrief me, unpicking each situation, untangling each crisis, explaining the theory behind my ever-increasing repertoire of responses. At the start, to be fair, he'd warned me about the way it would be, how he'd push me as hard as he pushed any other fighter pilot, stretching the flight envelope wider and wider, but I'd never imagined for a moment how physically and mentally draining this process would be. Most nights, I'd been in bed and asleep by half past nine. My world, quite literally, had shrunk to the cockpit of the Mustang. I ate, slept, dreamed flying. Nothing else mattered. Not Adam. Not Mapledurcombe. Not even Jamie.

Now, alone in the Mustang for the first time, I thought about it with a sense of wonderment. By being so ruthless, by making life so bloody difficult, Harald had given me immense confidence, and it was only now that I realised just how important that confidence would be. There were a million ways this aeroplane could still take me by surprise, but Harald had stretched me to the point where the basics – staying airborne, staying in one piece – had become second nature.

This was my very first Mustang solo. I wasn't required to bomb anything, or race around the sky after some lunatic from El Salvador or Honduras, or even climb up to 13,000 feet and induce a spin or two. But that, of course, was exactly the point. What should have been an ordeal was in fact turning out to be a pleasure. After an eternity of heart-stopping challenges and split-second decisions, I'd earned my just rewards. Thanks to Harald, I could take off, bimble around and then land again. All by myself.

He was waiting for me on the apron back at Standfast. He was sitting in Chuck's Jeep, his flying boots up on the dashboard, his peaked cap pulled low over his eyes. He watched me close down the engine, and when I hauled myself out of the cockpit he got out of the Jeep and helped me down off the wing. He didn't ask me how it had gone. That wasn't Harald's way. He just looked up at the open cockpit, and patted the warm panels behind the engine exhausts, and told me we were off for a picnic.

We drove down to the very edge of the airfield. A track I'd never seen before led through an open gate in the perimeter fence, and we bumped along for about a mile before stopping beside a tiny lake. I'd noticed the lake from the air. In the late afternoon, approaching from the north-east, the sun lanced off the water, and the lake became a puddle of molten gold that told me I was on track for a landing.

Harald, bless him, had taken me at my word. He spread a blanket in the shade of a big old cypress and produced a bottle of ice-cold Krug from a battered cool box.

'Real glasses?'

'Special occasion. They once belonged to my dad.'

I couldn't believe my eyes. Harald laid the two fine-stemmed crystal glasses side by side, giving them a wipe as he did so. The champagne cork made a splash as it hit the water. I watched the Krug bubbling in the first glass.

'And you?'

Harald smiled at me and shook his head.

'Orange juice,' he said, 'I'm afraid.'

We toasted my solo. When I told him how brilliant he'd been, he turned his head away, not saying anything. We'd become really good friends by now, a simple straightforward relationship tempered and burnished by something I can only describe as a deep mutual respect. I think he knew how much I admired his patience and his airmanship and in return I like to think he'd put aside the little scene I'd made in the restaurant. Since that evening, neither of us had mentioned either Adam or Jamie and for that I was profoundly grateful. Coming to terms with something as potentially lethal as the Mustang lends a certain sense of perspective. A lot of things matter in this world and one of them is survival. Going solo was a much bigger phrase than I'd ever imagined.

Harald was unwrapping the tuna sandwiches. I could see the mayonnaise oozing over the thick slices of rye bread.

'What next?' I enquired.

'Depends.'

'On what?'

'You.'

He handed me a sandwich. Service, I was glad to note, didn't extend to anything as un-Harald as plates. I took a bite of tuna, realising how famished I was. Harald was still waiting for an answer.

'I'm happy,' I wiped my mouth, 'to do whatever.'

'OK.' He nodded and looked away again. 'Then how about this.'

He outlined a flying programme. We had just under three weeks left. If the weather held and there were no serviceability problems, we'd be looking at another forty hours or so in the air. He'd like to put me in one of the Cavalier Mustangs, a single-seater with the full armament fit. He'd be flying alongside in another Cavalier and we'd be sticking to the brief-sortie-debrief pattern he applied to all the formal conversion courses. Forty hours wasn't a lifetime's flying but it should give me, in his phrase, 'a familiarity with the relevant SOPs'.

SOP means Standard Operating Procedure. Ten days at Standfast had given me a pretty good idea of what they might involve but I had to be sure.

'What exactly do you mean, Harald?'

'I mean putting all this to some use. Sure, it's nice to fly around once in a while and take a look at the view, but the plane was built for a purpose.' He began to doodle in the dust beside the blanket, using a bent old twig. 'The Cavalier's a workhorse. We hang stuff off it. Once you can fly the thing, you become the mailman.'

'*Mailman?*'

'Yeah, the guys who come here are in the delivery business. Bombs, Willy Pete, Hell Jelly. You name it, we teach them how to make the drop.'

A crude aeroplane was taking shape in the dust and I gazed down at it, realising just how easy it was to slip into this world of Harald's. Willy Pete was white phosphorus. Hell Jelly was napalm. Harald must have dropped tons of the stuff over Vietnam, and the combat skills he'd brought home doubtless formed part of the Standfast package.

I sipped at the champagne, thinking of the men I saw every morning, young pilots up from Central and South America, testing themselves against 12,000 pounds of vintage aeroplane.

'You want me to do the full course?'

'Bits of it.'

'Including dive-bombing?'

'Sure, and air-to-air, and tactical appreciations, and a little close-formation work.' He looked down at the shape of the aeroplane in the dust and then tossed the twig away. 'You'll get a taste, maybe a little more than that. It's just training really, dressed up as combat.'

Combat. He'd said it.

'You want me to fight in the Mustang? Become a man?'

'I want you to fly to your limits. This is one way of doing it.'

'The only way?'

'The best way.'

He reached lazily for the bottle and poured me more champagne. I'd had very little breakfast and the first glass had already begun to blur the edges of the day. I was made for this, I thought, stretching full-length on the blanket and trying to imagine what the dive-bombing course might entail. Away to the south, Standfast had a practice range, and when the wind was in the right direction you could hear the crump-crump of the little iron eggs I watched being loaded every morning.

I closed my eyes, waving away the insects.

'Why do you have to fight to fly well?'

'You don't. Not if you have good hands.'

'Do I have good hands?'

'You have wonderful hands. You fly very well. You're a natural.'

Good hands. Adam had used exactly the same phrase. Harald's compliments made me tingle inside. That, and the champagne.

'So why all this military stuff? The toys for the boys?'

I opened one eye, feeling Harald's shadow across my face. He was sitting with his back to me, his knees drawn up, and he began to muse aloud about fighter pilots, how competitive they were, how they were always keeping the score.

'Is that important?'

The question seemed to surprise him. He glanced round, his face shadowed by the peak of his cap.

'Of course it's important.'

'Why? Because it's all about winning?'

'Sure, but it's more than that.'

'You mean there's something more important than winning?'

'Of course.' Harald ignored the mockery in my voice. 'There's control, too. Planning the thing out, leaving nothing to chance, making sure that bit of sky stays yours. You know what they say about combat?'

I looked up at him, thinking suddenly of my glorious solo flight, the feeling of just hanging there, bathed in sunshine, weightless, immortal. Was this what Harald meant by control? Or was there a darker secret?

'Tell me . . .' I murmured, closing my eyes again. 'Tell me what they say about combat.'

'It's easy. You never fight a fair fight.'

'You don't?'

'Never. You stack the odds. You choose the time and the place. You make sure you're higher, tighter, smarter, faster. When I'm ready and you're about to die . . .' he laughed softly, '. . . that's what a fighter pilot dreams about.'

Something in his voice penetrated the Krug. I sat up, swatting away the mosquitoes.

'That sounds horrible,' I told him. 'That's not my kind of flying.'

'It isn't,' he nodded, 'and that makes you very lucky.'

'*Lucky*? Why? Don't people have a choice? Do you have to be a fighter pilot? Think about the odds all the time? Dream about killing people? Is that compulsory? Or am I missing something here?'

'You're missing nothing. Like I say, you're lucky.'

'And you?'

'I'm a fighter pilot.'

There was a long silence. Far away, I thought I heard the cough of a Merlin misfiring. I rolled over, still thinking about what he'd said.

'You make it sound like a life sentence. What have you done to deserve this, Harald? Is it some kind of punishment?'

I'd asked the question partly in jest, but the moment I saw him flinch I knew I'd touched a nerve. I wanted to apologise, to tell him that I hadn't meant to intrude, but when I tried to do just that he shook his head, telling me there was no need. He'd liked being a fighter pilot. It was one of the things he was good at. Never in a million years would he think of it as a punishment.

'And hey, I still get to do it, still get to fool around, thanks to that place.'

He nodded in the direction of the airfield and plucked at a stalk of grass. He was trying to lighten the conversation, turn it away from himself, but I wouldn't let him. I remembered something Chuck had said. Harald's strung out tighter than a bow, he'd told me. He seems buttoned-down real good but underneath he's pretty emotional and one day it just might all spill out.

'What happened, Harald?' I asked softly. 'What made you this way?'

'What way?'

'So competitive all the time? So much needing to win?'

He shook his head, brooding on the questions, refusing to answer, and I reached out and touched him gently on the shoulder, the way true friends do. We had a kinship. We were close. I wanted him to know that.

He looked up and for a second I thought he was going to tell me something important, something that might help explain this obsession of his with scores and kills and staying on top. Then, from the Jeep, came the trill of his mobile. The moment had gone. He was on his feet, checking his watch. Away to the east, the growl of the Merlin had grown louder. I swallowed the remains of my champagne and helped myself to another glassful. By the time Harald came back, I was practically asleep.

'What's the matter?'

Harald was standing beside me, staring out towards the east. He muttered something about an in-flight problem, and I got to my feet in time to watch one of the Cavalier Mustangs limping in towards the airfield. Smoke was feathering back from the exhausts, and as it flew low over us I could see that part of the rudder was hanging off. I watched it wallowing down the glidepath and I tried to imagine how tricky it must be for the pilot, fighting against the tug of the damaged tail.

Suddenly, in the wake of the plane, there was an overpowering smell of Avgas. A fuel leak as well, I thought. That's all the pilot would need.

'What happened?'

Harald was shaking out the blanket. Our picnic by the lake was evidently over.

'A dogfight turned nasty.' He picked up the empty champagne bottle. 'Couple of the guys had a row in the bar last night.'

I was looking for the Mustang again. From this distance it was impossible to judge whether or not he'd make the runway.

'They're using live ammunition?'

'Sure. They shoot at drogues, normally.' He shrugged. 'I guess it got a little out of hand.'

After Harald dropped me at the Casa Blanca, I went to my bedroom. Early afternoon was always the hottest part of the day, and four glasses of champagne had put paid to any flying. I pushed the door open, grateful for the air-conditioning and the prospect of a long nap. Only when I pulled the sheet down did I see the letters.

There were three of them and I knew at once that they were all from Jamie. The same green Pentel. The same thick trademark kisses scrawled across the back of the envelope. I slipped into bed, trying to work out the dates on the postmarks. Quite deliberately over the past week I'd neither phoned nor written. The realisation that Jamie had lied to me in that first letter was deeply upsetting, and no matter how hard I tried to make excuses for him I knew that something had changed. Maybe all the stuff about Andrea ripping up my photos was poetic licence. Maybe he'd never meant me to take it seriously. But either way, there was a part of me that didn't entirely believe him any more. If he'd lied about Andrea, what else shouldn't I take at face value?

It was questions like these that ate away at my concentration and I knew only too well that the last thing I should take with me every morning were worries about my love life. The Mustang was the most demanding partner I'd ever met. And unlike Jamie, it could all too easily kill me.

Now, though, it was different. The last ten days had toughened me immeasurably. I felt strong. I felt immensely pleased with myself. And – a real surprise, this – I felt a tremendous sense of independence. Adam had been right all along. Flying can change your life.

The letters, as it turned out, were linked. Jamie had helpfully numbered each envelope, and as the pile of airmail paper grew and grew on the bedside table it began to dawn on me that I had acquired yet another role in his young life. Not simply his lover, and flight instructor, and long-distance correspondent, but also – his word, not mine – his confessor.

The story, as far as I could gather, centred on a woman he'd met at university up in Aberdeen. She was older than him, nearly thirty, and German. Her name was Gitta and she was nearing the end of a two-year course in business studies. Back home in Munich, she worked for one of the big German oil companies and one of the reasons her bosses had sent her off to Aberdeen was to brush up on her English. Once she'd graduated, there was an important job waiting for her down in the company's London offices. Gitta was well-off, beautiful and newly divorced. Jamie, poor lamb, had fallen in love with her.

The affair had lasted nearly eighteen months. Gitta had been renting a big two-bedroomed flat up near the university, and Jamie had moved in. He'd never, he wrote, had any clear idea where the relationship would lead but the thought that it might one day end was inconceivable.

Gitta had come to obsess him. Sexually, she'd taught him every-thing he'd ever known. Mentally, she put him to shame. Every successive day had drawn him closer to her. Every night, he'd wanted more and more of her. He'd felt himself losing sight of the person he really was, a process of surrender that was both wilful and delicious. Gitta had swamped every last atom in his body. When he occasion-ally surfaced, and took an inventory, there was nothing left that was his. The word he used again and again was enslavement. He worshipped her. He followed her around. Pathetic. Needful. Lost.

Lost. I thought of Harald and his iron grip on life, on circum-stances, on himself. Then I read on, trying to imagine Jamie with this lustrous, talented siren, the woman who'd taken my puppy-lover and put him on a lead, and dragged him down to London.

They'd found a house in Chiswick. It had three bedrooms and a garden shed in the back yard where Jamie could keep all the stuff he used for tree surgery. At first he'd assumed that life in London would be Aberdeen with sunshine. They'd sleep late, make love at noon, take long walks by the river. The reality, though, was very different. Transformed by her job, and her brand-new degree, Gitta had disappeared every morning to some office in the City he didn't even want to visualise. When she came back it was late – often eight or nine at night – and she brought with her a life and a career that he found deeply threatening. People she worked with. Men she met for lunch. A whole cast of people who seemed to belong to something she called *Der wirklichen Welt*. The real world.

Poor Jamie. I sat back, thinking of him alone in Chiswick with his chain saw and his bewilderment and his big fat tubs of fairy dust. Every night, being Jamie, he'd try and revive a little of the old magic, and every night, being the bright young thing he undoubtedly was, he'd have to confront the terrible knowledge that whatever it was had gone. One of life's blessings had been Gitta. And one of life's crueller lessons was the realisation that she wasn't, after all, his property.

She'd asked him to leave only a couple of months ago. She'd turned up, unusually, in mid-afternoon. He'd been typing out some estimates in the little back bedroom he used as an office. She'd sat him down on the bed and told him that she'd fallen in love with a City trader called Tom. Jamie had been denied even the comfort of knowing she'd been swept off her feet by a fellow German. No. Tom was something big in sugar futures. And he was every bit as English as Jamie.

A couple of months ago. I kept my diary in my grab bag. I flicked back through April, trying to remember exactly when it was that I'd first laid eyes on Jamie. It had been down at Ralph's place. Jamie had been staying the weekend. I closed my eyes, leaning back against the pillow, remembering him coming in from his run, his face pinked with exertion, his runners caked in mud. It must have happened then, I thought. Heartbroken, homeless, sick of London, he must have fled south to the comforts of Ralph and his little bungalow by the sea. I thought of everything else that had happened to him – his father's affair, the step-family he'd never known, his mother's suicide – and I thought again of this German woman, Gitta, and everything he must have invested in her.

Gitta would have been the fresh start, the kind of headlong love affair that begins like a miracle and ends in a bitterness that I knew only too well. I returned to the letters. Losing Gitta, he said, was a blow so unexpected, so bloody unfair, that he'd seriously toyed with suicide himself. He could see no end to his grief, no point in carrying on, and it was only his contempt for his father that had kept him from following his mother's footsteps to the nearest station and chucking himself under a train. The Germans had a phrase for it. *Götterdämmerung*. The final curtain. Too bloody right.

I opened the third letter, as yet unread. Andrea had been right. After we'd said our goodbyes at Heathrow, Jamie had gone back into central London. He wasn't clear, even now, why he'd done it, but there were ghosts to be laid, and accounts to be settled, and much,

much sooner than he'd ever dreamed possible he felt strong enough, and dispassionate enough, to walk the half-mile from Turnham Green tube station and knock on the door and step back into Gitta's life. She'd been alone. The thing with Tom hadn't worked out. They'd talked for most of the night. He'd told her all about me, all about us, and at half past three in the morning Gitta had broken the news. She was four months pregnant. With Jamie's baby.

I stared at the words on the page. Jamie? A *father*? Back in the hotel, that first night on Jersey, he'd hinted of shadows in his past, and reading about Gitta, and what she'd meant to him, I'd begun to understand. But this was something else entirely. He'd loved this woman, given himself to her, and now she was carrying his baby. What next?

The rest of the letter tussled with exactly that. There was no question, he said, that he and Gitta would ever get back together again. Gitta, it seemed, was all for trying but Jamie was insistent that it wouldn't work. His life had moved on. There was me now, the relationship we'd built, the promises we'd made, the log book we'd jointly started for this new journey of ours. The phrases brought a smile to my face and I wondered what Gitta must have made of them. One day, I thought, Jamie might just take a risk or two with someone his own age. Not an ambitious divorcee. Or an even older widow.

I'd got to the last page now, and naturally enough the story took one final twist before the row of kisses waiting for me on the bottom line. Gitta had laid down an ultimatum. Unless Jamie was prepared to give them both another chance, she was going to have the baby aborted. Without a father, she had absolutely no intention of starting a family. I read the last paragraph again, not altogether sure that I understood what he was really saying. Was there a message here that he was too timid – or too young – to voice? Wasn't he really telling me that he'd like to go back, that he'd never really got Gitta out of his system? And in that case, mightn't the baby – assuming there was a baby – be nothing more than a pretext? A smokescreen behind which Jamie and I might disengage with honour?

I shook my head, at a loss for an answer, and when I read the last letter for a third time I realised that in all probability he didn't know either. Life, for Jamie, had piled confusion upon confusion, and just now the kindest thing I could do was talk to him.

The kitchen was empty. I took the cordless phone, and the local directory with the international codes, and returned to my bedroom. This time, I dialled my own mobile number, assuming that Jamie had hung on to it.

It rang and rang. I sat on the side of the bed, trying to picture where he might be. Down at Ralph's bungalow? Out on a run? At last, the number answered.

'Hallo?'

The sound of Jamie's voice brought the blood to my face, a big, whole-hearted, warm feeling that told me everything I wanted to know. I did miss him. A lot. And I wasn't quite as independent as I might have thought.

'Where are you?'

'In the car. Hang on, I'll pull over.'

There was a pause while he parked, then – within seconds – I found myself telling him about the adventures of the last ten days, partly out of excitement, and partly as an apology for not getting in touch. When I got to the more dramatic bits – bombs, rockets, dogfights – Jamie couldn't stop laughing.

'I thought the war was over?'

'Not here it isn't. Harald says it'll be good for my flying. He thinks every pilot should drop a bomb or two. He says it's like aerobics. He says it tones you up.'

At the mention of Harald, the laughter stopped.

'How is he?'

'He's fine. And before you ask, he's been the perfect gentleman. We go flying every day. He's taught me loads. He's made me realise what a lousy pilot I've been. But that's just about it. You've got him wrong, Jamie. He's old enough to be my father.'

I winced at the phrase. Jamie's letters were still all over the bed. Jamie was asking me again about Harald. He couldn't keep him out of the conversation. Why was he bothering to teach me all this stuff? What was the point?

'I don't know. Yet.'

'Will he ever tell you?'

'I'm not sure. He has this theory about stretching the envelope, but actually I think it's much simpler than that. It's boy's stuff. He never grew up.'

There was a long silence. Outside I could hear Monica's voice, and when I took the phone to the window she was out there again with the metal cage, alone this time.

'So when are you coming back?'

The date on my ticket was 5 June. I confirmed there'd been no change of plan. Jamie sounded relieved.

'Back for your birthday, then?'

'Absolutely. Bet your life.'

I asked him whether he was missing me. I was looking at the letters.

'Hugely. All the time. And the flying, too. Life's a drag at ground level.' He paused. 'You got my letters?'

'I just read them.'

'You don't mind, do you? Me telling you all that stuff?'

I frowned, thinking of that first letter. Should I get it off my chest? Give him a chance to explain why he'd had to stoop to fiction to explain how much I meant to him?

'Why didn't you tell me about London to begin with?' I asked him. 'Why pretend you'd been back to the island?'

'I . . . don't know . . .' I could hear his voice falter. 'I was just confused, I suppose.'

'But you could have told me, couldn't you?'

'Yes.'

'So why lie?'

He hated the word lie and he told me so. He hadn't tried to deceive me, hadn't tried to hide anything. Rather than broach what he called 'the whole bloody shambles', he'd thought it better to invent a bit. The fact that I might talk to Andrea hadn't occurred to him.

'OK.' I was trying hard to play the older woman. 'But next time you want to put me off the scent, just think it through, eh? Lying's not part of the deal, my love. We talked about it. Remember?'

I was referring to Adam, and I was cross, and he knew it. The affair with Gitta, he assured me, was over. The only problem was the baby.

'It's not a problem, Jamie. Not if you don't let it be.'

'How come?'

'She has an abortion. She gets rid of it. And she's right, too. If there's no father, no support, what kind of life could she offer?'

'Lots of single parents manage OK.'

'But she doesn't want to. Not as I understand it.'

'Who says it has to be her?'

I stared at the phone. Yet another little surprise.

'*You'd* take the baby?'

'Why not?'

I sat down on the bed again, robbed of an answer. Sometimes it occurred to me that Jamie himself was scarcely out of nappies. The thought of him bringing up a child of his own was a joke.

'It's a real commitment,' I heard myself saying. 'Have you really thought this thing through?'

'Yes.'

'You *have*?'

'Yes.'

'And what does she say?'

'She won't hear of it.'

'So where does that leave you?'

'I've no idea. I've been thinking of taking legal advice but I just don't know.'

He began to talk about abortion, how evil it was, how he couldn't bear to think of any baby, least of all his own, being torn from the womb and flushed down the pan. The language was pretty graphic – I could hear the emotion in his voice – and I asked myself yet again whether this baby was real. Jamie, beyond doubt, had a flair for the dramatic. Maybe this was just another way of getting close to me, just another torn-up snap in his rich imagination.

Abruptly, he said he had to go. He'd promised to pick up Ralph from the bridge club and he was already half an hour late.

'One thing I forgot to mention,' he said. 'Grandpa wonders whether you'd have time to go up and see a bloke called . . . I can't remember . . . I think it's foreign, Czech or something.'

I frowned, upset by this sudden change of subject. Why couldn't we carry on talking while he drove? What nerve had I touched now?

'Do you mean Karel Brokenka?' I said at last. 'The pilot who flew our Mustang?'

'That's him. I think he lives in Chicago. Grandpa says he gave Harald the address.'

'What does he want me to say?'

'I dunno. Apparently there's a letter on its way. It's all in there. Some stuff to do with the book as far as I can gather.'

'And this is urgent? Important?'

'I think so.'

I tried to place Chicago in my mind. It was way up north somewhere. I bent to the phone again and said I'd wait for the letter. One way or another I was pretty sure we could sort something out. Jamie said Grandpa would be pleased. Then he asked me whether I'd phone again.

'Of course.'

'Brilliant.' I heard the car engine starting. 'I love you. Remember that.'

I was looking down at the litter of airmail pages scattered across the sheet, the bold green Pentel, the cries for help. He was just as needful, just as young as ever.

'You too,' I said softly. 'Take care, my love.'

When I took the phone back to the kitchen, Monica was sitting at the table, stripping the flesh from an over-ripe mango. She waved me into a chair and offered me a piece.

'I want you to know that Harald's really pleased with you, my

257

dear. He says you're one of the best pilots he's ever put through the school.'

The compliment came out through a mouthful of mango. A thin trickle of juice was dribbling down her chin, dissolving the layers of make-up. I offered her a tissue from a box on the table but she ignored it.

'So what do you think about that, my dear?' She bent towards me, her voice shrill, demanding an answer.

I was thinking about the metal cage she'd carried out to her little patch of wilderness. What was in it? And why was this daily ritual so exactly timed?

'I think he's very kind, your son. And if you're looking for brilliant pilots, then you should be thinking about him.'

'*Harald?*' It was more of a scoff than a laugh. 'You really think he's any good?'

'He's better than that. He's excellent.'

'In the air? As a pilot?'

'Yes, and as a teacher too. I teach a bit myself. It isn't easy.'

Monica was poking at the mango with a knife. Her hands fascinated me, the stick-thin fingers, the perfectly painted nails, the rings encrusted with diamonds and little slivers of emerald. I wanted to know more about her. Where she'd come from. What had brought her down here to Florida. How long she'd been living like this with her son.

'Harald was a good boy.' She plunged the knife into the last of the mango. 'Always a good boy.'

'He's your only son?'

'Yes, my husband . . .' She frowned. 'Harald was the only child.'

'And you're close, obviously.'

'You think so?' The knife, raised, was dripping juice all over yesterday's edition of the *Christian Science Monitor*.

I nodded, trying to give the conversation a fresh direction. Harald had done well. Standfast was the living proof. She must be very proud of him.

'Perhaps. But compared to his father . . .' She shook her head and spread her hands wide, a gesture – I thought – of exasperation.

'His father died recently? Your husband, I mean?'

'Not so recently. Harald and I, we see each other through.'

It was a strange way of putting it. Was the world out there so hostile they had to stick together? As tactfully as I could, I tried to voice the thought. Monica rewarded me with a vigorous nod.

'Harald needs someone to look after him. Always, always. Me? I need someone to look after. So . . .' she beamed at me, '. . . there you have it.'

I nodded, pretending to understand, but the notion of Harald needing comfort and protection seemed, at the very least, unlikely. Most of the time I'd known him, he'd been a list of phone numbers on Adam's office pad – Jersey, Zurich, Moscow, Sofia, Belgrade – endless excursions to outposts of his business empire. Was I to believe that this elderly, bird-like woman with her walking sticks and her wardrobe of black dresses accompanied him everywhere? Watched over him day and night?

'He's a very busy man,' I murmured. 'You must be glad to have him home for a while.'

'Home?' She was amused again. 'Here?'

This, at least, was a clue of sorts. I was about to pursue it when I looked up to find Harald standing at the open doorway. I hadn't heard the Jeep.

'Mom keeping you fed?' He gestured at the wreckage of the mango. 'Only the boys across the way have been roasting a hog or two.'

Harald stepped across and retrieved the tissue I'd left on the table. Then he knelt beside his mother, mopping her chin. She might have been a cat, the way she tilted her face up, enjoying the attention.

'Boys across the way?' I queried blankly.

'Yep. First solo on a Mustang?' He got to his feet again and nodded towards the open door. 'We owe ourselves a little celebration.'

The party was taking place in a compound on the southerly edge of the airfield. Beyond a line of pine trees there was a big open square of low, flat-roofed chalets built around a swimming pool. I'd never been here before, and from a distance, bumping along the cinder track between the pines, it looked like a motel. The sweet pungency of charring pork drifted towards us on the wind and when Harald stopped the Jeep and turned off the engine, I could hear the hot, tropical rhythms of a salsa band. I was wearing denim shorts and a Standfast T-shirt and I suddenly felt as if I'd gone on holiday. Time to relax. Time to have a little fun.

The barbecue pit lay beside the furthest hut. The men were gathered round, drinking and talking. I recognised many of the faces but out of uniform they looked younger, just another set of eager young tourists up from the south.

Harald led me from group to group, doing the introductions. A lot of these men seemed to know my name already and they greeted me with extravagant Latin courtesies, bowing low and kissing my hand.

One or two of them spoke a little English but my Spanish was good enough to understand very quickly that this party of theirs was in my honour.

They'd been following my progress all week. They'd seen me taking off, or in the air, or back on the apron, waiting for the refuelling bowser. That a woman should fly such a plane was, to them, a revelation and as the days went by they'd laid bets on when I might go solo. To my immense satisfaction, not one of them had been brave enough to put his money on such a rapid conversion, and when a sweet young pilot stepped forward and toasted my lunch-time sortie, the clink of our bottles of Sol brought a huge smile to my face.

'*De nada*,' I murmured. 'You're welcome.'

The party lasted all evening. The men lived in the compound – the accommodation was part of the Standfast deal – and I drifted from chalet to chalet enjoying the small talk and the hospitality. The men, without exception, were gracious and attentive. They drank sparingly and they laughed a great deal, a laughter fuelled by that very special kinship that pilots seem to share. I'd met it back home with Adam and I'd often tried to work out just why it was so powerful. Maybe it had something to do with the tests that flying set us. How difficult it was. How we were always having to juggle height, and speed, and power, and wind direction, and the million and one other factors that always threatened to get out of hand. Or maybe it was infinitely simpler than that. Defy gravity, play God, and the laughter just keeps bubbling up.

Either way, it was a glorious evening. We swapped notes about the Mustang, and about how wonderful it was to fly here, and I listened to pilot after pilot telling me what a difference the Standfast course had made to them. None of these men was keen to talk about the uses they'd make of their new-found skills once they got back home, but I got an impression of small, rugged backyard wars – some of them declared, some not – and when one young flyer from Bogotá hinted darkly at the surprises awaiting some of the key honchos in the drugs business, I believed him. If you were wanting to stretch the arm of the law into the mountains of Colombia, there were worse mounts to ride than the Mustang.

Towards the end of the evening, Harald mounted a chair beside the pool and put two fingers in his mouth. The piercing whistle brought the conversation to a halt, and when he proposed a toast to the guy who'd roasted the pig there was a roar of applause. Throughout the evening, I'd had glimpse after glimpse of Harald as he moved from group to group. It was obvious – to me at least – that he loved these men, the respect they gave him, the way they smiled with pleasure as he traded a joke or a compliment, but it was obvious too that even here – amongst the music and the laughter – he was alone. Even Chuck, his lifelong buddy, was careful to preserve a certain distance. Not because of anything specific – a row of some kind – but because that's the way Harald was. A man apart. Way up at altitude. Forever keeping the score.

Now, from God knows where, he'd produced a cake. The men crowded around. It was a big cake, a square thing. On top, in blue icing, someone had carefully reproduced the Standfast logo – an outstretched hand clasping the torch of liberty – and underneath, in pink, was my name. *Ellie Bruce*, it read, *Mustang Aviator*.

I stared at it. I'd drunk rather a lot by now and it took me a while to realise that the cheering and the cries of 'Bravo!' were for me. I reached up for Harald's hand. Getting two people on to a chair isn't easy but we managed it. Harald had his arm round me. He was calling for quiet. Then he began to speak, very softly, in Spanish.

Harald's Spanish was much better than mine but the drift of what he was saying was obvious. I'd climbed a mountain. I'd joined a club. I was one of the boys. I gazed down at the sea of faces around me. I was acutely aware of being the only woman amongst all these men but I couldn't remember when I'd last felt so much warmth, so much simple human fellowship. Harald's speech came to an end. There was a silence. They expected me to say something. The faces began to blur.

I rubbed the tears from my eyes. Harald's grip had tightened. I did my best to clear my throat.

'I come from the Falklands,' I began haltingly. 'I grew up on a farm.'

It wasn't the most tactful way to begin, not when there were one or two Argentinians on the course, but I didn't care. This was an evening for home truths, and mine couldn't have been simpler. I told them about Smoko, my beloved piebald grey. I described the days we'd spent out by ourselves, miles from anywhere, a happiness so complete I thought I'd never find it again. I paused. I could feel how tense Harald had become. Everyone was looking up at me, watching, waiting.

I raised my bottle.

'To Smoko,' I said. 'And to our Mustangs.'

Applause broke out. First a ripple, then a storm. I could see one of the young pilots asking for a translation, wondering exactly what it was I'd said, and the expression on his face when he found out was an image I'll treasure for ever. They understood, these men. They understood about solitude, and challenge, and coming home safe at the end of it all. To have joined them was an enormous privilege.

An hour or so later, Harald drove me back to the Casa Blanca. I was drunk by now, and I hung on to the grab rail on the dashboard of the Jeep as we bounced across the grass towards the runway. I'd never seen Harald so relaxed. The party had also celebrated the certification of his rebuilt Messerschmitt and he was now making plans to ship the plane over to the UK. I was still on cloud nine, reliving those endless days on the Falklands, and mention of the Fighter Meet brought me back to earth. Harald seemed to be suggesting that I, too, might form part of the display team.

I tried to focus on his face.

'You mean flying? In our Mustang?'

'Yes.'

The bumping stopped as we crossed the runway. Somewhere in the darkness away to our left were three white lines and an awful lot of rubber. Was this why Harald was putting me through the hoop? Was he trying to turn me into a display pilot?

I tried to voice the question. Harald, I should have known, was rarely in the business of direct answers.

'Display flying is heavily regulated,' he said. 'It might sound simple but it isn't.'

I agreed at once. Living with Adam had taught me just how fussy the CAA people could be. Even with his experience, getting a display authorisation had taken months of effort.

'But that's the idea?' I reached out to Harald to steady myself. 'You're going to turn me into a circus act?'

Harald glanced across at me, amused.

'We'll see. Depends how you shape.'

I looked across at him, expecting more, but he refused to elaborate. So far so good, he seemed to be saying. I sat back, my legs braced, watching the lights of the Casa Blanca getting closer. What would it be like, doing what Adam had done? Stepping into his shoes? Displaying our Mustang in front of tens of thousands of people? Could it possibly be any more difficult than the tests Harald had been setting me? Wasn't it obvious that I could hack it?

Too many bottles of Sol wreck your better judgement. The Jeep came to a halt outside the Casa Blanca. Harald switched off the engine. I leaned over towards him, collapsing heavily against his shoulder. I could feel him trying to withdraw.

'I just want to say thank you,' I said thickly. 'For showing me a new life.'

Harald eased me back to the vertical. I kissed him on the lips.

'Thank you,' I repeated. '*Muchas gracias.*'

'No problem.'

'Has it been a pleasure?' I held him at arm's length, trying to focus. 'Be honest.'

He looked at me for what seemed an age. Then he led me very gently into the house. The next thing I remember was the click of my bedroom door closing behind me. I looked round. I didn't want to go to bed and I resented the suggestion that I should. Instead, I went across to the window. The dark shadows of Monica's wilderness loomed out of the night. I could hear the rustle of wind in the trees and the buzzing of a thousand insects. I headed back to the door. I wanted to know about the little cage she left there every afternoon. I wanted to know why she did it, what she put inside. There was a torch in the kitchen. I'd seen it.

I made my way back down the darkened corridor. Of Harald, there was no sign. I was tempted to find him, to invite him along for the ride, but I decided against it. Drunken lady pilots weren't altogether to his taste, far too wild, far too unpredictable.

Torch in hand, I left the house and made my way along the chain-link fence. The gate, when I found it, was unlocked. I pushed it open, the light from the torch pooling at my feet. I began to wobble along the beaten earth path, sweeping the torch left and right, not knowing what I might find. The Sol had robbed me of fear. I didn't even mind the clouds of mosquitoes settling on my bare arms. The path veered suddenly to the left, the vegetation pressing against me. It was noisier than ever in here and I began to giggle, wondering how insects ever got a decent night's sleep, when the torch settled on something metallic.

It was another fence. I stepped towards it. It looked pretty solid, heavy-gauge mesh wired to sturdy timber posts. Beyond it, I could see the dull glint of water. I steadied myself against the nearest post. I was drunker than I realised. I closed my eyes a moment, willing the world to stop spinning, then shone the torch along the fence, trying to find some explanation. Why go to such lengths to protect this little pond? What could possibly justify all these precautions?

In the beam of the torch, a flight of rough wooden steps led up to a little viewing platform. Halfway up I stumbled, gashing my leg beneath my knee. I tried to hold the torch steady, swatting away the mosquitoes from the trickle of blood. I could feel nothing.

I made it safely up the rest of the steps. The handrail around the platform at the top was sticky to my touch. I leant against it, staring down at the water. At first I thought the long black shape beneath me was a log of some kind. Then, very slowly, it began to move. I closed my eyes again and shook my head, annoyed with myself. I shouldn't have drunk so much. Harald had been right. Bed would have been a much more sensible option.

I opened my eyes, shone the torch down, then took an involuntary step backwards, rigid with shock. An enormous alligator was staring up at me. Its jaws were open and the flesh of its mouth was pink behind the savage rows of teeth, but it was the eye that I'll never forget. It was a yellowy-greeny colour, the colour of evil, and it was staring up at me, unblinking. Very slowly, I began to retreat down the wooden steps. This brought me even closer to the alligator. I switched off the torch, not wanting to look, but its jaws were still open and the sour fish-stink of its breath was overpowering.

At the foot of the steps I turned and fled, my heart still thumping. At the end of the path, the gate clanged shut behind me and I lay against it, breathing hard, trying to rid myself of the sight and smell of the alligator. I understood now about the need for all these fences. But why the afternoon visitations? And why the empty metal cage afterwards?

After a while, calmer, I turned the torch on and followed the fence around the property. Above the hum of the insects and the dry rasping of the cicadas, I could hear music, something classical and immensely sad. There was a clarinet in there, diving and soaring, and I made my way along the path that skirted the pool.

Harald's den was at the back of the far wing. His windows were open behind the insect mesh, and the light inside threw a soft white panel across the grass. I paused. I'd been badly frightened. There were questions I wanted answered. The Casa Blanca had begun to spook me. I stirred again and crept towards the window. Then I stopped. Harald was sitting at his desk, the chair swivelled sideways, his face in profile. In his right hand, held high, was a plastic model of an aircraft. It was a single-seater, propeller-driven, and at first I thought it was the Mustang he'd used when he briefed me. He held the little plane at arm's length and he was flying it in long, graceful turns, perfectly matched to the music. It was like a child's game, mesmeric, dreamlike, and I must have been watching for a couple of minutes before it dawned on me that this wasn't a Mustang at all. It was too small. The profile was all wrong.

The music was coming to an end now and I edged a little closer to the window as the aircraft soared upwards. At the top of the loop, Harald held it perfectly still, and at last I had a chance to recognise the tiny swastika on the tail. The plane was a Messerschmitt, a 109, just like Harald's.

The music ended. For a second or two the plane hung there, secure between Harald's fingers. Then he let the little fighter fall, and in the busy silence of the night I heard the splintering of the wings and fuselage as it disintegrated on the desk below.

Chapter fifteen

The memories of that night have never left me – the party, getting drunk, the nightmare that awaited me in Monica's wilderness – but the questions I wanted so badly to ask were quickly swamped by the rest of Harald's flying programme. From the start, he'd promised to stretch me in every direction, and over the next three weeks that's exactly what he did. The only physical evidence of that unforgettable evening was the gash in my leg, which quickly healed.

Item One on Harald's training schedule was something he termed 'precision targeting'. That meant sortie after sortie out to the bombing range, a ten-mile square boxed on to the Standfast air maps that Harald had specially printed at a little repro shop in Fort Myers. The range had once belonged to the Department of Defense and Harald had acquired what he called 'sole deposit rights' on a twenty-year lease, another little present from his friends in the Pentagon.

I never had the hours to turn myself into any kind of half-decent dive-bomber but I loved the disciplines it taught me. How to adjust the optical sight to the exact setting for – say – a forty-five-degree dive and a 3,000-foot release. How to calculate the slant range and then factor in the wind speed. And most important of all, how to suddenly change your mind and recompute all the settings and still arrive at the roll-in point in time to wing the Mustang over into a dive and then track the nose slowly up until the pipper in the bombsight was centred on the target. Put this way, it sounds easy. The fact that I never once dropped a bomb closer than 75 metres convinced me that it wasn't.

Alongside bombing, on alternate days, Harald introduced me to strafing. Strafing is the business of laying down machine-gun and rocket fire from the air. The Cavalier Mustang I was using had six .50 machine guns mounted in the wings. I knew from day one that Harald insisted on using live ammunition – the memory of those belts of shiny cannon shells for the Messerschmitt never left me – but on the sharp end, arrowing down from 3,000 feet, the kick of the machine guns made me think pretty hard about exactly what it was that took men so easily to war. Other pilots I know say it becomes addictive and I believe them, because nothing on this earth prepares you for the raw excitement of watching the tracers streaking way ahead of you, pocking the earth below with tiny little blossoms of dirt as you walk the bullets towards the big orange target.

The first couple of times I did it I was hopeless, not least because I forgot to take my finger off the firing trigger. A full load of ammunition lasts just under ten seconds but I was so fascinated by the patterns I was making in the dust that I never wanted it to stop. Addiction, again. So simple. So sexy. So indescribably satisfying.

Bombing and strafing, naturally enough, took me to air-to-air combat, an application I approached with considerable misgivings. It turned out that the damaged Mustang I'd seen the day I went solo in fact survived the landing, but I'd talked to the pilot since – a young guy from the Venezuelan Air Force – and it was obvious that the line between make-believe and the real thing was – at Standfast – dangerously thin. Harald, he said, believed in rattling a few cages. That was a phrase I recognised, the phrase Harald had used the morning I popped a smoke bomb at Chuck's flailing soldiers, and it made me aware yet again what kind of cage life had constructed for Harald himself.

The day I was due to become a fighter pilot began, as always, with a briefing. It was cooler than usual, a grey, overcast morning with the wind blowing down from the north. Harald and I were to fly as a pair, and we stood beside the wing of my Mustang while Harald rattled briskly through an introduction to air combat tactics.

Way back in the thirties, he said, squadron commanders had flown in triangular 'vics' of three aircraft. Then the smarter guys had dreamed up something he called a 'finger-four' formation, each aircraft covering the other. This, in turn, had led to a Luftwaffe variation called the *rotte*, which was basically a two-ship formation, with the pilots hunting in pairs. In the jet age, thanks to the Americans, the *rotte* had become known as 'loose-deuce', two aircraft flying side by side with lots of sky between them.

Harald's phrase for this was 'lateral separation', and when I looked bemused, he produced two little diecast models – both Mustangs – and weaved them around in front of me. Watching his hands, I was instantly back in the hot darkness outside his den, the night I'd ventured into Monica's wilderness. In my mind, the significance of that little episode was still unresolved. What would make a man fly a plastic Messerschmitt around? Was he a child at heart? Did he have an inexhaustible supply of little plastic 109s? To be honest, I hadn't a clue, but watching him now it occurred to me that the real answer was probably very simple. At some point in his life, Harald had lost touch with that glorious muddle that is – for most of us – real life. Flying, having to rely on no one but yourself, was infinitely safer.

Was I right? No, of course I wasn't, but it seemed a reasonable enough theory at the time, and when we finally got airborne that morning I was concentrating far too hard to give this strange man's motivation a second thought.

The object of the exercise was close formation work. I was to be Harald's wingman. We'd be flying against a couple of guys from Honduras. At all costs I was to stick to him, and stick close.

'How close?' I asked him.

'Like shit on a shovel,' he grunted, hauling on my seat harness and giving me a good-luck pat on the shoulder.

We were in the air for less than an hour but it felt like all day, and by the time I wobbled in for an untidy three-pointer, I swear I'd lost pounds in weight. My face was bathed in sweat. My pulse rate was still in three figures. And when Harald finally taxied to a halt in front of me I found myself physically shaking with what I can only describe as delayed shock.

I pulled back the canopy, sucking the air into my lungs. Harald was up on the wing and beside me in seconds. He looked excited. For reasons I didn't begin to understand, we'd evidently won the dogfight.

'We shot them down?'

'Smoked them both.' He nodded. 'Twice.'

The Hondurans had been practically invisible. We'd been way up above the thick eiderdown of cloud but I'd only spotted them a couple of times, twisting silver fish against the blue, blue sky. For the rest of the time they'd only existed in my headphones, brief clues from Harald. Five o'clock high. Eight o'clock low. Up-sun. Down-sun. I'm sure he was right, they were doubtless there, but I was concentrating far too hard on keeping formation, matching him move for move as he dived and banked and turned in his determination – in his phrase – 'to kick them in the nuts'.

The key, of course, was to get behind them, get in their six o'clock. A fighter pilot's love affair with the average timepiece begins and ends with six o'clock. Slide into his six o'clock, and your opponent's war is over. Let him get into yours, and it's goodbye world. That, at least, was the way Harald saw it.

'So how did I do?'

We were walking back across the apron. Just putting one foot in front of the other was suddenly very difficult. Inside the hangar, Harald patted me on the shoulder.

'My wingman,' he murmured.

Still dazed, I watched him heading for the stairs that led up to his office, and he'd disappeared before it occurred to me that I'd just won the ultimate accolade. Harald's wingman. Lucky old me.

It was later that day, in the kitchen back at the Casa Blanca, that I brought up the subject of Karel Brokenka. Ralph had written to me by now, enclosing a long list of detailed questions, and it was becoming important to fix some kind of appointment. I had another five days down here at Standfast. As soon as I could, I wanted to phone this man, introduce myself and find out exactly where he lived.

To my surprise, Harald had it all worked out.

'It's a nursing home called Shoreview. It's along the lake, west of Chicago.'

'How do you know?'

'I talked to the guy on the phone. Ralph gave me his number. We're going up there together, first thing next week.'

'We?'

'Yes, you and me. Any objections?'

Next week was June. I'd promised Andrea and Jamie I'd be back at Mapledurcombe by the seventh, well in time for my birthday. Wasn't this cutting it just a little bit fine?

'Not at all. I'll get you a ticket back from O'Hare. If that's really what you want.'

O'Hare is Chicago's main commercial airport. I blinked, listening to Harald detailing the trip he'd planned. We'd take the dual Mustang. We'd need to refuel en route but held arranged for the auxiliary tanks to be fitted and it should be a pretty easy go. If the weather was right, he was thinking of a little detour, a huge left-hand curve that would take us west over Texas and Arizona. It was, he said, a pity to have me leave the US without at least a glimpse of the Grand Canyon.

'Sounds lovely.' I was still thinking of his first remark. *If that's really what you want.* What did that mean? Why shouldn't I want to go home?

Harald was making space for his mother at the table. She'd come in from somewhere at the back of the house. She was wearing a pair of rubber gloves. I glanced at my watch. It was exactly half past four. Monica sat down, and mother and son exchanged glances before Harald got to his feet.

'Ralph says he's nearly finished the book.' Harald was heading for the door.

I followed him.

'That's right,' I said. 'He sounds quite excited.'

'You've talked to him?'

'A couple of times.'

'Recently?'

'Last night.'

'So how's he getting on?'

We were outside now. The sun had come out at last and the swimming pool looked especially inviting. Harald was heading for a long, low wooden shed out of sight of the main house.

'He's finished the picture research and he's done a couple of drafts on the text,' I said. 'I think he must have left a hole for this man Brokenka.'

'The Czech guy's that important?'

'Ralph thinks so. It was the only time our Mustang scored.'

Harald had produced a key for the padlock on the door of the hut. He paused, looking back at me.

'What about the other guy? The guy in the 109? Wasn't Ralph trying to get a picture or something?'

'That's coming.'

'It is?'

'Yes, he's been in touch with the German archive people. They've found the file now. It's just a question of getting the photo across.'

'And this Brokenka? He hasn't got a photo already?'

'No, but it's the account Ralph wants. He's talked to the man on the phone, of course, and I think he's written a couple of times, but what he really wants is a proper sound recording, me talking him through it. Ralph's really keen. It's the least I can do.'

'Of course.'

Harald opened the door. I used to keep rabbits back home at Gander Creek and I recognised the smell at once. There were dozens of them in a long wired-off run. The tiny ones looked adorable.

Harald was rummaging around in the corner. When he appeared beside me he had something in his hand. It was Monica's metal cage. He pulled the little door open. I stared at it.

'What's that for?'

Harald nodded down at the rabbits. Most of them had disappeared inside their hutch.

'Some of these little fellas. My mother does it most days.'

'Why? Why does she need them?'

Harald had opened the wooden door to the run. One of the rabbits he grabbed couldn't have been more than a couple of weeks old. It blinked up at me, wet button nose, twitching whiskers, perfect blue eyes.

'She feeds them to her pet,' he said.

'What pet . . . ?' My voice faltered. I knew the answer already. I heard the clang of the metal as he shut the rabbits in the cage.

'She's got a pet alligator.' He glanced up at me. 'She had an old Seminole Indian guy trap him. Down in the Everglades.'

I was still looking at the rabbits, remembering the unblinking yellow eye and the sour stink of the alligator's breath. No wonder he'd come to me. No wonder he'd opened those huge jaws.

'She does this every day?'

'Without fail.' Harald was heading for the door. 'I tell her it's unfair but she pays no attention.'

'Unfair?' Sickened, I could think of far stronger words.

Harald laughed, fumbling with the padlock.

'Sure. Damn reptiles are supposed to be out there hunting. Any more silver service and this one'll die of boredom.'

My last day's flying at Standfast nearly killed me.

The thunderheads had been piling up all morning and it was only my eagerness to fit in one last sortie that persuaded Harald to fuel up my Cavalier Mustang and let me have my way. The forecast, he said, was dire. I was to avoid the coastal area and keep well away from the towering stacks of cloud. When he asked whether I needed an escort, I shook my head. Greedy for one final hour alone in the Florida sky, the last thing I wanted was company.

I took off to the north-east. After ten minutes or so I was up at 12,000 feet. From here, just, I could see both sides of the Florida panhandle, the long appendage that hangs down into the Caribbean. The visibility, for once, was good – a sure sign of impending rain – and as we began to climb again I checked the settings on my camera. The souvenir picture I'd dreamed about would show the entire coastline of southern Florida. To achieve that, I needed to go south.

I winged the Mustang over, still climbing. The higher you fly, the thinner the air becomes, and I nudged the throttle forward, watching the airspeed push past 160 knots. Pilots will tell you that the Mustang is a very slippery aircraft and they're right. It's got a very thin wing, and poor manners at low speeds, but up here in the cold, thin air it was a joy to fly. I banked again, the gentlest of turns, checking the view. Below me, quite suddenly, there was nothing but haze, and as I watched – literally – the haze thickened into a blanket of ripply grey cloud. Like an idiot, I'd failed to keep a detailed note of my speeds and headings, convinced I'd be staying visual. With the cloud below me, I'd run out of landscape. Not only had my photograph disappeared but so had all the clues I relied upon to get home. In short, I was lost.

I throttled back and stored my camera in the starboard bin. That lovely warm feeling of euphoria I'd felt earlier had quite gone. In its place, the first cold stirrings of fear.

It was now 17.14. I checked the fuel gauges, calculating exactly how much I had left. If I called up Standfast, I thought, and they got a radar bearing on my transponder, they'd be able to give me a heading back to the airfield. Provided I could fly that heading, I'd be fine. If I had to divert for some reason, I'd have around half an hour's extra fuel to play with. I stared down at the cloud, trying to estimate how thick it might be. If I got low again, down below the cloudbase, then at least I'd be visual to the ground. Then, with a radar heading, getting home would be that much easier.

I throttled back, shedding height, then had second thoughts. I was still up at 12,000 feet. The longer I stayed here, the longer I'd eke out the fuel. Down low, in the thicker air, the Mustang drank Avgas.

I checked my transponder, then called Standfast. I asked the controller for my range and bearing but when he enquired whether I had a problem, my pride told me to gloss the truth.

'Negative,' I said briskly. 'Just a safety check. Over.'

There was a longish silence. Then the controller came back with the information I needed.

'You're one hundred and thirty-nine miles bearing at one five seven degrees. You need to fly three three seven. Repeat, three three seven. Over.'

'Roger, turning on to three three seven.'

I thanked him and signed off. The fact that he'd worked out my course for me meant that I hadn't fooled him. They'd be watching me now on the radar. Standfast's newest recruit was under surveillance.

I let go of the stick a moment, flexing my fingers. Ahead of me, the thick pillars of cumulus had closed, forming a dense, impenetrable wall of cloud. Just the time it had taken to talk to Standfast had brought it immeasurably closer. Inside these clouds, swirling up-draughts of superheated tropical air could tear the strongest aircraft apart. To risk it in the Mustang was suicidal.

My mouth felt dry. I began to talk to myself. At all costs I had to stay calm, stay in control. Panic, make a single wrong move, and the consequences didn't bear contemplation.

Dusk falls quickly in southern Florida, and already I could detect the colour draining from the sky. This was another complication, of course. I had absolutely zero experience of night flying, and even if I managed to grope my way home, the landing lights at Standfast were pretty rudimentary.

Up ahead, brilliantly neon against the looming grey cloud, I saw a flicker of lightning. Then another, further to the west. I checked my airspeed: 240 knots. I slipped back the cuff of my flying suit. My watch said 17.23. More lightning. Then the first fat drops of rain exploding against the canopy. I was in real trouble now and I knew it. I cursed my foolishness, my overconfidence, my greed. I'd been stupid to even think of cheating the weather. Harald, as ever, had been right. I should have been back in my room at the Casa Blanca, packing my bags, dreaming of England.

England. Jamie. Adam. Mapledurcombe. I shut my eyes a moment, trying to drive the images to the very back of my mind, but Adam, especially, wasn't having it. I could feel him here, with me in the Mustang, talking me through it, and the echo of his voice in my head made me feel even more vulnerable, even more alone. Was this the way it had happened for him? Back in February? Way out over the Channel? Had he made some hideous mistake and put the aircraft beyond his own competence? Or had it been something else?

We were closing on the cloud wall very fast now, the Mustang spearing through curtains of rain. Soon, perhaps in seconds, I'd have absolutely no visual reference at all. Just a grey formless world that would first swallow me up and then kill me.

I knew I had to do something. A glance over my shoulder told me that the way back was blocked, more clouds, more lightning. I checked the altimeter again. Somehow, God knows how, we'd lost 2,700 feet. The best way through it, the quickest way through it, was down. I pushed the stick forward, feeling my stomach rise. The airspeed was increasing dramatically and I felt a shiver of turbulence. At first it was like cobblestones in the sky, then we hit a vicious curl of windshear and the Mustang dropped like a stone then rose again, rearing up like the stallion she undoubtedly was. I was flying on instruments alone now, using the attitude indicator to try and keep the wings level. The needle on the airspeed indicator had passed 400 knots and the altimeter was unspooling so fast I thought it must have broken.

Then, suddenly, there came a searing light, incredibly white, incredibly bright, that seemed to start behind my eyeballs and spread and spread until it filled the entire cockpit. At the same time there was a huge bang and a funny acrid smell. I screamed. The stick went dead in my hands and for a second I thought we'd hit the ground. Then the controls began to answer again and I hauled back on the stick, my eyes scanning my precious instruments. A minute or so earlier, I'd switched on the dashboard lights. To my horror, the dials were now deep pools of black. The electrics had gone. We'd been hit by a lightning strike.

The key instruments in a Mustang are air-driven. That meant I still had the airspeed indicator, altimeter and artificial horizon, but without illumination they were as good as useless. It was so dark in the cockpit, I could barely see my hands. Once or twice in my life, people have told me about a fear so overpowering, so total, that it ceases to be fear at all. At the time I hadn't a clue what they meant, but now I understood them completely. Cold as ice, I relaxed at the controls. I had to sink the aircraft as tidily as I could. I had no idea whether I was upside down, or banked to port or starboard, or dead level. Whether or not I came out of the cloud in time to recover would be pure chance. There wasn't even any point in weighing the odds. All I could do was get on with it.

Seconds went by. I saw more lightning, though nothing close. I had the throttle at what I judged to be a conservative setting and I could feel the aircraft sinking through the seat of my pants. After the fear, I felt a deep, cold anger. Bitch, bitch, bitch, I thought. What a bloody stupid way to die.

Abruptly, the cloud parted. I looked down, or rather sideways, because I was in a shallow left-hand turn. A huge field of densely packed citrus trees looked horribly close. I levelled out and eased the throttle forward. The cloud base was maybe a hundred feet above me and for a few precious seconds it wasn't raining. I could see a road ahead and a tiny flatbed truck with its headlights on. I winged over, meaning to follow the truck, trying to work out whether it was wise or not to risk a landing. It looked like a country road. It looked pretty straight. Apart from the truck, there was no other traffic. Should I go for it?

I'd slowed as much as I dared, resigned to never finding Standfast, and I was still wondering about a landing when the road veered to the left and disappeared. My only other option now was a field empty and big enough for me to put down. My chances of surviving that were pretty bleak. My chances of keeping the aircraft intact were zero.

Houses flashed past beneath me, a small town of some kind. The rain was back again, thick beads of moisture tearing across the canopy, and what was left of the daylight had acquired an eery green-yellow tinge that made me wonder whether I wasn't already dead. Was this the afterlife? An eternity of little houses with their lights on and their curtains drawn?

Suddenly, off to port, something crept into my field of vision. Not on the ground, not part of this surreal blur of images, but up alongside me. I risked a glance to the right, then looked again, scarcely believing my eyes. I was hallucinating. I had to be. The plane was another Mustang. And the face staring back at me was Harald's.

Two days later, I was back in the air again, looking down at the low, brown sprawl of New Orleans. Two hours out from Standfast, we were on track for Flagstaff, Arizona. From there, after a ride through the Grand Canyon, Harald's flight plan would take us east again, to Denver, and then Chicago.

We were back in the dual Mustang, Harald in the rear cockpit, my luggage tightly strapped down in the stowage space aft. As New Orleans began to resolve itself into city blocks and a huge brown lake behind, Harald gave me a new heading. The islands of the Mississippi delta lay below us and he was keen for me to fly west, along the coast.

'Makes a nice picture,' he said drily. 'If you've still got the camera.'

I didn't bother replying. My adventures over southern Florida had earned me a debrief I'd never forget. By the time I'd called in for the radar fix, Harald had already been airborne, dodging the thunderheads, fearing the worst. The controller back at Standfast had vectored him on to my radar blip and he'd shepherded me back to the airfield. By the time we landed, I was down to less than ten minutes' fuel. Back in his office, cold as ice, he tore me to shreds. In sheer self-defence I wanted to point out that he'd sanctioned the flight, given me permission to go, but when he paused and gave me a chance to bite back, the only word I could think of was 'sorry'. The man had saved my life. What else was there to say?

'Up to the north is Baton Rouge. Next state along's Texas. We'll drop into Fort Worth for gas. Then route west for the Grand Canyon.'

'OK.'

I double-scanned the instruments. This was the first time I'd flown since I'd nearly blown it and to my surprise it felt wonderful. Three long phone calls to Jamie had helped me cope with the aftershock, and even Harald, I think, was impressed by my resilience. At the end of the debrief he'd softened slightly, telling me that training should always be a little scary, just to give me a taste of the real thing. Quite what the real thing might be was still a mystery, but when we met again later at the Casa Blanca, I confessed that my days of fighting it out with tropical thunderstorms were over. There was nothing I wanted more than a nice Atlantic low, rolling up the English Channel. Those I could cope with. Those I understood.

Harald had eyed me over a bowl of minestrone soup.

'You and Adam both,' he'd said softly. 'Next time, just have a little respect.'

The Grand Canyon was awesome. We got to the southern edge late in the afternoon. The sun cast long black shadows across the canyon floor and the photos I took were a thousand times better than anything I might have snapped over southern Florida. After two passes – one high, one way down at 300 feet – we climbed away to the north-east and an hour and a half later I was applauding Harald's landing at a small municipal airfield in the Denver suburbs.

He'd reserved us a couple of rooms in a motel about a mile from the airfield, and the restaurant nearby where we ate dinner was owned by a buddy from the Marine Corps. I studied the menu while the two men talked at the bar. I was longing to get home now. After we'd paid our respects to Mr Brokenka, up in Chicago, I couldn't wait to be aboard the overnight United flight Harald had booked for me. In my heart, I knew I owed him everything. A first-class seat back to Heathrow was the smallest of my debts.

Harald rejoined me at the table. His buddy's name was Al. Harald told me he'd come west in pursuit of a woman called Pamela-Ann who'd once been Miss Mardi Gras. He'd staked most of his Corps gratuity on the belief that she was crazy about him, and he'd lost the lot. They'd been married in three months, divorced after six. The relationship, in every conceivable respect, had been a disaster.

The man behind the bar gave me a rueful grin. He looked a little like Harald, I thought. Same build. Same watchfulness.

'Do you see him a lot?' I asked Harald.

'Couple of times a year. He comes down to Standfast once in a while. He was an explosives specialist in the Corps and he gets to talk to the guys about it.'

'Why?'

'Because I ask him.' He was looking at the menu. 'You need to wire a car? Have it blown up? Al's the man. You need someone out of your life? Ask Al. Only problem he never solved was Pamela-Ann, which I guess was pretty inevitable. That woman would make him go bang just by smiling at him.'

He looked up, gazing across at his buddy. There was almost a fondness in his eyes, something I'd rarely seen before, and again I wondered what the Marine Corps and active service had really done to Harald. I was used to men embellishing war stories – even Adam had occasionally done it – but Harald just wasn't the kind of person to exaggerate for the sake of effect. For one thing, it wasn't his style. And for another, he didn't have to. He really had flown fast jets in combat. And, for all I knew, he really had been part of a life where people got blown up or – in his phrase – 'wasted'.

The thought chilled me and I toyed with the food when it arrived. Harald asked me whether anything was wrong and I shook my head, sawing gamely through the huge rib-eye steak. This didn't fool him for a moment, but when he tried to enquire further, I quickly changed the subject, asking about his schedule for the next few months. What was he doing in the summer? Before the Fighter Meet? Would he be across in the UK at all? And if so, might there be space in his diary for a long weekend at Mapledurcombe?

The prospect seemed to attract him. He pushed away the remains of his own steak.

'Business is like war,' he mused. 'Did you know that? Business is war by other means.'

He began to talk about the deals he was brokering around the Russian Shuttle, the commemorative flight into the heart of the old Soviet Union. In my naïvety I'd somehow assumed that this little expedition had been cancelled or at least postponed – where would Harald find the time to organise it? – but the longer he talked the more obvious it became that he had a network of agents, men and maybe women whom he trusted, people perhaps like Adam.

When I asked him if that was the case, he frowned.

'I have a lot of money,' he said guardedly. 'It's not necessarily the same thing.'

'I don't understand.'

'I buy people, good people. But I don't have to like them.'

'Did I say that?'

'You implied it.'

'How?'

'By including Adam. Adam was a one-off. Adam was a friend.'

I looked at him and nodded. I'd felt that too. Exactly that.

'Don't stop,' I said. 'Tell me more.'

He hesitated a moment, twisting his signet ring around his little finger.

'I liked the guy a lot. I knew where he was coming from, what was happening inside his head. And I admired his judgement, too.'

'Adam was hopeless at business.'

'I didn't mean business.' He smiled softly. 'I meant you.'

The confession, coming from Harald, was a huge surprise. This past month or so we'd lashed together a pretty stable little raft. The relationship was close – of course it was – but it was practical as well. It had weathered some of the most intense, challenging flying I could ever have conceived. It had permitted him to be both a friend and a mentor. Why complicate it, so suddenly, like this?

Tomorrow's flight plan called for an eight o'clock take off. Harald, as far as I knew, never drank and I was stone-cold sober too.

'I'm not sure I know what you're talking about,' I said carefully. 'And I'm not sure I want you to explain.'

A frown briefly shadowed Harald's face, then he sat back, almost – I thought – relieved.

'You must have wondered about the flight programme, all the stuff we've been doing.'

'You're right, I have. In fact I've asked you a couple of times, you know, where it all leads.'

'OK.' He nodded. 'This is where it leads.'

'This?'

'Sure.'

I looked round. His buddy, Al, was back behind the bar. Was I Pamela-Ann? Was Harald in my six o'clock? His finger on the firing trigger? Me in his sights?

'We're friends,' I told him. 'Good friends. I'd do anything for you. You know I would.'

'OK.' He nodded again. 'Then I want you to become my wing-man.' That could have meant anything and I told him so. Harald frowned. 'You think I'm some kind of poet? Some candy-ass guy says one thing, means another?'

'No.'

'Then listen to me. I want to put together a display team. Nine Mustangs. I want to call them the Blue Angels. And I want you to fly as my number two.'

I tried to hide my confusion. Coming from Harald, this was a far bigger compliment than I could ever have expected. It meant that he really did rate my flying. There was no way I was up to that standard yet, but he obviously thought it was in me.

'You're sure I could hack it?'

'I'm certain.'

'OK,' I said carefully. 'So tell me more.'

Harald leaned forward across the table. He had a shortlist of pilots. He'd lined up eight machines. He had the makings of a display circuit, the team flying from country to country, continent to continent, performing in front of crowds of hundreds of thousands. Naturally, there'd be business spin-offs. He'd be crazy if he didn't integrate something like this with his commercial activities. But the heart of it, the *raison d'être*, was the Mustang itself. What it had done. What it represented. That's where the raw appeal lay. That's why I should say yes.

Something was bothering me. I put my hand on his arm.

'You said nine aircraft.'

'That's right.'

'And then eight.'

'Sure. That's because you own the other one.'

'You want our plane as part of this? *Our* Mustang?'

'Yes.' He smiled rather awkwardly. 'Please.'

'But what about . . .' I shrugged, '. . . Mapledurcombe? Old Glory?'

'You wouldn't need it.'

'I wouldn't?'

'No, you'd be with me, the Blue Angels, full time.'

'As what?'

'My wingman.'

'You mean your partner,' I said quietly. 'Don't you?'

There was a long silence. Al had disappeared.

'It's kinda the same thing.' Harald smiled bleakly. 'Isn't it?'

I withdrew my hand. At last I understood why Harald had been so provisional, so uncertain, about my departure date. It wasn't just the fact that my birthday was coming. It wasn't the thought that we might squeeze in a couple more days' flying. It was something infinitely more long-term. Most people would have called it marriage. But Harald Meyler wasn't most people.

'I can't, Harald.'

I said it as gently as I could. There was something so fatalistic in his face, so resigned, that he didn't even look disappointed.

'I had to ask,' he murmured at last. 'You know that, don't you?'

'Yes.' I looked at him for a long time. 'Tell me something.'

'What?'

'How long have you felt this way?'

'Years.'

'*Years?*' It felt like I'd only known him a couple of months.

'Yes, ever since Adam introduced us.'

'I see.' I was trying to remember the occasion but I couldn't.

'It was down in Devon. The Exeter air show. I was flying a Jug.'

Dimly, it began to come back to me. Jug is the American nickname for the P-47 Thunderbolt, a big unbreakable World War II fighter. Harald had pulled off a wonderful display. Adam, who barely knew him at all, had raced across to say well done. I, as ever, was in tow.

'You were wearing jeans,' he said. 'And you had the loveliest smile.'

279

'I did?'

'Yes. The one thing I always knew was that somewhere out there was the person I was going to fall in love with.' He ducked his head. 'Just happens it was you.'

'But did I ever . . .' I did my best to find the right word, '. . . encourage you?'

'Never. You couldn't.'

'Couldn't?'

'No, because that's not the person you are. You were married, happily married. You loved the man, you adored him. Everyone could see that.'

'And now?'

'Now?' He shrugged. 'Now you're not married.'

'And you think that makes a difference?'

'Sure. I thought it might.'

Thought. Past tense. He'd made his pitch. We knew where we stood. All I could say, for the second time in two days, was sorry.

My hand went out again, some small comfort. I could feel him trembling.

'It was probably my fault,' I said. 'I should have made things clearer.'

'No problem.' He produced a long white envelope and slipped it across the table towards me. I recognised the United Airlines logo on the front.

'Is this the ticket?'

'Yes.'

'Thanks.'

'That's OK.'

'I mean it, Harald.' I raised my glass to him. 'Here's to tomorrow.'

He studied me for a moment or two, the strangest smile curling one corner of his mouth.

'You mean the old guy? Brokenka?'

'No, I mean the future, yours and mine. We'll stay friends. Promise me that.'

'Sure.' He nodded. 'Oh, sure.'

Next morning, as planned, we flew up to Chicago. We landed at another tiny airport – windy and much cooler than down south – and I re-read Ralph's letter while Harald organised a cab to take us to the nursing home.

Shoreview was one block back from the road that ran beside Lake Michigan. The blooms in the immaculate flowerbeds were nodding in the breeze and the nurse who met us in reception asked us whether we'd prefer tea or coffee.

Karel Brokenka had a room at the front of the building on the second floor. The nurse had warned us that he was still recovering from a minor stroke, but when we met him I was surprised by how fit he looked. He was much smaller than I imagined, and he was completely bald, but as soon as he struggled to his feet and extended a hand, I recognised the lop-sided smile I'd seen in the photo that Ralph had shown me.

He'd obviously been looking forward to our visit because there was a huge stack of papers piled beside his armchair, and I kneeled on the carpet, going through his mementoes one by one, while Harald sat in an armchair by the window, watching us.

He'd said very little all morning. In certain ways he reminded me of someone recovering from a serious accident. Real life took a lot of getting used to. He didn't want to trip up again.

Karel was telling me about a sortie he'd done in our Mustang a couple of weeks after he'd shot the Messerschmitt down. He kept referring to it as *Little Ceska*, which was a bit confusing at first. The nurse was right about the stroke, because he kept losing the thread.

Harald suddenly bent forward, interrupting him.

'Mr Brokenka, I wonder if you wouldn't mind going through the story again. For my benefit.' He produced a small cassette recorder and I stared at it, wondering why he hadn't used it before.

'What story?' The old man was sounding vague again.

'The Messerschmitt. The 109.'

'Ah . . . so. You want me to . . . ?'

'Tell me what happened . . .' I saw Harald press the Record button, '. . . again.'

Karel gathered his thoughts a moment, then went through it all a second time. He was flying P-Popsie. P-Popsie was *Little Ceska*'s call sign. His squadron were supplying withdrawal support on a big B-17 raid. It was a lousy day, snow first thing. He remembered the weather because it was 1 January and snow was supposed to be lucky.

'Lucky?' There was a small, cheerless smile on Harald's face.

'Sure, and it was too. We found the bomber stream real quick. That didn't always happen.'

'And the 109s?'

'Five of them. Way over in the Ulzen area.'

'They were below you?'

'Yeah, but hard to spot against those damned trees.' He offered Harald a gap-toothed grin, warmed by the memory. Harald's smile had gone.

'You bounced them?'

'Sure.'

'They saw you coming?'

'At the end, yes.'

'The one you chased, the guy you shot down, he saw you coming?'

'Of course.'

Harald nodded, saying nothing. I could hear a slight squeak from the machine. Brokenka was looking blank again.

'Go on,' Harald prompted at last. 'What happened then?'

'He dived, like they all did. I went after him.'

'What kind of speed?'

'I don't know. Fast. I was in the dive, remember. Hell, you know . . .' he lifted a thin hand and waved it in the air, '. . . four hundred knots? More? I don't know.'

'And the 109?'

'Fast, too, and clever.' The hand began to weave and turn.

'A good pilot?'

'Yes, oh yes.'

'A brave guy? Stuck with it? Didn't bale out?'

'Not then, not for a couple of seconds, no.'

'But he could have done?'

'Maybe, I don't know. That kind of speed? It ain't so easy . . .' He squinted at Harald, trying to keep up with this volley of questions, but Harald had his back to the window and his face was masked by shadow. 'Anyways, I was firing pretty good, bam bam, and the stuff was socking into him. You could see it in the movie shots, the combat footage . . .' he nodded, smiling, '. . . bam, bam.'

'You've got this film?'

'Hell, no. It belongs to the Air Force.'

I glanced across at Harald.

'Ralph's got some stills. They must come from the film. I've seen them.'

'What do they show?'

I frowned, trying to remember the exact sequence.

'The plane's falling apart,' I said. 'It's disintegrating. You can see fire, flames. In one of them, the pilot's just baled out.'

Harald went back to the old man.

'He definitely baled out? You saw him?'

'Sure. Just like the lady says. It's all in the movie.'

'And you think he survived?'

'I don't know.'

'Any parachute?'

The old man stared at him, mystified. The expression on his face suggested he was having second thoughts about our little interview. He'd been expecting an hour or so of gentle reminiscence. Not the third degree.

'I don't know,' he said again. 'I was diving. Everything happens very fast. You say you fly Mustangs?' His hand was shielding his eyes as he looked across at Harald.

Harald nodded.

'Yeah.'

'Then you sure as hell know how it is. Four hundred knots? Ground coming up to meet you? This guy's buddies out there somewhere? No, sir.' He shook his head. 'I saw no parachute open.'

In the sudden silence I could hear the clatter of a trolley in the corridor outside. Finally, Harald stirred.

'But he flew well,' he said quietly. 'This guy?'

'Sure, they were good, these boys, all of them. I never met a guy who didn't fly the shit out of those 109s.'

The sudden violence of Karel's language gave me a jolt. Something had angered him and it showed.

Harald got to his feet. He stood over the old man for a long time. Then he extended a hand.

'It's been a pleasure to meet you, sir. I want to say thank you.'

Brokenka peered up. The anger had gone. In its place, fresh confusion.

'I didn't catch your name,' he muttered. 'What did you say your name was?'

'Harald. Harald Meyler.' He bent towards me and helped me to my feet. 'We should be going, Ellie. I don't want you to be late for that plane.'

Chapter sixteen

Jamie met me at Heathrow next morning. He told me he'd been camping all night in case the plane got in early but I didn't believe him. The weather back home had obviously been fabulous. He looked incredibly fit – tanned, lean, clear-eyed – and I was really surprised, because this wasn't at all the face I'd begun to associate with the lost little voice behind the letters.

We retrieved Ralph's car from the multistorey and made our way through the muddle of signs towards the exit tunnel. On the link road to the M4 I was still trying to explain the principles of dive-bombing when Jamie swung the Peugeot left, into the car park that served the huge Post House hotel.

I'd got to the roll-in point where you slap the stick sideways and stand the Mustang on one wing. The last thing on my mind was breakfast.

'I had something on the plane,' I told him. 'I'm not at all hungry.'

Jamie was laughing.

'I've been saving up,' he explained. 'I thought we could say hallo properly.'

He'd reserved a room on the top floor. We pulled the curtains shut and took a long shower together before tumbling into bed. He felt like a stranger at first – even his smell was slightly exotic – but the way he touched me was wholly familiar and afterwards I clung to him, stilled by the flooding warmth inside me. I slept until midday. My dreams were horribly vivid, lit by wild flashes of lightning, and seconds before I awoke the Mustang was upside-down, irrecoverable, plunging earthwards through an eternity of grey while I reached out, fighting certain death.

I had one arm round Jamie's neck. He was bent over me, telling me that everything was going to be OK.

'The radio,' I muttered. 'I should have called earlier. I should have known.'

'Known what?'

I sat up, rubbing my eyes. The feeling of relief was indescribable. Jamie had been up already. The tea he'd made tasted wonderful.

'I've really missed you,' I said thoughtfully. 'Did you know that?'

We drove south, to Mapledurcombe. By the time we arrived it was nearly seven o'clock, a beautiful June evening, the garden transformed by early summer. My sister met us at the front door. She'd hung strings of little American flags around the entrance hall and I was really touched by the gesture until it dawned on me that they were really for the benefit of our guests.

We split a bottle of Côtes-du-Rhône in the kitchen while she busied around with the evening meal. She'd put on a bit of weight since I'd last seen her and – like Jamie – she looked wonderfully well. Not only that but she'd very obviously got the business completely taped. The latest bunch of guests, she said, had taken to Mapledurcombe like ducks to water. They loved the feel of the place, the things she'd done to it, the little bits and pieces of antique furniture she'd managed to pick up through various local contacts. They were so appreciative, these Americans, so discriminating, so bloody *nice*. One wife from Milwaukee, herself some kind of society hostess, had been practically on her knees, demanding the recipe for Andrea's special *osso buco*.

I sat beside the window, listening to this flood of other people's compliments, the presents I'd brought back still unopened on the kitchen table. I was enormously grateful to Andrea for letting me go off like that but by the time Jamie and I had finished the Côtes-du-Rhône it occurred to me that I was virtually a stranger in my own house. Andrea, true to form, had grabbed Old Glory for herself. Without her very special touch, the business would plainly be in deep, deep trouble.

Tonight's menu featured *blanquette de veau* and Andrea was nearly ready to dish up. The girl she'd hired to help out – a nineteen-year-old called Katie from the village up the road – was draining the courgettes and tipping them into a hideous silver bain-marie.

'How about the flying?' I enquired.

Andrea was making cooing noises over her hollandaise sauce.

'The what?'

'The flying. The Mustang. The Harvard.'

'Ah, that's Jamie's department. Boys' toys.'

I looked across at Jamie. I'd asked him already, of course, on the way down but he'd seemed oddly vague about the details. In my absence, Dave Jeffries – our engineer – had been in charge of arranging flights for our guests, calling in one or other of the handful of pilots we trusted when their own work schedules permitted. Dave's link to our eager American veterans was evidently Jamie.

'Well?'

Jamie said the Harvard had been up a couple of times a week. The longest sortie had been over to Munster, and so far – touch wood – there'd been no maintenance problems.

'But what about the Mustang?'

Jamie and Andrea exchanged glances. Whatever little secret they shared was beginning to irritate me.

'It's been out for a bit,' Jamie muttered. 'Just recently.'

'Out? What do you mean, out? Has something happened? Has someone bent it?'

'God, no.'

'What's wrong then?'

There was another silence. I looked at my watch. It was half past eight, still plenty of daylight left.

'Well?' I was angry now. 'Aren't you going to tell me?'

Underneath his tan, Jamie began to colour.

'It's a bit awkward. Why don't you give it a couple of days?'

I stared at him. The Mustang was the very middle of Old Glory, the jewel in Adam's crown. He'd built the business around it. I'd just spent six extraordinary weeks learning to fly the thing. *Give it a couple of days?*

'Are you going to tell me? Either of you?'

Jamie was looking at his empty glass. Andrea was issuing instructions about her *pommes duchesse*. I left the room. The phone was still in Adam's study. I found the number of the local taxi firm and I was still waiting for them to answer when I became aware of Jamie standing behind me.

'What are you doing?'

'I'm going across to the airfield. What do you think I'm doing?'

'I'll drive you.'

'You can't. You've been drinking.'

It was my tone of voice that sealed it for Jamie. He looked at me for a moment, the surprise in his face giving way to a kind of wariness, then he shrugged and left me to it. Still waiting for the taxi people to answer the phone, I could hear him back in the kitchen, laughing at something Andrea must have said.

When I got to the airfield, the hangar was locked. Dave Jeffries lived in Shanklin, a couple of miles down the road, and I gave the taxi-driver his address. When I rapped on the door and demanded the key, all he wanted to talk about was Florida.

'Tomorrow, Dave. Just give me the key.'

'But was it good?'

'Brilliant. The key, Dave.'

He began to babble about Standfast again, how amazing it must have been for me, but I cut him short.

'What's going on?'

'Nothing, Ellie.'

'Give me the key then.'

With the greatest reluctance, he finally complied. When he offered to drive me back to the airfield himself, I said no. I could find my own way around. I even knew where the master switch was for the hangar lights. He'd have the key back in the morning.

The taxi dropped me at the airfield. It was getting dark now and I stood in the twilight behind the control tower, watching the gulls wheeling over a pile of scraps from the Touchdown Café. It seemed years since I'd last been here. So much had happened to me. To my flying. Even to the way I thought about my poor dead husband.

I walked slowly over to the hut Adam had used beside the hangar. I had the key on my own ring and the temptation was to go in and have a bit of a wallow, but I didn't need to open the door to remind myself what it looked like, what it smelled like. All those things were there, imprinted on my memory, along with the wretched photo I'd found in his drawer. Thinking of the latter still hurt, but the weeks away had somehow diminished its importance. It was part of an episode I wanted to put to rest. My life had moved on. I'd gone solo.

Access to the hangar is through a door on the side. The cold, oily smell of the place hit me at once. There are clear plastic panels let into the roof and what daylight there was left shed a pale ghostliness over the three planes inside. My old Tiger Moth was closest. I stepped across, running my fingers along the leather trim on the side of the open cockpit. I felt like a child who'd gone away to boarding school and returned to find a favourite old toy in the nursery. It looked so small, so primitive. Had I once been intimidated by this lovely old biplane? Had 135 knots once seemed the speed of light?

I stepped back. The Mustang was over on the far side of the hangar, beyond the bulk of the big old Harvard. I could see the long, sleek nose and the extended teardrop canopy. Even from here she looked poised, eager, sniffing the air, ready for anything. What could possibly have gone wrong?

I found the master switch for the overhead lights. The neon tubes flickered for a second or two before the hangar was bathed in a cold brilliance. I walked around the Moth, and the Harvard, and then stopped in front of the Mustang. It wasn't our plane at all. Wrong colour, wrong finish. I couldn't believe my eyes. This must be some kind of mistake, I thought. Dave Jeffries must have swapped our fighter for someone else's, just a temporary arrangement, helping a mate out, a favour of some kind. That's why he'd been so reluctant to part with the key. That's why Andrea and Jamie had been so secretive in the kitchen.

I gazed up at the aircraft. It was freshly painted in two shades of blue, a deep, rich navy for the underside of the wings and the bottom half of the fuselage, and a much lighter sky blue for the upper surfaces. I moved to the right, checking that it was, in fact, a dual cockpit, then my eyes went to the nose and I stopped again. It was, after all, our Mustang. In a flourish of deep red lettering, scrolled beneath the exhaust pots, it even had a name. *Ellie B*, it read. Ellie Bruce.

I walked slowly around the plane, inspecting her from every angle, wanting to know who'd done this, and why. Only when I got to the tailplane did I spot the vital clue. High up on the rudder was a logo I recognised: the torch of liberty, grasped in an outstretched hand, the trademark emblem I'd last seen in celebratory icing, half a world away.

It was Harald's doing, Harald Meyler. He must have contacted Dave, outlined a colour scheme and told him to get on with it. The excuse would have been my birthday, a surprise welcome-home present, lovely new colours for my trusty mount. I ran my finger over the leading edge of the wing. I'd lived with the company accounts for long enough to know just how much a repaint like this would have cost. The best paint jobs can take hundreds of hours of specialised work – stripping off the old paint, preparing the surfaces, applying primer, then layer after layer of top coat with light sandings in between. Add a final wash of protective polyurethane, and Harald would have been looking at a five-figure bill. Not that he'd have given the money a second thought.

I stepped back, half-closing my eyes, trying to work out why I was so offended. Given the work involved, Harald must have commissioned the repaint weeks ago. The very fact that he'd done it that early confirmed that he'd wanted me in his display team all along. That's why the flight programme had been so gruelling. That's why he'd insisted on testing me to the limits. He'd not only reserved me a place in the Blue Angels but he'd assumed – presumed – that I'd be only too glad to accept.

I nodded to myself, looking up at my shiny new toy. Harald had drawn a bead on me, chased me all over the Florida sky, welcomed me to his brotherhood of fellow fighter pilots, and left the rest to my better judgement. The fact that I'd said no, the fact that I was happy to go back to funny old England and pick up where I'd left off, must have come as something of a shock. No wonder he'd looked so crestfallen in the Denver restaurant. No wonder he'd barely summoned a smile when we'd said our goodbyes at O'Hare airport. Turning down the role of Harald Meyler's wingman simply wasn't in the script.

I called another taxi from Dave Jeffries' office, angry again. The fact that a major repaint like this would have kept the Mustang in the hangar for at least a month wouldn't have crossed Harald's mind. The fact that at least one set of Old Glory's guests had been short-changed was immaterial. The aircraft, and myself, were simply pawns, part of some far bigger gameplan. Our role, if we had one, was to be grateful. Money, in short, could buy anything.

When I got back to Mapledurcombe, Jamie was still there. I took him into Adam's study and shut the door.

'When did the repaint start?'

'A couple of days after you went.'

'And you didn't think to tell me?'

'I wasn't here but I gathered it was supposed to be a surprise. That's what I was told, anyway.'

'Who told you?'

'Dave Jeffries. He was the one who'd been talking to Harald.'

'And he just went ahead and did it? Without even asking me.'

'Harald said it wouldn't be a problem. He said you'd love it.'

'That's what he always says.'

'Really?'

Jamie couldn't keep the reproach out of his voice. I was sitting on the edge of Adam's desk. Most of the anger had gone now and the only thing I really felt was exhaustion. I held out my hand, tugging Jamie towards me. No wonder he'd been so insecure, so manic. No wonder he'd assumed the worst about me and Harald.

'When I said I missed you, I meant it,' I said simply. 'I'm a difficult old cow. Ignore me.'

It wasn't what he wanted me to say, and I knew it, but the rest could come later. Jamie kissed me, then nodded at the phone.

'Aren't you going to give him a ring, then? Say thank you?'

I shook my head, trying to smother a yawn.

'No, I'm bloody not.'

The rest of June came and went. Thanks to my sister, I had a fantastic birthday, crowned by the arrival of an enormous jiffy bag from Gander Creek. My mother had knitted me a really lovely sweater with wool from our sheep and I passed it around the dinner table that night, showing it off to our American guests. They were very taken with the idea of growing up on the Falkland Islands, and Andrea and I kept them laughing for hours with tales from our misspent youth.

As well, I got dozens of cards from family and friends, but – to my relief – nothing arrived from Florida. I was still pretty upset by what Harald had done to our Mustang, and although I was tempted to lift the phone and get one or two things off my chest, I thought it better to let the dust settle. He had, after all, taught me how to fly the beast, and for that I was more than grateful. As the days passed, and my anger cooled, I also warmed to the name scrolled so vividly beneath the engine exhausts. *Ellie B* had a lovely feel to it. My plane. My baby.

Ralph Pierson had been thrilled with the material I'd been able to bring back from Karel Brokenka – snaps, mainly, and a big sheaf of photocopies from a diary he'd kept during the war – but like an idiot I'd forgotten to ask Harald for the cassette tape he'd recorded in Karel's room at Shoreview. I had no secrets from Ralph – not as far as Harald was concerned – and when I told him how awkward it had been for me at the end, and how I wasn't keen to get back in touch too quickly, he said he quite understood. He had the Standfast number, and when the time was right he'd put a call through himself.

The one photograph that Ralph still needed for the book was the promised shot of the Luftwaffe pilot downed by Karel Brokenka. Ralph had been on to the people at the German archives yet again, and while it was true that they'd found the squadron file, there appeared to be some problem laying hands on the pilot's photograph. The girl in charge of this research had gone off to New Zealand for a month's hiking, so nothing could happen until she got back.

Ralph by now knew more or less everything about me and Jamie. His intuition had served him well, and when he touched on it at all – which was rarely – it was simply to let me know how much good I was doing his young grandson. He was much more stable, much more mature, an altogether happier lad than the wayward, rather adolescent Jamie of his university days. Put this way, I felt more like his mother than his lover, but the relationship between us was deepening all the time, helped just a little by a couple of outings in the Mustang.

Flying *Ellie B*, of course, was irresistible. The weather in June was off and on – a succession of Atlantic fronts with wonderfully clear, boisterous skies in between – but even so I managed a total of half a dozen flights. With the experience of Standfast behind me, I was now able to share Harald's admiration for Dave Jeffries' rebuild. Our Mustang, compared to the couple I'd flown over in Florida, was a pilot's dream. Little modifications Dave had engineered in the cockpit – a flap lever offset here, an instrument slightly repositioned there – made it a friendlier, safer aeroplane, and when I took it up to altitude and inched the boost forward against the stops, she was an absolute delight to fly.

It was on my second outing, flying back up-Channel after a sortie down to the Scillies, that I had the strangest experience. For once, the sky was absolutely cloudless. I was up at 9,000 feet, the sun behind me, the long chalk frieze of Lyme Bay off to my left. The Merlin was drumming away in front of me, and according to the map on my lap I was directly on course for that patch of mid-Channel where Adam had speared in.

As I got closer, I began to think through that sequence of events all over again – how it might have happened, the mistakes he might have made – and I was still trying to draw up a shortlist of what Harald calls 'adverse factors' when I heard Adam's voice. It was definitely him and it sounded so clear, so close, that I swear he was behind me, in the rear seat. At first, he was laughing. Not a laugh, really, more a chuckle. Then he told me that he was bloody pleased with what I'd done. I hadn't been silly about things. I hadn't bottled out. The trick now, he said, was to stay high, stay up-sun, and try not to lose it. There was a pause. Then he started chuckling again. Watch your six, he said. And keep the faith.

Watch my six. Up there in the Mustang I took a fevered look in the mirror. Half-blinded by the sun, I loosened my harness and tried to turn round, still convinced that Adam was actually up there, with me in the aircraft. He wasn't, of course, but when I landed back at Sandown and Dave Jeffries checked the rear cockpit, he found little crusts of mud on the floor beneath the pedals. They could have come from anywhere, but Dave is obsessional about keeping the cockpit clean, and when he swore that the back end had been spotless, I believed him.

Later, I recounted the incident to Jamie. His flights with me in the Mustang had, in his phrase, made him fall in love with me all over again, but we were also back in the Moth together, picking up the flying lessons where we'd left off, and I was so disturbed by Adam's brief reappearance that I made a point of taking the Moth out to that same point in mid-Channel, just to see whether it might happen again. It didn't, alas, not least because the Moth would have got a bit overcrowded, but I was grateful to Jamie for taking it seriously. As curious as ever, he made me write it all down, and I later discovered that he'd shown it to Ralph, who wasn't the least bit surprised. Flying during the war, aviators were forever bumping into the ghosts of their dead buddies, and when he mentioned it to me a couple of weeks later, he told me not to worry.

'It's a good sign,' he said. 'In fact it's a very good sign.'

'Why?'

'It means he's happy. Just like Jamie.'

Whether he was right about Adam, I don't know, but he was certainly right about Jamie. As it dawned on him that I'd no intention of getting in touch with Harald, a lot of his insecurities vanished. We went flying in the Moth as often as his working hours permitted, and I began to push him harder and harder, setting him some of the traps that Harald had taught me. Ninety per cent of the time Jamie sailed through without even raising his voice, and once he'd logged fourteen hours, I sent him off solo.

He did a couple of circuits at Sandown and then flew across the Solent and up Portsmouth Harbour before returning for a neat little three-point landing. We celebrated that night with a meal in a pub down in Ventnor, and for the first time since I'd got back we found ourselves having a sensible conversation about Gitta, his German girlfriend.

'I want you to meet her,' he said.

'Why?'

'Because you might make her see sense.'

'About the baby?'

'Yes. And about us.'

Talking about the baby made me feel uneasy. I'm passionate about kids, all the more so because I can't have any of my own, but I'm equally aware that a mother has rights too. If I was Gitta, and Jamie was so plainly in love with someone else, I'm not sure I wouldn't be talking about having an abortion.

'It's really nothing to do with me,' I said. 'It's her business. And yours.'

'Ours.'

'No, yours. My love, you have to face up to it. If it's over, and you keep telling me it is, then it's her baby, her body, her decision.'

'I don't want her to kill it.'

'So what *do* you want?'

He sipped at his pint. I was getting to know him really well by now and I could tell by the expression on his face that he'd rehearsed this conversation.

'What about adopting it?' he suggested at last.

'You can't adopt it. It's your child already.'

'I didn't mean me.'

I stared at him. The implication couldn't have been clearer. Jamie was asking me to become a mother. Of his child.

'Me?' I said weakly.

'Us.'

'But . . .' I spread my hands wide, '. . . living together? Bringing it up? Becoming a family?'

'Yeah, why not?'

This was such a contrast to my last proposal – Harald's laboured attempts to turn me into a Blue Angel – that I began to laugh.

'You're asking me to *marry* you?'

'Not at all. There's a problem with the baby. Rather than see it killed, we could give it a home. That's all I'm saying.'

I realised he was serious. The difficulties were obvious.

'What about Gitta?'

'I think she might agree.'

'Why?'

'Because it turns out she's Catholic.'

'She never told you?'

'I never asked.'

'But it matters now? To her?'

'Seems to.'

He described a recent conversation they'd had on the phone. It seemed she was resigned to losing him but getting rid of the baby wasn't as simple as she'd thought. A visit to an obstetrician had revealed an abnormality in her womb. It the abortion was to go ahead, it should happen very soon.

'And?'

'She's having second thoughts.'

'So what's the deadline? For the abortion?'

Jamie was grinning now. The fact that I hadn't said no, hadn't thrown a fit, was – to him – tantamount to agreement. He reached for my empty glass.

'Early August,' he said. 'How about another one?'

July was upon us days later. With it came a phone call from my accountant, Dennis Wetherall. The sound of his voice wasn't entirely welcome. Within seconds, I was back in the mess that Adam had left me to clear up.

'I've been drawing up the final accounts,' he was saying. 'I think you ought to come over.'

'Put them in the post,' I said at once. 'I'm really busy.'

'Really? I thought that sister of yours was in charge?' Dennis sounded vastly amused.

I lied for a moment or two about how we divvied up the work, but Dennis wasn't having it. He obviously spoke to Andrea a great deal, and the fact that she was running Mapledurcombe virtually single-handed was beyond dispute. The moment I'd left for America I'd surrendered control, and unless she died, or fell in love, or something equally unlikely, that's the way it was going to stay.

'These accounts . . .' I began guardedly, '. . . is there a problem?'

'Yes, I think there is.' I could picture Dennis scowling at the telephone. 'Come over and I'll show you.'

It was three days before Jamie could take the time off and I saw no point going without him. Another trip to Jersey wouldn't do his navigation any harm and if Dennis insisted on the normal boozy lunch, then my pupil could fly me back as well.

We left at eight in the morning. The crossing was a delight – a big high-pressure zone emptying the sky of clouds – and it was barely half past nine by the time Dennis picked me up at the Aero Club. On the way in to St Helier, he enquired about Harald and my trip out to Standfast. I told him a little about what we'd got up to – the flying, the facilities, the fighter pilot school he seemed to run – then said that Harald hadn't been in touch since.

'He's in Kiev,' Dennis grunted. 'Buying aeroplanes.'

'The Russian Shuttle thing?'

'Yeah, and lots else. The Shuttle was the key to the door. Just now he's inside, emptying all the cupboards.'

'Of what?'

'Anything that flies. Anything that goes bang. Jesus, you know the guy. He'll end up owning an air force at this rate.' He eyed me across the car, openly curious. 'He make any moves on you?'

'Not exactly.'

'What does that mean?'

'Nothing you'd understand.' I patted him on the knee. 'Tell me about these accounts. I have to be back at the airport by three.'

Dennis parked the Porsche and we took the lift to his new suite of offices on the Esplanade. They looked out across the harbour, a glorious view, and I was still watching a couple entwined around each other on the sun deck of a big fifty-foot motor cruiser when Dennis passed me a stapled sheet of papers.

'These are Adam's Amex statements. The key date's February the eleventh.'

I stared down at the list of credit-card transactions. The twelfth of February was the day Adam had speared in, the day I'd waited by the phone, hoping against hope that the radar people had got it wrong. My eyes went from purchase to purchase, following the footprints that Adam had left across those first ten days of the month: £12 to a garage in Newport, petrol probably; £19.27 to the off-licence we used near Mapledurcombe; £198.50 to settle his monthly invoice for landings at Sandown Airport. After Monday, the ninth, he'd been on Jersey. There was the charge from the sushi restaurant on the night of the eleventh, and then the bill from the Bon Accueil, settled on the morning he'd left in the Cessna. I'd thought of these places nonstop for months. Seeing them listed here, so cold, so matter-of-fact, was the strangest experience. Was this how Adam had ended up? As a list of entries on a credit card statement?

Dennis was getting impatient.

'Next page,' he said. 'Turn over.'

I flipped the page. The settlement date on Adam's account happened to fall on the twelfth of every month. The next page should have been empty. It wasn't.

I stared at the single line of type. On Friday 13 February, Adam had bought £83 worth of Avgas from the refuelling agency at Hurn Airport.

Hurn Airport serves Bournemouth. I looked up.

'He couldn't have done,' I said. 'He was dead.'

'That's what I thought.'

'Then it must have been a mistake. Wrong card, wrong account, whatever.'

'It wasn't a mistake. I've been through it with the Amex people. Twice.' He jabbed at the statement with his finger. 'On Friday the thirteenth of February, someone used his card at Hurn.'

'And you don't think it was Adam?'

Dennis shot me one of his looks. From the start, he'd dismissed any thought that Adam might have staged some kind of disappearence. He'd known him well, he'd rated his judgement, and in his book Adam didn't play games like that.

'He's dead, Ellie,' he grunted. 'That's the bottom line.'

Suddenly, something occurred to me.

'Did Adam have more than one card?'

'Not according to Amex.'

'But that's impossible.'

'Why?'

'Because his card was in the bag they fished out, the one that Harald's people found in the Channel. Harald showed me himself. They found the bag over a week later.'

'I know.' Dennis was nodding. 'You told me.'

'When?'

'February 22nd.' He tapped his diary. 'I made a note.'

I sat back, overwhelmed. The implications were horrible. I didn't want to think about them. I looked out at the sunshine, at the yachts in the harbour, half-listening to Dennis. Accountants, I thought, live in a very black-and-white world. Doubt wasn't a commodity they had much use for.

'Harald showed you the bag, Adam's bag . . . right?'

'Yes.'

'And the card in the side pocket was definitely his . . . right?'

'Yes.'

'So the bag couldn't have been in the aeroplane, could it?'

'No.'

'So Harald's blokes couldn't have found it, could they?'

'No.'

Something was snagging in my mind, something I'd half-felt at the time but had never pursued. I had my address book in my bag. The man I'd met from the AAIB was a Mr Grover and I'd made a note of his telephone number.

'May I?'

Dennis passed me the phone. When I got through to Grover's office, they said he was out on an investigation. They gave me a mobile number. He answered on the first ring.

'It's Ellie Bruce, Mr Grover. We had tea at Southampton airport a while back. My husband, Adam . . .'

The name finally registered. We swapped courtesies. Dennis was standing behind me, staring out of the window. The rattle of change in his pocket meant he was getting impatient. Mr Grover asked me how he could help.

'That bag I gave you,' I said. 'Have you still got it?'

'The Jaguar bag? The one they found in the sea?'

'That's it.'

There was a long silence. From his end, I could hear the whine of an engineering tool.

'I think I do,' he said at last. 'I think it's in a locker at the office. I'll check when I get back.'

'When's that?'

I listened to his answer, then thanked him and said I'd ring again. The moment I put the phone down, Dennis was back behind his desk.

'Well?'

'He'll be in his office next week, fingers crossed.'

'Next week? Phone him again. I'll talk to him.'

He pushed the phone at me but I shook my head.

'I have to think about this,' I said. 'I want a bit of time.'

'What is there to think about? We either go to the police or we don't. If we don't, we've got to have a bloody good reason why not.' He picked up the statements I'd left on the desk. 'This is *prima facie*, Ellie. The least we're looking at is fraud.'

I thought of the entry again. Eighty-three pounds buys you a tankful of Avgas. Provided it's a small plane.

'Give me a week,' I said. 'Please.'

'To do what? Have a think? Bit of a wobble? You don't need it, Ellie. What you need are the guys who know what they're doing. Round here we call them policemen.'

'No.' I shook my head. 'Can I have a photocopy of this?'

Dennis left the office. When he came back, he was carrying two sheets of paper. The second photocopy was a duplicate of the sales chit. The name of the agency at Hurn was Wessex Refuelling and the date, beyond any shadow of a doubt, was Friday 13 February. I peered hard at the signature but it really told me nothing. Anyone could have forged Adam's scrawl.

Dennis folded the photocopies and held them out. They might have been the Crown Jewels, the way he watched me slipping them into my bag.

'What about the AAIB guy's mobile number? You've still got that?'

'Of course.' I patted my bag.

Dennis looked at me a moment, then shook his head.

'Thank Christ for that.' He sank into his chair again. 'Phone me the moment anything happens.'

Jamie flew me back to Sandown that afternoon. He didn't ask me what Dennis had said and I didn't tell him. For the time being, I wanted to keep this shattering development to myself. If I'd misinterpreted Adam's death, if I'd got the circumstances all wrong, then I needed to be the first to know why.

That night, I tracked Mr Grover down to a small country hotel near Shrewsbury. He was investigating a series of hot-air balloon accidents and I told him just enough to make it plain that I needed the bag back in a hurry. The tests he'd done on it had all been completed so there was no problem in releasing it. When he finally offered to get someone to fish it out and put it in a Jiffy bag, I said I had a better idea.

'I'll fly up tomorrow and pick it up,' I said. 'Just tell me where to go.'

I flew up to Farnborough in the Moth next morning, alone this time. Mr Grover's secretary met me at the foot of the control tower. She was carrying a black plastic dustbin liner, held slightly away from her body. The bin liner was heavier than I'd expected and I strapped it down in the front cockpit. When she offered me coffee in her office, I thanked her but said I had to get back.

An hour later I was downwind in the circuit at Sandown. It says a great deal about my state of mind that I'd overflown the strip twice. I was looking for a red Yak trainer. The last person on earth I wanted to meet was Harald Meyler. According to Dennis Wetherall, he was in the Ukraine but even accountants can – just sometimes – be wrong.

Once I'd landed, I taxied over to the hangar, pulled the Moth into wind, and shut down the engine. This was almost exactly the spot where Harald had first given me the bag. I remembered his face when he'd handed it over, that expression of stony regret when he'd told me to look in the side pocket. I'd found the American Express card myself. I'd turned it over, seen the name, drawn the inevitable conclusion. Only then had he stepped across and put his arms round me. I remembered with absolute clarity how grateful I'd felt for his sympathy and his rough compassion, and I remembered too the very next thing he'd said. He'd offered to fly at the funeral. In Adam's Mustang.

I reached into the Moth's front cockpit and released the harness. I held the bin liner gingerly, just like Mr Grover's secretary, and when I upended it and shook the bag on to the grass, I stepped smartly back, as if it might explode.

It still felt damp to the touch when I picked it up. I turned it over and over, examining it from every angle, then I did what I'd been wanting to do since I'd sat in Dennis's office, staring at the sales slip from Hurn Airport. I found the zip fastener and pulled it up and down. The fact that it ran smoothly, and then made a snug fit with the little tongue of metal on the other side, told me everything I wanted to know. The zip on Adam's old bag had broken just before Christmas. One of the jobs I'd never got round to was mending it.

Chapter seventeen

That night, it took me nearly an hour to find the photograph album. Before I flew off to Florida, I'd had a giant sort-out, clearing the decks for what I wanted to be a brand-new start, and a lot of the treasures from my marriage had been boxed away in the little upstairs room we use for storage. Andrea had also been reorganising Mapledurcombe and it was gone eight before I laid hands on the battered cardboard box that held all the photographs.

I carried it downstairs to Adam's office, clearing a space on the desk and making it plain to Andrea that I'd welcome a little privacy. I'd have preferred to have used the tiny snug where Adam and I had so often spent our evenings, but this – like every other room in the house – seemed to have been annexed by the guests.

The album went way back to Gander Creek. I leafed slowly through the carefully stuck-on snapshots, following the path we'd trodden from the Falklands, back to the UK, up to Aberdeen, and then finally down here to Mapledurcombe. This was a journey I'd promised myself I'd never retrace – too upsetting, too self-indulgent – but what came back to me time and time again was the simplicity of the love affair we'd turned into a marriage.

From photograph after photograph came the sound of laughter, and that glad embrace of life that had been both Adam's strength and his weakness. His appetite for fun, for adventure, for getting things *done*, was limitless, while his patience for people or circumstances that got in his way was nonexistent. In this latter respect he was a bit like Harald, and I lingered over a particular shot I'd taken only last year.

They'd both been flying in the big Air Tattoo up at Fairford. Adam had just landed and taxied back to the flight line and Harald was up on the wing, squatting beside the open cockpit. It was a marvellous shot, full of sunshine and excitement and that special satisfaction pilots get from a nice display. At the time it seemed to me to capture exactly the bond between these two very different men – Adam passionate, disorganised, far too candid for his own good; Harald remote, obsessive, incredibly buttoned-down – but looking at it now I began to wonder. Harald, as I knew, never did anything without at least six ulterior motives. What really lay behind that rare smile he'd managed to conjure up for my camera?

The business with the bag was incredibly disturbing. At best, it meant that Harald had lied to me. He must have known that it wasn't Adam's holdall. Worse, given the tests that Mr Grover had carried out, he must have submerged the thing in saltwater and kept it there for days to get the right result. But what was the point in going to all this trouble? Why should he want to return something as grotesque and final as a replica of Adam's old kit bag? And how come he'd managed to lay hands on Adam's Amex card?

The answer, I imagined, was to convince me that my husband really was dead, and if I wanted to be benevolent I suppose it was just possible that he was trying to save me from myself. It was certainly true that the absence of a body had been extremely hard to accept. Maybe Harald believed that a lookalike bag – plus my husband's credit card – was the next best thing.

Really?

I flicked through the rest of the album, not beginning to believe it. I knew Harald was a control freak. I knew he'd tried to lay hands first on our Mustang, then on me. But there were lengths, surely, to which even he wouldn't go. Not unless there was something infinitely more sinister behind it.

I went back through the album, hunting for my favourite shot of Adam, and I was still gazing at it when Andrea walked in. The cup of tea in her right hand was nothing more than a pretext. Eternally nosy, she wanted to know what I was up to.

I felt guilty at once. I'd gone solo in the Mustang. I was reborn. Mooning over curling snapshots belonged to the old Ellie.

'Just looking,' I muttered. 'You know how it is.'

Andrea took the bait at once. Hamish, her estranged husband, had just initiated divorce proceedings and our conversations more or less revolved around the series of bitter little tableaux that seemed to represent her marriage. How he'd never lifted a finger around the house. How he never wanted to share her passion for modern art. How he'd never cared a stuff about anything she did. I was still looking at Adam, his face turned back towards the camera, and as I listened to Andrea banging on, the conviction grew that I'd badly misjudged him. He hadn't, after all, been unfaithful. He hadn't gone galloping after some windsurfing sexbomb in a tight-fitting wetsuit. I'd been right to trust him, right to believe he loved me, and now was the time to make amends. I thought of Harald again, and the scene

I'd made in the restaurant on Sanibel Island. Adam had been buying me a Spitfire, for God's sake. Is that the kind of present you give a wife you're bored to death with?

Andrea had got to the bit where she was about to instruct her own solicitor to counter-sue for adultery. I reached for my tea, interrupting her.

'I'm going over to Jersey for a while,' I said. 'I don't know exactly how long.'

Andrea looked horrified.

'But Jamie's so busy,' she said at once. 'I couldn't possibly spare him.'

'Who said anything about Jamie?'

'You mean you're going by yourself?'

'Yes, tomorrow.'

She looked at me for a long moment. When she bothers to take any notice of other people, Andrea can be much shrewder than she seems.

'You're not in any kind of trouble, are you?'

It was a good question. I put the tea down and then closed the photograph album.

'Not me, Andrea.' I smiled at her. 'Not yet.'

I was back on Jersey by lunchtime next day. I'd thrown enough clothes in the front of the Moth to last me for a week and I booked myself into the Bon Accueil, the little French-run hotel where Adam and I used to stay. The woman who ran it even gave me the room we always used, number 7. The sight of the double bed and the glimpse of geraniums behind the half-closed wooden shutters made me feel inexplicably better. Maybe Adam wouldn't limit his visits to the back seat of the Mustang. Maybe he'd deign to join me here tonight.

I'd brought the snap of Michelle La Page over from Mapledurcombe and I propped it against the vase of flowers beside the bed. I'd no idea where the next few days would take me but I definitely knew where I intended to start. I'd hired a small Renault from the Budget desk at the airport and after lunch I drove back to St Ouen's Bay. The high pressure was still with us, and when I got down to the windsurfing school the car park was nearly full. It was hot, way up in the high seventies, and I mingled with the students on the beach, hiding behind an enormous pair of sunglasses. Michelle was down by the water, rigging a board. A group of young kids were hanging on to her every word and I propped myself against a rock on the beach, watching from a distance, trying to work out what to do.

What I wanted was a specimen of her handwriting. Before I did anything else, I needed to be sure that the message on the back of the photograph had really come from her. But how could I lay hands on a sample of her script?

The afternoon wore on. Michelle and her group were afloat by now and I was impressed by her patience with the kids. Windsurfing was obviously harder than it looked and whenever one of them fell off – which was often – she was there in the water beside them, giving them a hand back on to the board, taking them through the manoeuvre again. Watching them, I couldn't help thinking about Jamie and his pregnant ex-girlfriend. Was he serious about adoption? Should I be?

Around four, I went back to the car and found a pen and an old envelope in my bag. By the time I got back to the beach, Michelle and her kids were packing up. She supervised the de-rig and shepherded them up towards me. At first, when I intercepted her, she hadn't got a clue who I was.

I took the glasses off.

'Ellie Bruce,' I said. 'Adam's wife.'

The expression on her face said it all. The last thing she wanted was another confrontation. I told her I needed ten minutes of her time. Not necessarily here. And not necessarily now.

'Where, then?'

'You tell me. Wherever it suits.'

The kids had gathered round her. They stared up at me, openly curious.

'This is ridiculous,' she said. 'You have no right.'

'I agree.'

'So why don't you –'

The kids began to stir. They could sense the aggression, the smell of impending trouble.

I produced the envelope and the biro.

'Here,' I said. 'Give me an address.'

'An *address*?'

'Somewhere we can talk, tonight preferably. Doesn't matter where. Café, pub, your home, wherever.'

Michelle looked dubious, then put her board down. She scribbled an address on the envelope and handed it back. Water from her wetsuit had blobbed the first line but the rest of it seemed pretty clear.

'It's a pub,' she said, 'in the village up the road.'

'Eight o'clock?'

'Seven. And you'd better mean ten minutes because I've got to pick up my daughter at half past.'

I went back to my rock in the sun. When the kids had disappeared into the sand dunes, I retrieved the photo from the top pocket of my shirt. Side by side, I compared the two sets of handwriting, feeling the relief flooding through me. The message on the back of the photo couldn't after all, have come from Michelle.

She was already in the pub when I walked in. She was sitting at a table in the corner, nursing a glass of what looked like Pils. Clothed, she was even more striking, her tousled black hair falling in wild ringlets around her bare shoulders. No wonder Steve Liddell had been in such a state. No wonder he'd missed her so much.

I sat down, not bothering with a drink. When I produced the photo, she picked it up.

'That's me,' she said at once. 'Last year.'

'Turn it over.'

She read the message. Her smile vanished.

'Where did you get this?'

'It was in my husband's office. In a drawer.'

'You mean Adam? Adam Bruce?'

'Yes.'

I sat back, waiting for an explanation.

'That's not my writing,' she said at last. 'I don't write anything like that.'

'I know.'

She began to ask how, then she obviously remembered the address she'd scribbled for me on the beach. I can't be certain but I thought I detected just the hint of a smile.

'All that stuff last time . . .' she frowned, looking down at the photo, '. . . all that was because of this?'

'Yes. That and other things.'

'Such as?'

'The fact that you left Steve. The fact that you started the windsurfing school. The fact that seventy grand of my husband's money went astray.'

Abruptly, she laughed.

'You still think he paid for it?'

I remembered her reaction to that same question last time I'd asked it. Then, she'd been outraged. Now, for some reason, she just found it funny.

'I'm here to be convinced,' I said quietly. 'Believe it or not, it still matters to me.'

She had the grace not to question my sincerity. When she asked whether I'd like a drink, I shook my head.

'You've only got ten minutes,' I pointed out. 'If you don't mind, I'd rather talk.'

She ran a hand through her hair and sat back. The reason she'd left Steve, she said, was none of my business but it certainly hadn't involved my husband.

'How do I know that? How can I be sure it's true?'

'You can't. Unless you ask Steve.'

'Does he know?'

'He knows that it wasn't your husband.'

'Was it someone else, then?'

She looked at me for a long time. Then she shook her head.

'No, he'd like to think it was but it wasn't. Men are funny like that, aren't they? When there's no one else involved, they wish there had been. When someone does drag you off, they wish it had just died of natural causes.'

Natural causes. I shivered. Had Adam died of natural causes? I was beginning to doubt it.

'So you just left,' I said. 'And Adam wasn't involved at all.'

'No. If you want the truth, I never even met him.'

I was amazed.

'Why didn't you tell me that before? When we met last time?'

'I couldn't. You wouldn't give me a chance.'

That wasn't true and she knew it. I'd accused her point blank of having an affair with my husband and all she'd offered in return were evasions. I studied her now, desperate to stay one step ahead. The clock was ticking and I knew I wouldn't get a second chance.

'Steve obviously thought there was someone else,' I suggested.

'He did but he's paranoid. It was one of the reasons I left him.'

'So who was it? Who did he think you'd gone off with?'

She eyed her glass, refusing to answer. Whatever had silenced her on that beach the first time, I thought, was still silencing her now.

I leaned forward.

'Was it Harald? Harald Meyler?'

I sensed she wanted to say yes. Instead, she told me I was being unfair.

'Why?'

'Because there are some things you shouldn't ask.'

'And that's one of them? Suggesting that you and Harald . . .' I sat back again, '. . . had some kind of relationship?'

'Have.' At last she looked up. 'And it's strictly financial.'

'He gave you the money for the school?'

'No, he gave me the introduction to the bank.'

'And the bank gave you a loan?'

'Yes.'

'Against whose guarantee? Harald's?'

She didn't want to confirm it but in the end she had no choice.

'Yes,' she said.

The light was beginning to dawn. I remembered riding the lift up to the waterfront offices of Gulf Services Banking Corporation. Much later, Dennis had told me that Harald was one of their biggest accounts.

'Was the manager's name Sant'Ana? Nice man? Tall? Dark, curly hair?'

There was something new in Michelle's eyes and it took me a moment to recognise what it was. I'd frightened her. By mentioning Harald, the bank, Sant'Ana, I'd touched a very raw nerve indeed. She was reaching for her glass. After she'd emptied it, she began to stand up. I put my hand out, stopping her. The photo still lay on the table between us.

'So how come this ended up in my husband's desk drawer?' I asked.

Michelle shook her head. She said she didn't know. She said she was late for her daughter. She said she was working her socks off trying to keep her business afloat and she really didn't want to know any more about all this Harald crap.

'Is he still guaranteeing the loan?'

She wouldn't tell me. Instead, she picked up the photo.

'You should ask Steve about this,' she said bitterly.

'Why?'

'He took it.'

There were seven Liddells in the Jersey phone book, none of them with a Christian name starting with S. Steve was the fifth I tried. It was barely eight o'clock, but by the sound of his voice, he was ready for bed.

'Why are you listed under M. Liddell, as a matter of interest?'

'Who's this?'

'Ellie. Ellie Bruce.'

There was a long silence. Then he told me he was back home with his mum and dad. His dad's name was Maurice.

'What do you want?'

'I need to talk to you.'

'Why?'

I thought about the question. Then I told him that I'd just spent six weeks at Standfast.

'Harald's place?'

'Yes.'

'*With* Harald?'

'Yes.'

He sounded astonished. Then I named a hotel on the harbourfront at St Helier.

'We'll meet you there at ten o'clock,' I said. 'There's a bar called the Casquets.' I gave him the name of the hotel again and then put the phone down, not waiting for a reply.

I was in St Helier by half past nine. I had a shower at the Bon Accueil and slipped into a dress. The hotel was a quarter of a mile away. I wanted to be there before Steve arrived. I'd no intention of letting him off the hook.

The Casquets bar is at the front of the hotel and the tables in the window have a perfect view of the street outside. I ordered a glass of red wine and an orange juice and soda and settled down to wait. Steve appeared a couple of minutes before ten. He'd lost even more weight since I'd last seen him and the dark-blue suit hung baggily around his gaunt frame. He spotted me the moment he walked into the bar.

'Where's Harald?' he asked at once, not bothering to say hallo.

I was signalling to the waiter. When I asked what he wanted to drink, Steve ordered a Guinness.

'Have a seat.' I indicated the orange and soda. 'Harald will be down in a minute.'

'I thought he was in Kiev?'

'He was.' I smiled. 'But now he's back.'

'And you're . . . ?' Steve was staring at Adam's wedding ring, '. . . together?'

I nodded.

'Yes.'

The news appeared to confuse him and I wondered why. Time for a long chat, I thought. Time to welcome young Steve to the family.

'So how's business?' I asked him. 'Harald's really thrilled with the Yaks.'

Bringing up the Yaks was a gamble but I knew enough about Harald's business methods to suspect that the odds were on my side.

'He thinks they're OK?'

'He thinks you've done marvellously.'

'Really?'

'Truly. He'd never tell you himself but you know how he is that way.'

Steve, poor lad, couldn't have looked more pleased with himself. I was right about Harald. On the ground, as in the air, he rarely believed in anything as sentimental as compliments.

I reached out, putting my hand on Steve's arm.

'And he's told me about the Spitfire, too.'

For a brief moment, Steve was lost. Then, to my inifinite relief, he caught up again.

'Adam's Spitfire, you mean? The one he was going to give you?'

'Yes. Sweet thought.'

'I know. I couldn't believe it.'

'Neither could I. It's just a shame it never happened.'

'I know. I'm really sorry, Mrs Bruce, really sorry . . .'

He ducked his head, staring at his knotted fingers, lost for words. I slipped out the photo of Michelle and laid it beside his glass.

'Did you take that?'

Steve's head came up. He seemed to be having trouble getting the photo in focus. The only word I can think of to describe the expression on his face is shame.

'Well? Is it yours?'

'It's Michelle.'

'I can see that. I'm asking you whether you took it.'

Steve was looking wildly across to the big main door that led to reception. I think it was beginning to dawn on him that Harald was still in the Ukraine.

'Turn it over, Steve.' He didn't move. I turned the photo over for him. 'Is that your writing?' He shook his head. 'Whose is it then?'

'I haven't a clue. Listen, I've got to go –' He began to get up, and for the second time that evening I reached out a restraining hand.

'I'm sorry, Steve,' I said softly. 'You're right, Harald's not here. I'm a widow, Steve. Someone took my husband and I need to find out who. I've got invoices of yours back home, some of them hand-written. You might as well tell me about the photo. That way we'll save ourselves a lot of trouble.'

Any moment now, Steve would snatch the photo and run. I could see it in his face. I reached forward, picking it up, and then stowed it safely in my bag. The last time I'd seen Steve in a suit was the night he'd turned up late for Adam's wake, and watching him now I could picture him slumped in the study, his face in his hands, wanting so badly to tell me something. It was Harald who'd intervened that night. Harald who'd cleared up the vomit and taken him away and spared me Steve's version of the truth.

The temptation now was to ask him about Harald, to put him on the spot, to try and get to the bottom of what had really happened back in February. Steve, though, had other ideas.

'How long are you staying?' he asked.

I blinked. The question was transparent. He wanted to know how long I'd be here on the island. Within minutes the information would be with Harald.

'I'm not sure,' I said lightly. 'I might go tomorrow. Or the next day.'

'Did you fly yourself over? Did you bring the Moth?'

'Yes.' I nodded. 'And actually it'll have to be tomorrow because I've got a meeting in Bournemouth last thing.' I paused, frowning. 'Do you know Hurn at all? Have they got a GA terminal?'

'Yes, they have, and it's a doddle getting in, too. They've got full ILS.'

ILS stands for Instrument Landing System. It's no use for something like the Moth but that didn't matter. Far more important was the fact that Steve obviously knew all about Hurn Airport.

'You go there a lot, Steve?'

'Twice a month.' He tried to force a grin. 'I've got half a dozen regulars there. I do all their maintenance. They stood by me when things . . . you know . . . got sticky. Without them, I'd have gone under.' He got to his feet again, eager to bring this conversation to an end. 'Have a nice flight, Mrs Bruce. Sorry I can't stay.'

He bolted for the door, weaving between the tables en route, and I leaned back in my chair beside the window, watching him disappear down the street. I was thinking of that last entry in Adam's Amex account. When Steve wasn't flying a Cessna, I knew he borrowed a Tomahawk. Empty, they'd take around £83 worth of Avgas.

It says a great deal about my state of mind that I double-bolted the door that night. There was absolutely no reason why anyone should know where I was staying – I hadn't even told Jamie – but events were galloping forward and I felt a good deal safer with the door firmly locked. Bad news, as Harald often used to point out, rides a fast horse.

Next morning, back behind the sunglasses, I took a walk around the harbour at St Helier. From the end of the long wall that encloses the seaward side of the harbour, I could look back through the forest of yacht masts to the office block where Dennis Wetherall had now pitched camp. He'd given me a week's grace to pursue my own inquiries. I had just four days left before he might lift the phone and talk to the island's police. Whether or not he really intended to do that, I'd no idea, but the threat seemed real enough and I still wanted the satisfaction of nailing one or two of the lies myself.

By far the most important, of course, concerned Adam. By now, thanks to Michelle La Page, I was convinced that he hadn't gone off on some wild affair. She'd told me she'd never met him and I not only wanted to believe her but I also thought it was true. Adam was too disorganised, too careless, to handle anything as complex as adultery. Just one woman in his life was quite enough. But that didn't begin to explain the photo. Just how had that bloody picture got into his desk?

The increasingly likely answer was Harald. He flew over to Sandown regularly. He was close to Adam. He got on well with Dave Jeffries. There was only one lock on the door to Adam's office and for all I knew there might have been half a dozen keys floating around, not least because Adam was always losing his. What if one of these keys had ended up with Harald? What if he'd stolen in one day and left the photo where he knew I was bound to find it?

I shook my head, walking back along the harbour wall. The implications of that particular question were too horrible to contemplate. Leaving the photo would mean foreknowledge of Adam's death. And foreknowledge of his death, unless Harald had the gift of prophecy, rather ruled out any notion of an accident. Might the Cessna have been tampered with? Might someone – Harald – have wanted Adam dead?

I couldn't believe it. It was too unlikely, too far-fetched. The two men had been friends. Killing your buddy just doesn't happen. Not in the real world. Not if you're normal.

Normal. I thought of Standfast, and the Casa Blanca, and that strange, silent household where I'd lived for over a month. After I'd discovered what went into Monica's little cage, her daily offerings to her pet alligator, I'd rather steered clear of her, but when we'd said our goodbyes I was struck by the relish with which she seized my hand and squeezed it and squeezed it as if my departure had been the answer to some private prayer. Quite what she'd been expecting before my arrival I didn't know but I was never able to rid myself of the feeling that I was under observation, constantly being put through some kind of test, not simply in the air but on the ground as well. Given the wild gleam in her eye when I finally bumped away across the airfield, I can only assume I failed, but the chill, air-conditioned silence of the Casa Blanca had stayed with me ever since. Tomb-like, it was exactly the kind of place that would breed a man like Harald Meyler. Emotionally, at least, he'd begun to strike me as half-dead.

I paused. Below me, aboard a sturdy wooden fishing boat, two youths in stained blue smocks were unloading the night's catch. I watched them winching the dripping plastic crates of glistening fish up on to the wooden pontoon. The boat reminded me of the vessel I'd seen from the front seat of Harald's Yak. I stood there in the sunshine, trying to remember its name. Harald had chartered it for the mid-Channel search. If the Jaguar holdall he'd given me had really been fished out of the water, then the crew aboard would certainly know.

I walked on slowly. At the end of the fish dock a middle-aged man in yellow waterproofs was hosing down the flagstones. He returned my smile but when I mentioned Harald's name and asked him about a chartered fishing boat he shrugged his shoulders and said he'd no idea. Undeterred, I mentioned the Cessna going down.

'That plane? Back end of last year?'

'February, actually.'

'Really?'

He pulled a face, then looked at his watch. The boat I was after was the *Frances Bevan*. Give or take an hour, she was due back any time.

I wandered back down the fish dock, found myself a perch in the sun and settled down to wait. Around noon, beginning to burn, I decided to find a drink and something to eat before coming back, but when I got to my feet and took a precautionary look over the seaward wall, I saw a stubby red hull pushing a big white bow wave towards the harbour. From this distance it was impossible to read the name but as the boat got closer, it began to resolve itself. My friend in the waterproofs had been right. The *Frances Bevan* was back.

I waited nearly an hour while the crew berthed and unloaded a vanload of fish. There seemed to be three men, and one of them – the oldest – was very obviously in charge. He was in his forties, small, squat, with a red bandanna wound round his head. His face, nut-brown and deeply lined, wouldn't have been out of place at Standfast and I'd almost convinced myself he was American when he clambered up the iron ladder from the deck and produced a thick roll of bank notes. I watched him counting the notes off and handing a bundle to each of the crewmen. When they'd gone, I stepped across. He looked at my extended hand with deep suspicion.

'Yes?' he said.

I introduced myself as a friend of Harald. I said I was interested in the plane that had gone down back in February and I wondered whether he'd been on board during the search.

'Who's asking?'

'I am.'

'So what's your name?'

I hesitated. Owning up to being the widow didn't seem the cleverest thing to do, so I settled for my maiden name.

'Ellie Tranter,' I said.

'You a journalist or something?'

'No.'

'What then?'

'A friend. I knew the pilot.' I smiled, 'And you're Mr . . . ?'

He ignored the question, looking me up and down. Whatever else I was going to find out wouldn't include this man's name.

'So what are you after?'

'I'd like to know what you found.'

'*Found*? Bits of the aeroplane, you mean? Or the pilot?'

'Either.'

For one giddy moment it occurred to me that there might, after all, have been a body.

'Nothing,' he muttered. 'Nothing much, anyway.'

'Nothing personal? Clothing? No bag of any kind?'

'Nothing like that.'

'No wreckage?'

'Yeah, some. Nothing valuable, though. Nothing worth having.' He nodded down at the boat. 'There's a sackful at the most, gash stuff, bits and pieces. We were going to dump it overboard but no one got round to it.'

I was staring at him. This was new to me, this crossfire of question and answer. Keep pulling the trigger, I thought, and one day you'll draw blood.

'It's still there? This sack?'

'As far as I know. You'll have to ask the skipper.'

'You're not the skipper?'

'No, he's across in France. Back tonight.' He wiped his hands on his jeans. 'That it, then? Only I'm away for my breakfast.'

I watched him walking off down the quay. He got into a battered white van and disappeared behind a cloud of blue smoke. I went to the edge of the quay and looked down at the fishing boat. I'd no idea whether boats were like cars. Do you lock them up? Was this one alarmed? For the first time in twenty-four hours, I wished Jamie were here. He'd know what to do.

I stood on the quayside a moment longer, wavering. The men had been paid. They'd be hungry. Thirsty. They'd been up all night fishing. They were hardly likely to come back. I looked round, wondering whether the harbourmaster's office extended to security. Were there cameras here? Men in Group Four uniforms with those little two-way radios? It was impossible to know and anyway I didn't much care. If it was true, if bits of Adam's Cessna were down there in that boat, then it was up to me to find them. That was the least I owed my poor dead husband.

311

The iron rungs of the ladder down to the pontoon were warm beneath my fingers. At the bottom, I scrambled up the side of the fishing boat, and steadied myself before jumping down to the deck. The wheelhouse was locked. I skirted the structure behind it, looking for another door. There wasn't one.

Forward of the wheelhouse, a grubby tarpaulin was stretched across the hold. It was secured only loosely and I pulled one corner back, peering down. The smell of fish and diesel was overpowering. I pulled a little harder, widening the gap. Sunshine flooded in, revealing a ten-foot drop to the bottom of the hold. This, I knew, was the moment of decision. Ten feet is a long way. And once in, how the hell would I ever get out?

I looked round again. No one seemed to be watching. I unfastened yet more of the tarpaulin and rolled it back. Then, on the other side of the deck, I saw a misshapen pile of wood and nylon that could only have been a rope ladder. This was how the guys got in and out, I thought. Stupid of me not to spot it earlier.

I dragged it across. The outside lip of the hold had downward-facing hooks to secure the tarpaulin and I used a couple of these to anchor the rope ladder. It was much heavier than it looked and I was breathing hard by now, my face bathed with sweat. I tipped the ladder over the edge, grunting with the effort, and watched it tumble down into the hold. The bottom rungs hit the metal floor, a hollow, booming noise that echoed and echoed. Committed now, I stepped over the edge of the hold and made my way down the ladder. The wooden rungs were still wet with fish slime and when I got to the bottom I had trouble keeping my balance on the greasy steel floor.

There was enough light from above to show me the four corners of the hold, and it was much bigger than I'd expected. It was empty, too, a dim, cavernous space with no sign of a sack.

I stood at the bottom of the ladder, still catching my breath, trying to work out what to do next. Forward of the hold, there might be some small compartment in the bow. Aft, there'd be a much bigger space for the engine room. Very carefully, I abandoned the sunshine and made my way towards the stern. I'd no idea whether there was any other access to the hold and I'd almost given up looking when my fingers began to trace the outlines of a door. I found the hinges, then the handle. The handle turned and I pulled the door open. In the pitch darkness beyond, the smell of diesel was even stronger. It was also much hotter, almost oven-hot, the engine still warm after the run back.

I began to feel my way around the knobbly steel walls. Somewhere there had to be a light switch. It must have taken me ten minutes to find it. In the dim light of the single bulb, the engine room was tiny and cramped. Behind the bulk of the engine, there was yet another door, open this time. I squeezed past a forty-gallon drum of fuel. I could see a sack already. It lay beyond the open door, half collapsed against a bulkhead, discarded, somehow forlorn. If this really was the sack he'd mentioned, if these men were lazy or careless enough to leave the evidence around, then I'd never been closer to finding out what had really happened to Adam.

I picked the sack up. It was surprisingly light. A twist or two of nylon rope secured it at the top and I had it open in seconds. I carried it through to the engine room, positioning it beneath the hanging light bulb. In the dim light I could see the dull glint of something metallic way down inside. I reached in, holding my breath, and my fingers snagged a jagged edge, something sharp and irregular. I gripped the thin metal and tried to pull it clear but it was entangled in the hessian sack. It had to have come from the Cessna. Had to.

I pulled again, and this time it came free. It was a tiny unpainted oblong of stainless steel, about the size of a playing card. On one side there were bits of foam insulation, stiff with salt. Quickly, I stuffed it into the pocket of my jeans then went into the sack for more. Seconds later, something heavy landed on the decking above my head. Then there were footsteps, someone big, someone in a hurry.

I froze, the sack still in my hand, not knowing what to do. The door to the hold was still open. I plunged towards it, still carrying the sack. If I could only get it closed, maybe even bolted, then I might be safe. I began to swing the door shut but the sack got in the way. I could hear the bottom rung of the rope ladder scraping on the floor of the hold. Someone must have seen me. Someone was climbing down. I bent to shift the sack, cursing my luck. Then I heard the footsteps again, much closer this time.

Abruptly, the door swung open, knocking me over. For a moment, everything went black. Then my vision began to clear. Still flat on my back, I stared up. Someone tall was standing by the open door. He seemed to be wearing overalls. It was hard to be certain but the moment he spoke I knew only too well who it was. Steve Liddell.

'What's going on?'

There was something in his voice I couldn't quite place. It was more than anger and it wasn't until I'd struggled to my feet that I recognised the expression on his face. He was as confused, as uncertain, as I was. He hadn't got a clue what to do next.

I tried to brush myself down but when I found the oil all over my jeans I gave up. I'd banged my left arm on something hard and it hurt like hell. My pulse was beginning to steady now, and looking at Steve

I knew I had to seize the initiative. He'd taken me by surprise. He'd caught me red-handed. But I had rights too and I wasn't about to abandon them.

'Harald chartered this boat to look for Adam's Cessna.'

'My Cessna.'

'OK, your bloody Cessna. Here –' I bent to retrieve the sack. The pain and the heat were beginning to make me feel dizzy.

Steve was staring at the sack.

'What's in there?'

The question, for some reason, made me flip. It was almost a physical thing, the feeling of a switch tripping way down in my subconscious. I was sick of all these games. I'd had enough of being lied to, and patronised, and pushed around. Adam was far too good a pilot to let himself just spear in. Accidents like that don't happen. Someone had helped him on his way. Someone had killed him.

'You didn't know about this?' I gave the sack a shake. I could hear the jagged bits of metal clanking around inside. Steve, poor pathetic Steve, just shook his head. 'You didn't? You didn't know about the search? This boat? Out twenty-four hours a day? Up and down? Looking for wreckage?'

'I knew about that.'

'But you didn't know they'd found something? This?'

I gave the sack another shake. We stepped into the hold now. The sunshine splashed down through the gap where I'd rolled back the tarpaulin and I could hear my own voice echoing back from the dimness beyond. It sounded shrill and very, very angry, pretty much the way I felt.

'Tell me about the bag, Steve,' I said. 'Tell me about that so-called bag of Adam's, the one with Jaguar on the side, the one with the credit card. Wasn't that supposed to be part of the catch? Or did you just go out and buy it?'

'Me?'

That single word told me everything I needed to know. I hung on to it, easy meat. Harald had been right all along. When I'm ready and you're about to die. Every fighter pilot's dream.

I up-ended the sack and shook it violently. Odd-shaped bits of metal, all backed with the same insulating foam, fell out, clattering on to the floor. Amongst them, bright yellow, was the torn bottom flap of a life preserver. I stooped, oblivious to the pain and the nausea, and picked it up. Adam's, I thought.

I held it inches in front of Steve's face. It was still sticky with salt.

'Tell me what happened, Steve.'

'I don't know what happened.'

'You're lying.'

'I'm not.'

'OK, then. Tell me how you came across the Amex card.'

'I don't know what you're talking about.'

'Yes you do. Adam must have given you the card, lent it to you, whatever. That's exactly the kind of thing he'd do. Bit silly using it after he'd gone, wasn't it?'

'I didn't. I'd never do something like that.'

'You did, Steve. My accountant picked it up. Someone used Adam's card to buy fuel at Hurn Airport. You go to Hurn. You told me yourself. Twice a month, you said.'

Steve took a tiny step backwards.

'Maybe it was Adam,' he muttered. 'What makes you so certain he's dead?'

I felt like hitting him. Instead, I stuffed the remains of Adam's life preserver into the top pocket of his overalls. He hated that, hated me touching him. So intimate. So personal.

'You know he's dead. You've known he was dead from the start. I just want to know how, how you knew.'

Steve was on his knees now, picking up the little pieces of wreckage. The first two or three bits he examined. Then he began to stuff the rest back into the sack.

'What are you going to do with those?'

'It was my plane. They're mine.'

'That's not what I asked.'

As he stood upright again, I tried a change of tack. Shouting at Steve didn't seem to work. Maybe that's what Michelle had done. Maybe the fact that he just stood there, taking it, was what had finally driven her away.

'Tell me about Harald, Steve,' I said softly. 'Tell me why you're so frightened of him. Tell me what he's done to make you like this.'

'Harald's been good to me.'

'I'm sure he has. He baled you out, after the fire.'

'That's right.'

'And he's still baling you out. Harald pulls the plug . . .' I aimed a savage kick at the sack, '. . . and you're history.'

'Maybe, maybe not. It's getting easier now. The customers are coming back.'

I nodded. It was true. Dennis had mentioned it only the other day. Steve Liddell Engineering, to everyone's surprise, was back on its feet.

'So does that make you independent again, Steve? Does that get Harald off your back?' I gave him a moment or two to answer but he didn't say a word. 'No, it doesn't, does it? He's still there. He's still bugging you, telling you what to do.' I gestured round the hold. 'What did he say last night when you gave him a ring? Did he ask you to check the boat? Make sure the guys hadn't left anything around? Because if he did, you're going to have to tell him.'

'Tell him what?' Steve was panicking again. I could almost smell it.

I reached for the sack. Steve refused to let it go.

'Give it to me,' I demanded.

'No.'

'Why not?'

'Because it's not yours.'

'But it is, Steve, it is. My husband died in that aeroplane, and he died for a reason. The stuff in that sack will tell us why. Give it back to me and I'll have an answer within a week. Then we'll all be happy. No?'

I tugged at the sack again, remembering the way that Mr Grover had put it, that afternoon he'd bought me tea at Southampton airport. The word accident was meaningless, he'd said. In aviation, at least, there was no such thing.

Steve was still standing there, mute, dumb, giving nothing away, least of all the sack. We glared at each other, a mutual stand-off so deadlocked it was almost comic. The possibility of violence, of Steve doing something irrational, was now remote and for that – at least – I was grateful.

'Why not?' I said, nodding at the sack. 'Why not get it analysed?'

'I will.'

'Is that a promise?'

'Of course.'

'Why should I believe you?'

He stared at me, volunteering nothing, the neck of the sack gripped tightly in his enormous fist, and I was on the point of beating a retreat when I heard the trill of a mobile phone. It was in the pocket of his overalls.

'Why don't you answer it?'

Slowly, he took the phone out. The stricken look on his face spared me the obvious question. It was Harald. It had to be.

I leaned forward, planting a noisy kiss on Steve's cheek.

'Give him my best, Steve. And tell him I look forward to getting the results.'

'Results?' He'd covered the mouthpiece with his hand.

'Of the tests they'll do,' I nodded at the sack again, 'when you hand that stuff in.'

I turned for the rope ladder and began to climb towards the

sunshine. When I looked down, seconds later, Steve was deep in conversation. I looked at his sagging shoulders, his hunched back, surprised at how much sympathy I felt.

By the time I got up to Dennis Wetherall's office, I think the shock had begun to hit me. It was exactly the same feeling I'd had after the near-disaster in Harald's Mustang. I couldn't stop shaking. I had trouble putting one word after another.

Dennis's secretary, aghast, made me a pot of tea. Dennis himself was locked away with an important client. After what seemed forever, he appeared from his office. I tried to get to my feet, wobbled horribly, then sat down in a heap. Dennis was staring at me. His nice new sofa was covered in diesel oil. The place stank of cod.

'Is this some kind of joke? Only I'm pretty busy just now.'

I told him what had happened. The moment I got to the bit about the sack, he forgave me everything.

'You got the sack out of there? You've got it with you?'

I shook my head.

'It's Steve's. He wouldn't part with it.'

'Shit. We need the police.'

'No, we don't.'

I stood up again, my one small moment of glory in this whole wretched story. I dug deep in my jeans pocket and produced the small oblong of stainless steel. Dennis turned it over several times. The metal was pitted on one side and there were strange shearing marks around the jagged edge.

'What's this?'

I sat down again. I felt indescribably weary.

'It's part of Adam's Cessna,' I said. 'My little souvenir.'

Chapter eighteen

I flew back to Sandown that evening. Jamie met me at the airfield and we stopped for a drink at a quiet country pub on the way back to Mapledurcombe. I told him more or less what had happened and the rest of it he was pretty much able to work out for himself.

'You think Harald had something to do with Adam going down?' Good question. I'd asked it myself, a thousand times. I didn't know why and I didn't know how but that made absolutely no difference to the answer.

'Yes,' I said, 'I think he did.'

'And you think that Steve's involved too? And this Michelle?'

'Steve, yes. Michelle, I don't know.'

'So why did she leave him?'

'Because he's a wimp.'

'You're sure about that? You don't think that Harald . . . she's a pretty girl . . .' He shrugged. He'd seen the photo of Michelle and it amused me that he'd drawn the obvious conclusion.

I shook my head.

'Harald's a one-woman man,' I said softly. 'He's quite principled that way.'

'But he's alone, isn't he? Unattached?'

'No, he's not. Not as far as he's concerned.' Jamie had put his Guinness down. There were bits of America I'd yet to share with him and this was one of them. 'You were right,' I said simply. 'He's got a thing about me.'

'What kind of thing?'

'He thinks he's in love with me. In fact he wants to marry me. He dresses it up in all kinds of ways but that's what it boils down to. He's an obsessive, Jamie. He lives in his head. He makes assumptions, and then just presumes you'll go along with them.'

I described our last evening together, the proposal he'd put to me. He wanted me in his team. He wanted me very close. The word he'd used was wingman.

When I'd finished, Jamie sat back and shook his head.

'Sad,' he said. 'Spooky and sad.'

'But he meant it, Jamie.'

'I'm sure he did.' He looked away, frowning. He was starting to put the clues together, just like me. 'You think he killed Adam? Because of . . . ?'

'Yes.' I nodded. 'Because of me.'

'You think he did something to the plane? The Cessna?'

'Either him or Steve.' I nodded again. 'Yes.'

'Bit extreme, isn't it?'

'Yes, but typical too. He's a means-and-ends person, Jamie. You have to be with him, to be around him, to pick it up. If something matters enough, he'll do anything to get it. He's like that in training. Chuck says he was like that in Vietnam. He says he's the classic fighter jock. Brilliant hand-and-eye skills. Bucketfuls of nerve. And absolutely no conscience.'

'Dangerous.'

'Very.'

I told him about Monica, about the ritual with the cage. What had really disturbed me, I said, wasn't this mad old woman feeding bunnies to her pet alligator but the fact that Harald had been part of it. The days when she couldn't be bothered to fetch out the offerings herself, Harald was the one playing God in the rabbit hutch.

I nodded.

'Never gave it a second thought. Never bothered him at all.'

Jamie shuddered. He liked small fluffy things and all Andrea's plans to take an air gun to Mapledurcombe's squirrels had come to absolutely nothing.

'Evil,' he said. 'The man's evil. You can see it in his eyes. It's a kind of blank look.'

I disagreed. I'd seen that look, too, but it wasn't evil.

'No? What was it then?'

'I don't know. Sometimes I think it's a kind of autistic thing. There's a bit of him that never got properly developed, never got a chance to grow. Things that would matter to you and me make no impact on him at all. He just doesn't think they're important.'

'You're making excuses.'

'Far from it. He killed my husband.'

It was the first time I'd said it so bluntly and the implications chilled me. If he could kill once, he could kill again. That's what fighter pilots did. That's what they were for.

'You really think he'd try?'

'I think he might.'

'Why?'

319

'Because he's obsessed with me. Because he wants me.'

'But can't have you? Is that what you're saying?'

'Exactly.'

Jamie looked at me a moment then shook his head.

'Jesus.' He pushed his glass away. 'So what do we do now?'

I sat back a moment, looking at him. Then my hand went to my jeans pocket and found the comforting little oblong shape buried amongst all that oil-stained denim. Dennis had insisted I put it in a polythene bag and he'd probably been right.

'There's a man called Grover,' I said softly. 'He works for the Air Accidents people.'

I flew up to Farnborough the following morning. Mr Grover was back in his office and the last thing I intended to do with my precious fragment of wreckage was entrust it to the post. By now, in twenty-four brief hours, it had acquired an almost religious significance. Not only might it defend me from the wrath of Harald Meyler, it was also, in a rather grotesque way, a very real link to Adam. This scrap of pitted steel had accompanied him to his death. It had been there at the end. It had a tale to tell.

Mr Grover was fussing around with a tray of tea when I laid it carefully on his desk. Busy making sure I got exactly the right amount of milk, he gave it barely a second glance. Only when I was settled in my chair did he pick it up. He turned it over several times, then produced a magnifying glass. I began to apologise for it being so small but he said it didn't matter. Size wasn't the problem. Its provenance was.

'Provenance?'

'Where it's come from. The fact that it *is* from the same plane.' He looked up. 'Can we prove that?'

This little detail hadn't occurred to me. I hadn't told him a great deal about my adventures aboard the *Frances Bevan* but he'd certainly picked up enough to gather that things hadn't been easy.

'Will they co-operate, these people? Will they testify to . . . ah . . . this little chap's origin?'

I said I'd no idea. The metal contained no serial numbers, nothing in the way of what Mr Grover termed 'positive identification'.

I held out my hand, wanting it back. I felt angry, as well as foolish. I'd wasted this man's time. I was sorry.

'Don't be, don't be, it'll tell us lots. In fact it looks remarkably promising.' He had the magnifying glass out again and he passed it across. 'You see where the metal's fractured? At the edges? Normally in an impact we're looking for a nice clean break, something like forty-five degrees.' One flat hand sliced through the air. 'Here we've got something very different. See how crinkly that edge is? And see how the very tips are almost rounded off?'

I looked. He was right. The torn metal was saw-toothed, the tips a soft blue colour, knurled over.

'We call it braising.' I looked again. 'See how the metal is all curling over in the same direction? That's pretty interesting too.'

'Why?'

'Because it may indicate an event of some kind. I'm not pre-judging matters, please don't get me wrong, but it's certainly worth a proper look.'

Event? What was he saying? Mr Grover shook his head, refusing to be drawn. Most of the analysis would be handled in-house at Farnborough. If he thought it appropriate, extra tests would be organised through a specialist facility down in Kent.

'Fort Halstead,' he said. 'Fascinating place.'

'What do they specialise in?'

'Explosives.' He beamed at me. 'Care for another biscuit?'

It was more than a fortnight before Mr Grover got in touch again. That first week, to my intense annoyance, I surrendered to Jamie's nagging and walled myself in behind a series of what he called 'sensible precautions'. We had the locks changed on the front and back doors at Mapledurcombe. I took unusual routes when I went shopping or drove over to the airfield. I even thought seriously about getting a dog. As the days went by, though, and nothing happened, my guard began to drop, and when Andrea darted upstairs one morning with news of a mystery voice on the phone, my heart barely skipped a beat.

'It's for you,' she said. 'And he sounds lovely.'

It turned out to be an old flying chum of Adam's, someone we'd put on the list of stand-by pilots for Old Glory. His name was Trevor and he now flew commercial jets for a living, ferrying holidaymakers to far-flung corners of the Mediterranean.

We nattered about the display circuit for a minute or two. He was flying a Spitfire for a wealthy owner and he'd heard all about my exploits over in Florida.

'How? Who told you?'

'Harald.'

Just mention of his name brought the conversation to a halt.

'You still there, Ellie?'

'Yes, sorry.'

'Something the matter?'

'Nothing.'

He wants me to fly in the Fighter Meet, I thought. He wants me up in the sky with Harald Meyler. My fears, though, were unfounded.

'We're having a get-together over at Goodwood,' he said cheerfully. 'They've got an event in August. Commemoration of Eagle Day. Battle of Britain. Usual piss-up.'

Goodwood is a lovely little aerodrome just east of Chichester, a fifteen-minute hop from Sandown. The flying programme, Trevor said, was pretty modest, nothing on the scale of Harald's September Fighter Meet, and he wondered whether I might be up to adding the Mustang to the afternoon's entertainments.

'You mean send it over?'

'I want you to fly it.'

'You mean display it?'

'Yes.'

'I can't, Trevor, you know I can't. I'd need a CAA permit. They'd need to check me out. They send an inspector, an examiner, God knows who. It takes forever.'

I could hear him laughing at the other end of the phone.

'What's the matter?'

'I *am* the inspector. It's guys like me they send to do the evals.'

Evals means evaluations. Trevor flew over three days later. He had CAA authority to check me out for what's technically called a Display Authorisation. The most basic of these would clear me for a simple fly-by – no bells, no whistles, just a simple pass in front of the crowd at a height no lower than 300 feet. A Stage Two authorisation, on the other hand, would permit me to indulge in simple aerobatics including various rolling manoeuvres in what we flying types call 'an upward vector'. For me, that would mean climbing rolls and barrel rolls, and I spent most of that morning putting our Mustang through my recently acquired repertoire of aerial tricks.

Trevor was waiting for me by the hangar when I got back. With the engine shut down, I unbuckled my seat harness and clambered out. Trevor had already expressed his admiration for Harald's paint scheme. Now he was even more effusive.

'He's taught you well,' he said. 'That was bloody impressive.'

I gave him a kiss. Life was getting back to normal.

'So what's the verdict?'

'Stage Two, definitely.' He grinned. 'I'll be in touch with the details.'

Three days later, beginning to wonder whether Mr Grover had lost my precious scrap of metal, I got a call from Farnborough. I recognised his voice at once. He said the report was complete.

'What does it say?'

'The metal was part of the fire wall, that's the bulkhead between the cabin and the engine bay.'

'And?'

'It exhibits all the signs of blast damage. Halstead found explosive residues. The direction of the blast indicates we should be looking in the engine bay.'

'Looking for what?'

'A device, Mrs Bruce. What kind of device, I'm afraid I can't say. The 172 isn't a big aircraft. It wouldn't take much to bring it down.'

I was still tussling with the first two words.

'A device?'

'Call it a bomb if you like. You'd only need a couple of ounces of explosive, some kind of detonator, it's pretty simple stuff.'

'And you're sure? You're absolutely certain?'

There was a brief silence. Andrea was upstairs with the Hoover, chasing elderly guests around.

'I'm certain there was an explosion of some kind, yes,' he said carefully. 'The residues indicate commercially available explosives. As far as I'm aware, these aren't standard issue on the 172.' I wasn't sure whether this was Grover's idea of a joke. Not that I was in the mood for laughter. 'The front of the aircraft would probably have separated from the cabin,' he was saying. 'If it's any consolation, your husband would have known very little about it. Fix a device to the fire wall, and he'd have been killed by the blast.'

I thanked him for the information, trying not to think about Adam.

'What happens now?' I heard myself ask.

'The analysis will form part of my report. In the mean time I'll be talking to the Jersey police.'

'You will?'

'Of course, Mrs Bruce. But remember what I said about provenance. The item we analysed tells a very clear story. Exactly where it came from will still be very hard to establish.'

It was Dennis, of course, who insisted that I, too, went to the Jersey police. He was so concerned that he flew over the day before and spent the night at Mapledurcombe, trawling through the evidence, drawing up a week-by-week diary listing everything that had happened since 12 February. Into this chronology, we wove all the loose ends that comprised Adam's estate – the guarantee on Steve Liddell's overdraft, the £70,000 he'd laid aside for my surprise

Spitfire, Harald's extraordinary generosity over the Harvard, the tell-tale fuel bill someone had run up at Hurn Airport. We finished way past midnight. What we were now calling 'the brief' ran to ninety-three pages.

My own contribution lay chiefly in the exchanges I'd had with Steve Liddell and Michelle La Page. I'd wanted to put in much more about Florida and my weeks with Harald but Dennis had limited this to a couple of brief paragraphs establishing that the man had expressed a desire to marry me. When I questioned this decision, trying to argue that motivation was important, Dennis told me to get a grip.

'We're talking facts,' he said, 'figures, dates, sums of money. This is a deposition. Not a bloody novel.'

Dennis had a contact at Jersey police headquarters, a cheerful-looking inspector called Alastair Roper, and I flew back with him for a formal interview. Forewarned by Dennis, Roper had already been through the file on the accident and was now waiting to speak to Grover. Dennis had been right. All my in-depth analyses of Harald Meyler – fascinating though they may have been – were strictly for the birds. As far as Roper was concerned, the investigation was about evidence.

'You say there's more wreckage?'

I explained about the sack I'd found aboard the *Frances Bevan*. The inspector scribbled notes.

'And you say Liddell has this material?'

'As far as I know.'

'Did you see him remove it? Take it away?'

'No.'

'So it might still be aboard?'

'I suppose so.' I shrugged. 'Though I doubt it.'

I watched his pen racing across the notepad. He looked up.

'And what about . . .' he glanced down, '. . . Mr Meyler? Where do we find him?'

'I'm afraid I've no idea. He's an American. He flies around a lot on business. The last thing I knew, he was in Kiev. To be honest, he could be anywhere.'

'You haven't talked to him?'

'No.'

'You're sure about that?'

I gazed at the man. Dennis had turned his head away. He loved rows, but only if he started them.

'I'm absolutely positive,' I said carefully. 'Mr Meyler and I really don't have a lot to talk about. We were friends, once. But what do you say to a man who probably killed your husband?'

Inspector Roper had a kind smile. He'd done his best to make me feel comfortable but his courtesy and good humour clearly didn't extend to wild assumptions like this.

'Can you prove that?' he asked. 'Because if you can't, you ought to be just a little bit careful.'

'Really?'

'Yes.' The smile at last returned. 'Disappointment can be a terrible thing, Mrs Bruce.'

I stayed two more days on Jersey. That same afternoon, according to Dennis, the Jersey police searched Steve Liddell's hangar, his camper van and the little house in St Helier that belonged to his parents. They took a number of items away and spent the best part of the next day interviewing Steve. Whatever came out of those conversations didn't include anything incriminating, because Steve was back at his parents' place by early evening. I know that because I went to see him. I wanted to know what he'd done with the rest of the stuff in the sack.

'I left it on the boat,' he said.

He was standing on the front door step. He couldn't wait for me to go.

'And the police? They've found it?'

'Apparently not.'

'They've looked?'

'So they say.'

'So where's it gone?'

'I've no idea. Maybe the guys ditched it. You know what they're like.'

I nodded. It was like talking to a child. Lies, lies, lies, I thought. And then more lies.

Back at the Bon Accueil, I phoned Dennis Wetherall. He'd asked me out to supper but I wasn't sure I could take another three hours of ear-bashing. I told him briefly about my encounter with Steve. Dennis listened without saying very much then told me not to worry. Roper might look like a bumpkin, he said, but in fact the guy was very sharp.

'He'll have to be,' I said wearily. 'At this rate.'

Dennis gave me another little lecture on the perils of high blood pressure, then said good night. About to hang up, I caught his voice again, an afterthought.

'By the way, some guy's been phoning for you. Jamie? That ring any bells?'

I tried to phone Jamie but there was no reply from Ralph's. I checked my watch. It was nearly nine, unusual for the bungalow to be empty. I put a call through to Andrea. My sister loves bad news, especially other people's.

'I've been trying to get you for ages,' she said at once, 'but your mobile's switched off.'

'That's right. What's happened?'

'It's Ralph. He's had a stroke.'

My phone calls eventually found Jamie at St Mary's hospital, over at Newport. He'd been there since early morning, waiting for word from the Intensive Care Unit. Ralph had woken up feeling dizzy. Trying to make his way to the bathroom, he'd collapsed in the hall. The noise had woken Jamie and he'd found his grandfather face down on the carpet, unconscious.

'Has he recovered at all?'

'Nothing. Yet.'

'Christ, I'm sorry.'

I could hear the tension in his voice, the disbelief that something so catastrophic, so sudden, could have happened to someone so close. February the twelfth, I thought. The voice on the phone from Newport police station. Your husband's overdue, Mrs Bruce. We may have to assume the worst.

'I know how you feel, my love, if that's any consolation.'

'Thanks. I wish you were here.'

I checked my watch again, pure reflex. I'm not cleared for night flying, and even if I was Sandown airfield doesn't have lights.

'I'll come across first thing tomorrow,' I said. 'Will he be staying at St Mary's?'

'As far as I know.'

'And you? You'll be there?'

'What do you think?'

I gave him my love and told him to be strong and rang off. My mobile was in my bag. I'd kept it switched off because even now I was nervous of a surprise call from Harald. It would be typical of him to ring me out of the blue, bounce me into a conversation and elbow his way back into my life. Watch your six, I thought, and hope to God that Dennis was right about the guileful Inspector Roper.

I flew back to Sandown the following morning. It was a ghastly day, low rags of dirty grey cloud racing up the Channel. We bucked and shied our way towards Sandown and I made a horrible landing in a strong crosswind.

I phoned Jamie from the car en route to Newport and he met me at the front door of the hospital. It was obvious from his face that the news was bad. He looked awful, pallid and grey, just like the weather.

'They say he may never wake up,' he muttered. 'I think he's half-dead already.'

The Intensive Care Unit at St Mary's is up on the second floor. Ralph had a tube down his throat and wires coming out of his chest. A ventilator was doing most of his breathing for him and a drip on a stand was feeding clear liquid into one of his arms. Jamie was right. His face had somehow slackened. He looked waxy and his flesh felt cold to the touch. We sat on either side of him, each holding a hand, and after an hour or so the sister in charge asked us to go. There was a nice coffee shop we could use. If there was any improvement, we'd be the first to know.

We went to the cafeteria. Jamie, for once, couldn't face food.

'Have you had anything since yesterday?'

He shook his head. He looked bereft, completely lost, and when I suggested he go home for some rest he barely seemed to understand me. I took his hand. It was nearly as cold as Ralph's.

'Go home,' I urged him. 'I'll stay here. If anything happens, I'll phone. I promise.'

He gazed at me, glassy-eyed with exhaustion. He couldn't go back to the bungalow. He couldn't face it. Not without Ralph.

'Go to Mapledurcombe then. I'll give Andrea a ring. Use my bed.'

Reluctantly, he agreed. He had Ralph's Peugeot and I walked down to the car park with him. He wanted to be sure I was staying at the hospital.

'Of course,' I said. 'Do you really think I'd be anywhere else?'

He stopped beside the car. I think he was close to tears.

'It's not just Ralph,' he said. 'It's everything.'

'Everything?'

I didn't know what he meant but it was pretty obvious to both of us that this was neither the time nor the place to ask. It had started raining again and I took the keys from his hand, opening the driver's door and helping him in. He might have been Ralph's age. Something inside him seemed to have collapsed.

I bent to the open window.

'Andrea's expecting you.' I touched his face. 'Get some sleep.'

For the next eight days we shuttled back and forth to the hospital.

Ralph stayed up in the ICU. His condition had apparently stabilised and he was certainly breathing without the help of the ventilator but there was no sign of any return to consciousness.

Occasionally, in the hot afternoons, I thought I could detect the ghost of a smile and quite often he'd make gummy sucking noises like a baby, but apart from that he remained beyond our reach. Watching him for hour after hour – the slow rise and fall of his chest, the little sigh he uttered after the nurses had turned him – I sometimes wondered whether he wasn't, after all, aware of what was going on around him. For that reason, I encouraged Jamie to talk to him and it was the oddest experience eavesdropping on these strange one-way conversations.

Jamie began by concentrating on things they'd been doing together recently – gardening talk mostly – but as the days went by he began to reach further and further into the past, recalling the days when he and his parents would spend long weekends at Ralph's house down in Dorking. Jamie floated these monologues on a thin raft of half-remembered incidents – little domestic things like a snowball fight in winter, or a birthday visit to a local stables – and listening to this version of Jamie's childhood it was impossible not to believe how secure and how happy he'd been, a contentment all the more precious because of the way it had so suddenly been destroyed. The morning he told Ralph about the face of his half-sister at the door, and then described how he got the news of his mother's subsequent suicide, had me close to tears and it was only then that I realised who Jamie was really talking to. It wasn't Ralph at all. It was me.

Every couple of hours we'd retreat to the cafeteria. Jamie had just spent the afternoon telling Ralph about Gitta. How much she'd meant to him. How she'd become the very centre of his life.

I'd treated us both to cream doughnuts. Jamie had eaten barely half of his. I pushed his plate to one side, the way you do with picky kids.

'She still matters to you, doesn't she?'

Jamie didn't bother denying it. I'd just got the itemised bill for the calls he'd been making when he still had my mobile, so I knew it was true.

'Yes,' he said, 'she matters hugely.'

'And you've been talking to her. About Ralph.'

'Of course.'

'But you're frightened to tell me. So you tell him.'

He had the grace to look shamefaced. I took his hand and told him it didn't matter.

'It's horrible, what's happening to Ralph. That's the important thing. The rest of it . . .' I shrugged, '. . . it'll all work out.'

'But nothing's happening to Ralph,' he said hotly. 'That's just it. He just lies there. It could go on for months. Years.'

He sounded petulant and bitter, as if he'd been the one who'd had the stroke, and I looked away, surprised. This wasn't Jamie at all. The man I'd tumbled into bed with had been young and strong and beyond intimidation. Not this hunched figure, picking at the loose skin around a blister, raging at the unfairness of it all.

I took his hand in mine, rubbing softly at the blister.

'Why don't you get her down here?'

'Who?'

'Gitta.'

Jamie looked startled, not at the suggestion but at the fact that I was the one who'd made it. He stared at me for a long time.

'Could you handle that?' he asked at last.

'Of course,' I said lightly. 'Could you?'

She came down the next day and I met her at the hospital. She was tall – much taller than me – and there was a little bit of Andrea in the way she talked, punctuating her conversation with delicate little actressy gestures with her hands. She was undeniably beautiful – long legs, creamy skin, and soft auburn hair tied at the back with a simple twist of black velvet – but what was immediately evident was the closeness between them. To this day, I still don't know how truthful Jamie had been about their relationship. Had it really ended? Had she really thrown him out for another man? Or had the crisis between them been triggered by something else? Like the realisation that she was pregnant?

Jamie, of course, had wanted me to believe that this was a late development but looking at Gitta, I wasn't at all sure. I'm no expert on pregnancy but to me she seemed infinitely more advanced than Jamie had suggested. Regardless of all the talk of abortion, I'd say that my carefree young aviator was very close to becoming a father.

Once Gitta had arrived, it was pretty obvious that she'd be around for a while. Neither of them explained how she could simply abandon her precious job – another mystery – but when I tactfully offered a spare bed at Mapledurcombe, Jamie didn't appear to hear. There were three bedrooms at Ralph's bungalow. After Gitta's exhausting journey down from London, the least he owed her was a decent night's sleep.

Was I hurt? Of course I was. The early weeks of our relationship had been so simple, so straightforward. Jamie had been a puppy, full

329

of sunshine and laughter and irrepressible energy. In some ways, as I was now beginning to realise, it had been like meeting Adam again, those first months down in the Falklands, except that Jamie had none of the steel that had made Adam – in the end – irreplaceable.

Jamie was sweet and good-natured and lovely company but it seemed to me now that he was still bogged down in a rather delayed adolescence. Confusion was too small a word to describe what must have been going on in his young head and I knew that I'd have to do what he'd never been able to put into words. Our affair – glorious and headstrong and wilful though it had been – was over. Whether or not she'd ever really left him, this beautiful woman was back in Jamie's life and I only had to register the look on her face to know what it was she wanted. The baby was for keeps. And so was Jamie.

That should have got me off the hook with Ralph but oddly enough it didn't. Ralph had been a very good friend of mine. When I'd needed someone to hold my hand, he'd been there, and the last thing I intended to do now was abandon him. One day, I was quite certain, he'd surface again and when that happened I wanted to be at his bedside.

The week after Gitta's arrival took us into August. It was the height of the season for Old Glory and I was doing what I could around the house to take the pressure off Andrea. This made me very much the unpaid helper – slave would have been a better word – and it felt odd to be in the chorus line at a show that was, after all, my own, but Andrea had made it plain that the price of her involvement in Old Glory was sole control, and for the time being – for me – that was an undeniable blessing. For one thing, I was getting more and more anxious about events in Jersey. And for another, I had to do some serious thinking about the Goodwood air show.

I was over at Sandown airfield, oddly enough, when Dennis Wetherall got hold of me on the mobile. A pilot we used, Simon Pettifer, had just returned from a cross-Channel flight in the Mustang with one of our guests. It was a glorious day, hot and sunny, and the three of us were sitting on the grass beside the aircraft, reliving the old boy's war.

I retrieved the mobile from my bag. I'd rarely heard Dennis so excited.

'They've arrested him,' he yelled. 'This morning.'

'Arrested who?'

'Liddell. Roper phoned me a couple of minutes ago. I thought you'd like to know.'

I thanked him for thinking of me but I wanted to know more. Did this mean that Steve Liddell had played some part in Adam's death? Was that why they'd arrested him?

'Roper won't say, not yet anyway. He needs a result first.'

'What kind of result?'

'A confession, I guess. Liddell's a heap of shit. A couple of nights without sleep and he'll cough to anything.'

I thought about it for a moment or two. Dennis was probably right about Steve's state of mind – he'd looked like a zombie for months – but there was part of me that felt almost sorry for the lad. The more I'd thought about it, the more I was convinced that he was the least likely person in the world to have sent Adam to his death. To do that, you had to be clever as well as ruthless, and on both counts I suspected that Steve was less than qualified. No, something else had happened, something that Steve probably knew about but – so far – hadn't chosen to admit.

'What about Harald?' I asked.

'Not a peep. Gone to ground. No one's seen him for months. Not round here, anyway.'

'Isn't that unusual?'

'Very. It's not illegal, though. He doesn't *have* to come to Jersey.'

'So where is he?'

'You tell me. Tony Sant'Ana thinks Florida but he might be bullshitting. How about you? Heard anything?'

I'd stepped away from the Mustang. The old boy was describing some long-ago episode, his Flying Fortress harried by dozens of Me109s, and as I watched his bony hands weaving and looping I couldn't help thinking of Harald. Was this why they'd pulled Steve in? Do you pressure the monkey to get to the organ-grinder?

Dennis didn't know but thought it was only too likely. Before he rang off, he promised to keep me in touch. Roper had just twenty-four hours before he had to apply to his superintendent to keep Steve Liddell in custody. After another couple of days, the remand would have to go before a magistrate unless Roper had the evidence to formally charge him. The latter, according to Dennis, was now a foregone conclusion. Maybe I'd like to pop over? Join the party? Be ready for the mediafest?

'What mediafest?'

'The papers, TV, radio, all that horseshit. This is one big story, Ellie. There's talk already of a movie. Some kind of documentary. If we play it right, it could mean serious money. You and that lovely aeroplane? Just think about it.'

My heart sank. I'd had quite enough media attention when Adam speared in. I hated the way that total strangers suddenly assumed they'd become my best friend. I loathed the hands on my arm, the cloying sympathies, the murmured requests for just one more shot. These people were every bit as ruthless as Harald, except they went to extraordinary lengths to disguise it.

I said goodbye to Dennis and settled on the grass again. Our guest was nearly in tears over the memory of a dead buddy, a waist-gunner called Mervyn who'd taken a cannon shell in the chest. He looked across at me, trying to apologise, trying to explain.

'You never get over it, Ellie,' he said. 'Even fifty years later, it's still with you.'

I glanced up at our newly painted Mustang, thinking yet again of Adam.

'Thanks,' I said.

That night, back at Mapledurcombe, I got another call from Jersey. I'd taken Simon out for a meal and delivered him back to the hovercraft at Ryde and I was feeling – for the first time since Gitta's arrival – moderately cheerful. Simon was in on the planning for the Goodwood air show and had talked me through the flying programme. The organisers had settled on the eightieth anniversary of the RAF as the show's theme and I was to appear after a quartet of Spitfires as part of the American tribute. Mustangs hadn't been around for the Battle of Britain but over the last two years of the war they'd shared the skies over Europe with the later marks of Spitfire, and it was altogether appropriate that *Ellie B* should do her bit in front of the Goodwood crowd.

Just thinking about tens of thousands of upturned faces made my pulse quicken, and I was trying to share a little of this excitement with Andrea when the phone went. It was a woman's voice, and for a moment I couldn't quite place it. Then I remembered the pub in the little village up from the beach on Jersey, and the tumble of black ringlets, still wet from the shower.

'Michelle,' I said. 'How are you?'

She said she was OK. She'd got my number from Steve Liddell's address book. She hoped I didn't mind her phoning.

'Not at all. How can I help you?'

'It's difficult. You know he's been arrested?'

'Yes.'

'Well, it's about that. I've got something for you, something you ought to take a look at.'

'What is it?'

She wouldn't tell me but I knew from the tone of her voice that it must be important. This was a different Michelle – subdued, apologetic, almost respectful – and I wondered what on earth had happened.

'Do you want me to come over?'

'Yes please. I can't send it. And I can't get away, not in August.'

I looked at my watch. Tomorrow's forecast was good. If I got up early, I could be on Jersey by – say – half past eight.

'How would that be?'

'Fine. I'll meet you at the airport. You know the Aero Club?'

'Of course.' I paused. 'Then what?'

I heard her quiet laugh.

'Then it's up to you. What I've got to say won't take five minutes. After that, you're on your own.'

She was more right than she could ever have imagined. I lay awake that night, sweltering in the heat, trying not to imagine what Jamie and Gitta might be up to down in Ralph's bungalow. I'd seen them only yesterday, over at the hospital. They'd been sitting in the coffee shop together, holding hands, and it spoke volumes that Jamie had beamed up at me, absurdly proud of this relationship he'd rescued from the dump bin. No longer his lover, I think he'd assigned me a new role, not unlike the one that Ralph must have played. I was older, and wiser, and doubtless had his best interests at heart. Next thing, he'd be asking me for advice.

In the end, at God knows what hour, I drifted off to sleep. Dawn woke me and by six o'clock I was over at the airfield, priming the Moth's engine. Flying in the early morning was outrageously beautiful and I tucked in a little detour over the middle of the island before picking up the heading for Jersey. There were little pockets of shadow amongst the maze of lanes and fields south of Brighstone Forest, and I winged the Moth over, feeling new-born. Real flying, this kind of flying, had nothing to do with combat manoeuvres and four-g turns and getting in the other guy's six o'clock. On the contrary, it was a glorious affirmation of all the best things in life and I swooped low over the little slate-roofed bungalow at St Lawrence before turning south. It was good to be free again. Good to be out on my own.

About an hour later, I booked in at the Aero Club at Jersey airport. The club room was already busy but there was no sign of Michelle. I settled down to wait and I'd nearly finished my second coffee when I spotted her over by the door. She'd had a problem that morning with her daughter. Under the tan, she looked drawn and anxious.

I bought more coffee. Michelle had a bag with her, a Berber design in lovely rich purples and reds, and she pulled out a thick brown envelope.

'It's in there.'

I picked up the envelope. The object inside felt like a book.

'What is it?'

She frowned at me, then looked round. I'd never put her down as nervous before.

'I just want you to have it,' she said. 'I was going to give it to the police but they're bound to ask me where I got it, and how long I've had it, and why I never gave it to them before, and quite honestly I don't need any of that. So you have it.'

She tightened the little leather noose on her bag and began to get up. I reached out, stopping her.

'But what is it?'

It was a question I could tell she didn't want to answer. I was in too good a mood to grind on about Adam, but if that was what it took, then I really had no choice. I began to tell her how much all this meant to me but she wasn't listening. She must have looked at her watch at least three times. Whatever she had to tell me wouldn't take long.

'You remember that fire Steve had in the hangar?'

I nodded. 'Harvey Glennister's Spitfire,' I said. 'Half a million pounds' worth.'

'Well . . .' Michelle was leaning forward, '. . . Steve knew it wasn't his fault.'

'How do you mean?'

'Everyone said he'd gone to sleep in the van outside. Left gear lying around, petrol, stuff like that.'

I tried to remember the details. Michelle was right. The fingers, certainly, had been pointing at Steve.

'And you think something else happened?'

'Not me, Steve. Steve said he'd cleared up for the night, and locked the place, too. When it was on fire, and he went back in, the hangar was wide open.'

'You mean unlocked?'

'Yes.'

'Because someone else had been in?'

'Obviously.'

'And set the place alight?'

'That's what he says.'

I was frowning now. Something didn't quite make sense.

'So why didn't he say? Why didn't he tell the insurers all this? Or the police?'

Michelle had gone quiet again, but this time I wasn't taking any chances. The fact that Steve might have been the victim of an arson attack was a major development. I had to know the rest of it, come what may.

Michelle must have seen the expression on my face. She beckoned me closer.

'Steve installed a security system,' she said. 'After the fire.'

'What kind of system?'

'A couple of cameras. He did it himself. He's not as thick as some people think.'

It was hard not to detect the anger in her voice, the feeling that her ex-partner had been underestimated for most of his life.

'Is that why you're here? You feel sorry for him? You want to help him out?'

She didn't say anything for a moment. Her face had hardened. These were questions I didn't have any right to ask.

'He's the father of my child,' she said at last. 'That's not something you can just walk away from.'

I thought at once of Jamie.

'Let's get back to the security system,' I said quickly. 'You're saying he installed cameras.'

'That's right.'

'So what's in the envelope?'

Again, for whatever reason, she wouldn't answer, so I tore the envelope open, up-ending it. A video cassette clattered on to the table between us. It didn't have a label, or even a box.

I picked it up.

'This is from Steve?'

'Yes.'

'He gave it to you?'

'Yes, for safe-keeping.'

'And it's part of that security system? The one you mentioned?'

'Yes.'

I weighed the cassette in my hand, asking myself a thousand questions. What kind of pictures were on this cassette? Why would Steve lodge it with Michelle, his ex-partner? And what, most important of all, could possibly justify this nervousness of hers? This determination to get rid of whatever evidence the cassette contained?

Michelle was on her feet now, her bag slung over her shoulder. Our brief relationship obviously didn't extend as far as a goodbye handshake.

'Just promise me one thing.' She was staring at the cassette.

'What?'

'If you take that any further, just leave me out of it.'

I was at Dennis Wetherall's office by ten. He had a video player at home and we walked the quarter-mile to his apartment. He was still telling me about Roper when he knelt on the floor in front of the TV set, slipped in the video cassette and pushed the Play button.

'They're laying the fuel on Liddell,' he was saying. 'The eighty-three quid's worth at Hurn Airport. Roper checked Liddell's log book. He flew over on the twelfth of February. Borrowed someone else's aircraft. Refuelled on the thirteenth. Had to be him. Had to.'

I was watching the screen. At first, it stayed black. Then, across the top left-hand corner, I saw two rows of figures. Top line, 02.16. Next line, 12/2/98. Time and date, I thought: 2.16 a.m., 12 February. The smallest hours of the worst day of my life.

An image appeared, black and white. For a moment I hadn't a clue what I was looking at. Then there was a flicker or two and the image jumped and settled again, and then shapes I recognised began to resolve. I was inside a hangar and I was looking at two aircraft. One of them was definitely a Yak. I recognised the big tandem cockpit. The other one?

I leaned forward, pointing at it on the screen for Dennis's benefit.

'That's a Cessna,' I said, 'a 172.'

The camera was mounted up high. We were looking down on the interior of Steve Liddell's hangar. I could see the black scorch marks on the floor from the fire. It was now 02.17. Something was about to happen.

Dennis saw it first. He was down on his knees beside me.

'There. Look.'

A door had opened across the far side of the hangar. A figure appeared, too far away to recognise. It came towards the camera, stepping around the tail of the Yak, pausing to examine something on the elevator. I bent closer to the screen. I'd seen that walk, that sudden pause, that same tilt of the head before. His hand was out, the fingers running over the trailing edge of the elevator. It was an engineer's touch, inquisitive, exploratory. He can't leave anything alone, I thought. Not then. Not now.

'It's Harald,' I breathed, 'Harald Meyler.'

He left the Yak and came across to the Cessna. He had a small cardboard box tucked under one arm. Standing beside the Cessna, his profile was unmistakable. The same set to the jaw. The same slight stoop. I even recognised the clothes he'd been wearing, exactly the same jacket and trousers as the night he'd turned up at Mapledur-combe to tell me how devastated he was.

Bastard.

He had the engine cowling off now and I could see the clutter of pipes and wires inside. He put the box very carefully on the floor and slipped out a pair of gloves. From the box he took a small package wrapped in dark paper. He unfolded the package on the floor, squatting beside it. The camera angle couldn't have been more perfect. Seconds later, I reached forward, fumbling for the Pause button. The image froze. Standing up again, Harald was examining an object about the size of a Psion organiser. Dennis was spellbound.

'That small?' he said.

I hit the Play button again. Harald reached into the engine bay, positioning the device on the fire wall that separated the nose of the aircraft from the cockpit. The device must have contained a magnet because it hung there without any visible means of support. Harald stood back a moment, his head cocked to one side, then he reached in again and adjusted it slightly. I was trying to imagine Adam sitting in the left-hand seat. The device would have been level with his knees, I thought. Poor lamb. My poor bloody lamb.

Harald was back beside the box. He was fiddling with something tiny, and even when I froze the picture again it was impossible to see exactly what it was.

'What else do you need for a bomb?' I was trying to remember what Mr Grover had told me.

'A detonator.' Dennis's nose was inches from the screen. 'And a power source.'

'Power source?'

'A battery. Look.'

He'd put the tape into Play again. Harald was working in the engine bay. When he withdrew, there were two other objects taped to the device. One of them, very clearly, was a battery, the kind Jamie used for the back light on his bicycle.

Dennis was showing off now.

'One and a half volts,' he was saying. 'Unbelievable, isn't it?'

Harald's work was done. He closed the cowling and latched it shut. As tidy as ever, he bent to retrieve the wrapping paper, folding it and folding it again before returning it to the box. As he headed back towards the door, I checked the time on the screen. It read 02.23. Seven minutes, I thought. Seven minutes, and a couple of ounces of some explosive or other, plus a trick or two he must have picked up from his years down in Central America. That's all it had taken. Wire the bomb. Close the cowling. And my husband's short, sweet life was effectively over. Only a change of plan or some

337

malfunction could save him now, and even that – I suspected – would be nothing but a stay of execution.

The screen went black again. I stared at it, my eyes hot with tears. Why had he done it? What purpose would it possibly serve to kill my poor dead Adam? Surely you couldn't fall in love with someone so obsessively, so *possessively*, that it justified blowing their husband apart?

Dennis was re-spooling the tape. He knew that Roper was still down the road at police headquarters. If we got a move on, we could deliver it in person. As soon as the tape rewound, he hit the Eject button. I was on my feet. I'd seen enough. The last person I wanted to talk to was Roper.

Dennis stared up at me.

'What's the matter? Where are you going?'

'Home,' I said briefly.

'But what about this?' He was still holding the cassette. 'What do I tell Roper?'

'Anything you like,' I said, 'But don't involve me.'

When I got back to Mapledurcombe, there was a message waiting for me from Jamie. He'd been called away to London. There was no mention of why, or for how long, but he'd left the key to Ralph's bungalow and an over-effusive note about holding the fort. Might I find time to pop into the hospital? And might I keep half an eye on Ralph's two cats?

Still dazed by the contents of the cassette, I drove over to Ralph's place next morning. For weeks, I'd been hunting for proof that Harald had played some part in Adam's death. Now that I knew for sure that he'd killed him, I felt nothing but a yawning hole inside myself. No amount of evidence could make the slightest bit of difference to what had happened. Adam was dead. He'd gone forever. And that was that.

I parked the car in Ralph's drive and let myself in. Jamie and Gitta must have decamped in a hurry. There was evidence of their stay everywhere and a quick check on the bedroom they'd been using did nothing for my peace of mind. The sheets on the double bed were strewn halfway across the room and there was a pair of rather nice black lace knickers lying beside the pillow.

I fed the cats, watered the handful of plants and retrieved the morning's mail from the front door mat. There were a couple of bills, and a subscription for *National Geographic*, and a bigger airmail envelope with a German stamp on the front. I turned the envelope over. On the back, in the space reserved for Return Addressee, there was an official-looking stamp. *Deutsche Bundesarchiv*, it read, *Fehrbelliner Platz 3, W 1000, Berlin 31.*

I gazed at it a moment, wondering what the envelope might contain, then I remembered all the conversations we'd had about the photo Ralph was trying to get hold of from the German archive people, the one that featured the pilot that Karel Brokenka had shot down. I felt the envelope, trying to guess its contents, then glanced at my watch. Our first flight of the morning was scheduled for half past eleven. I was the one ferrying guests to the airfield and it was already close to ten. Slipping the mail into my bag, I pulled the front door shut and locked it. Later this afternoon, I was supposed to be flying over to Goodwood for the final air show brief. All the other pilots would be there, and with only a couple of days to go it was our last chance to iron out any wrinkles in the display programme.

I sighed, heading up the path towards my car. Was I really in any kind of state to risk flying the Mustang? Could I hack the challenge of performing in front of God knows how many people? Wouldn't it be wiser to make my excuses and back out gracefully?

I tussled with the problem for the rest of the morning but it was a chance comment from one of our guests that decided the issue. He'd been at Mapledurcombe for the best part of three weeks and he'd loved every minute of it. He'd already had his trip in the back of the Mustang and he was only coming over to the airfield to watch. As *Ellie B* lined up on the runway, and our pilot gunned the Merlin, I felt a hand on my arm.

It was our guest. The smile on his face couldn't have been wider.

'We bomber guys used to call them "Little Friends" ' he said. 'And they looked after us just the way you have.'

'Really?'

'Yeah. And you know something else? About that husband of yours? He deserved a damn medal. A credit to your country. A credit to you. Finest rebuild I ever saw. Yessir . . .'

We were both gazing up at the Mustang. It was airborne now, soaring away to the west, and watching it I knew exactly the debt I owed to Adam. Backing out of the air show just wasn't an option. For his sake, as well as mine, I had to do it.

The briefing over at Goodwood went like a dream. It's a lovely setting, the grass strip and the encircling racetrack tucked beneath the soft green swell of the South Downs, and it was lovely to see so many faces I knew.

There were about twenty of us there in the briefing room – all men apart from me – and we each offered a brief précis of the key elements in our own display. In my case, it was pretty basic stuff – a run and break from the east, a slow pass with wheels and flaps down, a steep climbing turn bringing me downwind in front of the crowd, and then a fast fly-by at 300 m.p.h., followed by a couple of climbing rolls and a final pass before I winged over and rejoined the circuit for a landing. As a piece of display flying, it wouldn't hold a candle to the real aerobats but it wasn't every day that a woman – a *woman*, for God's sake – appeared at the controls of a hot American fighter and I could tell from their faces that these men were impressed as well as amused. Nearly all of them had been friends of Adam's and it was entirely in keeping with their own philosophy that I should have chosen this particular way of sorting myself out. Thank God for our American guest, I thought. Thank God I hadn't wimped.

At the end of the brief, the airfield manager took us through the safety routines. There'd be the usual ambulances on standby and plenty of helicopters for casevac should anything dramatic happen. The air show was attracting plenty of advance publicity, and given a spot of luck with the weather, he was expecting a decent crowd.

Afterwards, as he walked me out to the Moth, I asked him what he meant by a decent crowd.

He paused, looking back at the enclosures alongside the Aero Club, trying to come up with some kind of figure.

'Twenty-five thousand? Thirty?' He grinned at me. 'And another five because of you?'

'You're joking.'

'Not at all. Put a woman in a classic warbird and you'd be amazed who turns up.'

The moment I touched down, back at Sandown, I knew something had happened. I could see Andrea's four-wheel drive parked up beside the control tower. She'd had it for less than a month and it was impossible to miss. Lime green, you could spot it from 5,000 feet.

She ran up to me the moment I swung the Moth into wind. Only when the engine stopped could I hear what she was saying.

'It's Ralph.'

'What about him?'

'He's come round. He's conscious.'

We drove to the hospital at Newport. Ralph was still up in the ICU but his eyes were open and there was even a bit of colour back in his face. Absurdly, I felt that I'd got to know him even better over the weeks of unconsciousness and I took his hand at once and gave him a big wet kiss on his cheek. The kiss brought a smile to his face, and when a nurse appeared, I watched his eyes follow her around the

340

room, The sister in charge had warned me that he couldn't talk, or even lift an arm, but I think I only half-listened. If he could surface after barely a month, then it was surely only a matter of time before he became the old Ralph once again.

I settled down beside the bed, glad that Andrea had to go. The hospital had already contacted Jamie and they told me that he'd be coming down from London at some point in the evening. For now, I just wanted Ralph to myself.

With the arrangements for the air show still fresh in my mind, I told him all about Sunday's plans. How it was my first public display. How nervous I was already at the thought of all those people watching. How much I'd picked up from my six weeks away in Florida. Mention of Florida brought a flicker of recognition to Ralph's face and I found myself taking him through the training I'd done. The outings in the Harvard. My first solo in the Mustang. Even that hot, grey afternoon I'd flown into a tropical thunderstorm and only survived a lightning strike thanks to my very own Good Shepherd. The memory brought me to a sudden full stop. It was Harald who had done that. It was Harald who had saved my life.

'Harald? You remember Harald? Harald Meyler?'

Ralph had his eyes closed. For a moment, I thought he'd gone to sleep or – even worse – lapsed back into unconsciousness. I was aware of a nurse beside me. Normally busying from job to job, she was standing there, watching him.

Finally, Ralph's eyes opened again.

'Harald?' Another try. 'Harald Meyler?'

I swear he nodded. I swear it. I bent a little closer, remembering our trip to Chicago. Karel Brokenka. Why on earth hadn't I mentioned him before? The prize catch in Ralph's research trawl? *Ellie B*'s most distinguished pilot?

'I went to see him,' I told Ralph. 'We flew up there, to Chicago. Karel, Ralph. Karel Brokenka.'

The name drew another tiny nod of recognition. I described our visit to the lakeside nursing home and then went over Karel's story, telling it the way the old man had done, second by second, the Mustang plunging after the 109, reeling it closer and closer until the moment came to pull hard on the firing trigger and watch it disintegrate in the gunsight.

A hint of a smile ghosted over Ralph's face and it was then that I remembered the post I'd picked up at his bungalow. The airmail envelope had come from the German archives. If we were lucky, it might contain a photograph of *Ellie B*'s one and only kill.

I took the lift down to the car park. The envelope was still on the passenger seat. Back at Ralph's bedside, I opened the gummed flap at the top. The covering letter had come from an assistant called Gundren Hensch. Attached to it were three photos. I removed the paperclip, spreading them across the bed.

The first showed an Me109 drawn up in front of a hangar. The canopy was open and the cockpit was empty. There was snow on the ground and tyre tracks everywhere. The second photo was more formal, a squadron or perhaps a larger unit of pilots, three rows of rather drawn faces, staring at the camera. I turned the photo over, hoping for a guide to a particular face, but there was nothing on the back.

I picked up the third photo. It was black and white, like the rest, but this time there was a single face staring out. He was standing beside an Me109, the same plane and the same snow as I'd seen in the first shot. The pilot was wearing a long, double-breasted leather coat, but despite the cold he was bare-headed.

I stared at the face, meaning to show the photo to Ralph. For a long moment, everything seemed to go very quiet. I shut my eyes, then opened them again, looking down at the man in the leather jacket. I'd seen this face only a month or so ago. It had been there in the house in Florida, in the Casa Blanca, mounted in Monica's pretty little frames, and it had been there as well in Harald's study, propped against his laptop, the night I'd found him asleep. The same deep-set eyes. The same aggressive tilt of the chin. The same look of gaunt exhaustion.

Very slowly, I turned the photo over. This time, there was a name. Reinhard Mehler. *Staffelkapitan.* Killed in action, 1 January 1945.

Chapter nineteen

It took me most of the evening to find the card that the detective had left me, way back in February. His name was DC Perry. I was sure of it. And he'd told me to ring if there was anything he could do to help.

I called him on the mobile phone number he'd scribbled on the back of his card. By the sound of it, he was sitting in a pub. Very briefly, I explained what had happened. I told him about Harald, about recent developments in Jersey, and finally about the photograph from the Bundesarchiv. *Staffelkapitan* Mehler had gone down at the hands of Karel Brokenka. That's why Harald had subjected the old man to such a grilling in the Chicago nursing home. That's why he'd wanted to know every last detail of Brokenka's finest moment. Harald's father had been killed by our Mustang.

DC Perry seemed confused.

'But you say the Jersey police are handling it?'

'That's right. An Inspector Roper.'

'Then it's his case, his call. Why phone me?'

'Because I'm frightened.'

He was at Mapledurcombe within the hour. We sat in the kitchen and drank red wine while I went through it all again. My husband was dead. Harald had killed him. As far as I was concerned, he still wanted my plane and he still wanted me, and he just wasn't the kind of man who ever entertained the remotest possibility of failure. According to Roper, he'd disappeared. But what was likely to happen next?

'He'll be arrested.'

'Who by?'

'Depends where he is. It might be the Yanks. It might be the Russians. Or he might turn up in Europe somewhere . . .' He shrugged. 'There'll be a warrant out for his arrest. Then you have to go through all the extradition procedures. It can take months. Years sometimes.'

'But will he be locked up? Behind bars?'

'For murder?' He nodded. 'Almost definitely.'

Almost wasn't a word I liked, and I pressed him harder still. What if he came back to this country? What if he turned up on the Isle of Wight?

Perry laughed.

'After all the evidence he's left behind him? He'd have to have a death wish to do that.'

Perry left long after midnight. I'd been meaning to ask for some kind of police protection but the way he seemed so certain that Harald wouldn't be paying any surprise visits rather dissuaded me. Maybe he was right. Maybe Harald would be mad to risk coming back.

Saying goodbye at the front door, Perry had the grace – rather late in the day – to sympathise.

'Try and put it behind you,' he said, 'Sort out something to take your mind off it.'

We were standing beside the oil painting of the Mustang. Briefly, I told him about the Goodwood air show.

'Sounds perfect.' Perry was still hunting for his car keys. 'I might even pop over myself with the kids.'

Two days later, a little before three in the afternoon, I was sitting in the Mustang, the canopy open, the sun beating down from a near-cloudless sky. My slot time for the show was 15.18. In ten minutes' time, I'd have to fire up the engine. By 15.15, I'd be airborne.

The crowd were still swirling round the flight line, the dads with their cameras and their long lenses, the mums pushing buggies, the sniggering adolescents open-mouthed at the sight of a woman in a man's aeroplane. The airfield manager had been right. *Ellie B* was attracting a great deal more than her fair share of attention.

Earlier, at the prompting of the show's organisers, I'd done a longish interview with a video crew from one of the local TV stations. They'd positioned me carefully in front of the big four-bladed propeller and asked me endless questions about how difficult it must be for a mere woman to cope with so much horsepower. I'd done my best to explain about the ATA girls who'd ferried these planes around during the war but they hadn't listened, and in the end I'd given them the toss of the head and shots of me climbing into the cockpit that they'd so desperately wanted. The big story was little Ellie Bruce in this most macho of aeroplanes. Anything else was strictly for the birds.

The big story. I smiled to myself, wondering whether they'd ever know just how close they'd come to a real headline. The morning after DC Perry's visit, I'd phoned Dennis in Jersey. At first, Dennis had been slow to see the implications – to recognise how neatly all the ends tied up – but as soon as I'd reminded him about the way that Harald Meyler had first stepped into our lives, I could hear the eagerness in his voice.

'He wanted to buy the plane outright, yeah?'

'Yes.'

'And he bid silly money?'

'Yes.'

'Because he already knew the history. Is that what you're saying?'

'Absolutely. The rebuild had been in all the specialist mags. There were photos too, with the plane's production number. Harald must have been looking for the aircraft for years. It happened to be us that found it first.'

'But Adam wouldn't give him sole ownership?'

'Or even a majority share. So there had to be another way.'

On the phone, Dennis had whistled – a long, slow whistle that signalled disbelief as well as excitement. Would anyone be so crazy about an aeroplane that they'd kill for sole ownership? Wasn't that pushing obsession a bit too far?

'It wasn't just a plane, Dennis. It was the plane that had shot down his father. Harald was the only son. His mother told me that. He inherited a debt. He had to make restitution.'

'You mean a debt of blood?'

A debt of blood. I thought of the phrase now, watching the Spitfires that preceded my own display running in from the east, four abreast. One by one they peeled off into long, climbing turns, and as the last soared upwards, I thought of Harald's pre-flight briefings, the way he'd thrown down the gauntlet, daring me to join this strange brotherhood of warriors. Fighter pilots always keep the score, he'd said. Too damn right.

'So he killed Adam to get his hands on the Mustang?'

'Partly, yes.'

'And you.'

'Yes.'

At this point, Dennis had gone quiet. He was making notes. He needed the photo of Harald's father. He'd be talking to Roper in the morning. If the issue was motivation, then I was right. No one said no to Harald Meyler. Not unless they wanted to end up at the bottom of the English Channel.

The Spitfires were back again, in long-line astern this time. They slow-rolled in front of the crowd, one after the other, and I could hear Elgar's *Pomp and Circumstance* blasting out over the tannoy system.

This morning, Dennis had called back. Roper, he said, had been showing the video pictures to Steve Liddell and at last the young engineer had begun to talk. Michelle had been right about the security system. Steve had installed it because of the hangar fire, but after Adam had gone missing, it was days before he got round to reviewing the tapes. When he'd seen Harald planting the device in the Cessna and double-checked the date and the time, he'd drawn the obvious conclusion and then used the pictures to persuade Harald to bale him out with the insurers. That was blackmail, of course, but for the time being, Steve Liddell was back in business.

As a precaution, Steve had lodged a copy of the cassette with Michelle, knowing that she too had a financial link to Harald and might need to keep him in line. That was a neat twist, but I wasn't at all sure about the wisdom of what Steve had done. In the short term, certainly, he was back on his feet but one day I knew that Harald would get round to settling that debt too. Dennis was right. Harald Meyler wasn't someone you'd ever mess with. Not unless you had some kind of death wish.

'Did Roper mention the photo at all?'

'What photo?'

'The one I found in Adam's desk. The one of Michelle.'

'Yeah.' Dennis had laughed. 'Turns out you were right. It was a shot from Liddell's album. He wrote on the back and Meyler planted it for you to find.'

'Why?'

'*Why?* Because you'd be his for the taking. Betrayed by your husband. Mega upset. Flat broke. Three good reasons for falling into the bastard's arms. Clever, huh?'

I sat in the Mustang, staring out. The Spitfires were coming to the climax of their display, edging inwards into the Missing Man formation, their own tribute to the pilots who'd lost their lives in the Battle of Britain. On the tannoy, Elgar had given way to Churchill's recorded voice, booming out over the heads of the watching crowd. The four Spits were flying slowly down the display line and the sight of the hole in the formation reserved for the missing pilot brought a lump to my throat. I thought of Adam's memorial service and the lone Mustang as it breasted the down behind the little church, Harald up there at the controls. Afterwards, he'd winged the plane over, heading out to sea with my precious floral tribute. What had he been thinking about? Was there any hint of remorse? Of regret? Or was this just another test he'd had to put himself through? To prove that there was only room, in the end, for one top-dog?

Only Harald knew the answer to these questions, but when I asked

Dennis for the latest news – whether or not he'd been arrested yet – he, like DC Perry, said it was only a matter of time. Harald had too much profile, too many international deals on the go, to simply disappear. Sooner or later he'd surface, and when that happened, the rest of it would be a formality.

'They'll really lock him up?'

'Bound to.'

'You're absolutely certain?'

'I guarantee it.'

The thought of Harald behind bars was some small consolation, and I watched the Spitfires breaking formation, thinking about his mother, Monica, back in the chill, shadowed spaces of the Casa Blanca. What would she make of it all? And what would she do without him?

The lead Spitfire rolled lazily off the top of a loop and then swooped down towards a landing. The pilot was an old friend of Adam's, and I glimpsed a blur of white as he flashed past, waving to the crowd. I reached for the transmit button.

'Goodwood Tower, Golf Papa India. Clear start?'

'Golf Papa India, roger. Your display slot remains fifteen eighteen.' I steadied the check list on my knee and began to go through the start-up procedure. One of the marshallers had shepherded the crowd back into the public enclosure and when the prop was clear I pushed the start switch. The big Merlin coughed a couple of times and then burst into life, and I tightened my harness, knowing that the next few minutes would demand my total concentration. The weather had brought a big crowd and I was determined to do the Mustang justice. Harald Meyler was at last behind me. Solo, in Adam's precious aeroplane, it was time to settle some debts of my own. A woman could do this. A woman could fly like any man. Just watch.

I slipped the brake and inched the throttle forward. Bumping out over the grass, I weaved the Mustang left and right, aware of the crowd behind me. It was a calm, hot, cloudless day, virtually no wind at all, and we were taking off towards the west. I pulled the Mustang to a halt and went through the run-up checks before turning on to the runway. The canopy was still open and I could hear the commentator briefing the crowd as I did a last left-to-right scan of the instruments. *Ellie B* had seen active service with the mighty Eighth Air Force, he was saying. Her amazing range had taken her further than any other Allied fighter and the day Goering saw a Mustang over Berlin was the day he knew the war was lost.

'Ladies and gentlemen, Miss *Ellie B* . . .'

Over the growl of the Merlin, I heard the faint ripple of applause.

I'd been meaning to give the commentator a copy of Ralph's research but in the confusions of the last week or so it had somehow slipped my mind. Just as well, I thought, reaching for the throttle again. The last thing I needed was yet another reminder of Karel Brokenka's finest hour.

'Goodwood Tower. Golf Papa India. Request take-off.'

'Golf Papa India. Take off at your discretion. Runway two four. Surface wind calm.'

I gave the seat harness a final tug, kissed the tip of my left forefinger and then reached for the throttle. I kept my toes on the pedal-ends while the revs built up, then slipped the brakes. *Ellie B* responded like a true thoroughbred. A third of the way down the grass runway, I lifted the tail. Seconds later, we were airborne.

The undercarriage retracted, I kept her low until we flashed over the grey ribbon of racetrack that marks the edge of the airfield. Then I raised the flaps and pulled hard on the stick, winging over into a steep climbing turn. Below me, away to the left, I could see the jigsaw of streets around Chichester Cathedral. Ahead was the startling white of the grandstand overlooking Goodwood racecourse. The airfield was down to the right now, the sun dancing over the thousands of windscreens in the car park. Between the car park and the flight line, the dark mass of the crowd.

I throttled back, taking my time, waiting for the diving turn that would bring me racing across the airfield for the run and break that opened my display. I'd been practising exactly this manoeuvre over my home field back in Sandown and I knew how important it was to get the run-in exactly right. Leave the turn too late and I'd flatten the dive way before I was anywhere near the airfield. Wing the Mustang over too early, and I'd be in danger of overshooting.

I had my eyes fixed on a line of glasshouses about a mile east of the airfield. When they were in line with the cockpit, I smacked the stick over hard and squeezed in plenty of right rudder. For one glorious moment, the Mustang was vertical on its starboard wing. Then we were slanting down in a shallow turn while I trimmed and re-trimmed as the airfield rotated towards us. When the orange display line markers were perfectly aligned, I straightened up, checking my height and speed. The needle on the altimeter was dropping through 750 feet. With maximum boost *Ellie B* was nudging 330 m.p.h. At 400 feet, I levelled out, aware of the perimeter racetrack flashing past beneath. Perfect, I thought. Just perfect.

I sneaked a look at the crowd. They were down to the left, a blur of upturned faces. At 330 m.p.h., everything happens very fast, and seconds later I was hauling the aircraft up into the long climbing turn that fighter pilots use to shed speed. My next manoeuvre called for a slow pass, plenty of flap, undercarriage down, giving the punters a chance to have a proper look at my beautiful horse. I was still waiting for the speed to fall off when I saw something streak past. It happened again. Then a third time. I gazed at the little dots of yellow light as they disappeared in front of me. Under any other circumstances, I would have sworn they were tracer bullets.

My eyes raced across the instruments. Temperatures and pressures were fine. The Merlin was churning away. The stick was still as responsive as ever. Nothing appeared to be wrong.

My pulse began to settle and I was reaching for the flap lever when it happened again, much closer this time. Then, immediately below me, came a loud bang and the whole airframe shuddered. I heard myself gasp, first shock, then terror. At the same time, I heard the voice of the controller in my headphones.

'Golf Papa India. Conflicting traffic. Repeat, conflicting traffic.'

'Where, for God's sake?' I hadn't meant to shout.

'In your six o'clock. Closing. No radio contact. Repeat, no radio contact.'

My eyes went up to the rearview mirror and I felt a physical chill that started in the very middle of me. The head-on view of the Messerschmitt 109 is unmistakable. I'd seen it dozens of times in the hangar at Standfast, the black-and-white spinner on the prop, the brutal outlines of the cockpit, the underwing bulges that held the shells for the Oeliken cannon. On the ground, it looked sinister enough. Up here, in perfect fighter pilot's weather, I knew I was staring at death.

'So how do you like the new paint scheme?'

It was Harald. Somehow, he'd made it over to England. Somehow, he knew about me flying in the air show. And up here, in front of God knows how many people, he even had the right radio frequency.

'Golf Papa India –'

The controller was trying to butt in. He wanted to know what was going on. I told him to get off the air. Harald thought that was very funny.

'Telling them who's in charge,' he said softly. 'I like that.'

I couldn't take my eyes off the mirror. The Messerschmitt had eased away, riding high above my starboard quarter. I could see Harald's face. He was wearing a leather helmet and as I looked at him he waved. Then he came closer, and closer still, until I touched the stick to the left, widening the gap again.

'The wingman formates on the leader,' he said. 'Remember?'

The 109 crept in again. Any closer, and we'd collide.

'Something's happened,' I managed to say. 'What can you see?'

'You've got a minor coolant leak. I just winged your radiator. Lucky the shell didn't explode.'

Lucky it didn't explode? I swallowed hard, then looked in the mirror again. Harald was right. A thin white plume of coolant was feathering away behind me into the deep blue of the sky.

'Nurse her,' Harald murmured. 'She'll be fine.'

My eyes went to the engine temperature gauge. The needle was beginning to nudge upwards. How long before the engine overheated? How long before the big Merlin seized up?

Harald's voice again, that same even tone he'd used in the skies above Florida. He was telling me to circle the airfield in a long lefthand turn. I was to try and keep the Mustang within the perimeter racetrack.

'Why?'

'To give these good folks a look, of course.'

'At what?'

'Me and you. Me behind, you up front. Just putting the record straight.' He paused. 'I've got a couple of hundred shells left. Shouldn't be a problem.'

When I'm ready and you're about to die.

Was this it, then? Had Harald finally decided to level the score? Avenge his father's death? Shoot down the Mustang that had killed Reinhard Mehler?

I did what he wanted, easing the Mustang into a left-hand circuit, then gradually tightening the turn to keep the aircraft within the airfield, listening all the time for the first telltale signs of engine overheat. Harald matched me move for move, perfect formation. I glanced down at the crowd below. I felt sick with fear. They'd come to commemorate one of history's great aerial battles and they doubtless thought this was all part of the show. In a moment or two, when he was bored with playing cat-and-mouse, Harald would slip behind me, and line me up in his gunsight, and give them a finale they'd never forget. A little bit of history rewritten. With an execution thrown in at the end. Nice.

I put my thumb on the transmit button.

'Why didn't you tell me about your father?'

'My dad?' I wasn't supposed to know. He sounded shocked.

'Yes. Reinhard Mehler. Why didn't you explain all that?'

There was a long silence. Then the radio came to life again.

'It was none of your business,' Harald said.

'But it might have made a difference.'

'How?'

'We might have sold you the Mustang.'

Desperation breeds desperation. Anything, I thought. Anything to keep him circling here while I worked out what to do.

'Adam would never have sold it,' Harald said at last.

'You knew that?'

'Sure.'

'Is that why you killed him?'

I glanced over my shoulder. It might have been my imagination but I thought the 109 took a slight wobble. Maybe he doesn't know about the video, about Steve Liddell banged up in Jersey police station, about Michelle La Page. My finger was on the transmit button again.

'I've seen the security video, Harald, but there's something I don't understand. Why did you start that fire in Steve's hangar?'

It was a long shot but it turned out I was right. I thought I could hear Harald laughing.

'You really don't know?'

'No.'

'I needed the guy, I needed to get a lock on him. I needed him to need me. It's money, Ellie. With money, you can solve anything.'

'That's bullshit.' I swallowed hard. 'You killed my husband. You killed Adam. And you killed him because you couldn't buy him.'

Harald said nothing and I checked again over my shoulder. He was edging ever so slightly away. Any minute now, I thought. Any minute now he's going to get tired of this game.

We were still circling inside the airfield. Away to my left I could see the black mass of the crowd. I had a choice. I could simply sit here, waiting for the end, or I could try and do something about it. Put that way, it was no choice at all. Harald Meyler had taught me to think like a fighter pilot. I could hear his voice now, back in his office in the hangar at Standfast. One day, he'd said, all this may save your damn life.

I waited for the sun to come round, oh so slowly, and when it was full on the nose I pushed the stick forward and hit the throttle. The Mustang dropped like a stone and seconds later, as the grass began to fill the windshield, I hauled back, feeling the blood draining from my head, fighting to stay conscious. We were climbing now, the throttle hard against the stops, the engine howling in front of me. All my training told me to monitor the engine temperature but I ignored the dial. If the engine seized, so be it. Maybe that was a better death than another volley of cannon shells.

Following the sun would take me south-west, out over the coast, out over the Isle of Wight, I didn't care where, just as long as I slipped the long shadow of Harald Meyler. For the first time, I risked a look in the mirror. He was still there, nicely tucked in, about a hundred metres behind me, the 109 riding the thin trail of coolant. If he wanted to be sure, he'd have to drop back a little further. Two hundred metres. That's what he'd always told me. Two hundred metres for the cleanest kills.

'Good.' It was his voice again.

'What do you mean, good?'

'Nice flying. It's a textbook move. I can't recall ever teaching you that.'

You didn't, I thought grimly, it was pure instinct. I checked my airspeed, angry now at this game of cat-and-mouse. At 2,600 feet we were doing a fraction over 300 m.p.h. I looked ahead, recognising the long white crescent of Sandown Bay. In a couple of minutes, we'd be over *Ellie B*'s home airfield. Was this where I was supposed to spear in?

Suddenly, the Goodwood controller was back on the air. God knows what he'd been doing in the mean time but now, very definitely, he wanted to know what was going on. I was about to tell him but Harald got there first.

'Apologies, Goodwood,' he said. 'We're changing to one two zero decimal six five.'

I stared at my radio console. 120.65 was one of Goodwood's so-called quiet frequencies. How the hell did he know that? I toyed with staying on the tower frequency but decided against it. If I was going to survive this thing, then talking to Harald was more important than talking to the tower. I reached for the radio and changed to 120.65. Then I checked my mirror again. Harald was much, much closer. Head-on like that, a pale disc of face in the cockpit, he looked almost medieval, death with wings.

I closed my eyes a moment. Please God, get me out of this. Please God, wake me up.

'Maybe you've got a point. Maybe you should have sold me the Mustang. That might have been wise.'

It was Harald again. He was right. That was what we should have done. Sell Harald the bloody Mustang, and I might still have had a husband.

I felt for the transmit button.

'You did, didn't you?'

'Did what?'

'Kill Adam.'

'Yes.'

I tried to look behind me, an utterly reflex action. His acknowledgement was so matter-of-fact, so passionless, that it probably saved my life. On the very edge of panic, of losing it completely, Harald had hauled me back. Whether he'd meant to or not, he'd made me very angry indeed.

'Why?' I said. 'Why did you do it?'

'Because it was necessary.'

'But why?'

'Because I loved you.'

Loved. Past tense. Loved me enough to kill my husband. Loved me enough to wreck my life. Loved me enough to drag me across the Atlantic and try and turn me into a fighter pilot.

I reached up and made a tiny adjustment to the mirror. The nose and the cockpit of the Messerschmitt swam into view. Since I'd last checked, he'd got even closer. The perfect fighter pilot, I thought. Nerveless. Dispassionate. A killing machine.

'How did you do it, as a matter of interest?'

'Do what?'

'Trigger the bomb.'

'You really want to know?'

'Yes.' I felt myself nodding. 'Please.'

There was another silence. Then Harald was back.

'I wired a radio detonator,' he said, 'to the Southampton Control frequency.'

My eyes returned to the radio console. Flying up from Jersey, northbound aircraft pass from one control zone to another in mid-Channel. At that point, pilots are supposed to check in with Southampton Control, changing frequency and announcing their call sign.

'Fifty degrees north,' I said. 'That's where Adam went down.'

'Exactly.'

'How? How would that happen?'

This time there was no mistaking the sound of laughter.

'It's easy,' he said. 'You figure out the Southampton frequency, tune the detonator, and the pilot does the rest.'

'By calling up Southampton?'

'Of course.'

'Because the rules say he has to?'

'Yes.'

'You're telling me Adam blew himself up?'

'You got it.'

I looked away from the mirror, sickened. This man was psychopathic. He'd turned killing into an art form, an elegant mix of surprise, technology and God knows how much experience. I thought of those poor bloody rabbits in Monica's cage, of the waiting alligator in the hot darkness, and then of Adam, droning along in his borrowed Cessna, reaching out for the radio to change frequencies. All it would have taken was that split-second contact, his thumb on the transmit button, before the bomb triggered and the Cessna blew apart. *When I'm ready and you're about to die.*

I shuddered. Below me, our shadows raced across the top of St Boniface Down. I'd had enough. If Harald wanted to kill me, needed to kill me, so be it. But if I was going to be the rabbit, it was time to run again.

I smacked the stick forward and hard to port. The diving turn was so sudden and so vicious that I thought for a moment my head would explode with the pressure. My left hand, pure reflex, was pushing hard on the throttle. On maximum boost I wound the turn tighter and tighter, aware of houses revolving dizzily beneath me. I had the advantage of surprise. I'd never pulled g like this in my life. I must have lost him, must have. Not even Harald had reactions that fast.

'Unload, Ellie. Unload the stick.'

I was fighting the controls now. The Mustang was shuddering and bucking on the edge of the stall. Unless I eased the pressure, she'd flip over. Close to despair, I did what Harald had demanded, centring the control stick and feeding in a lot of opposite rudder. The Mustang came out of the turn, still nose down, but the crisis had passed. By 400 feet, I'd regained control. Harald was somewhere back there, waiting, watching. I didn't dare check. His voice in my earphones was evidence enough.

'Nice, Ellie. Very nice.'

The Mustang was flat out again, low, racing back across the south-east corner of the island towards the teeming beaches of Sandown Bay. There were people down there, holidaymakers, mums, dads, kids, hundreds of upturned faces as I flashed past. Ahead, I could see the looming white wall of Culver Cliff. I banked hard to the left and for a moment I thought I'd left the turn too late. We were way below the top of the cliff and I had the briefest impression of the shadow of the Mustang, black against the chalk, before the windshield filled with the soft greens of Bembridge Down.

The land fell away again and for a split second I toyed with trying for landing at *Ellie B*'s home strip. I could see the tower and a row of parked aircraft directly ahead of me, but the moment I checked my airspeed I knew it was hopeless. Putting the flaps and gear down at 320 m.p.h. would tear the aircraft apart.

I thundered over the airstrip at 250 feet, still trailing coolant, hunting desperately for Harald. My mirror appeared to be empty. I looked over my right shoulder. Nothing. About to check my port quarter, I heard his voice again.

'Above you, Ellie. In your six o'clock.'

Above me? I tried to twist round but the harness wouldn't let me. I tried pushing my head back until I was looking almost directly up through the canopy but all I could see was sky. Harald probably knew more about the Mustang than any man alive. Inch-perfect, he was now riding in one of its few blind spots. It was like fighting God or gravity. I'd never win.

'Go right and pull up.'

Instinctively, I hauled back on the stick. The top of St Boniface Down flashed past below me. I had a glimpse of houses, roads and then a stubby little pier before we were over the sea again, racing due south. Ventnor, I thought. And now the Channel.

How far would we go? How long a rope was Harald prepared to let me have? I stole a glance at the fuel gauge. If the coolant held out, fifty gallons would take me to France. Did I want to be buried there? Or would it be more appropriate to end it all in mid-Channel? To call it quits and join my lovely husband?

I shook my head. I'd lost the plot. I simply didn't know. All that mattered was urging the Mustang onwards, faster and faster, trying somehow to outrun the terrifying shadow above me. I began to climb, saying a prayer for this sturdy old engine, wondering whether I might bale out. There's a quaint little tradition amongst fighter pilots that forbids shooting at parachutes but I wasn't at all sure that Harald had much time for that kind of sentimentality. If he wanted to kill me, he would. The only puzzle was why he was taking so long to do it.

I checked the mirror again. To my surprise, Harald had reappeared, abandoning my blind spot. He was now some 600 metres behind me and for a moment I wondered whether he couldn't keep up. It was a thought I clung to, my only hope. I glanced at the altimeter and as I did so I became aware of the first signs of a lumpiness in the engine. Instinctively, I throttled back and levelled out. To punish the engine now would be madness.

I risked another glance in the mirror. Harald was catching up fast. The 109 looked bigger, squatter, more menacing. I tensed, transfixed by the shape in the mirror. Any moment now, I'd see the cannons winking on the wings, see the tracers reaching out for me, feel those sleek, glossy shells thumping into my poor sweating horse. I steeled myself, knowing I couldn't carry on like this, trapped dead-centre in Harald's gunsight. I owed him, at the very least, a difficult kill.

I winged the Mustang over again, plunging down. From 5,000 feet, the sea was a huge bowl of blue, splintered with sunshine. The airspeed was passing 400 m.p.h. The control stick was light beneath my fingertips and another glance in the mirror told me that I hadn't lost Harald. He was still there, closer than ever, arrowing down through 4,000 feet, 3,000 feet, 2,000 feet.

I tried hard to swallow to ease the pain in my ears. Was this the way it had been for Harald's father? For Karel Brokenka? Locked together in a near-vertical dive? I couldn't believe the needle on the airspeed indicator. I'd never been so fast in my life. The whole aircraft was shaking now and I fought to read the numbers dancing in front of me: 440 m.p.h.? 460? I didn't know. All that mattered was the throb of the engine, and the pale disc of the propeller, and the onrushing blue of the sea.

Instinctively, I hauled back on the stick, bracing myself for the pressure, the iron hand that would push me down into the seat and squeeze the air from my lungs. My eyes dimmed and the sunshine faded to black and white and then a strange chill mistiness. I tried to breath but couldn't. Very slowly, I became aware of a horizon, a thin grey line out there beyond the windshield. We were climbing. I could almost breathe again. Colour flooded back into the cockpit. The sky was blue, faint at first then richer and richer as I sucked the air into my lungs. It tasted slightly aromatic, the taste of high-octane fuel, the sweetest taste in the world. Then, far away, I heard a cry, or perhaps a gasp, barely human. It seemed to register surprise. It came from the radio. It was Harald.

Very carefully, the way you nurse an invalid, I levelled out at 3,000 feet, desperate to spare the engine further punishment. The mirror above the windshield was empty, and below me, when I looked down, I could see the ripples still spreading outwards, a perfect circle, the ocean gashed white where Harald had speared in.

I circled as long as I dared, looking for wreckage. Away to the west I could see a long feather of wake from an outbound tanker. At length, still dazed, it occurred to me to radio back. The VHR emergency frequency is 121.5. For a second or two my finger hovered over the transmit button. Then I shook my head. Harald wasn't going to haunt me. I wouldn't let him. Not now. Not ever.

I gave my call sign and reported what had happened. The rescue people have an amazing radar set-up. They can pinpoint your position within seconds.

'I need a heading for Sandown.' My eyes were glued to the engine temperature. 'I need to get home.'

There was a brief silence. Then the voice returned.

'You're plumb on the fifty-degree north line. Squawk 7700 and steer zero three zero. Forty-four miles to run.'

I made it back in one piece. Later, when Dave Jeffries took the engine apart, he reckoned I got the Mustang down with five minutes to spare. By then, it was academic. Harald, very definitely, was dead. While *Ellie B*, with her rebuilt Merlin, would be airborne again within months.

Christmas at Mapledurcombe that year was magical. Andrea had made very big friends indeed with the young director who produced the documentary about Adam and Harald, and he stayed with us until the New Year. I'd done a lot of the flying for the aerial sequences, which in some respects was more terrifying than the real thing, but by Christmas we'd had a chance to see what the director called the rough cut, and we were relieved, as well as pleased. Andrea's new beau had done a very fine job indeed.

The film was transmitted in February, on the anniversary of Adam's death, and the first phone call after the closing sequence came from Jamie. He and Gitta were living up near Oxford and he told me how moving the closing sequence had been. I'd only agreed to let the film go ahead on the condition that it ended with some kind of montage of my favourite photos of Adam. The way the director handled it was incredibly sensitive, the slowly dissolving images scored to a piece of Ravel, and Jamie told me that he'd cried, too. I could tell from his voice that all was far from well between him and Gitta but I resisted the temptation to enquire further. When I asked about the baby, he said they'd finally decided to name it after his grandfather. Poor Ralph hadn't survived the year. We buried him in October. I can't believe how much I miss him.

Six months after the film was transmitted, a package arrived for me from Florida. Inside was a videotape and a letter from Monica. She'd seen the film on cable TV and hadn't regretted her refusal to take part. It hadn't done justice to either her husband or her son, and if I was really interested in the truth then perhaps I should take a look at the video. I did so. It contained eighteen seconds of black-and-white combat footage. The Messerschmitt 109 gets bigger and bigger. Bits of the tail and part of the wing fall off and a small black package, barely human, tumbles out of the cockpit. Then the plane disintegrates. We'd spent months trying to trace the footage for use in the film but an exhaustive search of the USAF archive failed to turn it up. Harald's reach, it seemed, was infinite.

The day after I watched Monica's video, I drove back to St Lawrence and walked up the narrow path to the old church where we'd said goodbye to Adam. It had been raining all morning and there was a blustery wind up the Channel stirring the stands of iris that lined the path from the churchyard gate.

I sat on a bench for a long time, thinking. Adam would have loved it here. He'd have loved the sigh of the wind in the big old trees, and the way that the church nestled so comfortably amongst the shadowed gravestones. He'd have loved the silence and the feeling of peace. Most of all, I like to think, he'd have loved being with me.

I got up from the bench and walked down to the corner of the graveyard, remembering his touch and the way that he grinned when he was really happy. Harald had been right about the Mustang. He'd never have sold it. Not for all the money in the world. I smiled to myself, thinking for a moment that I could hear him laughing, then I looked up, half-expecting the swans to reappear, but I all could see were the tumbling clouds and a single shaft of watery sunshine, far out to sea.